SAMANTHA KANE

BROTHERS IN ARMS

AT LOVE'S
Command

ELLORA'S CAVE
ROMANTICA PUBLISHING

What the critics are saying...

An Ellora's Cave Romantica Publication

www.ellorascave.com

At Love's Command

ISBN 9781419957727
ALL RIGHTS RESERVED.
At Love's Command Copyright © 2007 Samantha Kane
Edited by Raelene Gorlinsky.
Cover art by Syneca.

This book printed in the U.S.A. by Jasmine–Jade Enterprises, LLC.

Electronic book Publication December 2007
Trade paperback Publication May 2008

Also by Samantha Kane

෨

Brothers In Arms 1: The Courage to Love
Brothers In Arms 2: Love Under Siege
Brothers In Arms 3: Love's Strategy

About the Author

෨

Samantha Kane has a Master's Degree in History, and is a full time writer and mother. She lives in North Carolina with her husband and three children.

Samantha welcomes comments from readers. You can find her website and email address on her author bio page at www.ellorascave.com.

Tell Us What You Think

We appreciate hearing reader opinions about our books. You can email us at Comments@EllorasCave.com.

AT LOVE'S COMMAND

Dedication

※

This novel is dedicated to my family. First to my husband, who is my biggest fan, and that was before I became a published writer. He is the very definition of partner. Next, to my two sons and my little girl, because they are so patient when mommy has to "do her email", and "work on her computer". To my parents, who worry where the ideas come from but support and brag about me anyway. To my two sisters who are just too cool, and think I am too. And for my Smokin' Hot Big Brother, who has spent most of this year weathering the storm of losing his wife to breast cancer, and is learning how to sail his ship again. And to my late sister-in-law, who taught me the valuable lesson of living and loving every minute of every day.

Acknowledgments

※

There are quite a few people I'd like to thank for their assistance with this novel. First, Julie Gupton for her invaluable support and advice as my critique partner. She's spent almost as much time with Ian, Derek and Sophie as I have. Thanks also go to Nancy Mayer and her online class on the Regency gentleman. Raelene Gorlinsky was, as ever, gracious and patient with me through the entire editing process. She is an editor beyond compare. Thanks also go to Mary Altman for her editing expertise. Thank you to K. Manzella for her help with translations. An anonymous thank you goes out to the many people who dedicate their time to sharing their knowledge and love of history on the internet. And last but not least, thanks to Deb Dixon and her GMC workshop. It helped me through a dry patch in the final edits.

Chapter One
ဢ

Ian Witherspoon was rather amazed at how calm he was considering he had just left his lover to go meet his bride. For all that he'd been betrothed to her for nearly twelve years, he couldn't recall having seen her since that long-ago day. She'd been a mousy little thing of ten years then, thin and blandly brown—hair, eyes and clothes. He had been a very immature eighteen, reluctantly agreeing to the future marriage in order to stay in his father's good graces.

Then the war, and Derek, had come along and he'd forgotten about little brown Sophia Middleton. Ah yes, Derek. His lover was less than thrilled at Ian's upcoming nuptials. Ian had tried everything to make Derek understand why he was doing this. But Derek refused to listen, he refused to talk about the past or the future. Derek wanted to live in the present, with no thought to causes or consequences. Ian couldn't blame him, really. He'd seen too much of consequences in his short life. Hadn't they all? But his stubborn refusal to even discuss the situation had Ian tremendously frustrated.

As he walked up the stairs to the drawing room Ian thought about their friends Jason Randall, Tony Richards and their wife Kate, Lady Randall. Jason and Tony had fought beside Ian and Derek on the Peninsula, and they had suffered in the same way Ian and Derek had from the war. Yet they had found happiness with Kate. Why couldn't Derek see it was that elusive happiness that Ian sought for both of them with Miss Middleton?

Ian put Derek and their problems firmly from his mind. Right now the neglected Miss Middleton was awaiting him with her papa in the salon. Not only had she been kept waiting this morning, but she'd been cooling her heels here at his

London townhouse for over a week, awaiting his return from the Lake District where he had gone to help a friend in need.

Ian stopped long enough to check his cravat in the hall mirror. Assured that his cravat, indeed his entire person, was suitably groomed to beg Miss Middleton's pardon, Ian stepped purposely down the hall to the drawing room. A footman opened the door for him, so he didn't even need to break his stride as he entered the room. The two occupants turned to the door expectantly and Ian stopped to bestow a polite smile on them.

"Good morning, Sir Middleton, Miss Middleton," he offered. He had decided not to be too contrite before them. A small amount of sheepishly apologetic behavior was required, of course, but for the most part he thought he ought to behave as he felt—sorry they'd been kept waiting but not sorry he'd gone to see his friend Jonathan Overton through a rough patch. As it was he worried that they'd left Jonathan too soon.

Ian saw that Sir Isaac Middleton was unabashedly sizing him up. Sir Middleton had been knighted for making an obscene amount of money in trade. Oh, they claimed it was for some terribly important service he'd done for the crown of course, but everyone knew it was the money. That's why Ian had been betrothed to his daughter. Ian's father was Lord Thomas Witherspoon, the youngest son of the Earl of Wilchester. Granted, Ian did not have a title himself and was rather out of the running for Earl seeing as his cousins were amazingly prolific, but he was *connected*. Lord Thomas Witherspoon needed a large loan, and Sir Middleton wanted an entrée into society. Thus Sophia and Ian were matched and the two proud papas were happy.

Ian had been miserable about it at the time. He'd been picturing himself dazzling some diamond of the first water when and if he decided to settle down. He had arrogantly assumed his dashing good looks would overcome his complete lack of income. That lack of income had enabled his father to successfully threaten to cut off his meager allowance unless he betrothed himself to the girl. Little brown Sophia had done nothing to ameliorate Ian's displeasure. The only consolation was that he would not have to wed her for at least eight years. He'd made sure that provision was in the marriage contract, and in return Sophia received a very large marriage settlement. Everyone ignored the fact that the money would almost certainly come from her own dowry.

Over the years Ian had forgotten about her. When he asked his father to buy him a commission in the army, Ian had been surprised when the old man had asked him, "What about Miss Middleton?" He had nearly replied, "Miss Who?" In his own defense he hadn't thought he'd be at war longer than a year or two, and as Miss Middleton was only sixteen at the time he assumed it would work out well.

He'd been at war for four years. And when he came back he had Derek with him and a whole host of demons at his heels. Rushing to Sophia Middleton's side for a lavish wedding did not appeal. He didn't think she cared too much; he'd written to tell her of his commission and hadn't heard a thing from her, not in four years. She'd known where he was, she could have contacted him. And she hadn't sought him out in the two years he'd been back, either.

Ian thought back on why he'd finally decided to marry her. It had nothing to do with her charms—he honestly didn't know if she had any. What he wanted was a new beginning. He had love with Derek, but it hadn't made either one of them truly happy. They were too mired in the past, in a war they rarely talked about. Even more than Ian, Derek was haunted by the war. Ian wanted them to have a new start with someone not associated with the war and all that happened there. Sophia Middleton was the way to do that, he just knew it. Finally they could put the past behind them and live fully in the present, planning for a future. Ian wanted a family. He wanted children. And he wanted to give those things to Derek, too.

Since he'd decided he wished to marry, Ian logically concluded that the wife he'd had waiting in the wings for twelve years would do as well as any other. He thought after twelve years he at least owed her a wedding.

Ian finally allowed himself to study Miss Middleton. She'd looked at him briefly when he came in, but turned away almost instantly. He noticed now that she was biting her lower lip nervously, her cheeks red. She was clutching her hands together in front of her tightly enough to whiten her knuckles. She was as brown as ever. Dull brown hair scraped back in a utilitarian bun, brown dress better suited to a day of work than an auspicious occasion such as meeting the fiancé you haven't seen in twelve years. He assumed, with an inward sigh, that her eyes were still brown as well. He caught her glancing nervously at him, and just at that moment a small beam of sunlight crept through the window to strike her face. Her eyes glowed warm amber, and copper highlights in her hair warmed her skin tone from pale to cream. Interesting. She wasn't so brown then.

"Well, Mr. Witherspoon," Sir Middleton barked, capturing Ian's attention, "it was good of you to invite us here before the wedding. Glad to see you're a man who lives up to his promises after all. Been wondering if you were going to let Sophia wither on the vine before marrying her."

"Yes," Ian drawled, "as to that—"

Sir Middleton interrupted him. "Ah well, no explanations necessary. A young man with seeds to sow, and after the war, well, I daresay you had some seeds stored up, eh?" Sir Middleton's laughter was as coarse as his humor. "No matter, we've kept Sophia at home these years. Saw no need of her gallivanting about when she was already spoken for, so you needn't worry about her, if you know what I mean, even at such an advanced age. She's had no beaux to speak of. We've kept her for you, to be sure."

Ian's eyes widened at this crude assurance. He reflexively looked at Miss Middleton and saw her wince in horror, her features pinched into a frown, her cheeks going from red to white. What on earth had he done to the poor girl, leaving her to Middleton's tender mercies all these years? If she'd been a virtual prisoner in her home her behavior was most likely caused by shyness and inexperience. Ian sent her a small smile of understanding and he saw her eyes widen with surprise before she looked down.

"Miss Middleton may require an explanation," Ian told her father, still looking at the young woman staring fixedly at the Aubusson carpet beneath her feet.

"What?" Sir Middleton exclaimed. "Sophia need an explanation? I daresay not. She'll do what she's told and make no mistake, sir. She don't question her elders nor her betters like some of the young women these days. She knows her place. No, Sophia don't require an explanation."

Ian hadn't looked away, and so he saw her close her eyes and bite her lip harder. He wished she'd speak up for herself. What was she thinking? Did she want this marriage? It had never occurred to Ian that she might not. He had assumed she'd be as anxious to marry as any other young woman. He was still attractive at thirty, and he'd made quite a bit of his own money in the years since their betrothal. He was, by anyone's standards, a rather good catch. He got the impression Miss Middleton was not just anyone.

Sophie wished the floor would open up and swallow her whole, even if she dropped straight down to hell. Surely the Devil was preferable to spending even one more minute in the company of her overbearing, pompous, callous, ignorant toad of a father. Sophie always felt better after she called her father names, even if it was only in her head. Sometimes she got so angry she couldn't even think of a name foul enough for him, so she just chanted to herself, *I hate him, I hate him, I hate him*. It settled her nerves and cleared her head so that she was able to bear his awful presence for another day.

Today's mantra was different. Today it went something like, *please let him marry me, please let him marry me*. It was a shorter version of the prayer she'd been sending to God every day for the last twelve years. She knew nothing about him. As a matter of fact she hardly remembered what he looked like she'd been so frightened that day he and his father had come to sign the papers for the betrothal. She'd assumed then that he was like her father and her brother Harold—crude, mean and vicious. She'd thought he was going to take her away that day and she was scared. She knew how to deal with her father and Harold, where to hide from them and what to say to avoid the worst when hiding wasn't possible. She didn't know how to protect herself from Mr. Witherspoon or his father.

But they had left her there that day. Before leaving he'd spoken directly to her, the first and only time. She remembered his words quite clearly, she'd repeated them to herself so often since.

"Well, little girl," he had drawled with a smile, "so we're to be married, hmm? I daresay it won't be that bad. I'm not such an awful character, after all. I shall try to make you happy and treat you very well, I suppose. But first we both need to grow up. When you are grown, Miss Middleton, I will come for you and you shall be my wife."

In the years after he left her there, Sophie's life in her father's house grew worse and worse. The only thing that had kept her sane all these years was the memory of his words and the promise he had made. She knew she was no bargain. Harold had told her often enough that she was not attractive. She was too plain, too thin, too intelligent to be thought of as pretty. Harold had told her Mr. Witherspoon was never coming. That he would never want a girl like Sophie for a wife. Harold tortured her with his taunting, his threats to tell Mr. Witherspoon all about her, and then surely he would never come. Sophie couldn't help but think it was a good thing she hadn't remembered that he was beautiful. Tall, with golden hair, classically chiseled features and kind blue eyes the color of the summer sky. If she had remembered she would have had no hope to sustain her through her long wait.

Then two months ago his letter came. Harold had been gone for almost a year, the most wonderful year of Sophie's life. He was on the Continent gaining polish, as Sir Middleton put it. Personally Sophie didn't think there was any amount of polish that would shine up Harold's tarnished soul. When her father had come to tell her that Mr. Witherspoon had finally decided to marry her after all, she was numb with shock, sitting in the small solar she claimed for herself for hours, unable to believe it was true. That night at dinner Sir Middleton had informed her they were to go to London in two months time to visit with Mr. Witherspoon and plan the wedding. Sophie had been forced to excuse herself early and barely made it to her room before she broke down. She'd cried until she had no more tears, until her chest and her throat ached. She was leaving her father's house. She was getting *out*.

The last two months had been harder than the previous twelve years. She now knew that freedom awaited her and it made her chains that much harder to bear. Each morning she woke up wondering if that was the day that Harold would return and ruin everything. But Harold never came, and finally, finally the day arrived when they could leave for London. Sophie had very carefully not spoken more than a dozen words to her father since Mr. Witherspoon's letter arrived. She gave him no reason to postpone the trip or, God forbid, cancel it.

And then they were here, in his house. But Sophie's wait was not over; he hadn't been here. A whole week he'd left her wondering if he was going to go through with it. The footfall of a servant in the hallway made her flinch, prepared for a letter from him saying he'd changed his mind. Her father had settled into the townhouse as if he owned it, conducting business out of Mr. Witherspoon's library and drinking his spirits and berating his servants. And Sophie had waited quietly, just as she had for the last twelve years. *Please let him marry me, please let him marry me.* And now here he was.

"Miss Middleton?" Mr. Witherspoon was speaking to her, and she realized he expected an answer from her. He wasn't going to just accept her father's words as her own. He wanted to hear *her.* It was a heady experience.

"I…" She had to stop to clear her throat. She wasn't expected to talk very often. "I do not require an explanation, sir. I am glad you are well and finally arrived." There, that ought to do all right. There was nothing in her statement to take offense at, surely. It was polite and noncommittal.

"I hope your wait was not unpleasant?" Mr. Witherspoon inquired as politely. "You have been made comfortable by my servants, have you not?"

"Ignore her, sir!" Sir Middleton angrily replied. "'Finally arrived', indeed! Are you complaining, girl?" He stalked across the room to grab her arm, and Sophie stiffened her back in preparation. She didn't move away, that always made it worse. Before he could touch her, Mr. Witherspoon intercepted him, deftly leading him over to the settee.

"Could I interest you in a drink, Sir Middleton? I have quite an impressive collection of scotch. A friend in the Highlands sends it to me, you know. It is early, but finally seeing this marriage through is cause for celebration, is it not?" He smoothly rang for a servant while he spoke. The butler materialized in the doorway.

"Scotch, please, Montague," Mr. Witherspoon told him, and the servant turned away without another word.

"A drink would be welcome, Witherspoon. Your butler kindly let me sample some of that scotch in your absence. Excellent stuff, excellent."

Mr. Witherspoon beamed at him. "Thank you, Sir Middleton. It is quite my favorite beverage as well."

Almost immediately Montague reappeared with two glasses and a bottle on a tray. "Tea, miss?" he asked Sophie quietly as he poured the scotch.

Montague had been unfailingly polite to her, even almost kind, and Sophie secretly liked him. She didn't let it show of course—he was a servant and her father got very upset if she was too familiar with the servants. She didn't want her father to tell Mr. Witherspoon and get Montague sacked. When she replied, she kept her tone impersonal. "No thank you."

Mr. Witherspoon looked at her oddly when she answered Montague. Her features remained neutral, but inside she was panicking. Oh God, what had she done? Should she have taken tea? Ignored Montague? What?

Mr. Witherspoon looked back at her father without speaking to her. "Here is your scotch, Sir Middleton. Do enjoy it while I discuss some ideas about the wedding with Miss Middleton. Boring stuff, really. I shall return her after we've made some decisions."

While he'd been talking, he kept in constant motion. He handed her father his drink and glided over to take Sophie's elbow and urged her toward the door. She was stiff and clumsy next to him, surprised at his ability to manipulate her father, shocked at the heat and strength of his hand on her arm. She was prepared for his grip to get tighter, to bruise as he pulled her in his wake, but it remained gentle yet firm.

Sophie's father was frowning. "Plan what you like, Witherspoon. Sophia doesn't need a large wedding—too old for that. I've not a lot of time or blunt to waste on her, anyhow. Spent all I'm going to spend in that department on her sister's wedding. Corrina, now, she did well. Married to Lord Applesmith, she is," he said crassly.

Mr. Witherspoon stopped in the drawing room doorway and smiled politely at her father, clearly refusing to take offense. "Applesmith, you say? Good man, good man. Excellent. Well, Miss Middleton may have what she likes, I daresay."

17

Before her father could answer, the footman closed the door behind them. Sophie expected to hear him bellow after them, but silence greeted their departure. She demurely followed Mr. Witherspoon, but inside she was rejoicing. Her father let her go. He was already giving up the irksome responsibility of her to Mr. Witherspoon. Now if only she could be sure that was a good thing.

Ian kept a gentle grip on Sophia's arm as he led her to his study, but inside he was seething. Wasn't she even allowed to have tea, for Christ's sake? What an utterly graceless baboon her father was. He had no recollection of that. If he'd had any idea he certainly would have rescued poor Sophia by now.

If she wanted rescuing, that was. He was as unsure of her thoughts and feelings now as he had been when he walked into the salon. She gave nothing away, other than her obvious dislike of her father, who was oblivious to it. Ian couldn't really blame her there, anyway. No, what she failed to reveal was how she felt about him and this marriage. That was what he intended to find out once he got her alone in his study. Hopefully she would talk more there. He'd actually counted her words this morning. She had spoken less than twenty in the entire conversation.

He led Sophia to a comfortable chair directly across from a deep burgundy velvet chaise. Ian and Derek had spent many an hour ensconced in the study reading in those two chairs. After seating her, Ian returned and closed the door to ensure their privacy. When he turned back around Sophia looked a little frightened. Marvelous, his bride-to-be was scared to be in the same room with him. This just got better and better.

She had not said a word, nothing. If she were frightened she apparently wasn't going to talk about it. Sighing inwardly, Ian carefully walked over and sat down on the chaise facing her.

"Miss Middleton…" he began and then paused. "Do you mind if I call you Sophia?"

She nodded. Well, it was a response anyway. "Is that a yes you mind or yes I may call you Sophia?" Ian asked teasingly, trying to draw her out.

"You may call me whatever pleases you, Mr. Witherspoon," she answered quietly. Her voice was low and husky, probably from lack of use, Ian thought wryly. Nevertheless, he was pleasantly surprised to find that he liked it. It raised the hairs on the nape of his neck in a sure sign of desire. How odd to actually want her, Ian mused. Amber eyes, copper hair, velvet voice—little Sophia Middleton was turning out to be not at all what he had expected, in both positive and negative ways. He frowned at the thought.

In an absentminded way he watched Sophia's mouth tighten. He looked up into her eyes and she quickly looked down. Damn, she must have seen him frowning and assumed he was angry at her.

"Sophia, I wanted to get you alone to ask if this is all right with you." Ian kept his tone gentle and schooled his features into a pleasant mask.

Sophia just looked confused. "If…if what is all right with me?"

Ian waved a hand vaguely in the air. "All this, the wedding, the marriage, me. Do you want to marry me? You needn't go through with it if you don't want to, you know. I won't make you."

When you are grown, Miss Middleton, I shall come for you and you shall be my wife. He didn't want to marry her, Sophie thought, horrified. It was a promise made by a young boy who was forced into a situation he had no control over. Now that he was a man, he didn't want to marry her. Oh, she'd known it all along, really. Harold had tried to warn her but she hadn't wanted to believe him. She'd convinced herself it was more of his emotional torture, but he'd been telling the truth. She supposed when Mr. Witherspoon waited four years past the specified date in the marriage contract to even contact them, she should have suspected as much. And now here it was—he was going to toss her off.

Sophie closed her eyes. After the first two or three times Harold had touched her, she'd stopped begging. She wouldn't give him the satisfaction, no matter what he did. But here she would beg if she had to. She had no pride left, nothing to lose. She would beg Mr. Witherspoon to marry her. Slowly Sophie sank down to her knees.

Derek had slipped out the French doors to the terrace when he heard Ian and his fiancée coming down the hall to the study. He'd been hiding in there trying to take comfort from one of his and Ian's favorite rooms. Now it, too, was to be tainted by that bitch.

She sounded like an idiot. "You may call me whatever pleases you, Mr. Witherspoon," and, "if what is all right with me?" God, how could Ian stand it? Derek was tempted to peek and see what she looked like. He could picture her now with her perfect brown hair and vacant brown eyes, dolled up in the very latest, most expensive fashions. Her papa had bought her a noble connection. Bah! She was a slut fucking her way into the nobility.

When Ian asked her if she wanted to marry him, Derek held his breath. Perhaps she would say no. Ian wouldn't make her, he was telling the truth. He'd set her free and play the blackguard to save her reputation. She was silent so long Derek leaned over to look through the door.

"What the hell?" Ian suddenly exclaimed from inside the study and Derek moved faster to look through the glass. He didn't know what to make of the scene that greeted him.

Ian was standing in front of the chaise and Miss Middleton was kneeling before him. As Derek watched, she lowered her head to the floor at Ian's feet, clasping her hands before her as if in prayer.

"Please, Mr. Witherspoon, if you have any charity in your soul, please, I beg you, marry me." Her voice was low, muffled by the carpet, but Derek could hear the tremor in it, could almost feel her sincerity. *She isn't perfect*, was all he could think.

"Sophia, Sophia, please, get up," Ian implored her, reaching down and grabbing her shoulders to lift her. He managed to raise her head and torso though she remained kneeling. Derek jerked back at the sight of the tears on her face.

"I swear to you, Mr. Witherspoon," she said fervently, her voice rising, "I will be a good, biddable wife. I will do whatever you want, I swear it. You can send me away once you don't need me anymore. You can send me to the country—I'll go quietly. I know I'm not much of a bargain, but you'll never regret marrying me, I promise." She hesitated, but rushed on when Ian started to speak. "I know about your lover, about Mr. Knightly. I don't mind, I swear it. I'll stay out of your way, I won't complain. I'll just give you an heir if that's all you need me for and I'll fade into the background." She obviously didn't realize that the revulsion she felt at the idea of Ian getting her with child showed on her face.

"Please, please, don't send me back. Don't, I beg you." The last was said with a sob as she collapsed and Ian bodily lifted her off the floor and sat her down on the chaise. He sat next to her, still holding her shoulders, and she visibly flinched.

"Sophia, I have every intention of marrying you if that is what you wish. Shh, my dear," he crooned, pushing a handkerchief into her hand, "stop crying. I will not send you back, even if you don't want to marry me. I will find a place for you. You needn't ever go back, Sophia, I swear."

"Sophie," she whispered so quietly Derek almost didn't hear her.

"What?" Ian asked, confused.

21

"My name is Sophie," she said, wiping her eyes. She looked at Ian as if he hung the moon. "And I want to marry you, Mr. Witherspoon."

Ian took her hand in his. "Then we shall, Sophie," he told her quietly, "as soon as possible." He gently held her hand between his. "Will you do me the honor of being my wife, Sophie?" She nodded stiffly and started crying again. Ian rose to sit next to her, awkwardly patting her on the back as she sobbed into his kerchief.

Derek quietly moved away from the door and leaned back against the rough brick wall. Bloody hell, how did he fight that? Miss Middleton was turning out to be a more formidable foe than he could ever have imagined.

He stalked off across the terrace and down into the gardens on the back lawn. Why did Ian bring her here? Why did he insist on changing everything? They'd been happy the way they were, hadn't they? They lived quietly, enjoying their free time, and they had plenty of it! Why would any man give that up for a wife and a squalling infant? Ian had tried to tell Derek this marriage was as much for him as it was for Ian. That Derek needed a woman in his life, a family of his own. With Miss Middleton, Ian claimed, they could have those and still stay together, just like Jason and Tony and Kate.

Derek sat down on one of the benches, and then turned and lay down on it. He rested one booted foot on the bench and raised his arm across his forehead, blotting out the sun while he stared at the clouds. His inner turmoil made a mockery of the relaxed pose. He thought again of Ian's reasons for this marriage. Was Ian so very unhappy then? Perhaps their life had no highs or lows, so what? He'd seen enough of those in the war. He deliberately blocked the memories. And if Derek had no thought of the future, again, so what? The war had certainly taught them that any future was uncertain. It was best to live for the present and let the future take care of itself.

He liked his life this way. People left him alone and he left them alone. He had time for his books, and Tattersalls. Perhaps one day he'd buy some racers. Yes, that's what he'd do some day. And it wasn't as if they needed Miss Middleton's money now. Brett Haversham had made them a tidy little fortune on the 'Change, and Derek had learned enough from him to continue to do quite well there on his own. He'd parlayed the modest inheritance from his father into a rather immodest income.

That was another thing. Family, family, family. Ian was always going on about wanting a family. Derek didn't understand it. He'd been an only child, as had his parents. His mother died when he was young and he and his father hadn't been particularly close. When he'd died before Derek came back from the war he felt a small measure of regret, but it certainly hadn't devastated him. It wasn't as if Ian's numerous relations had done so well by him. They'd broken off with him over Derek. Derek felt a stab of guilt over it every now and then, but it had been Ian's decision. Derek knew Ian missed his brothers, missed the huge gatherings of the Witherspoon clan that occurred several times a year. He'd grown up with so many relatives he couldn't go to the loo without tripping over one. And now there was just the two of them.

Derek sat up suddenly as a horrific thought occurred to him. Good Lord, how many children did Ian want? Surely not enough so they'd be tripping over them. He moaned and hung his head. What the fuck was Ian doing? Had he lost his mind?

Chapter Two

೫

After their emotional meeting in the study, Ian suggested Sophie go upstairs to rest. He didn't even bother informing Sir Middleton that they were done. He sent a footman to tell him Ian and Sophie would be busy the rest of the day. If he saw him, Ian was afraid he'd kill him, literally. He could almost feel the man's throat slowly being crushed beneath the pressure of his hands, silencing his crude, vicious words forever. He hadn't pressed Sophie for details about why she would beg a virtual stranger to marry her. It was enough she had done so. She was his responsibility now.

Not wanting the wedding to be too much of a burden on Sophie, Ian penned a note to Kate, Lady Randall, the wife of an old friend. In it he informed Kate of his upcoming wedding and asked her to please help his fiancée get ready. He knew Kate would come. Then he went in search of Derek.

He found Derek upstairs in his bedroom. Derek hardly ever used it. When he slept, which was rarely, he slept with Ian in Ian's room each night. It was not a good omen to find Derek haunting the little-used chamber.

He closed the door behind him when he entered. If he and Derek were going to have a row, he'd rather not advertise it to the servants or Sophie. Derek surprised him by turning away from the window he had been rather assiduously staring out of.

"So is it all settled, then?" Derek asked in an uncharacteristically neutral voice. Ian's sixth sense for trouble was sounding the alarm immediately.

"Yes, Sophie has agreed to be my wife," Ian answered cautiously. "I'd like to proceed with all due haste actually. I was thinking of getting a special license."

Derek looked at him for a few moments as if expecting him to continue. When he didn't, Derek looked away, his façade cracking just enough to show Ian a hint of frustrated anger. He looked back at Ian after gaining control. "Nothing interesting happened, then?"

Ian debated telling Derek about the scene in the study but decided against it. Derek despised weakness in anyone. He'd learned that in the war. Weakness meant you didn't live very long. He didn't want Sophie to start out with a mark already against her, so he shook his head.

"No, not really. Her father is a boor, however. The sooner we can get rid of him, the better."

Derek angrily undid the buttons on his coat, placing his hands on his hips aggressively. "So you're quite eager to marry her just to get rid of her father. There's a good reason. Yes, I can support that logic."

Ian sighed. "Derek…" His voice trailed off because he didn't know what to say anymore. He'd said it all and Derek hadn't listened.

"Don't 'Derek' me." He stomped over to a chair beside a small reading table in the corner and threw himself down on it. Ian winced. The chair was Louis XV and looked as if it would snap in two at Derek's rough treatment. Derek gestured wildly about the stale, impersonal bedchamber.

"Am I to be banished here, then? Shall I move my things today?"

Ian barely stopped himself from barking an affirmative at him. Why was Derek making this so hard? Ian had tried everything he could think of to get Derek to talk about this marriage but Derek refused. He ran away every time, not willing to hear Ian's explanations. Ian had stopped trying. He was desperate and damn frustrated now. He didn't know how else to make Derek accept it except to just do it and deal with the consequences later. He knew in his heart it was right for them. Why wouldn't Derek trust that Ian was doing this for both of them? Hadn't Ian always taken care of Derek, done what was best for him?

"No," he forced himself to be patient yet again, "I don't want you to move in here. I want you to stay in our room, where you've always been welcome and will continue to be so."

"By 'our room' are you referring to your new wife? I know how you prefer to keep your lovers close at hand. But she may not be so eager to share her lodgings with me." Derek came up off the chair with the same violence he'd used to sit down. He began pacing in front of Ian. "She's going to take over, it's what women do. Pretty soon you'll be dancing to her tune. 'Yes, Sophie,'" he simpered. "'No, Sophie.' It's enough to make me sick."

Ian's denial died in his throat. Instead he asked, "How did you know her name was Sophie?"

Derek spun around to look at him guiltily. This time Ian did sigh. "So you heard the entire conversation?"

Derek immediately went on the attack. "It's a good thing I did, since you clearly were not going to share it with me. I can't believe she begged you to marry her! And you fell for it, every word. I pity you for a gullible fool. And if she really is that pathetic, I pity you more." He ran his hands through his hair in frustration. "I'm trying to save you, Ian, from making a terrible mistake! Pay her off and send her away. If you marry her we will all be miserable."

Ian wearily walked over and sat on the edge of the bed. It smelled musty from disuse. "I can't, Derek. If what I suspect is true…I just can't. You didn't see her face. She was desperate. She needs me." He looked up at Derek hopefully. "She needs us. And we need her."

Derek backed away, waving his hands defensively. "Oh no, don't drag me into this. You wanted to get married, not I. I am the victim here. She's the spider luring the unsuspecting fly—that would be you—into her web of guilt and pity. I see through her. Ian, she won't be able to resist you, no one can. You watch, she'll be after you to get rid of me next." He stopped backing away and shook a finger at Ian. "Oh yes, that was a very affecting part of her little speech you know, where she claimed not to mind that you had a lover."

"Derek—"

Once again Ian was cut off. "Don't," Derek warned, narrowing his eyes at Ian. "Don't try to make me feel sorry for her. She's fucking marrying you, isn't she? What the fuck have I got to feel sorry for her for?" Derek ripped off his coat and threw it across the room.

"I'm well aware—"

"You are completely oblivious!" Derek shouted. "She is manipulating you. I'm not arguing that her father isn't a horse's arse and has probably browbeaten her from the cradle. But she's using you, Ian. To her you're just a way out of her personal hell. Damn it, you could be me and she wouldn't give a damn. You're a warm body to drag in front of a parson and unlock her jail cell. She doesn't know *you*, she doesn't love *you*."

"I fail to see—"

"Exactly! You fail to see everything!"

Derek continued to rail against Sophie and the marriage. Ian had been listening to the same arguments for months now. Derek wasn't saying anything new. Ian got distracted watching Derek. God, sometimes he forgot how incredibly handsome Derek was. He was extremely tall—no matter where they went he was the tallest man there. He had thick, wavy, dark brown hair and hazel eyes, a beautiful mix of green and gray. His arms were thick with muscle, his shoulders broad, his chest deep. Derek's waist and hips were lean, but his ass cheeks were nicely rounded and firm with muscle. They fit perfectly in Ian's hands. The dark hair on his chest tapered down to a thick nest around his cock. Ian loved to bury his nose there and smell that musky Derek scent that drove him mad. Derek's legs were a mile long, thick with hard muscle and covered in coarse, dark hair. When Ian was riding Derek tight and hard, the hair on his legs rubbed Ian's smoother thighs and sent shivers straight to his cock. Derek was all man and all his. Suddenly Ian realized Derek had stopped talking.

"God damn you," Derek whispered. "How can you marry her when you look at me like that?"

"Are you actually going to let me speak?" Ian asked teasingly.

"If you've something worthwhile to say," Derek replied, his belligerence returning. He held out a hand and gestured for Ian to speak.

Ian smiled. "I love you." Derek snorted and Ian's smile became a lopsided grin. "I have nothing else to say. I can hardly think straight. I was sitting here thinking how incredibly attractive you are, and that you're mine, and now I'm hard as a pike and can't think at all."

"Aargh!" Derek growled. "I'm ready for battle and you disarm me again with your fucking charm. That really pisses me off, Ian."

"I know. Come and do something about it." Ian leaned back on his elbows on the bed, his erection straining against the front of his trousers.

Derek ripped his cravat off and threw it to the floor. As he was opening his shirt he snarled, "If you think I'm going to come over there and suck that hard cock you're showing off, you can think again."

"All right." Ian was being very agreeable. "If not here, then where?"

Derek was standing in the middle of the room with his shirt open and hanging off his big shoulders, framing the perfection of his chest and stomach. His trousers were riding low on his hips and when Derek put his fists on those hips it pushed them lower so that Ian could just see the beginning of the bush of pubic hair he so loved. Ian felt his cock jerk. He looked up at Derek and raised an eyebrow. "Are you done showing off that body for my benefit? I'm already hard. Are you trying to make me come all by myself over here?"

"Over against the wall, by the door," Derek ordered.

Ian pushed himself up off the bed. "Today your wish is my command, Derek." He sauntered past Derek and over to the wall. He turned and leaned against it, narrowing his eyes. "But tomorrow it's my turn again."

"Oh ho, so you're going to do whatever I want today?" Derek crowed, rubbing his hands together. "I didn't know you knew how to let go of the reins."

"You've never wanted me to. You love being ridden hard too much." Ian ripped open his trousers, pushing them down to free his cock. It was so hard it bounced against his stomach as he settled back against the wall. "Forget what I said. You'll do as I command, and right now I want you to get over here and suck this."

Derek padded over to the wall like a predatory cat. He was so goddamn graceful. Christ, everything about him excited Ian, even after five years together. Derek placed one forearm on the wall next to Ian's head and leaned in to whisper in his ear.

"And what will you do for me, lover, if I suck that cock?" Derek's words were accompanied by a featherlight touch along the length of Ian's erection.

Ian turned his head so that he was looking at Derek, their faces so close together he could have kissed him almost without moving. "Do it right and I'll fuck you with it later."

"You always know the right thing to say," Derek teased, and he moved the fraction of an inch required for their lips to meet.

Ian immediately opened his mouth and devoured Derek. He ate at his lips, sucked his tongue, caressed the inside of his cheeks. His teeth nipped Derek's lower lip and Derek pressed in against him. Ian bent his knee and let Derek ride his thigh, his cock a hot ridge against it. Ian reached around and grabbed Derek's ass, those tight cheeks filling his palms, and ground Derek's cock against his leg. Derek pulled away from the kiss with a shudder.

"Steady there, Captain," Derek said shakily, "you can do permanent damage that way." His breath hissed as Ian squeezed one ass cheek hard and traced the hot valley in the center through his trousers with the fingers of the other hand. God, Derek loved that, the tease of what awaited him later driving him deeper into the well of desire.

"God, you're round-heeled," Ian laughed huskily. "You could at least pretend to be hard to get."

"I thought I was," Derek testily replied, his argument undermined by a hard thrust against Ian's thigh and another shudder.

Only here, with Ian, was Derek able to show weakness. It was one of the things Derek loved about being with him. His weakness was a trigger for Ian's passion. Ian craved his surrender, and by surrendering, Derek conquered. He possessed Ian's soul as completely as Ian owned his.

Ian just laughed again. He took his hands off Derek's ass and Derek started to complain until Ian rested his palms on his stomach and caressed his way up to Derek's shoulders. "Take that fucking shirt off."

Ian's voice was low and deep, and when Derek looked at his face, Ian's eyes were hard and hooded by desire. That look had precluded so many bouts of lovemaking and sexual satiation that it alone would have made Derek hard and ready even if Ian weren't touching him like this. Derek gasped as he felt his cock jerk.

"Jesus, are you going to come now?" Ian's voice was amused, with an underlying thread of indulgent satisfaction.

"I might as well," Derek ground out, "since it's your cock that's about to get sucked, not mine."

"Do unto others…" Ian muttered with a sly grin.

"You are going to hell, Ian Witherspoon," Derek chastised him mockingly.

At his words Ian roughly pushed Derek's shirt off his shoulders and helped him tug it off his arms and drop it to the floor. "Heaven first," Ian told him. Derek groaned as Ian leaned in and bit down on a nipple hardened with arousal. Ian pulled back slightly and licked the stinging nub with the flat of his tongue, then he ventured off to the side and began indiscriminately swirling his tongue along the muscles of Derek's chest, his fingers tangled in the hair there, tugging gently. Derek's head fell back and he bit his lip to keep from moaning as he clutched Ian's shoulders. He reveled in Ian's worship of his body. He knew he could make Ian hard and reckless with just a glimpse of his chest or arms. Ian became positively feral when he saw Derek naked.

Ian slowly wrapped his arms around Derek's chest, his fingers caressing Derek's spine as he raised his head and licked along Derek's lips. Derek opened his mouth to let Ian inside and was treated to a deeply tender kiss, soft yet possessive. When Ian pulled back, Derek found his own arms wrapped around Ian's neck, his fingers buried in his baby-soft hair. He clung as Ian slowly pushed him away until he had to let his arms drop.

"Take the rest of your clothes off." The order was issued in a firm voice, one that brooked no disobedience. Derek languidly complied.

It was an especially erotic thrill to be naked in Ian's arms while Ian himself remained almost fully clothed. It made

Derek feel a little like a sex slave, and secretly he liked it. Well, not so secretly. He'd told Ian as much once, and it was one of Ian's favorite games now.

When Derek stood proud and naked before him, Ian let his escalating desire show. He licked his lips and reached down to wrap his fist around his cock and pump it slowly several times, clearly enjoying the view. Derek stood docilely before him, the object of his desire, Ian's to command.

"Masturbate for me. I want to see you come."

Derek's breathing hitched. Christ, Ian had him on fire today. When Ian watched him like this, made Derek perform for him, Derek felt his own power over his lover. He stared at Ian and slowly ran his hands over his chest, stopping to tweak his own nipples hard. He rubbed the palms of his hands over them and savored the sting. Ian watched it all avidly, his breathing unsteady.

"Are you going to come just from watching me?" Derek sounded almost bored, but his labored breathing belied the impression.

Ian smiled wickedly at him as he made a great show of letting go of his cock. "Oh no, darling. I have no intention of denying myself the pleasure of coming in your mouth."

Derek's head fell back and he ran his hands down his stomach until he reached his cock. He fisted it tightly in one hand while the other sought his balls and rolled them together. The pleasure brought his head up and hunched his shoulders.

"You love to play the tease, don't you?" Ian whispered throatily. "You love to show your body to me, to make me want you ferociously when I see how much you enjoy pleasuring yourself."

"Yes." Derek's tone was harsh and defiant as he watched Ian stare in fascination at his finger slowly rubbing over the leaking end of his cock, spreading the pre-cum on the plum-shaped head until it glistened in the sun coming through the window to his left. At the sight Ian leaned against the wall, closed his eyes and swallowed. When he opened his eyes he laughed weakly.

"If you keep that up, lover, you're not going to get to suck my cock, and I know you want to."

Derek stopped and completely let go of his cock. "Bastard," he whispered. He slowly walked forward until he was so close to Ian he could see the pupils in his eyes dilated with desire. "Permission, Captain, to suck and masturbate at the same time." He smiled wryly. "I'm not going to last either, I'm so fucking close. I want to taste you in my mouth when I come, Ian. I need to taste you." He didn't wait for permission, but fell to his knees in front of Ian, grasping both his own cock and Ian's in his hands. He leaned forward and sucked on the warm, firm head of Ian's cock.

"Yes," Ian hissed, his hands going to either side of Derek's head. One gripped his hair tightly, the other lay tenderly along Derek's cheek. "Yes, bring yourself while you taste me, Derek. Bring me with you."

Derek needed no further encouragement. He slid his lips down Ian's length as far as he could comfortably go, then placed his fist there as a marker. He pulled back and then sucked down to his fist again, making Ian shudder and lay his head back on the wall. It took a moment to find a rhythm that worked for both him and Ian as the hand on his own cock kept time to his mouth on Ian. He sucked deeply on each downward stroke and swirled the flat of his tongue along the underside as he pulled back. Ian squirmed and moaned, especially when Derek's tongue hit the sensitive spot just below the head of his cock. Derek knew how he liked it and he enjoyed doing it.

Ian's breathing grew heavy, each exhalation a growl as Derek felt his cock harden more in his mouth. Derek's climax was hovering just out of reach, almost painful in its reticence. He pumped his fist harder, unconsciously sucking deeper on Ian in counterpoint.

"Christ, Derek, I'm going to come. It's so good. You are so good." Ian's hands were gripping his shoulders, the fingers digging into his muscles, and Ian hunched over him, fucking in and out of his mouth as Derek sucked him. Suddenly Ian's hands were gripping the back of his head, pulling him down hard on his cock until the tip was almost touching the back of his throat. It was nearly too much, and would have been if Derek hadn't taken the precaution of placing his fist so that Ian couldn't choke him. He knew from experience that Ian got carried away when he was coming in Derek's mouth. He wanted to ram his cock down Derek's throat and tried, not to hurt or intimidate him, but because it felt so good. Derek loved that it felt that good to him. Ian groaned his name and Derek tasted the first wash of his cum on the back of his tongue. He swallowed convulsively around Ian's cock, causing Ian to groan and jerk, more cum spurting into Derek's throat. As he swallowed, Derek felt his own climax burst on him. As he ejaculated, the pleasure was almost painful and he felt his cock jerk and burn with the heat of his cum. He kept hold of Ian, kept him in his mouth, tasted and rolled him on his tongue as he moaned his own satisfaction.

After he came, Derek unwrapped his fist from around Ian, but kept his softening cock in his mouth and gently sucked on it, laving it with his tongue. Ian gasped and hunched over him again. His hands ran down Derek's shoulders, petting him, caressing his strong upper back tenderly. When Ian was small and soft in his mouth Derek finally set him free.

"Derek," Ian said softly, running his hand through Derek's hair.

Derek looked up at him as he knelt before him, a sexual supplicant. "Don't forget what I can do for you, Ian," he said, his voice unsteady. "Don't for one minute think she can give you this."

Ian blinked slowly several times, tipping his head to the side and then laid his hand on Derek's cheek. "I could sooner forget to breathe than forget how you devastate me, Derek." For a change, he said nothing about her, and Derek tried to be satisfied with his answer.

* * * * *

The following afternoon in the drawing room, Ian turned to greet Lady Randall and her niece with a genuine smile. As he had hoped, Kate, as Lady Randall preferred to be called by her friends, had agreed to help Sophie get ready for the wedding and had rushed over as soon as she was able.

Ian hadn't seen Derek since last night. He hadn't appeared at dinner and Ian had had to endure an evening of his future father-in-law's crude, self-aggrandizing conversation and verbal bludgeoning of Sophie. He'd intercepted the worst of it, but the evening seemed interminable and Sophie retired immediately after dinner. He couldn't blame her. He'd escaped as soon as politely possible. Politeness with Sir Middleton was getting harder and harder to maintain. This morning Ian had taken breakfast in his room and had ordered the same for Sophie so she wouldn't have to suffer alone with her father. Ian wished he'd had the opportunity to speak with her again.

Derek had mysteriously reappeared in Ian's room about an hour after Ian retired last night. Ian hadn't inquired where he'd been and Derek didn't offer the information. When he'd climbed on top of Ian, he'd smelled suspiciously like he'd been drinking, a lot. He was voraciously aroused however, and Ian had no problem living up to the promises made during their morning liaison.

"Ian, my dear," Kate said, coming over and kissing his cheek, "I'm so glad you asked for my help. I didn't get to plan much of a wedding for myself, if you'll remember, so this will be the wedding I didn't get to have." She smiled with delight. "So just open your coffers and promise not to get shot before the wedding." Kate, Jason, and her other husband Tony had been married at what they all thought was Jason's deathbed.

Jason, however, had other ideas and woke up in the middle of the ceremony to make his promises. He'd fully recovered from the gunshot wound he'd incurred during a duel over Kate.

"I hope it isn't too much of a burden, Kate, considering your condition." Ian hadn't even thought about Kate's pregnancy when he'd penned his note yesterday. She looked marvelous, however, tall and lithe and blonde. Her stomach was only slightly rounded with child.

Her niece, Veronica Thomas, snorted inelegantly. "You must be joking, Ian. Look at her! She is disgustingly glowing. She's never looked or felt better in her life. If this continues, they'll have her breeding every year." Very's eyes had a mischievous twinkle as she sat down in a delicate armchair.

Kate took the bait. "Veronica Thomas! That is beyond rude. You'll have poor Ian blushing and thinking I don't know what about us." It was Kate who was blushing, and Ian took pity on her.

"She is right, Kate. You look absolutely stunning. Motherhood seems to agree with you." To his dismay, Kate got choked up and had to dig a handkerchief out of her reticule.

"Oh Ian, never mind me. I'm a veritable watering pot these days. Mother tells me it's the baby and it will pass." She sniffed delicately and tucked her handkerchief into her sleeve. "Good heavens, I burst into tears when Cook made my favorite soup the other day. Can you imagine? The poor woman was beside herself."

Very laughed and got up to lead Kate to a chair. "It's true. It's driving Jase and Tony mad. They're afraid to say anything for fear of Kate having a breakdown. It's the only reason we were able to get out of the house alone today."

The drawing room door opened and Derek sauntered in as if he hadn't been in hiding. "Why hello, ladies! And to what do we owe this pleasure?" He intercepted Very and Kate and enveloped Kate in his arms, giving her a smacking kiss on the cheek which made her laugh and then cry again.

"Oh, look what you've done, you darling man!" Kate laughed through her tears. "And I'd just stopped."

Derek looked alarmed. "What did I do? Did I hurt you? Sometimes I forget what a big ox I am. I'm so sorry, Kate."

Very came to his rescue by punching him on the arm. "You big lummox, she's just overly emotional because of the baby. Why don't you ever kiss me? I'm younger and available, and quite pretty if I do say so myself."

Everyone laughed at Very's comment, as she'd wanted them to. "That's exactly why I don't kiss you," Derek teased. "I don't want to find myself dragged in front of the preacher by Jason and Tony. Not to mention Kensington and Wolf would probably kill me before I got there. And your head is swollen enough with your own charms, I don't need to contribute to it."

"My head is perfectly proportioned to my body, ape, and these days I think Kensington would gladly sell me to the gypsies. As for Wolf, he does whatever Kensington wants him to." Lord Michael Kensington had had an on-again, off-again courtship with Very for the last year or so. Every couple of months he decided she was too young, or too argumentative, or too something and then after a few weeks he came crawling back because he clearly couldn't live without her. It amused the rest of them no end. Wolf Tarrant was Kensington's lover, and rather an enigma to everyone else. Ian didn't think Very's assessment was right, but he really had no reason for his belief, just a feeling.

"And who could blame him?" Kate said archly. "You are a trial, Very. If I'd been thinking clearly when you were younger, *I'd* have sold you to the gypsies. I needed the money then." Everyone including Very laughed with Kate.

Derek led Kate to a chair and after she was seated started to sit down on the settee facing her. He stopped in mid-motion and sprang back up at Kate's next words, however.

"We're here to help plan the wedding, of course. Ian said poor Miss Middleton has no one to help, and so here we are."

"Well, it was good to see you both," Derek said, walking briskly to the door. "I'm sure we'll see each other again soon. Good day, ladies."

"Derek," Ian began, but the other man was out the door and gone before he could say more.

Kate sat stunned. Even Very was struck speechless. "What did I say?" Kate asked anxiously.

Ian sighed and sat dejectedly on the settee, his head dropping onto the back of the elegant piece of furniture. "Derek has yet to meet Sophie. He keeps disappearing, and avoids any situation where they might cross paths."

"Oh dear," Kate murmured. "That doesn't bode well. Are you sure this marriage is a good idea, Ian?"

Ian sat up and placed his elbows on his knees, clasping his hands together between them as he stared at the floor. "I can't cry off now, Kate. I've set it in motion and I can't leave Sophie in her present situation." He looked up at Kate bleakly. "You'll understand when you meet her. If only Derek weren't so stubborn. If he'd stop viewing her as the enemy and instead try to understand that she needs us. Why can't he see what I'm trying to do here?" Ian stopped. "Never mind. Let's focus on making this a beautiful wedding for Sophie. I'll deal with Derek. He'll come around."

"But Ian," Very said heatedly, "you can't just make him accept her. You and he have been together so long, you have so much you've shared together. I don't think it's right you're bringing this Sophie here if Derek doesn't want her." Very took a belligerent stance in front of Ian, her arms akimbo as she glared at him. "You owe him that much, Ian."

Kate had been watching Ian closely. She spoke softly but firmly. "Very, you are jumping to conclusions again. Haven't we talked about the danger of doing that? Come and sit. Let us reserve judgment until we meet Miss Middleton. We owe Ian that, I think." Very reluctantly sat down with a final glare for Ian.

"Thank you," Ian told her sincerely. "And I think when you meet Sophie you'll understand, Very. She needs all the friends she can get."

Sophie approached the drawing room door with trepidation. Montague himself had come to knock on her door and inform her that Mr. Witherspoon was waiting for her with some guests. Sophie didn't like to meet new people. One never knew how to act around them or how to please them. It made her extremely uncomfortable. Harold and her father were forever telling her she had no social skills.

She had about decided to turn around and send her regrets when Montague opened the drawing room door and announced her. She was clear across the landing at the time and had to hurry to the door. It was almost as if he'd known she was going to run. She allowed herself to frown at him. He merely blinked benignly and stepped behind her to crowd her into the room, closing the door after her.

Sophie looked into the room and saw Mr. Witherspoon standing up. He walked toward her and she couldn't see around him although she sensed the presence of other people in the room. She could feel herself getting tense and uneasy. What did he expect of her?

"Hello, Sophie," he said quietly when he stopped in front of her. "I trust you are well today?"

His manner was calm and Sophie found it soothing. Mr. Witherspoon had so far shown himself to be a gentleman, and his reassurances in his study yesterday had alleviated many of her earlier fears. She was still quite embarrassed about how she broke down in front of him, however. What must he think of her? She straightened her spine and tried to speak confidently.

"Good day, Mr. Witherspoon. I am well, thank you. And you?" There, that sounded polite and self-confident. His answering smile told her she'd done well.

"I am fine, Sophie." He turned back to the room and indicated two attractive, well-dressed women sitting there. "Let me introduce you to some friends. This is Kate, Lady Randall, and her niece, Miss Veronica Thomas." He took Sophie's elbow and led her farther into the room. "They have come to help you plan the wedding, my dear. I hope you don't mind my asking for their assistance."

Sophie felt herself blanch. Oh God, he didn't trust her to plan the wedding. Of course, she knew nothing about planning a wedding. She hadn't thought that far ahead, she'd been so focused on just getting him to agree to marry her. What on earth did one do at a wedding? The only one she had ever attended was Corrina's, and she'd only witnessed the vows. She'd not been allowed to attend the festivities after. She could feel a crushing weight in her chest knowing she was already a disappointment to him. She looked up at Mr. Witherspoon. Before she could apologize, Lady Randall spoke.

"How do you do, Miss Middleton? May I call you Sophie? And you must call me Kate. It is so wonderful to finally meet you. Ian told us of your upcoming marriage weeks ago. How exciting! Very and I can't wait to help plan the wedding with you. I was married in a bit of a…hmm, situation, shall we say, so this is a first for me. You don't mind, do you? I'd hate to impose." Lady Randall stood and Sophie could see she was tall and beautiful, and exquisitely dressed. Sophie felt even more of a frump than ever in her plain brown dress.

"How do you do?" she murmured, keeping her face a polite mask. Everyone seemed to be waiting for her to speak some more, so she continued nervously. "I'm very glad of any assistance you can give me, ma'am. I'm not well versed in planning social events, I'm afraid." A discreet look at Mr. Witherspoon showed him smiling at her encouragingly. She mentally relaxed.

The younger woman who'd been introduced as Miss Thomas finally spoke. "How do you do, Miss Middleton? Congratulations on your upcoming marriage." She eyed Sophie in a confused way. "I hope you don't mind my asking, but how long have you been out in society?"

Sophie's cheeks burned with embarrassment. "I've never had a come-out, I'm afraid. Father didn't want the expense since I was already betrothed."

"Veronica!" Lady Randall chastised. She turned back to Sophie. "Ignore her, my dear. She's terribly jealous. Ian is a wonderful catch, you know." She smiled teasingly at Sophie, and Sophie had no idea how to respond. Did Miss Thomas want Mr. Witherspoon? Had Sophie unknowingly interfered in their love affair?

Mr. Witherspoon stepped into the breach. "Veronica is no more jealous of me than she is of the dog next door, Kate. She knows I'd never put up with her wild ways." Sophie's eyes flashed to him in alarm. Was he trying to tell her she needed to behave or he would punish her? He sensed her distress but seemed at a loss as to what to say.

"Sophie, I didn't mean…" he trailed off and Sophie bit her lip.

"I didn't mean to offend, Miss Middleton," Miss Thomas spoke up, more confused than ever. "I just thought your father was rather wealthy, is all. Ow!" She jerked as Lady Randall hit her in the arm with her fan. "What? Isn't he?"

Sophie was mortified. She realized now Miss Thomas was talking about her old, unattractive gown, not suitable for a young debutante. She bit down harder on her lip.

Lady Randall walked over and took Sophie's arm, leading her to the settee. Sophie looked frantically at Mr. Witherspoon, but he seemed relieved that Lady Randall was taking over.

"I'm sure Miss Middleton will tell us all about herself as we plan the wedding, Very," she said firmly. "There's no need to interrogate the poor girl today."

"One little question is hardly an interrogation," Miss Thomas muttered, spinning around indignantly to take a seat in a huff. Louder she said, "How are we to know what she wants if we don't ask her about herself?"

"What I want?" Sophie asked, alarmed. "Want for what?" She couldn't believe the young woman was talking to her aunt in such a manner. Surely she was going to get into trouble. Lady Randall tugged Sophie down to sit next to her.

Miss Thomas looked at her like she was a lackwit. "For the wedding, of course."

"Yes, well, I'll leave you to it, then," Mr. Witherspoon said, backing toward the door. Sophie started to shoot up from her seat, unable to believe he was going to leave her alone with these two women. What on earth was she supposed to do with them?

"Yes, run along, Ian," Lady Randall said officiously, placing a hand on Sophie's arm to hold her down. "Men have no place in these affairs. A wedding is all about the bride."

"No!" Sophie burst out, "Don't leave." Mr. Witherspoon froze and looked at her stricken face. Lady Randall slowly let go of her arm while Miss Thomas looked at her in shock. She tried to keep the panic out of her voice as she continued. "I mean, I don't know anything about planning a wedding. Father has said he won't pay for a big wedding. What am I to do? Where shall it be? I...I don't know who to invite. I don't...don't you have people to invite?"

Her voice was rising, but she couldn't control it. Mr. Witherspoon looked pained at her outburst and Sophie tried to backtrack, tried to think how to repair the damage. "What I mean to say is, I don't require a large wedding or an expensive one. Couldn't we just get married here? With a few witnesses? Or no one, not if you don't want them." By the look on his face she was just making things worse. She looked down and noticed she was wringing her hands and forced herself to stop. She looked at Lady Randall and saw pity in her face. When she glanced at Miss Thomas, the young lady's face had gone from shock to horror. Oh God, what a mess! She should leave. She stood jerkily and took a step toward the door. "I should just go. Yes, I'll just go."

Mr. Witherspoon came up and took her hands gently. "Sophie, stop. Take a deep breath." His voice was calm and soothing, his face soft with an emotion Sophie couldn't decipher. She took several deep breaths and did feel better. She concentrated on his face and let the panic subside.

"All right?" he asked quietly with a squeeze of her hands.

"Yes, yes, I'm better. I'm sorry." She clutched his hands, still not wanting him to go.

"Now, about the wedding," he began and Sophie's eyes widened in alarm again. "Sophie," he said admonishingly, and she forced herself to relax. "Good girl." He squeezed her hands again. "You may spend as much as you like." He looked at Lady Randall when he said it, and Sophie glanced over to see the other woman nodding in agreement. He continued and Sophie looked back at him. "I will draw up a list of friends to invite. I know they will want to be here."

"Of course they will," Lady Randall murmured in agreement.

"As for where we get married," he paused to make sure he had Sophie's attention, "I don't care where it is. All I know is I want to marry you, the sooner the better. As a matter of fact, I'm going to get a special license. I didn't want to force your acquiescence by obtaining a license before we'd had a chance to meet and talk, Sophie. With a special license we won't have to wait." He looked over at Lady Randall. "Kate, would it be possible to have the wedding as soon as next week? Perhaps Thursday next?"

Lady Randall looked a little shaken, but nodded her head. "Yes, it's possible. We'll be extraordinarily busy to pull it off, but we can do it, can't we, Very?" she asked her niece. "It will be a beautiful wedding, Ian."

Miss Thomas answered her aunt, her eyes on Sophie. "Yes, we can do it. We'll get Kitty to help, and Mrs. Jones." She turned to look at Mr. Witherspoon. "You're right, Ian. I do see it now." And with those enigmatic words, Miss Thomas smiled purposefully at Sophie. That smile, for some reason, made her think of a protective guard dog. She wasn't sure she felt entirely comfortable being the object of it.

Chapter Three

છ

Sophie was shocked at how quickly the week went by. She was getting married tomorrow. She had almost accepted that it was indeed going to happen—almost. Kate and Very had been wonderful to her, and Kitty Markham as well. She was Kate's best friend and she owned a dress shop. Apparently the dress shop used to belong to Kate, but after she married Lord Randall she sold it to Kitty. Not only had Kate and Kitty designed a beautiful wedding dress for her, they had also helped her order a lavish trousseau, insisting that Ian had the money to pay for it and would not mind. Ian...even now it was hard to think of him that way although he'd practically begged her to use his first name.

It was the trousseau that had finally caused angry words between Ian and her father. Sophie had been so embarrassed because Kate and Very and Lord Randall had witnessed the scene. After they returned from Sophie's first fitting, Kate had made the mistake of offhandedly telling Ian about the trousseau while Sir Middleton was in the drawing room.

"Ian dear, you'll be happy to know that we've ordered an entire trousseau for dear Sophie. She simply isn't used to how many clothes are required for London, I'm afraid." Kate had accompanied her comment with a smile at Sophie, who thought it very dear of her to phrase it that way instead of pointing out how outdated her ugly brown dresses were.

Sophie had made the mistake of relaxing too much here. She'd forgotten how her father could be.

"What do you mean, Sophia, ordering clothes without Witherspoon's approval?" Sir Middleton had asked, outraged. He'd stalked across the room, grabbed her arm and started to

45

drag her to the door. Sophie had immediately fallen back on years of training. She'd closed down her face, she'd said nothing and she hadn't resisted. She'd avoided looking at everyone else in the room, stoically hiding her shame behind that blank face.

Suddenly Ian was there in front of them. The look on his face frightened Sophie. She'd never seen anyone so mad, not even Harold or her father. When he spoke she actually flinched at the anger in his menacing tone.

"Unhand her this instant, Middleton." What did Ian mean to do to her?

Her father had tightened his grip and pulled her roughly to his side. "I'll handle this, Witherspoon. You needn't fear that she'll be doing this kind of thing again. You've got to take a firm hand with Sophia. She's the devil's own temper and a mind of her own. If you let her get away with something like this she'll be out of control in a month."

"I said let her go." Sophie was staring intently at the carpet, tracing the beautiful red swirls around and around, imaging she was lost there in the maze of them, far from that room and her awful, horrible pig of a father. Ian's command made her jerk slightly, and her father shook her.

"A good beating will put her back in her place. Like all women she thinks to rise above her station every now and then. But she's been trained well, Witherspoon. It's just this loose atmosphere here in London, more license than she's used to, I daresay. Well, she's not your responsibility yet. I'll not have you thinking we've let her run wild, no sir. She's been taught to be seen, not heard, to carry out her duties to her master and stay out of the way when she's not needed."

"If you touch one hair on her head in my house I will kill you." Sophie's head jerked up and she stared at Ian incredulously. She'd never heard anyone threaten her father.

Sir Middleton was frowning, not understanding. "What do you mean, sir? Not discipline my own daughter? You are not her husband yet, sir, and you haven't got the right to do it."

Ian reached out and grabbed Sophie's other arm, yanking her away from Sir Middleton, who tried to hold on tight. Ian's grip was firm but he took care not to hurt Sophie. Her father had no such compunction. His fingers dug into the soft flesh of her upper arm as he fought with Ian over her.

"What do you mean, Witherspoon, interfering between me and my daughter?" He was beginning to grasp that Ian was angry at him and not Sophie.

Sophie could feel her face burning with humiliation and she couldn't stop her gaze from darting across the room to the other occupants. Kate looked ready to cry and both she and Lord Randall were holding Very's arms. Very looked as if she wanted to hit someone, and with shock Sophie realized it was her father. From the look on Very's face, if Kate and Lord Randall let go she would attack Sir Middleton. Sophie's heart melted in gratitude. Ian's voice brought her back to the confrontation between him and her father.

"Sophie is to be my wife in less than a week. We are betrothed, and I have met all my obligations in the marriage contract. In the eyes of the law we are already legally bound. Dowry be damned, if you hurt her again I will throw you out of this house and the wedding will go on without you."

Sir Middleton let Sophie go and she stumbled into Ian, who wrapped his arm around her protectively. "Fine," Sir Middleton said gruffly, "take her. I wash my hands of her. She's been a trial since the day she was born, and no amount of beating made her mind her betters. You'll see. You'll rue the day you let her get away with this. And don't come crying to me for the blunt for all her fripperies, no sir. If you want her to dress like some high-class whore, you are paying for it, sir, not I." He marched indignantly to the door but threw one last parting shot back. "I'll not be leaving this house until she's legally wed. I'll not let the world call my daughter slut if I let her stay alone with you. I've worked too hard to gain a foothold in society, sir, and I'll not let some bitch I had the misfortune to whelp ruin it."

The door clicked shut behind him and Sophie stood stiffly in Ian's loose embrace, her eyes focused intently on the blue superfine of his expensively tailored jacket. She was drowning in so many emotions she didn't know which to feel, so she felt nothing.

"Sophie?" Ian asked, his voice concerned. "Are you all right?" He put both hands on her shoulders and pushed her back slightly as he lowered his head to look at her face. She couldn't meet his gaze. Humiliation and gratitude overwhelmed her.

Her voice seemed small and fractured to her ears when she spoke. "I...thank you, Mr. Witherspoon. I never had anyone defend me from Father before. I...thank you." She was horrified to feel tears on her cheeks. She was crying again. Oh Lord, her father was right. Ian was probably already ruing his decision to marry her. "I'm sorry." She stepped back and fumbled for a handkerchief. "I always seem to be crying around you, Mr. Witherspoon. I honestly don't know what's wrong with me lately. I'm not a watering pot, I swear. You needn't worry that I shall cry all the time. I won't, really I won't. It's just...just things, I suppose."

She abruptly turned her back to him and to the others. It was all just so humiliating. At home at least no one had seen it but the servants. But now, now they all knew. Her own father thought her worthless—no, less than worthless. She was a troublesome slut was what they all must be thinking. Suddenly something barreled into her from behind, nearly knocking her down, and Sophie couldn't quite contain the "Oof!" that escaped her. She was spun about and Very crushed her in her embrace.

"Oh, Sophie! Sophie!" was all she said, but it was enough. Of their own volition, Sophie's arms came up and clung to the taller girl, and she found herself sobbing against her shoulder.

Kate had hurried over and bustled the two of them out and they had somehow ended up in Sophie's room with tea and cakes, and a cold compress for Sophie's eyes. She'd spent nearly every day since at Lord and Lady Randall's, or shopping for more clothes and accessories and wedding necessities. She hadn't seen her father once, and she hadn't asked about him.

Sophie was brought back to the present by a knock on her door. "Come in," she called out, so excited she could barely sit still. Kitty was bringing her wedding dress today and Kate and Very were coming over to watch the final fitting.

"Hello, darling!" Kitty called out as she came into the room. Behind her one of the maids was carrying the dress carefully wrapped up, and Mrs. Jones, the seamstress from the dress shop, brought up the rear. "We've brought your wedding finery, my dear. I think I heard Kate and Very downstairs just now, so go on and take off your clothes so we can see it on you."

Sophie didn't need to be told twice. She kissed Kitty exuberantly on the cheek and disappeared behind the screen to take her morning gown off. She still didn't like to undress in front of others. The first time at the dress shop no one had said anything about the two or three scars on her back, so they must not be as noticeable as Sophie thought. She'd been relieved not to have to lie about them. Harold's riding crop was small and must not have left large marks in spite of how much they'd hurt at the time.

"Did you bring the underthings too, Kitty?" she called out. "I don't think my shift will fit right under it."

"Of course, silly, they're right here," Kitty told her, peeking around the screen. "Shall I help you with them?"

Sophie blushed and grabbed her discarded dress to hold in front of her. "No, no, I'll be all right. Just put them there, Kitty. Thank you." She smiled at the older woman to take the sting out of her words, not wanting to offend.

As soon as Kitty put them down and disappeared, Sophie heard the door open again and voices raised in happy conversation.

"We're here! We're here!" Very called out excitedly. "Where's the bride? Has she run yet? I know I would if I were marrying Ian and Derek."

Sophie paused, confused. Ian and Derek? She must have misunderstood. She heard Kate shushing Very.

"Very, do shut up. You'd run straight to the altar if you were lucky enough to marry Ian, you little scamp, and you know it." Kitty was laughing as she said it.

"Children," Kate said mildly, helping Kitty and Mrs. Jones unwrap the wedding dress, "behave. You'll have Sophie thinking she's fallen into a nest of Bedlamites. Here Very, grab the bottom and help us lift it over Sophie's head."

"I haven't seen Derek in ages, Sophie," Kitty said conversationally a few minutes later as they helped her into the dress. "Where is he?"

Sophie spoke from inside the dress. "I don't know, Kitty. I haven't met him." The dress glided down around her and Sophie looked up into three incredulous faces.

"You haven't met him?" Kitty asked slowly. "Not at all?"

Sophie shook her head. "I believe he's avoiding me. I sent him a note the other day, but I don't think he read it. I tried to assure him that Ian and I getting married needn't change anything for him. I've told Ian that too." She looked away from them all. "I mean, I assume you know that they are, um, close."

"Close?" Very repeated. "Sophie, they are—"

Kate interrupted her. "Yes, well, I'm sure he's been busy getting ready for the wedding too. Now do look at yourself, Sophie, really you must."

Kitty wouldn't let Sophie look until the dress was on properly. Kate started crying again and Sophie gave her a handkerchief. She'd taken several out and left them on the table since Kate invariably needed one every hour.

"Oh Sophie," Very breathed, her eyes shining. "You're beautiful. Look."

Sophie was afraid to look. Kitty nodded at Very's words and gestured to the mirror behind Sophie. "Look," she urged with a huge smile. Sophie slowly turned around.

Who was that? It surely wasn't Sophie Middleton. The woman in the mirror was beautiful with shining copper hair and luscious curves encased in silk and lace. The dress was heavy gold watered silk falling from the bodice to pool on the floor around her feet slightly. The overdress was a rich cream Valenciennes lace which came to a vee between her breasts, leaving a triangle of the gold silk exposed. The lace covered her shoulders and back and ended in small, formfitting sleeves on her upper arms. It fell shorter than the gold silk to end about a foot above the floor. The effect was ethereal and bold at the same time. Sophie looked like a flame lit from within. The woman in the mirror looked like someone who should be marrying handsome Ian Witherspoon. That had been one of Sophie's greatest fears. That she would appear next to him at the wedding in front of his friends and she'd see by the looks on their faces that they were wondering why he was marrying her. But this Sophie, yes, she could marry him and no one would question it. Her eyes met Kate's in the mirror.

"Yes," was all Kate said, as if she knew what Sophie was thinking.

"It fits perfectly, miss," Mrs. Jones said, beaming. "Not a stitch needed."

"Ian will be totally besotted," Very laughed, "if he isn't already. He'll hardly be able to wait through the day to ravish you."

Sophie watched herself flinch in the mirror and the color drain from her face. Oh God, all this week she'd been trying not to think about the wedding night.

"Let's get you out of this before something happens to it," Kate said briskly, stepping up behind her. "Very, why don't you go and make sure the staff has all their instructions for tomorrow."

Very looked at her suspiciously. "Why? What are you going to talk about while I'm gone?"

Kate gave her a look over her shoulder that Sophie couldn't see.

"Are you going to talk about the wedding night? Because, honestly, Aunt Kate, I'm sure you aren't going to tell Sophie anything I don't know already."

"Veronica Thomas!" Kate said reprovingly. "As an unmarried young lady I certainly hope you don't know all there is to know yet."

From where she was kneeling down at Sophie's feet checking the hem of the dress, Kitty spoke up. "I don't know, Kate, she's got half the men wrapped around her little finger. I'm willing to bet they've told her anything she wants to know. And lord knows Kensington and Wolf don't look like they need lessons in it."

Sophie tried to steer the conversation away from sex. "Who are Kensington and Wolf?"

Kate's answer was meant to put a damper on that line of questioning. "You'll meet them tomorrow. Very, out."

Sophie's tension level escalated. "No, Kate, honestly, I don't need to talk about, you know, that." She tried not to babble and lost the fight. "I'm sure I'll be fine tomorrow night. Honestly. I've lived in the country, you know. I've seen, well, animals and such." God, she was sweating. She had to get out of the dress. She did not want to talk about sex. She knew sex. She knew the ripping pain of it, the humiliation of it. She knew how to think about something else when someone was doing that awful thing to her. She could go so far in herself that she almost didn't feel it. She started grabbing at the dress, trying to get it off.

"Sophie!" Kate's voice was loud and firm, and Sophie stopped, her breathing ragged. She looked at herself in the mirror and saw her stark white face, her too large, panicked eyes. She looked at Kate and she knew the other woman saw it, saw what she didn't want anyone to know.

"Sophie?" Very said, confused.

"Very, get out," Kitty said quietly, and when Sophie looked at her the same knowledge was staring back.

Kitty raised the dress up. "Kate, hurry up and get the tapes undone." Sophie felt the dress go slack and she automatically raised her arms to let Kitty pull it off over her head. When she could see again, Very and Mrs. Jones were gone.

Sophie nearly fell as she rushed behind the screen to change her clothes. When she was hidden from sight she covered her face with her hands and tried to block the thoughts crashing through her head.

"Sophie?" Kate's voice was quiet from the other side of the screen. "Are you all right? Do you need help?"

"No," she said, but it came out muffled by her hands and she lowered them and tried again. "No, I'm fine, Kate, honestly. I'm fine. I'll meet you downstairs." If not for her shaky voice she might have believed it. Kate did not.

"I'm not leaving, Sophie. You may as well come out."

"Kate," was all Sophie said. She didn't know what else to say.

"Either you come out or I come in. Your choice." Kate sounded determined.

Sophie heard Kitty folding her wedding dress and laying it on the tissue to keep it from wrinkling. Her wedding dress—the words were enough to bring back the tremors she'd almost conquered. Her wedding night lurked like the veritable monster under the bed. Sophie knew the monsters where real, and she was scared of them.

She pulled on the simple blue dress that Kitty and Mrs. Jones had altered the day they'd gone for her first fitting. Kitty had taken one look at her awful brown dress and nearly swooned in horror. That's why Sophie liked her so much, Kitty didn't dissemble. If she liked something everyone knew, and if she hated something the same applied. She knew, intellectually, that she could trust Kate and Kitty. But emotionally she was terrified that someone had figured out her secret. When she was dressed she slowly stepped out from behind the screen.

She took one look at the mixture of pity and concern on their faces and she turned away, walking over to the window to pull the curtain aside and stare unseeing at the street below.

"Do you want to talk about it?" Kate asked quietly. Sophie shook her head. God no, she never even wanted to think about it again. This marriage to Ian, it was insurance that she'd never have to, or so she'd thought. She was distressed to realize that the idea of consummating the marriage with Ian was bringing back the horrible memories and feelings. She hadn't thought that far ahead.

"How long ago was the rape, Sophie?" Kate's question made her wince. Rape, yes, that's exactly what it had been, every time.

"The last time was over a year ago," she whispered. "I'm fine now, I am." She still couldn't bring herself to look at the other two women.

Sophie was so tense it wasn't until Kate's hands came to rest on her shoulders that she knew the other woman had moved. She forced herself to relax against the gentle touch.

"Sophie, I know something of what you're going through. I myself was raped almost two years ago." Sophie couldn't restrain her gasp of disbelief as she spun to look at Kate. The tall, cool blonde nodded, and Sophie saw the memory in her eyes and knew she spoke the truth. "I can tell you honestly, Sophie, that making love with your husband is nothing like the act of rape. It can be a beautiful experience, Sophie. It is meant to be. Do not fear what will happen between you and Ian. Let him ease the memory of your pain and replace it with memories of pleasure and love."

Sophie felt the panic flood her. Kate was going to tell Ian, she was going to tell him! She grabbed Kate's hands tightly, beseechingly. "Please don't tell Ian, Kate, please." She was shaking her head over and over, frightened. Harold said if he knew, he wouldn't come, he wouldn't marry her. No man wants a used bride. "He mustn't find out, Kate, oh God, please don't tell him."

Kitty had risen from the small stool where she had been listening. "He doesn't know?" she asked cautiously. "You must tell him, Sophie. If he knows he'll be able to treat you accordingly tomorrow night."

Sophie's eyes were huge. Accordingly? What did that mean? That he wouldn't need to be gentle because she wasn't a virgin? "No! This is all I have, don't you see? He's practically being forced into this marriage, and he knows about my father already. If he finds out about this, he'll throw me out, I know he will. He won't want a wife who isn't a virgin, no man does."

"Was it your father?" Kitty asked matter-of-factly.

"My father? No, it wasn't Papa." Sophie was genuinely shocked. She couldn't imagine her father doing something like that at all.

"It doesn't matter who it was, Sophie," Kate said sympathetically. "You must tell Ian, and if you can't then I will do it for you. Do you want me to tell him?"

Sophie started to cry desperately. "Please Kate, I'll tell him, I will, in my own time. Please. This marriage, it's my last chance, Kate. If Ian doesn't marry me I'll have to go back with my father, and…and he's waiting there, Kate. It will happen again and again and I'll never be free. Oh God, Kate, please help me be free."

Kate took her in her arms, rubbing her back soothingly. "All right, Sophie, all right. We'll let you tell him. But Sophie, Ian won't care. He would marry you anyway, Sophie, whether he knew or not. Ian cares for you, he does, you'll see. Tell him before tomorrow night, Sophie. Give him the chance to make it good for you."

* * * * *

"Ow! What the hell was that for?" Derek rubbed his arm where Very had punched him. He was hiding in the study. He'd been sitting in his favorite chair trying to read as he listened to the women upstairs exclaiming and chattering like magpies. That was what happened when you let women in the house, they cut up your peace and now here was one abusing him for no good reason.

"You utter, completely selfish clod," Very hissed at him.

Derek slithered out of the chair and put it between him and the very angry woman glaring at him.

"I may be, but that hardly gives you the right to come in here swinging." Derek didn't like how pathetic he sounded, so he stood up straighter and glared back at Very.

"I can't believe you haven't even met Sophie yet, you little worm. Don't you know how nervous she is? How scared of everything that's happening? Her whole life is changing. She's entrusting it to strangers, and you can't even be bothered to say how do you do? What do you think, you'll just march into the bedroom on their wedding night and say let's fuck? Do you think she's going to roll over and take that?"

Derek could see how mad Very was, and he knew how volatile she could be, but she was pissing him off too. He tried not to think about the image she'd just painted for him, but the fact that he could indeed imagine fucking Sophie with Ian made him even angrier. He'd been avoiding those mental images all week, ever since he'd seen her in the library.

"She's got you championing her now, has she? Can't she even fight her own battles? First Ian and now you. She must be amazingly good. And no, I have no intention of bedding her. If Ian wants her, he can have her, but I have no interest. She's getting what she wants. She wants Ian and she's got him under her manipulating little thumb. She'll not get me. She may not like it, but Ian was mine first and I'm not going anywhere. So you and she can just take your poor little Sophie act somewhere else because I'm not buying it."

"God! You are such an ignoramus! Can't you see anything beyond your big, fat, selfish nose, you idiot? Sophie is so fragile a good, stiff wind will break her. If you'd bothered to pull your head out of your arse for five minutes in the last week you'd know that she's spent most of her life being horribly abused by a father who has no feelings for her whatsoever. She's afraid to trust, afraid to care for someone, she's afraid to be touched, for Christ's sake. She needs you, Derek, you and Ian. She needs all of us, but especially you. Do not, and I mean this sincerely, do not make me regret trusting her with you. If I think you're no good for her, Derek, if I see you hurt her, I will make your life hell. Do you understand? Do you?"

Derek was shaken by Very's words, though he tried not to show it. Was it true? It would explain why she'd begged Ian to marry her. Or was it just part of her act? Had she told them all this to get their sympathy, win their trust?

"I don't know what she's told you—"

Very cut him off. "Nothing. She won't say a word, won't talk about it at all. I watched her father try to drag her off and beat her the other day, Derek. And blithely talk about how hard he's tried to beat the spark out of her for most of her life. And Sophie stood like a statue, her beautiful eyes dead while he said it. I never want to see her look like that again. Or look the way she did this morning." Very turned away abruptly, hugging herself. Her voice was barely a whisper when she continued. "Oh Derek, I think something awful was done to her, even more awful than her horrible father beating her." She spun back around and walked over to him, clutching his arms tightly. "Please don't hurt her anymore, Derek. Please."

"What are you talking about, Very? I'm not likely to hit her, you should know that much about me." Derek was wounded that Very would think that of him. He knew he had a bit of a reputation as a bully, but he'd never hit a woman, never.

Very shook her head. "No, Derek, I know that. I'd never think that about you." Suddenly she hugged him tight. "But there are other ways to hurt someone, deeper ways. Please be kind to her, Derek."

Derek hugged her back. "All right, Very, all right. I'll try to be nice to little Sophie. There, see? Feel better?"

Very pulled back and smiled tremulously. "Yes, yes I do, because I know you'll never break your word, Derek." She backed toward the study door. "I've got to go see about the preparations for tomorrow or Aunt Kate will have my head." She turned and opened the door, calling back over her shoulder as she went. "And stop hiding in here, you coward. You're pathetic."

"Shrew!" he called after her lightheartedly.

She laughed, closing the door behind her. He heard her feet skipping down the hall.

Derek walked back around and fell into his chair. Why hadn't Ian told him? If what Very said was true, why hadn't Ian confided in him? It didn't take a great deal of soul-searching for Derek to figure it out. He'd been a bloody bastard to deal with the last couple of months, ever since Ian had decided to marry. Especially since Sophie and her father had arrived. Ian probably realized that Derek was in no mood to be forgiving or sympathetic. He'd been so ready to hate her, to fight her for Ian. When he realized there would be no fight, that from that first morning she'd owned part of Ian already,

Derek had moved beyond reason and into survival, and Ian had paid for it. He could see that now.

Bloody hell, Derek didn't like all this introspection. It made a fellow deuced uncomfortable to recognize he was a damned selfish prick. It pained him more to realize that, even knowing some of Sophie's background, he still resented her — resented every moment she spent with Ian, every future moment, every touch of his hand on her, the children they'd have, the love they would share. Jealousy was an ugly thing, and he was too full of it to let it all go at once, maybe too full to let it all go ever. But for Ian he'd try. Derek didn't need to love her, he didn't even need to be her lover, he just needed to find a way to live with her and not kill her.

Chapter Four

𝕊𝕆

Ian was in his dressing robe staring out his bedroom window at the stars. There were so many of them. He'd heard many theories on what they were, literary musings on what they represented—lovers, broken hearts, fish in the ocean, raindrops in a storm. To Ian they were just stars, they simply existed. They were bright, they were beautiful, they made mysterious things possible in the night. He was not an astronomer and didn't want to be. He preferred to live simply, to take what was given him and enjoy it as much as possible before it left or was taken away. He didn't dissect things, he didn't quantify or qualify them. It was a philosophy he'd been taught by war.

So why was he standing here evaluating his life? He was getting married tomorrow to a sweet, beautiful girl who would be the mother of his children. He had a magnificent lover whom he adored even if he was a bit moody. Ian felt his lips curve in a reluctant smile at the thought. Derek's moodiness was one of the things Ian adored about him. He'd always loved the challenge of dragging Derek out of his black moods, forcing him to be happy and to live life to its fullest. He sighed. He'd hoped that his wife would be able to help him do that for Derek.

Perhaps it was standing on the cusp of a new life that made him look back at the past. He had few regrets. Derek was one of them. He often wondered if he'd done right by the young soldier who had suddenly appeared at his side one day and never left. If he had pushed him away, if he had never made Derek his in every way, would he be happier now? Would he have a wife and children, a home of his own, a profession? He owed Derek more than just his love and adoration. He had, in his own selfish way, ruined Derek's life. He'd stolen his future, his peace. But he was going to give it all back to him.

He thought back to those early days, trying to figure out when the decision had been made, if it ever really had. Was there one moment when he said I can either love this boy or I can send him away? It seemed as if they had drifted together until being lovers was simply another step, another part of who they were. And one day he'd woken up and thought *I can't live without him.*

* * * * *

1811, Torres Vedras, Portugal

"Who the hell are you?" Ian was tired and dirty and in a foul mood. He'd been slogging through the mud for days on patrol. Ever since Fuentes De Oñoro, he'd been unable to sleep, again. Christ, would this war never end?

"Lieutenant Knightly, Sir," the gangly youth replied, staring at him. He was ungodly tall and nearly as dirty as Ian. He was also blocking the way to the officers' tent where Ian had every intention of sleeping until doomsday or the next engagement, whichever came first.

"Get the fuck out of my way, Lieutenant," he snarled, shoving past him. "Whatever you want can wait. I'm tired."

"Yes Sir," was all he said, and Ian forgot about him. He stumbled into the tent and fumbled out of his wet, grimy boots and damp jacket. He put his rifle under the cot before he fell on it and soon the blackness of utter exhaustion took him.

When Ian awoke he was disoriented. Where was he, what day was it? He swung his feet over the side of the cot and sat up, rubbing his face. He could see sunlight through the tent flaps. So it must be day, he thought, scratching at his naked armpit. Naked? What the fuck? Ian looked down at himself. He still had his breeches on, but was naked from the waist up.

He never completely undressed so he'd never be caught unaware if called to battle. Quickly he looked around and had to look twice before he could believe what he saw. His shirt and jacket were draped across a stool next to his cot and they looked dry and clean. His boots were next to them on the floor, looking dry and so highly polished they shone in the weak sunlight.

Ian grabbed his shirt and started to put it on but hesitated when he got a good whiff of himself. It seemed a shame to put clean linen on when he was ripe as bad cheese. No sooner had the thought entered his head than he saw a chipped basin covered with a thin cloth under the stool. He pulled it out and removed the cloth to find clean water. When he dipped the cloth in he was startled to find the water not hot, but still warm. When he found the sliver of soap on a piece of paper next to his boots he was beyond shock. It seemed only natural that where there was water, there must be soap. He scrubbed his face and hair and torso with the thin soap and rough cloth. The water was nearly black by the time he was finished, but he felt like a new man. He pulled on his shirt and jacket, delighted at the feel of dry clothes after weeks of damp, dirty wool. His boots were dry as well, and that actually made him whistle with delight.

"Captain." Someone greeted him from behind and Ian swung around to find Major Richards eyeing him speculatively. "Clean clothes? And those boots, good God, old Boney will find us just by their shine. To what do we owe the welcome relief of your improved toilette?"

Ian laughed, and it sounded rusty even to him. Major Richards' eyes went wide. Ian shrugged good-humoredly. "Apparently someone found my stench so offensive they went to the trouble of cleaning me up while I slept."

"Sir." The voice at Ian's back sounded vaguely familiar. Ian turned and saw the young officer he had barked at the day before.

"What is it, Lieutenant?" Ian asked impatiently. The fellow was certainly persistent.

"Request permission to transfer to your command, Captain." The request surprised Ian. He'd never seen the young man before, and not many men wanted to ride with Ian. He had a tendency to take every suicide mission that came along. It was that bloody rumor, that ridiculous tale that he couldn't die. It was as if Ian had to test his mortality every time he went out. He knew it was folly, but he wanted to get shot. He wanted everyone to stop looking at him as if he were the second coming. It was sheer luck he hadn't been wounded yet, not divine intervention.

"I'm not shorthanded right now, Lieutenant. I don't need a new officer."

"With all due respect, Sir, your appearance yesterday indicated that you do."

Ian started with surprise. The boy actually had the audacity to sound amused at Ian's condition the day before. "Well, as you can see, today I'm fine."

"And how do you suppose that happened, Sir?" the young lieutenant asked wryly with a raised eyebrow.

Ian was getting pissed. "Thank you, Lieutenant," he forced out between gritted teeth, "but you are an officer, not a batman."

"Well, word is you haven't got one." The lieutenant had the effrontery to lean against the tent pole with his arms crossed aggressively.

Ian glowered at him. "He died."

Lieutenant Knightly spread his arms. "Well, here I am."

"As I said, I haven't need of a new officer."

The young man stood and narrowed his eyes at Ian. "I say you do. Most of the men in your command can't wipe their own arses, much less cross enemy lines on patrol or find simple supplies for you." He walked over and picked up what was left of the soap. "This was not bartered for gold, Captain, but close to it. You owe me."

Major Richards stepped into the conversation. Ian had forgotten he was there.

"Whose command are you in now, Lieutenant?"

Lieutenant Knightly looked at him, his posture improving at the major's rank and demeanor. "Crossingham's, Sir."

"I'll speak with your commander. Unless there is some impediment you are unaware of, consider yourself assigned to Captain Witherspoon."

"Major!" Ian exclaimed, aghast. "Perhaps we should discuss this further." He looked at the smirking lieutenant. "Privately."

Major Richards looked at him from his impressive height, his lips pursed in contemplation. "I don't think so, Captain. The lieutenant is correct. Your men need a kick in the arse and, apparently, someone to teach them how to wipe it after. Your young lieutenant looks like he could do it." Richards turned and walked to the tent entrance. Turning back he added with a grin, "And I think we all owe him a debt of gratitude for the soap. You were worse than ripe, Captain."

Ian glared at Lieutenant Knightly. "You sorry little son of a bitch. Trust me, you will regret this."

"No more than you, Captain, I assure you," the lieutenant replied sarcastically. "And I had no idea you knew my mother." His reply surprised a laugh out of Ian. The lieutenant smiled wolfishly. "Now, give me a list of things you need. I'm a bit of a collector, you see, if you don't inquire too closely how I acquire them."

It didn't take long for Ian and his young lieutenant, as everyone called Derek Knightly, to become the scourge of camps on both lines of battle. Derek was almost as good as Ian at sneaking around across enemy lines, sabotaging French camps and gathering information. He was even better at collecting supplies from around the British camps. Ian was living like a king, as were most of his men. Hot food, clean clothes, wine, women—Derek acquired it all for them. Ian knew Derek gambled for quite a bit of it. The boy had the devil's own luck. Somehow, and Ian wasn't sure when it had happened, they'd become friends; more than friends, actually. They were damn near inseparable. It became commonplace for people to see them together everywhere. If they weren't, people asked where the other one was. They shared a tent, food, liquor and women.

The first time they shared a woman was similar to their friendship, somehow it just happened, without a plan or discussion. Derek showed up at the tent one night with a rather pretty Spanish whore, still young if a little jaded. When Ian got up to leave the tent, Derek stopped him with a hand on his arm.

"Don't go, Ian." Ian looked at him inquiringly. "Just shut the flap and douse the lamp." He'd done as Derek asked.

"Now what?" Ian asked, but he knew, and he wanted it. He'd heard some of the other officers talking about sharing women. He wanted to do it with Derek. No one else, just Derek. It seemed a natural progression of their friendship somehow.

"Now we fuck." Derek's matter-of-fact statement made Ian laugh.

"Well, that sounds good, but how?"

As his eyes adjusted to the dark Ian could see Derek's perplexed look. "What do you mean how?" The whore was hanging on Derek's shoulder, caressing his chest through his open jacket. "We could take turns, I suppose. Or she could suck one of us and fuck the other."

Ian thought about it. Yes, both of those were options. But if they were going to do it, they might as well do it right. "I want to fuck her together, at the same time."

Derek's eyes widened at Ian's suggestion. "Can she do that?" His voice had a little boy quality to it, as if he'd just found out girls were good for something after all. Ian found himself smiling widely in anticipation of Derek's reaction to what he was going to say next.

"From what I've heard," Ian told him, rubbing his chin thoughtfully as he circled the girl and assessed her attributes and willingness, "one of us fucks her cunt and one of us fucks her ass."

"Christ Jesus," Derek whispered in awe, "that's bloody ingenious. Who thought of that?"

Ian burst out laughing. "I've no idea, Derek, but it sounds pretty damn good to me too." The whore had figured out what was going on, and she was standing there sizing the two of them up. She held up two fingers and pointed at both of them. Ian nodded and she made a gesture for more money.

"Well, it looks as if she knows what she's doing," Derek said cautiously. "I say let's give her a go." Ian pulled the money out of his kit and handed it to the whore, who counted it carefully. Then she took off her shoe and stuffed the money in the toe. She then proceeded to take off the rest of her clothes.

Ian looked at Derek and he shrugged as if to say why not, and then he began to undress as well. Ian found himself anxious to see Derek nude. He was so big, tall and rawboned, with a thick pelt of hair on his chest. What did the rest of him look like? So as not to be obvious, Ian also undressed as he divided his attention between Derek and the whore. She finished first, and Ian was impressed.

"How the hell do you get all the young, pretty ones, Derek?" he asked conversationally as he watched her get comfortable on his cot.

Derek sat next to her and kissed her on her shoulder while he pried off his boots. "I'm young, clean, good-looking and I've the blunt to pay them. Why wouldn't they choose me over some old, fat, smelly officer?" The whore responded to Derek's attention with a smile and she came up to her knees to caress his muscular shoulders and back. She slid behind him and rubbed her large breasts against his back and Derek closed his eyes and smiled. "Is there anything better than the feel of a woman's naked breasts against you?"

Ian had his own boots off and was taking his breeches off, careful not to be too rough as he was pushing them over his erection. The thought of what they were going to do had him hard and aching. "Probably, but I haven't found it yet," he agreed. When he was nude he looked over at Derek and found him openly staring at Ian's cock.

"Bloody hell, Ian, how do you walk around with that beast between your legs?"

The knowledge that Derek was looking at him and admiring him made Ian's cock quiver, and he felt a small drop of liquid leak out. "I'm sorry to disappoint, but it doesn't look like this all the time," he told Derek wryly, trying not to let the other man see how his attention was affecting him. God, he hadn't thought that it would be Derek and not the whore who would have him so hot to fuck.

When Derek stood up and pushed his smalls off, finally standing nude before him, Ian was shocked speechless. He was absolutely beautiful. He was sculpted of thick muscles from his shoulders to his legs, his torso and hips lean, his buttocks firm. His cock was as hard as Ian's, although Ian had to admit not as big as his. Ian had never really compared his penis to another man's. If Derek's was any indication then he supposed he was rather large. His hand actually itched to bury itself in the thick bush of hair surrounding Derek's cock.

Christ almighty, what was wrong with him? He had never been attracted to another man, never. It must be their friendship. He cared very much for Derek. He was probably the best friend he'd ever had. Ian had realized some weeks ago that Derek's appearance in his life was fortuitous. He'd been the lowest he'd ever been, and those suicide missions had been just that—attempts at suicide by enemy fire. Because of Derek's friendship those dark days were over. These feelings, whatever they were, must be attributable to that. With everything going on, the whole bloody world turned upside down with this war, was it any wonder he'd confuse friendship with desire? The thought reassured him.

Ian moved to the bed where the pretty whore was sitting waiting patiently and he sat next to her. "What's your name, sweetheart?" he asked, and she frowned at him, not understanding.

"She's pretty and clean, but she doesn't speak English," Derek said. "I'm good, but I can't work miracles."

Ian smiled at him. "That means she hasn't been at this long. In my book, that's a plus." He turned back to the girl. "Name?" he said slowly. "Nom?" He placed his hand on his own chest. "Ian. Ian." He pointed at her. "Name?"

"Ah, *si*," she said, smiling. She placed her hand on her chest, imitating Ian. "Dolores." She said it slowly, pronouncing each syllable as he had said his name. "Ee-an," she repeated with a hand on his chest. She turned to Derek expectantly.

"Derek," he told her with that wolfish grin of his, and Ian's heart rate sped up. He quickly looked back at Dolores.

"Der-reek," she said slowly and smiled triumphantly, making both men laugh.

"Yes," Derek said, smiling. "Now, kiss." And he leaned in to kiss her mouth. She tried to avoid him and Derek frowned.

"Most of them won't let you kiss them," Ian told him, leaning back on his hands. "You know that. It's some trick of the trade."

Derek gave Dolores a heart-melting grin as he sat down on her other side and snuggled her hand between both of his, bringing them to his chest beseechingly. "Please, Dolores, kiss?" he asked.

Clearly Dolores had not been at her trade for long because she was not immune to Derek's charms. "*Si*, Der-reek, keess," she said and rose to her knees as she leaned over to give him a peck on the lips.

"I don't think she knows how," Ian said wonderingly. "She knows how to fuck two men and has no idea how to kiss. That seems so wrong." He turned Dolores to him. "How old?" he asked pointing at her. He touched his chest. "Twenty-five." She tilted her head, obviously trying to understand. Ian flashed his open hands twice and then held up five fingers. "Twenty-five."

Derek turned her to him. "Twenty," he said, and flashed his hands twice.

"Ah, *si*," Dolores said, smiling. She pointed to herself. "*Diecisiete*." She flashed her hands once and then held up seven fingers.

"Seventeen," Ian whispered. "Should we be doing this?"

Derek was looking at Dolores with ill-concealed lust as she brushed his hand over her pebbled nipples. "If not us, then someone else. Someone else already, actually." He looked up at Ian. "At least we know we'll be gentle and treat her well." He looked back at Dolores and kissed her softly and the girl went willingly into his arms. Derek caressed her cheek with his hand and used his thumb to open her mouth. He kissed her harder, his tongue going deep in her mouth. After a shocked moment, her arms wrapped around his neck and she moaned. Even to Ian's jaded ears it sounded real. Ian ran a hand down her long, smooth back, across her full buttocks and down to the rich delta between her thighs. Her heat and wetness convinced Ian of her sincerity. His touch there caused her to tremble and moan again as she pulled away from Derek's kiss. The look she gave them was a little panicked.

Derek caressed her cheek again and gave her a tender smile. She tentatively smiled back, and then gasped as Ian's finger entered her, going slow and deep. She was smooth and hot and wet, like wrapping damp silk around his finger. Her hips jerked as he swirled his finger, looking for her sweet spot. He knew he found it when she shuddered and bit her lip. Ian moved to his knees behind her to reach her better.

"*Madre de Dios*," she moaned as he pressed against her silken inner wall.

Ian grinned against her hair behind her. "Oh yes, sweetheart, that's right, tell me how good it feels," he whispered, knowing she couldn't understand the words but hoping he was conveying his meaning with touch and tone.

"I love to kiss," Derek whispered, pressing light kisses on Dolores' face and jaw. "I love to kiss a woman's mouth, her body, that sweet, juicy spot between her legs."

Ian chuckled, slowly moving his finger in and out of the girl pressed between them. "Well, she certainly has a juicy cunt." He placed delicate nibbles along her shoulder.

"Is that what you call it?" Derek asked. "I never know. It's got so many damned names." He rubbed noses with Dolores and smiled. "Do you have a cunt, Dolores, or a pussy? What do you call it?"

She smiled. "Keess, Der-reek," she whispered.

Derek's laughter passed through Dolores and into Ian. Ian gasped lightly at the incredible intimacy of it, feeling Derek's laughter during sex when he was so aroused. It damn near brought him right there. He pulled up from Dolores' shoulder and was inches away from the two mouths dancing in the intricate moves of a heated kiss. He avidly watched Derek's tongue delve into Dolores' mouth, watched her surrender to the wet, tender invasion, her eyes fluttering shut. Yes, Derek loved to kiss. It was in each touch of his lips, each thrust of his tongue, each little nibble on the corners of her mouth. Ian's own mouth watered at the sight and sounds of the kiss. He couldn't stop his mind from imagining being on the receiving end of one of Derek's kisses. His hips involuntarily thrust at the thought, jarring Dolores so that Derek broke off the kiss. He looked over at Ian with eyes gone glassy with lust, and Ian's stomach muscles clenched in response.

Ian quickly looked away, laying his forehead on Dolores' shoulder, moving his finger more forcefully inside her until she gasped and shuddered uncontrollably.

"Christ, Ian, what are you doing to her?" Derek asked in wonder as he watched Dolores' uninhibited pleasure.

"I've found her woman's spot," Ian whispered, in enough control now to look up at Derek.

"Her what?" Derek's perplexity was obvious.

Ian's grin flashed in the darkness of the tent. "This is all so I could teach you how to fuck a woman, isn't it?"

"I know how to fuck a woman." Derek sounded offended. Then his grin flashed. "I just don't know how to fuck one as well as you."

Ian's laughter burst out of him. Derek always made him laugh with his brutal honesty, sometimes at his most awful or awkward moments. It was one of the reasons he liked him so much. Ian felt on safer ground here, talking about fucking a woman instead of imagining kissing Derek.

Ian shook his head and then explained. "Every woman has a sweet spot inside her channel, one place that if you touch it they go wild. For some it's near their entrance, for others it's deeper, maybe even so deep the only way you can touch it is with your cock. But they'll come like a wildcat if you find it."

"Now that is the sort of thing every young boy should learn," Derek said seriously, making Ian laugh again. "They need to teach that in school."

Ian snorted. "I'm pretty sure most of my professors were sorely lacking in that respect. There aren't endless, boring treatises written on the subject."

At that moment Dolores grabbed Derek's shoulders tightly, thrusting down on Ian's fingers harder in an age-old rhythm. He moved one finger forward and rubbed the hard nub of her desire, at first gentle but then increasing the pressure until she gave a breathy little moan that quickly escalated into a soft cry as she threw her head back. Ian could feel her vaginal walls pulsing around his finger, and he thrust in another. Dolores cried out loudly and pressed hard against him.

"Christ, her nails are leaving permanent marks in my shoulder," Derek laughed. "I'm definitely going to practice finding that spot on sweet Dolores." Ian leaned over and spread kisses along her nape as she collapsed into Derek's arms.

Ian felt the girl trembling and he leaned over her shoulder for a kiss. It was then he noticed she was crying. He raised his hand and wiped a tear off with his fingers. "What's the matter, sweetheart?" She said something in Spanish that Ian didn't understand, but Derek was able to translate the general idea.

"I don't think she's ever done that before." His voice held wonder and pure male satisfaction. "She's never come before, and we did it." He smiled ferociously at Ian. "Damn, we're good."

Ian laughed. "We? I believe I did most of the work."

Derek licked along Dolores' lips. "My kisses helped tremendously." When she opened to receive him, Derek devoured her mouth.

"Yes, I believe they did," Ian agreed in a whisper.

He pulled his fingers out of Dolores, leaving her wet and swollen, and she moaned. His fingers were soaking with her juices and he glided slowly back to her ass and the tight entrance there. He eased one wet finger in to the first knuckle and Dolores broke from Derek's kiss to cry out in surprise.

"What the hell are you doing now?" Derek asked in exasperation. "I can't see a damn thing in here. Next time we're doing this during the day."

"Would you stop making me laugh?" Ian complained with a chuckle. "This is supposed to be a thoroughly erotic experience, not half-penny theater."

It was Derek's turn to laugh. "Yes, oh great professor of fucking. Now tell me what you're doing."

Ian pulled his finger back and then inserted it a little deeper, gently fucking it in and out. Dolores gave a deep moan and clutched at Derek. "I'm getting her ass ready to fuck."

"Goddamn, I like doing this with you." Derek's voice was deep with desire and rumbled along Ian's nerves, making him shiver.

"Good. Does she?" Ian was being as careful as he could be with her. At this point everything he did was instinctual or theoretical. He'd never fucked a woman in the ass before. The more he played with Dolores' ass, however, the better the idea sounded. "She's so fucking tight and hot here. Jesus, I'm not sure I can wait."

Dolores' head fell back on Ian's shoulder, her movement pulling Derek forward a little bit so the two were bent over on Ian. Derek looked up at him with an irreverent grin. "Oh, I think she likes it." Derek sobered at the look on Ian's face. "Ian?" he asked, desire throbbing in his voice.

Ian tried to disguise how he burned for Derek, how the sight of him lying against Ian's chest looking up at him with desire written in each line of his face made Ian ache for him. "Kiss her, Derek. Kiss her breasts. I want to watch you."

Derek's eyes stayed on Ian as long as he could hold his gaze as he lowered his head to her breasts. He finally looked away as he turned to kiss first one then the other.

"Lick them," Ian quietly ordered him.

Derek circled Dolores' nipples with the tip of his tongue and then placed openmouthed kisses on the sides of the firm mounds. She grabbed his head and moved him to the nipple on one breast. He laved it with the flat of his tongue and Dolores squirmed with a little cry.

"Suck them." Ian's voice was rough.

Derek opened his mouth and took in Dolores' nipple and sucked hard. She nearly came off the bed. While he'd been kissing her breasts, Ian had been slowly working his finger deeper into her ass. As Derek sucked hard, Ian pressed his finger in all the way and Dolores cried out, spreading her legs wide and pushing back against Ian's hand.

Ian's breathing was hard and erratic. He had never wanted to fuck so much in his life. The entire situation was pushing him beyond all the limits he'd known and obeyed since he became a man. He desired the young, pretty Dolores. He was going to fuck a woman with another man, share her in the most intimate way with Derek, whom he desired more than Dolores. The sight, sound and scent of Derek's passion were driving Ian mad. He was going to fuck a woman in the ass for the first time, and in the back of his mind was the knowledge that he could do the same to Derek. Sweat beaded his upper lip as the image of he and Derek locked together in that embrace filled his thoughts. He was confused, aroused, frightened, excited; the combination of all these emotions had him walking a tightrope of desire. His senses—touch, taste, smell—were more sensitive than he'd ever felt them. He wanted to remember every moment of this so that years from now he could look back and think of it with perfect clarity. The three of them, young, healthy, lusty, exploring and pleasuring one another in ways that before tonight, before Derek, he had only thought of vaguely in a fantasy.

"She's so tight, Derek," Ian whispered. "I don't want to hurt her."

Derek broke off from Dolores' breast, licking and soothing with gentle kisses. He looked up at Ian again, all laughter gone. "Use one or two more fingers in her, Ian, the same as stretching a woman's cunt. You're too big to go in before she's ready." He looked back at Dolores and smoothed the back of his fingers down her cheek. "I think I like her too much to rush this. I want her, I want this." He closed his eyes and leaned over Dolores' shoulder so his face was close to Ian's chest and breathed deeply. His forehead rested on Ian as he kissed Dolores' ear. "Am I making sense anymore? Christ, I'm hurting for you. Hurry Ian, hurry."

Ian needed no more encouragement. He pressed another finger into Dolores and slowly scissored them, stretching her. She sobbed and clutched Derek, kissing his neck, his cheek, blindly seeking his mouth. He gave it to her and swallowed her cries as Ian worked her ass.

"Now, now," Ian panted, pulling his fingers out. Derek grabbed Dolores' thighs and lifted her, spreading her ass cheeks in the process. Ian placed his cock at the tight rosebud there, finding his way by touch. He started to enter her, but Dolores started shaking her head.

"No, no!" She pushed away from Derek with her arms and pulled away from Ian's embrace.

Ian fell back on the bed. He wanted it, but he wouldn't force her. "All right, Dolores, all right." He watched in confusion as she turned to him. "*Mira me*," she said, but Ian didn't understand. She leaned over him and quickly took his aching cock in her mouth.

"Oh God," he groaned, his hand burying itself in her hair as she used her lips and tongue on him. She was licking his hard length, making him wet and slick.

She pulled back and pointed at his cock. "*Mira aqui, si*?" she said. He shook his head, uncomprehending. She ran a finger down his cock and pulled it away to show him the wet residue of saliva and Ian suddenly understood.

"You're making it easier," he whispered with a shaky laugh. "*Si*, Dolores," he said, nodding with a smile. "*Si*." She licked him again and then turned and rose to her knees, holding on to Derek again, who had silently watched their exchange.

"Der-reek," she said, smiling, and slid her arms around him as she kissed the side of his neck. When he didn't respond she pulled away and placed his hands back on her thighs as they were before. "Der-reek," she tried again, indicating he was to lift her up as he had done earlier.

"Ian?" he asked.

Ian moved behind her. "She got my cock wet, Derek, so it would go in easier. Lift her up again."

"Jesus, I think I'm in love," was all Derek said as he grabbed her thighs and spread her for Ian.

Ian laughed but it was cut short as the thick head of his cock slid into her tight passage. He clutched Dolores' shoulders too hard and she cried out. "I'm sorry, it just, God, it feels so good." He let go of her, but then had nothing to hold on to.

"Hold on to me, Ian," Derek said softly. "Hold on to me."

Ian looked over Dolores' shoulder into Derek's eyes and slowly raised his hands to Derek's biceps. The feel of the hard, smooth muscles beneath his hands, the hot, slick skin made Ian's stomach muscles clench. *Yes*, he thought, *this is perfect now. I needed to touch Derek when I was doing this. I needed him to be a part of it.* He pushed his cock slowly into Dolores and the feeling was so exquisite that he closed his eyes and locked his jaw with the effort not to come.

Holding on to Derek's arms brought the three of them closer together. Dolores was pressed tight between the two men, and the sound of their breathing filled the tent like a chorus of passion. When Ian's cock was buried almost to the balls in Dolores' ass, he stopped.

"Derek," he panted, "now. Enter her now."

"How does it feel?"

Ian opened his eyes and smiled at Derek. "Fucking amazing. You have got to try this."

Derek lifted one of Dolores' legs high, making her moan. "I plan on it. Here, hold this." He passed the leg to Ian, who let go of Derek's arm and held it up. From where he was kneeling in front of Dolores, Derek tried to enter her but the cot started to wobble. With a curse Derek stopped. "Move onto the floor."

Derek carefully climbed off and lay down on the floor. Ian kept his cock buried in Dolores as he followed, he and Dolores straddling Derek. She moaned and grabbed Ian's hands where they were wrapped around her stomach. When they were in place it took Derek only a moment to get his cock into position.

"Lower her, Ian, put her on my cock." Ian lowered Dolores, and found he had to bend her forward and lean over her to keep himself inside. As soon as Derek started to enter her, Ian could feel him, could feel Derek's cock sliding along his own through the thin wall of Dolores' vagina. Derek stopped with a moan.

"Do you feel that, Ian, do you feel me?" Derek said, his voice strangled.

"Mmm," Ian mumbled, nodding. He couldn't speak past the lust crashing through him as he felt Derek's cock jerk inside Dolores. His eyes slammed to Derek's when the other man's hands came up and covered his on Dolores' hips.

"More," Derek whispered. "I want more of both of you."

The words made Ian cry out as he pushed Dolores down on Derek. She gave a short scream, quickly stifled with her hand as her head flew back, her hair streaming down her back. She thrust down hard and Derek's upper body jerked off the floor.

"God, yes!" Derek cried out, grinding against her.

"Slow down, slow down," Ian panted, trying not to join them in their uninhibited fucking. They all froze for a moment, their breaths slashing through the quiet of the tent.

Derek's head fell back on the floor. "Do something Ian, quick. I can't stay like this. I—God!" Dolores had moved on Derek, pulling up until he was almost out of her.

"Ee-an," she moaned. "Ee-an." She tried to push him back awkwardly.

"Yes, *si*, I understand." As she moved back down on Derek, Ian pulled out, the two cocks sliding past each other inside her, the added layer of sensation making Ian shiver and Derek moan. Without words, the three began an intricate dance, one cock in as the other pulled out, fucking Dolores and each other. Sensations and words murmured in desire all blended until who was fucking whom became blurred around the edges.

Through Dolores Ian tried to show Derek how he felt, while at the same time he tried to please Dolores, to give her a sensual experience that perhaps she had never had before. He wanted her to reach her woman's pleasure again and again, he wanted to feel her contract around him. He wanted to hear her cries. But he also waited breathlessly for Derek's climax, to feel his cock spill inside Dolores against Ian's cock, to hear Derek's cries fill the night. He was wild for it, and his thrusts became harder.

Suddenly Derek rose up to kiss and suckle Dolores' breasts. Ian stopped his movements, glad of the reprieve. He wanted this fuck to last forever. He ran his hand through Derek's sweat-slick hair unselfconsciously, and then down to caress Derek's broad shoulders, also damp with the heat of their sensual play. Derek arched his back into Ian's touch like a cat and then slowly pulled away from him and Dolores to lie back on the floor. Without speaking they began to move inside Dolores again.

Each time the pressure built until Ian thought he would fly apart they pulled back and began again, over and over. Dolores came, and then came again until she was limp and liquid in their arms.

"Ian," Derek cried out at last, "I can't wait anymore. Please, God, Ian," and then he thrust into Dolores deeply and spilled his hot seed as she contracted around them one more time. She fell forward on Derek's chest and the two of them kissed voraciously as they came. The heat and ferocity of Derek's release combined with the tight spasms of Dolores' climax finally brought Ian. He came inside her so hard he felt lightheaded. It was the most incredible climax of his life. He fell forward on Dolores, but tried to keep most of his weight braced on trembling arms.

After he collected himself, Ian pulled slowly out of Dolores, prompting a moan of relief from the slight woman.

Ian chuckled as he fell off to the side and lay down on the floor next to Derek. He threw an arm over his eyes, feeling each ragged breath he drew into his lungs. He was physically exhausted, but he was more content than he'd been since he went to war. What started out as an experimental fuck with his best friend and a whore had turned into the most emotionally exhilarating sexual experience of his life.

"Ian?" Ian turned his head and found Derek looking at him. Dolores was snuggled up against him, her head on his chest, her eyes closed as Derek stroked her hair. They looked beautiful together and Ian's chest tightened remembering what they'd just done.

"What is it, Derek?" he whispered, a small smile curving his lips.

"How soon do you think you can do that again? I want to switch places."

Ian bit his lip to smother his laughter, not wanting to wake Dolores. "Let's let her rest a little bit, Derek. And then, if she's able, we will definitely do it again."

"Fucking yes we're doing it again," Derek said reverently. "I never want to do it any other way again."

Ian closed his eyes. "Neither do I, Derek," he whispered. *Not without you*, he silently added.

The following morning they allowed Dolores to sleep off their night of passion in their tent. Somehow one night turned into two, and in the end Dolores never left. Their camp moved on and she moved with them. Ian and Derek taught her English and bought her trinkets and clothes, and in return at night she taught them how to love a woman, and inadvertently, how to love one another.

She was theirs. Everyone acknowledged it. No one tried to buy her services after Derek beat the hell out of a soldier whose offer Derek chose to treat as an insult. They spoiled her in bed and out of it, and she took care of them like a good army wife following the drum. They loved her in their way, and she them, but theirs was not a grand passion. They all knew that when Ian and Derek left, Dolores would stay. She was saving all the money they gave her for a dowry, so she could make a good marriage after they were gone. They contributed to her fund faithfully.

Dolores became more a best friend than a lover, although their nights continued to be filled with the kind of passion experienced only by the young and healthy exploring their sexuality for the first time. Anything and everything was permitted with Dolores. Ian and Derek only touched one another peripherally when they were fucking Dolores, in spite of the fact that Ian's desire for Derek grew more compelling with each encounter. He kept his feelings to himself and tried to be satisfied with these fleeting moments of intimacy.

Dolores was with them during that god-awful year of 1812 that saw the Light Dragoons in action nearly every time Ian turned around. Physically spent, emotionally drained, horrified at the carnage they'd witnessed, Ian and Derek would return to Dolores' companionship and tenderness. Many nights Ian awakened to the sounds of Derek and Dolores fucking in the cot next to his and he would watch them. Watched Dolores taste Derek's skin with her tongue and bite his hard, flat nipples until he moaned. Derek loved it when she licked and sucked the delicate skin of his inner thigh and ran her nails down his back to dig them into his buttocks as he was riding her. More often than not he'd be on the bottom by the time they finished. He liked her to suck his cock, but he preferred coming inside her cunt or ass instead of her mouth. Ian watched all this and stored the information away.

Ian knew some nights Derek awoke and watched him and Dolores fucking. When he knew Derek was watching Ian went wild. He would fuck Dolores so hard he was always afraid after that he'd hurt her, but he never did. He thought he saw understanding in her eyes but they never talked about it. On those nights Ian would make sure to have Dolores do the things he liked the best, like suck his cock until he came in her throat. The first time she did it Derek unabashedly watched.

"What's she doing?" he asked as she slowly took as much of Ian's cock in her mouth as she could and then wrapped her hand around him where her lips stopped. She then began to freely move her head up and down, never moving her fist from that spot.

"I think it's her way of marking how much she can comfortably take," Ian surmised, never having seen this method before. "I'm rather large, I guess. This way I won't accidentally hurt her." His breathing became erratic as she expertly sucked and licked his cock.

"Our girl is fucking brilliant, Ian," Derek marveled.

They lost Dolores in July of that awful year, at Salamanca. A stray French artillery barrage wiped out a small section of the retreating British camp on their way to Cuidad Rodrigo. Several women and children were killed as well as troops. Dolores was one of them. When they heard about the attack they raced back only to find chaos. Someone had covered Dolores' body with a blanket and before Ian could stop him Derek had ripped the cover off her. Ian knew he would never forget the sight of their beautiful girl burned beyond recognition. He'd thrown up to the sound of Derek's anguished screams. They'd had to haul Derek away from her and he'd bloodied several men in the process. Their commanding officers Majors Randall and Richards came to help bury her and they'd cried with Ian. Derek had stood silent and stoic as Reverend Matthews prayed over her grave. Then he'd gotten on his horse and ridden away without a backward glance.

For the next few months Ian and Derek had barely spoken, each lost in his own grief. Ian felt as much guilt as grief. He missed Dolores, but he grieved more for the loss of Derek and the intimacies they'd shared. God, he missed Derek. Missed him so much he ached with it.

By November, at a small skirmish near Matilla, Ian had reverted to his suicidal ways, jumping into danger without a care, riding into the path of stray bullets. His heart was broken and he felt numb inside. Suddenly Derek was there hauling him off his horse in the middle of the battle.

"What the hell are you doing?" Derek screamed at him. "Are you trying to kill yourself?" At the look on Ian's face Derek turned ashen and his eyes widened in horror. "What about me? Are you going to leave me too?"

Before Ian could answer he glanced over Derek's shoulder and froze in terror. A French soldier whom they'd presumed dead on the ground had his pistol raised and pointed at Derek's back. The moment seemed to last an eternity. Ian shoved Derek down and fell on top of him, every second waiting for the impact of the bullet, either in Derek or himself. It never came. The soldier was too injured to get off a decent shot and the bullet whizzed past harmlessly far above them.

Ian clutched Derek to him and Derek held on tightly. Ian couldn't catch his breath. He was panicking, he knew it but couldn't stop. God, he'd almost lost him. If Derek had died Ian knew with a sudden clarity that he too would have been dead by the end of the day, by a French bullet or his own hand. He felt Derek shake and rolled off to the side, raised on his elbow to look down at him. Derek was crying.

In that moment Ian realized that he would never leave him. He could not live without him.

Chapter Five

ଶ

Derek saw Ian's head jerk sharply to the side as he opened the bedroom door. He walked silently into the room and closed the door behind him. When he saw Ian staring at him he stopped and leaned his shoulders against the door.

"Should I leave?" he asked gruffly, trying to hide the vulnerability he was feeling, letting the anger rise instead as he pissed himself off with his weakness.

Ian was smiling softly. "Of course not. I never want you to leave."

Derek chose to interpret the statement narrowly. "You say that now, but tomorrow night you'll be singing a different tune."

Ian sighed. Derek rushed to speak. "Yes, I know, don't start." He pushed away from the door and walked across the room. "You're right." He snorted at Ian's look of astonishment. "Don't you start either," he said with a trace of his old humor. He lowered himself onto the windowsill next to where Ian was standing, resting just on the edge of it, his right knee bumping Ian's thigh.

"I want it to be just us tonight, Ian," he whispered, looking down at the floor. "It's our last night, our last chance for that." He finally found the courage to look at Ian and was rewarded by the warmth and tenderness in his gaze. "No more fighting, no more Sophie." He held up his hand to halt Ian's response. "Just for tonight. One last time."

Ian's look turned serious and Derek thought he saw panic quickly disguised. "Are you leaving me?"

Derek started in surprise. "Hell no. You'll have to drag me out kicking and screaming, I'm afraid. You know I hate to lose."

"Lose?" Ian looked confused. "What are you talking about?"

"I'm not going to let her win. If I leave, she wins. So I'm going to try, Ian, I really am."

Ian ran his hand over Derek's shoulder and down his arm. The touch was tender but underlying the tenderness was the heat that had always simmered between them.

"You're wrong, Derek. If you leave Sophie loses, and so do I."

Derek turned to Ian and slid over on the windowsill until he was close enough to rest his head on Ian's chest. The other man began to run his fingers through Derek's hair, his touch soothing and erotic all at once. It had always been that way for Derek. Ian's touch had aroused and comforted from the first, before they were ever lovers.

"I want to make love with you tonight, Ian. I need to be yours tonight, because tomorrow I have to share you and it's killing me."

"When the three of us are together—"

Derek cut Ian off. "No!" He was shaking his head and dislodged Ian's hand. He pulled back and looked up into Ian's eyes. "No. I'll learn to live with her, I may even learn not to hate her, but I will never love her, Ian. I will never be her lover."

Ian looked out the window at the night sky. "I was thinking about Dolores."

Derek felt an ache in his gut at the reminder of their beautiful girl. "She will never be Dolores."

When Ian turned back to him Derek didn't like the look in his eyes. "No, she will be more." The words chilled Derek to the bone. It was precisely what he feared, that she would be more—more than Dolores, more than Derek, more than anything Derek could give Ian or do for Ian.

Ian continued, each word like an arrow in Derek's heart. "She will be my wife and the mother of my children. She already has a place in my heart. I want to share this with you, Derek. Please let me."

Derek shook his head again and Ian smiled sadly. "You are leaving me."

Derek stood abruptly and faced Ian angrily. "I told you I wasn't, I won't. Are you trying to push me away?"

Ian grabbed him and pulled him into his embrace. He spoke into the curve of his shoulder where he rested his head. "Not physically, but inside you're pulling away from me, Derek. I need you. Don't leave me." Ian looked up at him. "You promised to take care of me. Do you remember?"

* * * * *

April 1813, Torres Vedras, Portugal

Derek was reluctant to go back to camp. It made him feel guilty and that pissed him off. But Jesus, it was so hard to be around Ian these days. He was so polite, so solicitous and so aloof. At night Derek lay on his cot listening to Ian breathe in the dark next to him and he was assaulted by memories of their passionate nights with Dolores when their ragged, mingled breaths cut through the darkness.

He wanted Ian so badly sometimes he thought he'd go mad with it. Couldn't Ian see it? How could he not be aware of Derek's feelings when every time he turned around Derek was watching him? When he used any flimsy excuse to touch Ian? It had been months since Derek had had any kind of release. Not since Dolores was killed.

Dolores—another reason for Derek to feel guilty. If he hadn't brought her back to their tent that night, if he hadn't begged Ian to stay, she'd probably still be alive. But he'd wanted Ian so desperately and sharing Dolores was the only way he could think of to have him. Now he was lost to Derek, so far out of his reach that those idyllic nights with Dolores seemed like a dream.

He'd thought after Matilla that Ian might return his feelings. The way he'd looked at him that day, right after the Frenchman had fired at his back, for one moment he thought he saw an almost wild look of intense emotion in Ian's eyes. Then his look had changed to dismay and even though he'd saved Derek's life and they still rode together and lived together Ian had slowly been pulling away.

Derek felt Ian's withdrawal like a physical pain, as if an arm or leg were being slowly ripped off. He knew he was surly as hell, nearly impossible to live with these days, but he couldn't seem to do anything about it. He'd lost so many people in this fucking war that when he saw Ian charging recklessly into battle at Matilla he'd nearly gone insane with fear. He wouldn't be able to bear it if he lost Ian. What would he do when Ian left him? He knew he'd leave, they always left. But Ian mustn't die, he couldn't die. That was why Derek had sought out his command in the first place, because everyone knew he was lucky, so damn lucky bullets and cannon shot couldn't even touch him.

As he rode slowly back to camp with his pilfered goods, food and wine from a nearby camp, he thought about all the friends that they'd lost in the last year. Dolores was the hardest to bear. But Harry Collier had gone down, and Bertie Thorne. Brett Haversham had gone home after he'd been injured. God knew he was lucky to be alive although he might not walk again. And Gideon North, who wished he hadn't been so lucky, who'd screamed and begged for Doctor Peters to kill him when he awoke with most of his leg missing and his right side burned so awfully. Dolores had helped care for him until they found him transport out. She'd stayed by his side with his young sergeant and made every man in camp love her for her compassion. Ian had written to Gideon of Dolores' death, and he'd written a one-line letter back, the handwriting shaky and scrawling. *She deserved better.* Yes, she had.

Before he knew it, he arrived back at their camp. They'd been here for months. Last year had been a waking hell, one battle after another. They'd been idle for months nursing their wounded and waiting for reinforcements while other battalions bore the brunt of the fighting.

The inaction made suffering Ian's indifference even harder. Day after day they sat around trying to find ways to amuse themselves until night fell. He'd won a bloody fortune in cards it seemed. But all those hours spent with Ian acting so cool, showing no emotion were beginning to tell on Derek. Last night he'd nearly broken down and begged Ian to touch him, to fuck him. He literally ached with want, the space between his balls and his ass tight with desire. He knew what he wanted, what his body wanted. It wanted Ian inside him fucking him like he used to fuck Dolores—hard and wild with that huge cock of his. He'd never had a man before, never wanted one, but he wanted Ian. He'd known he wanted him almost from the first. He'd had to content himself with friendship. Now he wasn't sure he had even that.

An hour later he'd taken care of his mount and delivered the food where it would do the most good. He turned for his tent with a sigh. He was bringing a hot meal and several bottles of wine with him. Maybe he could get Ian drunk and seduce him. He snorted with the improbability of that. Ian was rarely in his cups. He valued control too much to voluntarily give it up to a bottle.

"Get the fuck out of my way," he snarled at a couple of people who made the mistake of getting within ten feet of him. Most people stayed out of his way these days. He'd taken to picking fistfights when he was good and pissed, and he was good and pissed a lot lately. The anger felt better than this pathetic weakness over Ian. It felt a hell of a lot better than the choked, panicked feeling that he'd been getting lately in the middle of the night after a nightmare.

When Derek reached their tent, Ian wasn't alone. Majors Richards and Randall were there sharing a drink with him.

"Derek," Ian greeted him, his voice cool, his stare intense. "Where have you been? I haven't seen you all day."

"Oh, I've been out collecting. I'm sick of the swill we've been eating around here lately." He picked up the bottle the three men were drinking from and looked at the wine in disgust. "I'm also sick of this piss that passes for wine."

Major Randall raised an eyebrow at him. "That, Lieutenant, is my piss so you will show a little respect."

"Major piss is still piss," Derek said with a shrug.

"Quite the little toad-eater, aren't you?" Randall said as he lifted his glass for another drink.

Ian laughed hard at that little sally. "Toad-eater? Derek? He hardly knows how to give a genuine compliment much less flatter someone's ego." Still laughing, Ian took a drink.

"Is that what you want, Ian? Do you need me to flatter your ego?" He pulled off his light blue jacket, the uniform of the Light Dragoons, and threw it on his cot in disgust. "You're the fucking rajah of the Peninsula, Captain; the stinking Supreme Prince of this shithole. You are brilliant and beautiful and so funny I piss myself over your jokes. There, feel better?"

He grabbed a bottle of the wine he'd brought back and pried the cork out. Without even looking for a glass he sat on his cot and drank straight out of the bottle.

"Well, rajah," Richards said, touching his hand to his chest, then his mouth and finally his forehead in a parody of the foreigners' greeting of respect, "I almost feel bad leaving you in such rotten company." He looked at Derek for a moment and then smiled. "Almost."

"Leaving? Where the hell are you going?" Derek demanded, wiping his mouth with the back of his hand.

"Home," Randall spoke reverently, "England. 'This royal throne of kings, this sceptered isle,'" he quoted. "'This earth of majesty, this seat of Mars, This other Eden, demi-paradise,' —"

"Yes, yes," interrupted Derek impatiently. "'This blessed plot, this earth, this realm, this England.'" He took another swig of wine then looked up into the astonished faces of the other three men. "What? I'm not a cretin. What kind of Englishman can't quote his Shakespeare?"

"Who the hell are you?" Ian asked, bewildered. "Every time I think I know everything about you, you surprise me."

Derek stared at him. "You don't know anything about me, Ian. You only think you do."

"How dare you address his majesty the Supreme Prince of this shithole that way," Major Randall mocked.

Derek looked over at him and feigned shock. "You're still here? I thought you were leaving for your sceptered realm."

"Sceptered isle, toad-eating cretin," Randall said with a sly grin and even Derek smiled as the others laughed.

Major Richards stood up. "Well, we've got to make the rounds and tell everyone goodbye."

"A toast first." Ian stood up and raised his glass, but before he could speak Derek got up from the cot.

"Not with that French piss." He dumped their glasses in the dirt outside the tent and refilled them with wine from his bottle.

"Good God, Derek, were did you get this?" Major Randall asked in astonishment as he took an appreciative sip.

"The less said about that the better," Derek told him, topping off Ian's glass last. "Let's just say a certain commander will be going without for a while."

Major Richards held up his hand. "Enough. We don't need the details."

Ian held his glass up again. "I wish you luck, gentlemen. Here is to your success in obtaining your objectives in England." They all drank to the toast.

"Are they invading England? What exactly are their objectives?" Derek asked lightly, sitting back down.

"Marriage, my boy," Major Randall told him with mock gravity.

"Really? Who are you going to marry?" He wasn't that interested actually. He'd probably never see Major Randall again.

"Mrs. Katherine Collier." Major Randall said her name in the same tone he'd said home and England, as if she were one and the same to him.

"Harry Collier's wife?" Well, that was news. He had no idea they'd been carrying on. He wondered idly if it had started before old Harry's death last year.

"Yes, one and the same," Major Richards said, putting his glass down.

Derek turned to him. "Are you getting married too, Major?"

Richards smiled like a man with a secret. "I hope so, Derek, I hope so."

"Who's your lucky bride?"

"Mrs. Katherine Collier."

Derek stared at Major Richards for a moment then looked over at Major Randall, who seemed amused at his consternation. "Aren't you upset about his courting your intended?"

"On the contrary, she is intended for both of us."

Derek very nearly fell off his cot. "What? You can't do that!" It took quite a lot to astonish Derek, but this had definitely done it.

"You did. You and Ian and Dolores." Major Richards had picked up his shako and walked over to the door.

Derek was standing now, incredulous. "It's one thing for a Spanish whore to live with two English soldiers in a tent in the middle of a war. It's quite another thing for a respectable English woman to do it in some fancy manor in good old England."

"I don't see why. I should think that the fact that we love her and plan on marrying her would make it more acceptable than your temporary arrangement with Dolores." Major Randall's voice had gone cold.

"She'll throw the both of you out on your arses, that's what going to happen," Derek predicted with pity. "Mark my words, you're only in for heartache if you pursue this."

"It is what we wish, Derek." Major Richards looked at him hard. "You of all people should know and understand how short life is, both you and Ian. Jason and I believe that it's too short not to pursue that which we desire most. We've been here too long." He shook his head sadly. "We've seen too much death and too much heartache." He looked over at Major Randall. "But we've been together so long that the idea of living apart is unconscionable." He looked back at Derek. "So we shall pursue Kate and win her together. We will not be denied this happiness. We have earned it."

"Has she got the kind of courage it will take to defy all the rules of society in order for you to have that happiness? Have you?" Derek asked the question seriously. "I don't know anyone who has. No one ever really gives everything up for love, Major. That only occurs in fairy tales and Shakespeare."

"And what kind of Englishman can't quote his Shakespeare?" Major Richards asked with a sad smile. "Goodbye, Derek. I hope to see you again back in England. I think you're going to be very interesting when you grow up."

"If I grow up anymore I won't fit in England," Derek joked, taking the olive branch he offered. They all laughed, though it was a little forced, and shook hands before the two older men left.

Derek offered Ian some of his hot dinner and they ate in silence. Afterward they finished off another bottle of wine outside, watching the sun set. When the sky was the purple-gray of almost night, the bath Derek had ordered arrived.

"What's this?" Ian asked idly, setting his glass aside.

Derek stood up to direct the men where to put the tub in the tent. "I almost forgot I hired MacAllister's trull to wash out our things. Then I figured if our clothes are going to be clean, we might as well be." He looked down at Ian as the men went for some hot water. "I know you stink, so I must be as bad if not worse."

Ian leaned over and sniffed under his arms. He came up blinking. "Bloody hell, I reek. A man forgets among the stench of an army camp, I suppose." He struggled to his feet. "What the hell. I'll do it for you, since you're the only one who gets close enough to smell me." He stumbled a little going into the tent and Derek caught his arm.

"How much have you had to drink today?" he asked in surprise. He couldn't recall ever seeing Ian the worse for drink.

Ian smiled at him crookedly. "Apparently too much." He laughed, although the sound was strangely without humor. "It was that damned Richards, and Randall too. They spent half the day here maundering on about how awful this war was and how they couldn't wait to get back to Mrs. Collier. Those two will drive a man to drink."

Derek barked with laughter. "Well, don't come crying to me tomorrow with your headache. I've warned you about drinking that god-awful shit."

"Oh, shut up, Derek." Ian collapsed on his cot. "You take the tub first since you ordered it. Then I'll wash."

Derek shrugged. "Seems fair. I'll wake you when I'm done."

The men were back with water and the tub was steaming by the time they left. Derek told them to come for the tub in the morning and closed the tent flap behind them. He undressed and was about to climb in the tub when a voice called in to them.

"'Ere now, have ya got them smalls for me, Lieutenant?"

"Oh Christ, it's MacAllister's girl. Ian, will you hand her my things? And yours too." He called out to her. "Hold on, Millie. The captain needs to take his off. Then he'll hand them to you through the flap."

There was a cackle of laughter through the tent walls. "'Ere now, I don't mind if'n I have to come in there, dearie. Are ya both in the buff then? Who wouldn't mind that, I tell ya? You two luvs are the best thing to look at around 'ere with your clothes on, never mind off." She laughed again and Derek joined her.

"Never you mind, Millie. MacAllister would come looking for us to be sure if we stole his girl. You stay respectably on that side of the tent if you please." He smiled at Ian and sobered when he saw the strange look the other man was giving him. "Hurry up, Ian. The poor woman probably has to pick up several things all over camp."

Ian shook his head and undressed quickly. He wrapped his blanket around his waist and took their things to the flap. Derek heard Millie on the other side.

"Well bless your 'eart, Captain, aren't you the shy one? Got something Millie ain't seen yet, have ya?" Derek smiled at her comment.

"Thank you very much, Millie," Ian told her quietly. "We appreciate it very much."

The woman was obviously flustered when she replied. "Oh, well then, it's how I make my livin' then, isn't it? I'll take good care of ya, Captain. Have 'em back by tomorrow."

"Don't worry, Millie," Derek shouted out at her as he stepped into the tub. "We've a set to wear already. We won't be needing those for a couple of days."

"All right then, Lieutenant," she called in to him, her voice receding as she walked away, "thank you very much. You'll have 'em by Wednesday."

Ian turned back into the tent with a frown. "We have another set?"

Derek didn't bother to look at him as lowered himself into the water. "We do as of today. I was collecting, remember?"

"Ah," Ian said. Derek heard him walk over and sit back down on his cot.

The tub was too small for Derek by far. He was practically eating his knees in there, and was splashing around trying to wash himself.

"Why don't you just stand up?" Ian asked, his voice flat.

Derek glanced over in surprise. Ian appeared asleep laying there with his ankles crossed. It was hard to tell in the low light of one lamp but his eyes looked closed. "I thought you were asleep." He got up but felt a little self-conscious standing there nude in front of Ian. He knew it was stupid. Ian had seen him naked plenty of times, but something seemed different now. Perhaps it was just that he was different. He wanted Ian so much it was making him awkward. He hated it, and as usual any kind of weakness on his part pissed him off. He scrubbed himself hard and splashed around, rinsing himself off. He sat back down to wash his hair.

"Do you want me to pour some water on your head?"

Derek dropped the soap he was so startled. "God damn it, Ian! Are you or are you not asleep?"

"Clearly I am not." Ian was amused, and Derek got even angrier. He was in an agony of want and awkwardness and Ian was enjoying himself at Derek's expense.

"Then yes, get over here and help me rinse this soap out of my eyes." Derek lathered his hair once more, rubbing the top of his head as he watched Ian stand up out of the corner of his eye. From Ian's vantage point it must have looked as if Derek couldn't see him, because for the first time since Matilla

Derek saw emotion flashing across Ian's face like lightning. Longing, sadness, desire all tumbled in his eyes and pulled his mouth into a thin line as he stared at Derek in the tub with a burning intensity. Derek felt the smoldering fires inside him ignite. He was suddenly an inferno of need, conscious of his own nakedness and Ian's under the thin cover of his blanket.

"Hand me the bucket," Ian said, his voice emotionless. But he couldn't fool Derek anymore. He felt the same things as Derek, wanted the same things. Here was his chance and Derek didn't know what to do. How did one go about seducing one's reluctant best friend? He slowly picked up the bucket and started to fill it from the tub, but at the last minute handed it to Ian empty. "Here, you fill it. I've got soap in my eyes."

From under his lashes he watched Ian take a deep breath, and as he moved to fill the bucket with water his hands were shaking. Ian's eyes wouldn't rest on one part of Derek. Instead they kept darting from one spot to another. Nervous, unable to believe his own daring, Derek parted his legs as if making room for Ian to dip the bucket there. Ian froze. Derek tried to be nonchalant. "Is there room? Here, I'll move." He came to his knees, the water dancing just below his semi-erect cock, his legs spread. "There. Hurry up, Ian, before the water gets cold." He watched Ian close his eyes for a moment and came close to feeling guilty for deliberately enticing him, but the moment passed and all he felt was elation. He was so close, Ian was almost his.

Then in one swift movement Ian filled the bucket and dumped it over Derek's head. Derek was sputtering as Ian dropped the bucket and backed away.

"There," Ian said, "you're done. Get out and get dressed."

Derek stood and shook himself like a wet dog. "What the hell did you do that for?" he bellowed, rubbing the soap and water out of his eyes for real this time. "Hand me a cloth, you fool." Some rough linen was shoved into his hand and he wiped his face off. When he could see again he glared at Ian.

Ian stared dispassionately back at him. Just as Derek was sure he'd missed his chance he saw Ian's gaze dart down and then back up as if he couldn't stop himself.

Derek took a deep breath and he saw the pulse in Ian's throat leap. He slowly wiped the cloth down his chest and Ian's eyes followed. Very slowly and very deliberately, Derek dried himself off, running the cloth up and down his arms, his chest and stomach. He stepped out of the tub and dried his legs, and as he stood he placed the cloth just beneath his cock, in the thick mat of pubic hair between his legs and rubbed slowly. He looked up at Ian surreptitiously and saw sweat beading his upper lip as his eyes locked on Derek's hands. He thoroughly dried his cock and balls and then turned his back to Ian and held the cloth out.

"Would you dry my back?" He looked over his shoulder and saw Ian take a step forward, his eyes glazed. He jerked to a stop.

"No," he croaked.

"Why not?" Derek asked, injecting his tone with just the right amount of petulant confusion.

"Dry your own damn back," Ian snarled, and Derek had to turn away to hide his smile. Oh yes, he was going to have him. Before this night was through Ian would be his.

"Fine," he grumbled, making a great show of flexing his muscles as he tried to reach his back. He turned this way and that, giving Ian a show. Ian turned away abruptly when Derek faced him.

Derek couldn't stop the sharp little grin from cutting across his face. He wiped it off before he spoke. "Well, get in," he told Ian harshly. "I'm not paying good money for you to let the water get cold."

He saw Ian's shoulders rise as he took a deep breath. He walked over to the tub, and keeping his back to Derek, Ian dropped the blanket from around his waist and stepped into the tub. He lowered himself to sit and found he had the same problem as Derek.

Derek let him flounder for a minute or two as he retreated to his cot. It was strategically placed in front of Ian, who watched Derek in dismay, clearly regretting his miscalculation.

"Just stand up like I did," Derek suggested, keeping his tone neutral.

"Get dressed," Ian ordered him, his voice quiet but firm.

"I'll get dressed when I feel like it." Derek sat on the cot facing Ian. He spread his legs wide and placed his elbows on his knees. He leaned his head to one side and rubbed his hair briskly with the linen, drying it. He pretended he couldn't hear Ian's ragged breathing cutting the air.

When his hair was dry enough, Derek threw the cloth on the cot next to him and slowly leaned back, resting his weight on his hands. Without looking at Ian he spread his legs farther apart, aware of how his body was displayed, his cock now hard and erect. He reached one hand down and idly adjusted it, rubbing his balls slightly. He could feel each beat of his heart there in his engorged sex. It pulsed in time to Ian's breathing. He forced himself not to look at Ian, to continue to stare at his own erection. He ran his thumb over the slit in his cock head and shuddered. He had to stop touching himself then. He was too close. He could feel Ian's eyes burning into him like a brand. Casually he ran his hand up his stomach and rubbed it over his chest, pebbling his nipples. He shifted his gaze to Ian without warning and caught him staring, his nostrils flared like a predator sensing the wind.

"Would you like me to rinse you too?" Derek asked, his voice deliberately casual. "I know how damned hard it is to maneuver in that tub." Without waiting for a reply he rose and walked over to pick up the bucket. He made sure to stand in front of Ian, his cock right in front of his face. Let's see what he makes of this, Derek thought smugly. "I won't drown you as you did me," he teased.

Ian finally looked up into his face. "No." Derek understood he was talking about more than the rinsing, but he chose to act as if he misunderstood.

"Don't be such a ninny. Get up on your knees and let me rinse you. I swear I won't toss it in your face."

Ian was left with two choices—either to directly address the sexual tension choking the air or to do as Derek asked and pretend it was just about the rinsing. Derek was betting on the second choice and he won. Ian rose to his knees.

"Let me fill the bucket," Ian said, reaching for it.

"No, that's all right," Derek responded, pulling it out of reach and then dipping it quickly into the water between Ian's legs. His breathing became as ragged as Ian's as he saw the other man's huge cock full and hard, riding his stomach he was so aroused. When he pulled the bucket out of the water he let his arm "accidentally" brush the hot, engorged flesh and Ian shuddered with a gasp.

"Derek," he choked out, a warning in his voice.

"Close your eyes," Derek told him quietly, his voice soothing. Ian obeyed. Derek slowly poured the water over Ian's head, gently rubbing the silky strands of his hair to wash the soap out. He ran his hand down the back of Ian's head to his strong shoulders and brushed along the smooth, firm skin there, caressing him in the guise of rinsing him off. Ian's hands gripped the sides of the iron tub. When he was done, Derek put the bucket down on the floor.

"Stand up," he told Ian, unable to keep the desire out of his voice. "I'll dry you off."

Ian's eyes were closed, and he shook his head. "No." His denial was weak, and he stood, not looking at Derek. Derek walked over and picked up the dry linen he'd gotten for Ian. He walked back to Ian, who had his head bent down and wouldn't look at him.

He started with Ian's back, slowly dragging the cloth from his nape down along the strong, sinuous length of his back to the high curve of his ass several times. Ian's head came up and he leaned into Derek's strokes. Derek stepped close and ran the cloth over the cheeks of Ian's ass and along the bottom curve into the snug crevasse between cheek and leg, then back up along the tempting crease separating the firm globes. He felt Ian shiver and thought he heard a low whimper. He was beyond enjoying Ian's discomfort. Derek was so aroused his hands were shaking. He was aching and breathless and the desire was almost painful in its intensity.

"Turn around," he rasped. Ian shook his head again but did as Derek commanded. Derek ran the rough linen across Ian's chest, watching the play of the lamplight in the whorls of blond hair lightly dusting his pectorals. He rubbed the cloth softly over his pebbled nipples several times until he saw Ian's stomach quiver. The tremor distracted him and drew his attention to other things.

Derek lowered himself to his knees in front of Ian and began to dry his legs. He ran the cloth down and around thighs thick with muscles from his years in the cavalry. The same blond hair that gleamed on his chest lightly covered his legs. His feet were long and graceful with a high arch. The only thing Derek hadn't dried was Ian's cock. He looked up and Ian's face was turned away, his eyes closed. Quietly Derek put the cloth down, and reaching out he slowly wrapped his hand around the thick width of Ian's hard erection. Ian's entire body jerked. Derek started to lean forward, his mouth watering in anticipation of tasting Ian's hot, hard flesh.

"Derek, no!" Ian's cry was hushed but fervent. He grabbed Derek by the hair and painfully jerked his head back. Instead of deterring him, it aroused him more.

"Yes, Ian, yes," he moaned, fighting his grip, trying to reach Ian's cock with his mouth.

Ian sobbed and his other hand joined the first in holding Derek's head back. "No, Derek, I can't let you. Please stop."

His words registered and Derek relaxed into his hold and looked up at him questioningly, letting all his love and desire show in his face.

"Derek, God, Derek," Ian whispered, the fingers of his right hand gently smoothing down Derek's cheek. He shook himself and tried to pull away from Derek's hold on his cock, but Derek tightened his grip slightly and Ian gasped and shuddered.

"Derek, I can't do this to you. It's just…I haven't had a woman in too long. Please let me go." Ian's voice broke and a terrible sadness was on his face. Derek felt choked by emotion, unable to breathe.

"You know that's not it, Ian. You want me, admit it." Derek heard the desperate plea in his voice and inwardly winced. He'd never begged for anything, but he would beg for Ian. "Let me take care of you, Ian."

"You're so young, Derek." Ian's voice was laced with regret. "So young. You don't know what you're doing, the repercussions. I don't want you to hate me, Derek, and you will. You'll hate me and yourself."

Derek took a deep breath, trying not to get angry. It took a moment for him to find the words to express what he felt, and still when he spoke he believed them inadequate. "Ian, I have wanted you from the first moment I saw you. You're right. At the time I didn't understand what I was feeling. Now I do. I've seen you in the throes of passion, I've seen you fuck someone so deep and hard you owned them. I want that. I want you to own me. There is nothing you can do to make me want you more, and there is nothing you can do to make me want you less. What is, is. I want you. I want to take care of you, of this." He caressed Ian's hard length. "Let me take care of you, Ian. You will never regret it, and neither will I."

"No, just…no, Derek. You're so young, too young—"

That did it. Derek let himself get good and pissed. "God damn it, Ian! Would you quit saying that? I wasn't too young to know what I wanted when I was fucking Dolores with you. Why am I too young when it's you I want to fuck?" He let go of Ian and stood up. "I was out there in the fucking face of death with you. I wasn't too young to die for King and country, was I? But I'm too young to know that I love you and want you. I'm too young to know that I will feel that way until the goddamn day I die." He shoved Ian back in anger. "Arrgh! You really piss me off, Ian."

Ian laughed. Derek couldn't believe it. "What the fuck is your problem, Ian? Don't you dare laugh at the way I feel."

"Derek," Ian said in exasperation, shaking his head. "There you are. I was wondering who that man was kneeling at my feet begging." He grabbed the back of Derek's head with one hand and pulled him forward until their foreheads were resting against one another. "This man I believe," he whispered. "This raging lunatic, him I know. I thought I was going to save you, save you from me. What the hell was I thinking? *You* saved *me*, Derek. You saved me."

Derek wrapped his arms around Ian, feeling protective and vulnerable at the same time. He couldn't speak. Ian's words meant yes. Yes, he would have Ian, they would have each other. His blood pounded in anticipation, in trepidation, in love. He was in love for the first time in his life and he wanted this man so much. Christ, he was weak-kneed with it.

Ian's skin was still warm and moist from the bath. He smelled of soap and linen and wine. Derek wanted to remember everything, every touch, every smell, every sound. He had seen Ian in every situation imaginable, shared almost every experience men can share. And yet it all felt new and wondrous. Ian pulled back just enough so that their heads no longer touched but their faces were still close, still aligned. Derek trembled at the warm brush of Ian's breath against his lips. He could see the shadows cast by Ian's lashes on his cheeks in the lamplight as he narrowed his eyes, gazing at Derek's mouth.

"I'm going to kiss you, you know," Ian whispered.

"You'd better do it damn quick or I will," Derek whispered back.

Ian's smile made Derek's stomach clench, made that vulnerable spot between his balls and his ass tighten in longing. Ian's smile was feral and blazing with erotic promise. "No, you'll do as I say." The words were softly spoken but carried an arrogance that should have angered Derek, not thrilled him as they did. His breath caught in his throat. Ian's hand gripped Derek's hair and dragged his head the inch or so required to bring their mouths together. There was little tenderness in the kiss. It was dominant and ravenous and arousing.

Ian's tongue was long and clever. He sought out the corners of Derek's mouth languorously, licking along the roof and tracing the soft tissue behind his lower lip. Derek couldn't stop the ragged moan that was dragged from the bottom of his soul at Ian's taste. Hot, wet, slick, Ian was everything Derek had been dreaming of for over a year. The kiss lived up to the dreams and then moved beyond them into a realm of pleasure Derek hadn't even known existed. Ian gave no quarter, refused to let Derek lead in any way, only follow. He dueled with Derek's tongue, subjugated it and finally drew it into his mouth. Derek could only cling to him, needing him with an ache that permeated every fiber of his being.

Ian held Derek's head in place while he was kissing him, and after a minute his free hand started to roam possessively over the terrain of Derek's body. He ran his palm over Derek's chest and shoulder and down his arm, stroking his muscles and tracing their lines. On Derek's chest he buried his hand in the dark, thick hair that covered the heavy musculature there. Ian seemed to revel in Derek's body, his kiss becoming more aggressive as he caressed him. When he took Derek's nipple between his fingers and pinched and plucked it roughly, Derek cried out, not in pain but in arousal. Derek felt Ian smile against his mouth and then Ian bit his lower lip gently at the same time he pinched Derek's nipple hard. The dual sharp sensations went straight to his cock like lightning racing through his veins. Ian chuckled at Derek's gasp of pleasure, pulling away from the kiss almost reluctantly.

"Do you want to take care of me, Derek?" Ian asked quietly, suggestively. "Do you?" His lips lay against Derek's cheek as he spoke, and as he waited for an answer he tenderly kissed him there.

Derek's hands came around to rest against Ian's chest. He could feel Ian's heart racing and thrilled to the knowledge that he did this to him. "Yes, Ian, yes." His voice trembled, his hands shook.

Ian caressed the length of Derek's arms, took his hands and then stepped back, leading Derek to the cot behind him. Ian sat on the edge of the cot and pulled Derek down until he was kneeling between Ian's legs. Derek was panting in excitement. He wanted to reach for Ian's cock again, hold it, caress it, taste it, swallow it whole. But instinctively he knew to wait. Part of his pleasure, and Ian's, was letting Ian control their passion. Derek had never really thought about how they would fuck, only that they would. He didn't really have enough experience to know how to give the most pleasure. He'd learned much from their lovemaking sessions with Dolores, but this was different. This was a level of carnality that he'd never reached before. It was a hunger, a craving the likes of which he'd never felt. He was empty, so empty, a vessel waiting to be filled by Ian, reveling in the feast laid before him.

It seemed always, everywhere, Derek was the aggressor. He was wallowing in the decadent pleasure of being submissive to Ian. He gladly, lovingly let Ian dominate here. Ian gripped his head tightly with both hands and drew it down to his cock. Derek had to lower himself completely so his ass rested on his heels because he was so tall. There was no hesitation in Ian's hands. He pulled Derek inexorably toward his cock with a firm grip and pressed the head against Derek's lips until he opened them. Ian pushed inside his mouth with the same arrogance with which he'd kissed him.

Ian threw his head back and groaned deep in his throat as Derek's mouth closed around his cock. Derek had to take a deep breath through his nose to calm himself. The salty taste and velvet texture of Ian's sex was intoxicating. It was hard to maintain a train of thought through his arousal but Derek still had the presence of mind to remember how he'd seen this done before. He moved his mouth slowly down the length of Ian's cock as far as he could comfortably go, then wrapped a fist around it right below his mouth. He felt Ian chuckle and pulled his mouth up and off the hot, hard penis to look up at him with a grin.

"Dolores," they both whispered and their smiles turned sad for a moment.

Ian broke the sadness first with a blink that revealed eyes a smoldering blue. "Take more, Derek. I know you can. Take just a little more." He pushed Derek's head down roughly, thrusting his cock into Derek's mouth. Derek bumped up against his fist and stopped. "Come on, sweetheart, more. Relax your throat, Derek, and take some more for me." His whispers were raspy, deep and throbbing with need. He goaded and demanded, his words not a plea but a command.

Derek could do nothing but obey. He tentatively moved his fist another inch down Ian's cock and slowly relaxed as he slid his mouth after his fist. It was uncomfortable at first but Ian sat motionless, patiently waiting for Derek to adjust. When he was ready he pulled his mouth up at the same time he swished his tongue back and forth along the underside of Ian's cock, ridged with pulsing veins. Ian tasted deliriously good. Derek gave himself over to the pleasure of it, to the knowledge that he held Ian, tasted Ian, he was at long last loving Ian as he'd wanted to for so long. He shivered in suppressed desire, clamping a lid on his own lust until he sated Ian's. He began to rhythmically move his head up and down, fucking Ian with his mouth and tongue. He gently scraped his teeth along the sides and Ian groaned gutturally, thrusting hard. Derek let his mouth fill with his saliva, smoothing Ian's movement in and out of his mouth until Derek couldn't stop his own groan of pleasure. He cupped Ian's balls with his free hand, rolling them and squeezing gently. Ian swore as he fucked wildly into Derek's mouth, his hands pulling on Derek's hair hard enough to help keep Derek's own arousal from overwhelming him.

"I want to come in here, Derek, in this mouth of yours, down your throat. I love that I've shut you up with your mouth full of my cock. Always talking, swearing, threatening, bragging, now all you can do is suck me and moan as I fuck you. You're mine, Derek, mine and you know it." Derek did moan as Ian thrust into his mouth so hard and fast all he could do was lean his head back and open his mouth wide to take it. He wanted to drink Ian down, was desperate for the taste of him. "Christ yes, Derek, yes," Ian gasped and then thrust hard and deep as Derek felt the first splash of hot cum in his throat. He swallowed around the long, thick cock with difficulty, determined to take it all. Ian's cum tasted salty and thick and hot, so hot it burned, and the heat filled his own cock until he thought he'd burst.

When his cock stopped jerking, Ian pulled it from Derek's mouth and slid to his knees on the floor, straddling Derek's legs. He still held Derek's head in his hands and he pulled him close and kissed him passionately. Derek knew Ian could taste himself in his mouth, that the kiss was a way for them to keep sharing the moment. It was also a reward for Derek for how good he'd been. He whimpered in the back of his throat, amazed at how he felt, that he could even make such a needy, desperate sound. Ian pulled his hands from Derek's hair and slid them down his chest and stomach. The muscles there quivered in anticipation and Derek held his breath as Ian paused. Then Ian plunged his hands down into the thick pelt of hair around Derek's cock and Derek shouted out in pleasure. One of Ian's hands held Derek's balls firmly, the other wrapped around his cock and pulled once, twice and that was all it took. He started to cry out as his climax gripped him but Ian's mouth swooped down again and swallowed his cries. He felt his cum shoot out on his stomach and chest and realized that it must be getting on Ian as well, as close as they were. The thought made him shudder and another ripple of pleasure shot through him, making him moan. A few seconds later Ian slowly broke the kiss. Derek opened his eyes to stare into Ian's burning blue ones.

"I will always take care of you, Ian," Derek promised hoarsely, "always."

"And I will take care of you," Ian whispered back, "always."

Chapter Six

ഇ

"Derek?" Ian interrupted his memories, his voice soft, and Derek realized he'd been quiet too long.

"Yes, I remember, Ian," Derek answered his earlier question. "And I have, haven't I? I've taken care of you." He glided his hand up Ian's back and into the hair at his nape, tangling his fingers there, gently rubbing the soft strands.

"Yes." Ian leaned his head back into Derek's caress, closing his eyes. "We've taken care of each other."

Derek leaned down and nuzzled his lips against Ian's throat.

"What were you thinking of just now?" Ian's voice was getting deeper, softer, falling into tones of desire. Derek loved Ian's bedroom voice, it zinged along his nerve endings until he felt it lodge in the head of his cock as it grew hard. He had to think a moment to process the question.

Derek pulled away as he answered. "I was thinking about the first time we were together."

He could see Ian's puzzlement. "The first time we...oh." His face suddenly cleared and amusement took the place of puzzlement. "You mean the first time we fucked. God, what a disaster that was."

They both laughed softly at the memory. "No, the first time we touched, after Dolores. When I sucked your cock for the first time. That was marvelous, and a good thing too considering how awful I was at the fucking." Derek shook his head with chagrin.

Ian ran his hand across Derek's chest and under his jacket to caress him through his thin linen shirt. "I believe it was I who contributed the most to the disaster. I was too big and in too much of a rush. You weren't ready for it yet." He looked somber and a little sad.

"Ian," Derek said softly, raising his face with a finger under his chin. "You've more than made up for that first time in the ensuing years, trust me." He deliberately smiled wolfishly and Ian laughed. Ian pushed away to turn and look out the window again.

"Yes, well, I do wish our first time had been memorable in a better way." He stuffed his hands into the pockets of his robe. "I know you said you didn't want to talk about her, but I've no one else to talk to, Derek."

Derek winced. "Bloody hell. Can't we even have a conversation anymore without having to bring that goddamn—"

"Derek." Ian's voice was hard though he spoke softly and Derek knew to tread lightly.

Derek gestured in an exaggeratedly polite motion. "Go ahead. What about her?"

Ian sighed so deeply his chest noticeably rose and fell. "I've never been a woman's first. I'm not entirely sure Sophie isn't scared of me. How am I to do this?" He looked over at Derek with a half smile. "The only virgin I've taken is you, and look how that turned out."

Derek closed his eyes, pain lancing through him. And so it begins, he thought to himself. He just wished his new resolution to try to live with Sophie wasn't being tested so quickly, and in such a way. Fuck, he cursed inwardly. Trust Ian to try to make him a part of his fucking wedding night even if he refused to be there.

"Well, I've never fucked a virgin either." He hoped the smile he sent Ian was convincingly teasing. Ian continued to look somber. Derek sighed. "I suppose you just take it slow and, I don't know, let her get used to it."

"'Let her get used to it.' Yes, that's brilliant, Derek, brilliant."

His sarcasm grated on Derek's already raw nerves. "She's such a fucking little mouse, Ian." He stalked across the room and then paced back. "She'll probably fuss and cry and bleed the hell all over and think she's dying. Just do it quickly and get it over with. You can try for soul-shattering ecstasy the second time around."

Ian sat down on the windowsill in Derek's place with a disappointed sigh. "I was hoping for a little more constructive help, Derek. I hardly want my wife to remember our first time as a painful 'getting it over with'. I'd like to make it romantic and pleasurable if possible."

Derek looked at him in disbelief. "She's going to be fucking *you*, Ian. Trust me, it doesn't get any better than that. If she's not pleased by that reality, roses and poems won't make it more palatable."

Ian chuckled morosely. "Yes, 'palatable'. You're just full of cheery descriptions this evening, aren't you?"

"For Christ's sake, you are a fucking god, Ian! You fuck like it's the be-all and end-all. I've seen you fuck women, seen their reaction to it. They goddamn love you! Eat her cunt first, they seem to like that, and God knows you've a sinner's mouth. Then cram her full of that huge cock of yours and fuck her like there's never been anyone else and never will be. That always works for me." He had to turn away as he said the last, force his voice not to choke as he thought of Ian fucking anyone the way he fucked Derek.

Suddenly Ian was there at Derek's back, pressed against him, his mouth on Derek's neck, his hands on his hips. "Derek," he whispered, "Derek. There is someone else. There always will be. How will I fuck her when I can't stop thinking about you? How will I fuck her without you?"

Derek shook his head. "I don't know, Ian." He lost the battle and his voice cracked. "But I intend to be rip-roaring drunk while you're doing it, so don't come looking for me tomorrow night to help. I won't help her take you from me."

Ian rested his forehead against Derek's shoulder and his hands traveled from his hips to his stomach. Derek's breath caught.

"Help me now then. Show me, show me how you like to be fucked." Ian's voice went deep again, suddenly becoming almost harsh as he reached up and slid Derek's coat off his shoulders. "You came here to be fucked. Fine. I'll play the stallion for you, Derek. And tomorrow night, make no mistake, I will play it for my wife." His hands came back around Derek and he roughly pulled his shirt from his trousers. He spun Derek around. Then he stepped close and grabbed Derek's shirt in both hands and yanked hard, ripping it open.

"You come to me for reassurance, for me to prove my love with a fuck? If that's all you want from me, you'll have it." Ian wrapped his hand around the back of Derek's head and pulled him into a rough kiss, bruising his lips and then forcing them apart so his tongue could spear into Derek's mouth. Derek moaned at the hot, wet assault. He grabbed on to the lapels of Ian's robe trying to hold on to his sanity but Ian's suddenly violent lust made his head spin. Just as he surrendered to the kiss, Ian broke away.

"That's not all I want from you," Derek said, as harsh in his desire as Ian. He pulled the torn remnants of his shirt down his arms. "But it will do for a start."

Ian stalked away, tearing at the ties on his robe, ripping it off and letting it fall unheeded to the ground. He turned to face Derek.

Derek couldn't breathe. Ian was so goddamned beautiful. His body was sleek and muscular, his stomach flat, his thighs thick. He was dusted all over with blond hair gleaming in the moonlight, from the small triangle in the middle of his chest to the curly nest of darker hair around his erection. Ian's cock was ridged with veins, red with the blood filling it, the full head plump and nearly purple. His sac rode beneath it, large and full, balancing the thick, weighty length above it. It made Derek's mouth water and everything inside him clench in anticipation.

"I want you naked. Now." Ian's voice brooked no argument, and Derek was not inclined to give any. When he was bare he stood there in the moonlight waiting. He saw Ian looking at him, felt his eyes devour him. "I want you as much tonight as I did the first time we were together. My desire for you has not abated. Why, Derek, why? What is it about you that makes me love you so?" Ian sounded genuinely perplexed. "You can be such an ass, but I will make every excuse for you just for the chance to fuck you again, to hold you and kiss you and love you. You have bewitched me." Suddenly he lost his fierceness. He held out his hand and Derek felt compelled to walk forward and take it, as if he were the one bewitched. "I will love you, Derek, always." Ian pulled him toward the bed. "Remember that whatever I do, I do because I want what's best for you."

Derek tugged on his hand and Ian stopped, looking over his shoulder at Derek. "Shouldn't I be the one to decide what's best for me?"

Ian just smiled. "Not tonight."

Ian had his nose buried in the thatch of hair at Derek's crotch and he inhaled deeply. He opened his mouth against Derek's inner thigh and sucked at the skin there, making Derek cry out as he marked him. Christ, he loved the scent of Derek. Just a whiff of it and Ian would be hard as iron in seconds. He'd thought and thought about it and decided part of its allure was that it was his, Ian's. No one else had the right to bury their face there and inhale the essence of Derek. Derek smelled of desire for Ian alone. Briefly Ian wondered if he would be jealous when Sophie shared Derek's scent. In spite of all Derek's protestations he knew that if Sophie agreed, one day soon the three would share a bed. Derek was too sensual not to crave the experience and too possessive of Ian not to invade his marriage bed.

He sucked harder on Derek's thigh and at the same time worked his fingers into Derek's ass. He would mark Derek here, and then again on his ass. Added to the marks he'd put on his chest, Ian was relatively sure that Derek would carry a reminder of his possession for days to come. They should help Derek rein in his jealousy over Ian's marriage for the first week. He pulled his fingers out of Derek while Derek moaned, and added more cream. Derek was deliciously tight, and as good as it felt they'd learned through experience there had to be a certain amount of preparation before Ian could fuck him. He was just too tight to rush into it.

He stopped sucking and laved the bruised skin with his tongue soothingly. Derek liked it just a little rough, just the way Ian liked it. He supposed that was a good thing because his penis was just large enough that fucking was rarely a gentle affair. He worried yet again about Sophie. Would she like it that way too? Would she be able to take Ian? Suddenly Derek's hand fisted in Ian's hair as Ian licked him.

"Hands above your head, Derek," he ordered quietly. With a whimper Derek obeyed. God, he loved that. He knew everyone wondered about them. Who was dominant? Who was on top? Derek was so loud and brash it was hard for anyone to imagine him surrendering to Ian, but surrender he did, in every way, and Ian made him love it. "Roll over, Derek," he told him, and Derek did it immediately. Ian kept his fingers in Derek's ass while he rolled, scissored them as they twisted with Derek's movement. Derek cried out and Ian laughed. He had to take them out to pull his arm out from underneath Derek's leg and Derek gasped, making him laugh again.

"Keep your hands above your head, Derek. I'm going to mark your ass, darling. A huge love bite right here." He licked a spot on Derek's muscular left cheek and Derek shivered. He bit down on the choice piece of flesh just as he thrust his three fingers back in Derek's ass. Derek moaned and his hips jerked back, taking the thrust expertly. Ian pulled his mouth off and lightly slapped his ass. "Don't move, Derek. I need to suck."

"God damn it, Ian, I can't help it. You can't expect me not fuck back when it feels so goddamn good." Derek's voice was harsh and breathless. Ian had been working him for almost half an hour, lovingly torturing him as he marked his territory. Ian slapped his ass again and Derek groaned. "If you keep doing that I'm going to come. I'm warning you." Ian swooped down and sucked hard on Derek's ass, relishing the clenching of the tight muscles there. Ian always made sure Derek's trousers were cut snugly. He loved his ass, loved to watch him walking or riding, the muscles flexing. Just the thought made him bite a little rougher as he sucked and Derek swore again, but he didn't move.

"Fuck, fuck, fuck. Yes, god damn you. Don't stop." The words were harsh, but his tone was pleading.

Ian finally broke away. The taste and feel of Derek's salty, firm flesh in his mouth, the musky scent of him, the tight little whimpers he made had pushed Ian to his limits. He needed to fuck, he couldn't wait any more. He yanked his fingers out and rolled Derek over unceremoniously.

"What the…" Derek was startled by Ian's abrupt movements. He lay sprawled, his arms spread over his head, his legs wide. He was breathing hard and his cock was rigid, pre-cum glistening on the tip.

"I want you now." Ian could hear the growl in his voice. He was on edge and he tried to rein himself in, pull back from the precipice of desire but he couldn't. He wanted. No, he hungered plain and simple. He'd been a seething mass of pent-up emotions for days with worry over Sophie, over Derek, over the wedding, over the wedding night. Somehow it was all boiling to the surface here, in this fuck.

He grabbed the pillows from where they'd been tossed to the end of his huge bed. He partially rolled Derek over to shove the pillows under his hips and then hauled him back over them. Derek didn't say a word. He knew better.

Ian crawled over him, predator and prey. He settled himself between Derek's legs, his hands on Derek's thighs, spreading them apart. Derek's ass was raised high by the pillows, perfect for Ian to penetrate deeply, effortlessly. At the same time Ian could watch Derek while he fucked him, play with his cock. He loved fucking Derek in this position. He grabbed the cream and rubbed a generous amount on his aching erection. While he rubbed he stared at Derek and their eyes locked.

"I'm going to fuck you this way so you can see me, Derek. I want you to see the look on my face when I'm inside you. I want you to see how much I need you. I want you to know, once and for all, that you are mine and I will never let you go."

Ian rose to his knees and leaned over Derek, supporting his weight on his fists by Derek's shoulders. He adjusted his hips and pressed his cock into Derek's ass. The first few inches were the hardest, pushing his head past the tight ring of muscles that guarded Derek's passage so well. It was a sweet, vicious torture for Ian every time. If he could get past the entrance without coming, he knew he'd last for a good, hard fuck. But there had been times when he'd barely gotten inside and he'd come before thrusting even once, the tight, burning heat of Derek's ass driving him over the edge.

Derek's neck and upper back arched sharply, pushing his chest into the air as he grabbed at the bedsheets above his head. "Ian," he cried out, his voice strangled. Yes, it was a sweet torture for him as well. He'd told Ian that those first few inches frequently crossed the line between pain and pleasure and then back again. For Derek, short of climax it was one of the best parts of fucking Ian.

Ian was breathing heavily, his nostrils flared, his eyes narrowed in concentration. He focused on the pulse in Derek's neck as he pushed until he was halfway inside, then he paused. He closed his eyes and relaxed for a moment, just enjoying the overwhelming sensations of heat and tightness. Derek relaxed with him as he slowly adjusted to Ian's width.

"More," Derek whispered, bringing one hand down to grip Ian's forearm. Ian opened his eyes and looked directly into Derek's intense stare. "More," he repeated. Ian's eye was caught by the glitter of a drop of sweat running down Derek's temple. He looked and saw Derek's hair was wet and curling with perspiration, and suddenly he could feel the heat and sweat of their passion on his own skin. It added a new layer of sensation, of decadence, to their intense fuck. He didn't answer Derek with words, instead he gave him what he desired. With a strong thrust he slid the rest of the way into Derek.

Derek's neck arched again and he groaned loudly.

"Is that what you wanted, Derek?" Ian's question was soft and menacing. "I'll give you what you want, what you beg me for." Ian pulled back and then thrust in again and Derek angled his hips more to take Ian deeper. Ian laughed darkly at Derek's complete surrender to him. "Spread your legs wider and bend your knees more. I want to get closer, deeper." His commands harsh, Ian pushed forward, forcing Derek's legs farther apart. Derek whimpered and Ian felt the beast inside him stir and stretch. "Cry for it," he told Derek roughly at the same time his thrusts became less controlled, faster and harder.

Derek cried out and clutched at Ian's arms with both hands now. "Put your hands above you, against the headboard." Derek didn't obey, and Ian repeated the order louder, breaking through Derek's sexual haze. Slowly Derek complied while Ian stopped moving and waited.

"Why?" Derek questioned breathlessly.

"Because I don't want you to hit your head on it." Derek shuddered and closed his eyes. Ian would have none of that. He reached one hand over and fisted Derek's hair tightly, pulling it hard enough to make his eyes fly open. "Don't you close your eyes. Look at me. Watch me fuck you. Watch me."

Derek kept his eyes open and trained on Ian's face as Ian began to fuck him again. His motions were smooth, practiced, but each thrust increased in intensity until Derek's whole body was jerking with each one, only his arms braced over his head keeping him from sliding forward. At that point, Ian adjusted his angle just a fraction and Derek couldn't stop the loud, harsh cry that ripped from his throat. Oh yes, Ian knew just how to fuck Derek until he cried with the pleasure of it.

The pleasure, however, was a double-edged sword. The rippling of Derek's muscles with each plunge of Ian's cock, Derek's throaty cries, the heat, the sounds of flesh slapping flesh, the feel of Derek's balls and hard cock caressing his lower stomach with each thrust drove Ian closer and closer to his own climax.

"Who owns you, Derek?" Ian panted demandingly, rising to his knees, grabbing Derek's thighs and spreading them so he could watch his cock go in and out of his ass. "Who owns you?"

"Ian," Derek groaned.

"Come for me, Derek. Do it, now." The command was all Derek needed. He cried out harshly and bent forward as cum shot from his cock to cover his stomach. He jerked over and over until he was spent and fell back. Ian slid his arms under Derek's thighs and gripped his hips. He fucked hard into him, pulling Derek down on his cock with each thrust and Derek grunted with each harsh penetration. In moments Ian roared wordlessly as his semen filled Derek and he could feel its heat and wetness surround his cock inside him. The pleasure was so intense Ian's vision wavered, and when the waves of orgasm quieted he felt weak as a babe.

He gently collapsed on top of Derek. He gripped Derek's hair again, shaking him out of his post-orgasmic lassitude. When Derek opened his eyes and focused on him, Ian leaned over and lay his lips against Derek's before he spoke.

"I love you, you fucking idiot. Do you believe me now?"

Derek laughed weakly. "Right now you could tell me the moon was made of cheese and I'd believe you, Ian. Ask me again tomorrow after your wedding."

Ian sighed and rolled off Derek to pull him close. Derek curled into him, his head on Ian's shoulder and his arm and leg across Ian as if to hold him there. Right before falling into a deep sleep, Ian spared one more thought to worry about Sophie.

Chapter Seven

₰

Ian woke up abruptly, disoriented but quite sure something was amiss. It took him a moment to acclimate himself and inventory before he discovered what it was. Derek had gotten out of bed and was even now trying to slink out of the room with a handful of clothes.

"It's been years since we felt the need to sneak out of one another's beds in the morning, Derek," he said quietly, clearing his throat when he heard how tired and raspy his voice sounded.

Derek froze in place, his hand arrested where it was reaching for the doorknob.

"I can't do it, Ian," Derek said, and Ian was surprised by the anguish in his voice. Had he missed something? Do what? He rolled to his back and sat up, rubbing his face to clear the cobwebs from his brain.

"I'm still half asleep, darling. You're going to have to be a little more specific. What exactly did I ask you to do?"

Derek turned slowly to face him, and Ian was alarmed to see tears on his cheeks.

"Good God, Derek, what the hell is the matter?" Ian quickly rose from the bed and started across the room to his lover's side. He stopped when Derek held up his hand.

"What day is today, Ian?"

Ian shook his head, trying to follow the conversation, but he was so bloody tired. He and Derek had loved long into the night. He looked out the window and saw a weak sun just over the horizon. And then he remembered.

He looked back at Derek, at a complete loss as to how to make things better for him. "It's my wedding day," he said softly.

Derek's eyes closed and he took a deep breath. He opened them before speaking again, but wouldn't look at Ian. "I know I said I'd try, but I can't be there, Ian. I'm sorry, I just can't." He tried a smile and it was painful for Ian to see the effort it took. "Besides, I'll hardly be in a celebratory mood. I'd more than likely turn the event into a wake instead."

Ian couldn't stop his burst of hurt laughter at Derek's words. "Yes, I suppose you probably would. My bride is frightened enough as it is. It is the height of chivalry for you not to subject her to your misery." He was angry. He tried not to be, but he was.

"I'm sorry, Ian—"

"I am too, Derek." Ian turned and walked stiffly over to his robe lying on the floor. He picked it up and donned it with jerky movements. "This is probably one of the most important days of my life, and you, as usual, refuse to support me. I don't know why this comes as a shock."

Derek ran a hand through his hair in frustration. "I have every right—"

"Spare me your pathetic excuses, Derek." Ian's voice was cold. "I've heard them all. Hell, I've made most of them for you in the last several years." He turned his back and crammed his hands in his pockets. "So when shall I see you again? The next time you need me to act as stud? Will you send a note 'round when you need a good fuck?"

Derek cursed and threw the clothes he was holding at Ian's back.

"Don't act the fucking victim, Ian. This whole marriage mess was your idea. I'm the one who's suffering. I'm the injured party."

"Ballocks." Ian turned angrily to face Derek, kicking at the clothes now around his feet. Derek stood in nothing but his trousers, feet and chest bare. "You're the selfish bastard here, Derek, not the victim." Ian grabbed handfuls of his blond hair and pulled as he growled his frustration and rage. "I don't know what else to do to prove to you that I love you! I'm doing this for us! Derek, we can't go on this way. You can't go on this way. You refuse to listen to me." Suddenly defeated, he collapsed into a chair before the cold hearth. He felt tears gathering and closed his eyes. "I'm sorry, I'm sorry I want more. I'm sorry I want children, and a wife. I'm sorry I want to make you happy. I'm sorry I'm hurting you. I'm just so bloody sorry, Derek."

"Ian," Derek's voice was no longer angry.

"I'm sorry I'm losing you," Ian choked out. "I'm sorry that I tried to force my vision of our future on you. I'm sorry that I thought it would be wonderful to have another person love us, a new beginning. I'm sorry, I'm sorry, I'm sorry." He opened his eyes and let a tear leak out of one. "Is it enough? Am I sorry enough?"

Derek sighed. "You manipulative bastard," he said calmly.

Ian sat forward in his chair and with lips thinned raked his hand through his hair. "Do you think I'm happy about how low I've sunk here?" he cried.

Derek studied him shrewdly. "You must want this very badly, Ian."

"Why do you say that?"

"You've never used tears on me before." Derek walked over and bent down and retrieved his clothes.

"They're genuine?" Ian tried hopefully.

Derek snorted in disgust.

"All right." Ian sighed. "What will it take, Derek?"

"Don't bother. The tears worked." Derek started to walk away but spun back around. "Call it off, Ian. There's still time."

"And then what?" This was where Derek balked every time Ian had tried to talk to him.

Derek deliberately misunderstood the question. "You don't have to send her back with her father. We can find somewhere else for Sophie."

Ian shook his head. "No, Derek. I'm not talking about Sophie. I meant what then for us?"

Derek looked at him blankly for a moment. "We go on as we were. Life goes back to normal."

Ian put a hand over his eyes. Derek wouldn't believe the tears now, anyway. "I don't want that."

"You want her," Derek spit at him.

Ian shook his head again. "Not at first. At first it was about the life that she could give us. A home, children, boring, blessed peace." He looked at Derek. "I never lied to you, Derek. Marrying Sophie has always been about a new start for us. A beginning far removed from the war."

"This has nothing to do with the war," Derek snarled. "Why are you always trying to get me to talk about that bloody war?"

"It has everything to do with it," Ian cried. "You're not happy, Derek. I can't make you happy."

Derek stumbled back a step. "What the hell are you talking about, Ian? Of course you make me happy."

Ian shook his head and Derek believed the tears in his eyes were real now. "No, Derek, I don't. When was the last time you laughed? Not with sarcasm, or in anger, but really laughed?"

"You can hardly blame me for not laughing since you took this idiotic marriage scheme to heart." Derek's heart was pounding erratically.

"How often do you sleep through the night?" Ian didn't wait, he answered for Derek, who remained silent. "Never. Not since the first day I met you." Ian rose from his chair.

"Derek, I want those things for you, things I can't give you. Happiness, peace, stability."

Derek turned away in confusion. "I'm happy, Ian. You are the one not happy with our present arrangement."

"No, Derek, I'm not." Ian sounded tired and defeated. "I love you with all my heart, but it's not enough. You're dying inside and I can't help you, and it's killing me."

Derek turned around and stopped himself just before he let out a sarcastic laugh. "Don't be melodramatic, Ian. That's more my style than yours."

Ian took a deep breath. "I'm asking, Derek. I'm asking you to please come to the wedding."

"Declare a cease-fire and fete the enemy?" Derek allowed the bottled-up sarcasm to infiltrate his words.

Ian sighed and walked over to him and ran a hand down his bare arm. "It's a wedding, not a war."

"You're always trying to get me talk about the war. This is the one I'm fighting now."

"There is no battle, Derek. You won my heart long ago. But I owe it to Sophie to try with all my heart to make things work."

"You can't give all your heart to two people, Ian. It's mathematically impossible." Derek felt his control slipping.

"We're not talking about your mathematics, Derek. There are no rules in love."

"Then it *is* war," Derek told him. Ian sighed and closed his eyes wearily. Derek gave in. "I'll try, Ian. I'll come to your wedding and I'll try not to hate her. That's all I can promise."

* * * * *

Sophie was so nervous she thought she might throw up. She'd been up most of the night, pacing to and fro and fretting. She hadn't spoken with Ian as she'd promised Kate and Kitty. It wasn't necessary. She'd play the virgin for him and he'd be pleased and everything would be fine, *fine*. She didn't need kid gloves, for heaven's sake. She wasn't broken, she wasn't. She could handle one little wedding night.

She thrust her arms into her heavy robe, determined to find a book in the library to occupy her until her maid came with breakfast. The sun had barely risen, she was sure everyone was still abed. She'd go mad if she had to stay in this room for one more minute. She quietly opened her door and snuck into the hallway. She was almost at the stairs when she heard a door open behind her. She scurried into the shadows of a small alcove with a bust atop a pedestal and looked in the direction of quiet voices.

A man she'd never seen before was leaving one of the bedrooms and being very obvious about trying to be quiet. He wore nothing but trousers and Sophie's heart literally stopped in her chest. He was without a doubt the most beautiful man she had ever seen. She'd thought that of Ian, but there was something so primitive about this man he was in a category by himself.

He was extraordinarily tall and had wavy dark brown hair, although it was hard to see in the dimly lit hallway. What color were his eyes? His shoulders were so broad they filled the doorway and she couldn't see the person behind him with whom he was talking. His chest was full and covered in dark hair that tapered down to the low waist of his inexpressibles. He had what looked like two strange bruises on his chest. She had never seen so many muscles in her life, not even on the laborers on her father's land. He was huge and magnificent and frightening.

"Of course I'm being quiet," he hissed over his shoulder, and then he turned to whoever was behind him. Sophie caught a glimpse as he turned and was shocked to see that it was Ian. She listened harder.

"You'll be there?" Ian was saying.

"I said I'd be there and I will," the tall man snarled, and Sophie flinched.

"Derek, it means so much to me. I love that you're doing it for me, and I know ultimately it will mean a great deal to Sophie as well."

Derek! So this was the elusive Mr. Knightly, Ian's lover. Well, she could certainly see why he lusted for him. Sophie's hand flew up to cover her mouth as a nervous giggle tried to escape. Good Lord! Where had that thought come from? Sophie couldn't imagine lusting after anyone, not knowing exactly what the consequences entailed.

"You know I don't give a damn about that," Derek told him as he reached out a hand and wrapped it around the back of Ian's neck. Sophie tensed. Was he going to hurt Ian? "But I'd do anything for *you*, Ian, you know that." Sophie couldn't stop her gasp of shock when he pulled Ian's mouth to his and the two men kissed passionately.

Her shock was so great at what happened next she fell back against the wall and had to grab for the bust before it fell to the floor. Ian grabbed a handful of Derek's hair and pulled the other man's head away, keeping a hold of his lower lip somehow until Derek whimpered. Then Ian let go. Ian's hand leisurely trailed down Derek's strong back until it cupped his buttock. "I know you'll do anything I want, Derek," Ian purred and squeezed the full, round cheek he held, making Derek gasp, "and you'll like it."

"God damn it, Ian," Derek growled, "don't start something you can't finish." He reached back and removed Ian's hand from his backside and Ian's laugh was low and seductive. Ian murmured something she couldn't hear, and she saw the dazzling white of Derek's answering smile as he leaned down to kiss Ian again, quickly this time.

"You can order me around some more later," Derek hissed as he pulled away, looking furtively up and down the hallway. Sophie pulled back, trying to blend into the wall behind her. He began to walk quickly away from her down the hallway, turning halfway down to look back longingly at Ian as he walked backward. Ian leaned casually against the doorframe until Derek ducked quietly into a guestroom at the end of the hall, then he went into his own room and closed the door without looking in Sophie's direction.

Sophie waited for several minutes to make sure they didn't come back out of their rooms, then she quietly drifted back to her own chamber. She'd known about Mr. Knightly, of course, but she hadn't really known, had she? It was one thing to think the two were lovers, quite another to see the reality of it. She smiled with glee and threw herself down on the comfortable wingchair in front of the small fireplace filled with glowing embers from last night's fire. Ian certainly wouldn't want Sophie very often with Derek around, would he? She'd make sure to make it perfectly clear it was absolutely all right with her if he wished to bed Derek frequently. Surely it wouldn't take that long to get her with child? And then Ian could leave her alone completely. She would take the first opportunity presented to assure Derek of this, as well. She'd heard servant gossip and knew he was jealous of her. Well, there was really no need, was there? He could have Ian if he wanted him, in that way. She just needed Ian to give her shelter—yes, that was it, a place to live her life quietly so she would never have to return to her father's house. She'd never go back, never. And she would do whatever was needed to make sure Ian never had reason to send her back.

* * * * *

Sophie didn't have a chance to speak with Ian before the wedding. Kate and Very and Kitty arrived and spent hours primping her for "her big day" as they called it. Their kindness and excitement only served to make Sophie more nervous than ever. According to the three, all of Ian's friends would be here today. What would they think of Sophie? She winced to imagine what they might think of her father. Hopefully he'd leave as soon as he was sure Sophie was off his hands for good.

Her preparations for the wedding had seemed interminable, but when Sophie stood at the doors of the large drawing room waiting for the footmen to open them so her father could escort her in she couldn't believe the moment was here. Her heart was pounding in terror. Any minute she expected Harold to come charging through the entry, decrying her as an unworthy slut and dragging her back to the country. A cold trickle of perspiration made its way down her spine and she shivered.

"Stop your sniveling," her father snarled. "I'll never be so glad as when I finally wash my hands of the likes of you. Your pervert husband and his lover can have you. As soon as I've made sure this wedding goes off and he doesn't try to back out at the last minute when he realizes what he's getting, I'll be out the door. And don't cry for me to save you, missy, when you're missing your home and family. You've been nothing but a trial since the day you were born. Why I listened to Harold and didn't marry you off to someone else sooner, I'll never know. It's clear Witherspoon would have settled for any woman he could get a child off of."

Well, what a heartwarming wedding day speech from a loving father to his daughter, Sophie thought acerbically. At least one of her prayers had been answered. He'd be leaving soon, thank God, and hopefully she'd never see him again. Her father wasn't done however.

"And don't think I'll be giving my hard-earned money to that ungrateful bastard you're about to marry. He said, in front of witnesses, that he didn't want your dowry. Well, he'll not be getting it, not after the way he's treated me. Ha! I'd like to see him try."

Sophie was horrified. If her father didn't give Ian her dowry, Ian might send her back! "Father, please," Sophie whispered frantically, "you must give him the dowry! It's in the contract. He could nullify the marriage, couldn't he?" She clutched at his arm and he yanked it away from her.

"He can try! I'll not be taking you back, so you'd better whore your way into his good graces if you don't want to be out on the street," he told her viciously, his eyes gleaming with satisfaction. "Always thought yourself better than your family, didn't you? All the times Harold lied for you, I knew! I knew you'd been out, acting the slut. Well, I'll not stand for it anymore. You're Witherspoon's problem now."

Sophie was aghast. Was that the only way to make Ian keep her? To whore for him? She shuddered in revulsion. She couldn't do it, she couldn't! And how she longed to tell her father of Harold's lies—that he was covering up his own horrifying, shameful behavior, not hers. She'd never wanted it, never.

Someone cleared their throat and Sophie looked up at Montague standing by the drawing room doors, close enough to have heard their exchange. She colored in mortification. Montague smiled encouragingly and she nearly cried in gratitude.

"Are you ready, miss?" he asked quietly.

"Ready?" her father asked incredulously. "Of course we're ready! Open the damn door, you idiot, so we can get this farce of a wedding over with. Is Mr. High-and-Mighty's lover going to be here, you think?" he asked Sophie snidely. She winced at how loud his voice was.

Montague opened the doors and Sophie couldn't raise her eyes above the floor. She knew everyone in the room had heard her father's words. Oh God! What must they think of her? She could barely walk as her father moved forward, dragging her into the room. She blinked back tears. Halfway to Ian she felt the calm descend over her that had been her refuge for years. She could get through this. She wouldn't let any of them know how embarrassed she was. She would not show them how much she cared about their opinion, how much she wanted Ian's friends to like her. She raised her head and squared her shoulders with a deep breath, and she met Ian's gaze.

He was furious, she could see it. She felt her lip tremble and tightened her mouth in determination. Ian smiled at her. His smile was forced, but it was a smile. Sophie risked a glance at the people standing around the room to witness the wedding. She saw Kate crying and Sophie smiled weakly at her, which set Kate off on another crying jag. Very handed her a handkerchief and then winked at Sophie. Lord Randall tapped his hand under his chin as if telling her to raise her head and so she did, and he smiled at her with a nod. She darted her eyes around the rest of the room, looking for one person in particular. She didn't want to look too closely at all the strangers there. She didn't want to see condescension in their faces, or pity for Ian over the monstrously ill-bred mouse he was marrying. She looked around once, twice, and then realized that he wasn't here. Derek hadn't come.

Suddenly she was in front of Ian and her father was handing her off, none too gently. He turned and walked a few steps away with a scowl at the people there as they backed away and gave him a generous berth. Ian took her hand and pulled her close to kiss her cheek. When he whispered in her ear, she jerked her head slightly in surprise.

"If I kill your father after the ceremony, darling, will you hold it against me for a very long time?"

Sophie was shocked by the sharp burst of laughter that she couldn't contain. Ian pulled away, smiling a genuine smile, and she returned it. Furtively looking at her scowling father out of the corner of her eye, she looked at Ian and shook her head. His grin widened. She said very, very quietly, "He is leaving immediately after the ceremony."

Ian glanced over at the attractive young minister standing before them. "Did you hear that, Stephen? Please make it as brief as possible." Sophie actually shook with laughter at the man's grin as he nodded.

"I think it best for all concerned," Stephen said solemnly, and Sophie nodded her head in thanks with barely suppressed mirth. What was wrong with her? She was never this merry.

The minister began with a short speech about the beauty of love and commitment, and Sophie's eyes grew blurry with tears. Yes, yes, that's what she wanted—someone to protect her, to care whether she lived or died, to actually concern themselves with her happiness. Was that so wrong? Ian suddenly squeezed her hands and she realized he was about to repeat his vows. She looked up into his eyes as he spoke.

"I, Ian Churchill Witherspoon, take thee, Sophia Terèse Middleton, to be my wife..."

The rest of the words were lost as he repeated after the minister. She clutched his hands in hers tightly and the world narrowed down to just the two of them. He spoke fervently, and Sophie so wanted to believe the promises he was making. Without realizing what she was doing, she stepped closer to him and held their bound hands to her heart. She heard her name and looked over at the minister.

"Are you ready?" he asked quietly. Sophie nodded and began to repeat the words after him.

"I, Sophia Terèse Middleton, take thee, Ian Churchill Witherspoon, to be my husband..." Something caught her eye and she turned to the French doors open behind the minister. Derek stood there, staring at her. And without thinking she began to repeat the rest of her vows to him.

* * * * *

She was bloody gorgeous. How dare she? Where the hell was the little mouse that'd prostrated herself on the study floor and begged Ian to marry her? This woman was a flame, a beautiful, mesmerizing flame of walking desire with her copper hair and full breasts and shining amber eyes. He hated her with a passion that surprised even him. And then she did it. She looked at him. She looked at him and repeated her wedding vows, *to him*.

"With my body I shall worship..." Derek's stomach clenched in a wave of unexpected, unwanted desire.

"To love, honor and obey…" She spoke so earnestly, her expression guileless, he had to fight to hold on to his anger.

When she was done there was a moment of absolute, utter silence in the room. Derek had to drag his eyes away from hers, the sensation like a physical separation. He saw their clasped hands pressed to Sophie's breast, barely a breath of space between them. From their hands Derek's eyes followed the line of Ian's arms up to Ian's face. Ian was looking at him with a mixture of gratitude, hope and joy, emotions suited to a man's wedding day. In that moment he knew, as hard as it was for him, that he'd made the right decision to come today.

Derek had to look away as he felt tears in his eyes — goddamn fucking tears. Suddenly he saw how he'd been acting the last several months in a decidedly negative light. What a fucking selfish bastard he'd been. He was mortally ashamed of how hard he'd made things for Ian, and Sophie too. He got himself under control and turned back to find most of the room staring at him. He crossed his arms defensively and glared at Stephen Matthews, the minister. Stephen quickly turned around.

During the presentation of the ring, Derek was disgusted with himself. He hadn't even bothered to look at the wedding ring Ian had bought for Sophie. Ian had asked him to come with him to help choose it, but Derek refused. For what? So he could stand here at Ian's wedding, an outsider? Well, it was his own damn fault. His determination to find a way to live with Sophie solidified. He did not want to feel this way again.

He watched as Stephen declared them man and wife. Sophie looked at him before she turned to accept Ian's kiss. Derek's stomach lurched again, and with a sinking heart he recognized that this marriage would irrevocably change his future.

* * * * *

Sophie was in a daze. Immediately after the ceremony Ian ushered her into the study with the minister, a Mr. Matthews whom Ian had known since they'd been on the Peninsula together. Her father joined them and they all signed the appropriate papers. Her father had been unforgivably rude, as usual, and as soon as she'd written her name Lord Randall had appeared and whisked her back to the drawing room to accept congratulations and meet all of Ian's friends. Ian had yet to appear, and Sophie hoped with all her might that her father would make good on his promise to leave.

Lord Randall, Kate, Kitty, Very, Mr. Richards, Lord Kensington and Mr. Tarrant were guarding her like a pack of dogs surrounding a sheep. They moved everyone along quickly and kept shoving glasses of champagne in her hand. They really needn't bother anymore, she was quite tipsy already and inured to the stares and whispers. Actually everyone was being quite solicitous, clearly having a genuine affection for Ian and honestly wishing them well. She couldn't blame them for their curiosity about her, not if they were his friends in truth.

She could only smile wryly at their efforts to block her view of a rather morose Derek in the corner on the opposite side of the room. What would they all think, she wondered, if they knew she completely sympathized with him? She didn't begrudge him his misery at all. She just wished she'd had a chance to talk to him before the wedding, to set his mind at ease. As much as she'd like to do it now, it was not the appropriate time or place. Poor Derek, she did wish her efforts to escape her family had not meant his unhappiness.

The thought made her a little sad, so she drank another glass of champagne, cheerfully supplied by the dashing Lord Kensington. It had been intriguing to meet Very's Lord Kensington and her Mr. Tarrant. They seemed totally captivated by Very, who accepted their adoration as her due. How very, well, Very, Sophie thought with an inner giggle that made her smile. She looked over and saw Kate watching

her with a worried frown. Sophie sighed and gave Kate a
pointed look meant to convey her exasperation. Clearly it
conveyed something else, as Lord Randall plucked the
champagne glass from her hand and Kate rushed over to put
an arm around her.

"Oh dear," Kate said, fretting, "you're not going to be
sick, are you, Sophie darling?"

"What?" Sophie asked with a frown. It took a great deal
of concentration to make the frown, and somehow that seemed
wrong, but Sophie shrugged it off. She felt amazingly carefree,
actually. Why was everyone looking at her like that? She
looked down at herself and noticed nothing amiss. Oh God,
what had she done now? All the old fears came roaring back,
and she retreated a step, her arms hugging herself as they kept
staring. "Have I done something wrong?" she whispered to
Kate.

Mr. Tarrant came to her rescue. He was a quiet one, so
Sophie was a little surprised by his support. "Not at all, my
dear. Kate and Lord Randall are merely worried that you've
had too much to drink and may be feeling ill as a result. But
clearly you are not."

Sophie took a deeply relieved breath. "No, no, I feel fine,
Kate, honestly. I feel wonderful, as a matter of fact." She
accompanied the reassurance with a huge smile, and it did feel
wonderful. Sophie couldn't remember the last time she'd
smiled like that. Kate visibly relaxed.

"Oh, Aunt Kate, leave her alone. If a girl can't get foxed at
her own wedding I don't know when she can." Very put her
arm around Sophie from the opposite side. "But you ought to
refrain from here on out, Sophie dear. You wouldn't want to
be too far gone to enjoy your wedding night." She
accompanied the remark with a lascivious grin and suddenly
Sophie did feel ill. She felt the color drain from her face.

"Oh yes, that was just the thing, Very," Lord Kensington
said dryly. "Nothing like terrifying the drunk bride."

Kate dragged Sophie behind her out of the room. They adjourned to the retiring room and Kate checked to make sure no one else was about before confronting Sophie.

"Have you talked to Ian yet, Sophie?"

Sophie closed her eyes and struggled to swallow her bile. She shook her head, incapable of speech.

"Oh, Sophie," Kate said with a weary sigh, sitting down next to her on the small fainting couch. She took Sophie's hands. "Would you like me to talk to him?"

Sophie stood up so fast her head spun, and she had to place a hand on the wall. "No! No, Kate. Everything will be fine. Ian is a gentleman, and I'm sure he will act appropriately. This has nothing to do with what may have happened in my past. It is completely different. You and Kitty said so. I have nothing to fear, remember? And of course there's Derek, so really, I needn't worry at all, really. Right?" Somehow her speech had made more sense in her head. Kate was looking at her with a great deal of concern. "You must promise not to say anything to Ian, Kate, you or Kitty. Promise me. Promise!" Sophie grabbed Kate's hands and only realized how tight she was holding them when Kate winced.

"All right, Sophie. All right, I promise." She pulled Sophie down next to her again and pressed Sophie's head to her shoulder. "I promise that neither Kitty nor I will say anything to Ian about it. Now take a few deep breaths and we'll relax here for a few minutes." She frowned down at Sophie. "Very is right, my dear. No more champagne. You've had quite enough."

* * * * *

Ian walked back into the drawing room with a sigh. He'd had to have Mr. Middleton forcibly removed from the house, via the servants' entrance. The man had actually had the audacity to try to blackmail him, threatening to expose his affair with Derek and Sophie's apparent past indiscretions unless Ian paid him a rather handsome sum. Ian had refused to even comment, instead summoning two burly footmen to escort him off the premises. Mr. Middleton had railed and cursed, but they were far enough from the party that no one heard.

He scanned the crowd. Sophie was holding court in the far left corner, surrounded by Very and her two gallants, as well as several others. She was shaking Dr. Thomas Peters' hand and holding a glass of champagne in her other hand, smiling happily. She seemed a bit unsteady on her feet. When she saw him, she frowned at the other corner with a nod of her head. He turned to look. Derek was there doing his best to be sociable, which was not very good on the best of days. He was listening to Freddy, the Duke of Ashland, and he was smiling and nodding absently. Freddy's constant companion, Mr. Brett Haversham, was standing beside Derek with a hand on his arm. Ian was glad someone was comforting him, because he simply didn't have the patience today.

Oh happy day, Ian thought with an inner grimace. *I've just booted my blackmailing new father-in-law out of the house, I think my bride is drunk, and my lover looks like his dog just died. Ring the bells, it's my wedding day.* He shook his head, pinching the bridge of his nose at the feeling of a headache coming on. He looked around yet again and noticed Kate and Kitty huddled in another corner, whispering furiously to Jason and Tony. What the devil was that about? The two men looked as if they wanted to bash someone's head in, and Kate kept wiping her eyes and blowing her nose, crying again. Had Derek done something?

Ian was at a loss as to which corner to go to. He thought about simply retreating to his study to get as drunk as Sophie. Before he had to make a decision, Jason and Tony walked over to him.

"May we have a moment of your time, Ian?" Jason asked rather formally. His tone did not bode well.

"Whatever he's done, it can't be that bad," Ian said with a sigh.

Jason looked perplexed. "Who?"

"What are you talking about?" Tony asked. "Has something happened?"

It was Ian's turn to be confused. "I don't know. Hasn't it? I thought Derek had done something."

Tony turned to scan the room. "No," he pointed to Derek, "Derek's right there."

"What are you talking about then?" Ian was completely at sea in the conversation.

Jason lightly grabbed hold of his arm and steered him to the door. "Let's talk in your study."

When they reached Ian's study, Ian walked right over to the bottles of spirits and poured three drinks. He gave one to each of the other men and then raised his in a toast.

"To Dolores," he said and drank the entire glass in one gulp. Jason and Tony repeated the toast and followed suit.

Tony raised an eyebrow. "That's an odd toast on your wedding day, Ian. Not that Dolores wasn't a beautiful girl, but what made you think of her?"

Ian stared at his empty glass as he spun it in his hand. He turned to pour himself another one. "I've been thinking a lot about Dolores in the last few days." He turned back to Tony. "She taught me how to love a woman, and in her own way, how to love Derek. But more importantly, she taught me how to love a woman with Derek. I think all of those lessons, particularly the last, will come in handy in the ensuing weeks." He took a sedate sip of his whiskey, his desire to get drunk slowly fading.

"He'll come around, Ian." Jason sounded so sure and Ian turned to him in surprise.

"What makes you so sure?"

Jason sat down in Derek's big chair. "Derek needs two things desperately. He needs to be loved and he needs you. Both of those will bring him to you and Sophie. Give him time." Jason held up his empty glass for more whiskey. He looked a little ill, and Ian's trepidation about their little talk increased.

"What's going on, Jason?" he asked suspiciously.

Jason sighed and Tony took the bottle from Ian's hand, filling everyone's glass. Then he pushed Ian down into the chair opposite Jason. "Those lessons of Dolores'? I think you're going to need them more than you anticipated, Ian."

Chapter Eight

🔊

Ian walked back into the drawing room and didn't know what to do. He felt numb. He'd been so worried about tonight with Sophie. Now he felt sick about it. How was he to make love to her when all she knew of sex was violence and violation? He looked at his beautiful bride and wanted to rage and scream and hit someone. The idea that someone had done that to her after everything else she'd had to endure made him sick to his stomach. She looked at him then, her smile turning to a frown.

He smiled weakly at her, determined not to ruin her wedding day. She frowned harder and made a small, furtive gesture to the far corner. He turned and saw Derek looking at him. Ian turned back to Sophie, sure for once that Derek could take care of himself, but Sophie would have none of it. She kept making shooing motions with her hands and rolling her eyes and nodding her head in Derek's direction. Kensington and Wolf were watching the exchange avidly, fascinated. Ian sighed and gave in, turning to walk over to Derek. All eyes in the room, of course, were on him, but he tried to ignore them. He couldn't believe he'd been married less than a day and already he was henpecked about his lover. Only he was henpecked to go to his lover, not leave him. He didn't think Derek would enjoy the irony.

As he approached the corner, Brett came over to meet him.

"Congratulations on your wedding, Ian," Brett said with his usual solemnity, although he accompanied his comment with a genuine smile. "She's a beautiful girl, and rather unusual."

Ian looked at him questioningly, cocking his head to the side.

Brett laughed softly. "Very introduced Freddy and me in her usual dramatic way and made some comment about how we loved to mother hen you all. Mrs. Witherspoon very seriously took my hand and asked sweetly if we wouldn't mind mother henning Derek a little today, as he might be in need of it." Brett looked over at Sophie wistfully. "I rather wish I'd met her before you."

Ian closed his eyes at the guilt that stabbed him. "God, Brett, so do I," he whispered.

"What?" Brett sounded distressed. "What are you saying, Ian? Surely it's not that way."

Ian opened his eyes and looked at Brett in confusion and then realized how his comment had sounded. "No, no, I didn't mean it that way. Just that if you had met her, then she wouldn't have been—" He stopped, aware of what he'd almost said. He had to get himself under control. Brett misunderstood, although what he assumed was also true.

"You mean her father? Yes, we heard him before the wedding. Poor girl, what an awful childhood she must have had. It's a wonder she turned out as she did, I think."

Ian could only nod. He looked at Derek, suddenly longing for the other man desperately. He needed to talk to Derek, to tell him about Sophie, to share this god-awful guilt eating him alive.

"Go on," Brett said softly. "Freddy and I shall go and join the throng of your new wife's admirers."

Ian looked at him gratefully and walked slowly up to Derek where he leaned against the wall in lonely exile.

"Come to toss me a few crumbs?" Derek asked with his usual asperity. Then he winced and did something very un-Derek-like. He apologized. "Jesus, I'm sorry, Ian. That was uncalled for."

"I'm glad you came." Ian's voice was soft. He didn't feel like sharing this conversation with the rest of the room.

"I heard her father's little speech before the wedding. Quite the charmer, eh? What a swine, and Sophie's only role model. Are you sure your little bride isn't," he paused to tap his head, "a little unstable?"

"Derek," Ian said with disappointment.

Derek looked away and took a drink of champagne. "The vows, was that your idea?"

It took Ian a moment to realize what Derek meant. "You mean how Sophie was looking at you when she said them? No, I had nothing to do with it. I wasn't even sure you'd come, and I didn't see Sophie today before the wedding."

Derek looked at him, perplexed. "How did she know it was me? We've never met."

"I don't know." Ian took a deep breath, the image of Sophie making those sacred promises to him and Derek causing a tightness in his chest. "I've never even talked to her about you, about us." He shook his head and covered his eyes with his hand. "Derek…" He couldn't go on as his voice choked.

"Ian, Ian, what's wrong?" Derek straightened and touched his arm in concern. "Are you all right?"

Ian shook his head again. "No, no I'm not." He looked at Derek's beloved face full of worry and felt his emotions settle a little. "I've got to talk to you, out on the terrace." He moved off toward the doors and felt Derek follow.

Once on the terrace, Ian placed both hands on the railing and leaned over, taking several deep breaths to steady himself. Derek leaned his back against the railing next to him.

"What's going on?" Derek was as serious as Ian had ever seen him, and Ian realized he must look quite shaken.

"It's about Sophie."

Derek snorted. "Well, it's your wedding day. I thought everything was about the bride on her wedding day."

"She was raped, Derek. More than once apparently, as Kate understood it." Just saying the words made Ian feel like he was going to throw up.

Derek reached over and gripped Ian's forearm tightly. "When?"

Ian didn't look at him, just shook his head. "I don't know. I don't know anything. Sophie refused to speak to me according to Jason, who got it from Kate, whom Sophie swore to secrecy."

Derek exhaled in amazement. "Could this turn into more of a tragedy? Or is it comedy? No, tragedy, with our own Ophelia." He placed his hand on his chest and threw out the other hand dramatically. "'Get thee to a nunnery!'" he cried softly, and then he froze.

Ian was alerted to Sophie's presence by Derek's sudden stillness. He looked up and saw her horrorstricken face.

"I…I was worried," she whispered. "Ian looked so upset, and…" She sobbed and quickly covered her mouth with her hand. Ian took a step toward her. She backed away. "You weren't supposed to know," she cried out. "Does everyone know?" She glanced frantically behind her at the open French doors. "Do they?" She spun on her heel and raced back along the terrace for the doors, Ian close behind her.

"Sophie!" Ian called out, chasing her. He heard Derek right behind him. When he rushed through the doors, he heard people calling out and had to push through them trying to get to Sophie. He burst out of the crowd in time to see her stop in front of a weeping Kate.

"I thought you were my friend!" Sophie accused her, crying so hard the words were an anguished howl. She ran out the drawing room doors.

"Sophie!" Kate cried after her. Ian rushed after Sophie, leaving Kate to her husbands.

* * * * *

Derek wanted to follow Ian, but knew it was not a good idea. He was frustrated and angry, and this helpless feeling in his gut pissed him off. In the silence that followed Sophie's and Ian's dramatic exits, he resorted to one of his favorite defenses, sarcasm.

"And thus ends Act One of our tragedy, ladies and gentlemen," he said harshly. "Refreshments will now be served." He turned and retreated to the terrace.

Derek stood there for a moment once he was outside, completely at a loss as to what he should do. His indecision and uselessness made him furious. He swung quickly around, throwing his fist at the wall. Instead of brick, his hand met the flat palm of another outstretched hand with an unsatisfying smack.

"Ow!" Freddy cradled his abused hand on his chest. "God damn it, Derek, that hurt! I should have let you break your damn hand on the brick." He shook his hand fretfully in the air, trying to soothe it.

"Yes, you should have," Derek growled unsympathetically. "I don't need you or Brett shoving your noses into our business, Freddy." He glared at the young duke. "Whatever pieces of wisdom you think you have to impart, stuff them. I've heard your opinions about Ian's wedding already and don't need a reminder." He transferred his glare to Brett, who was standing silently next to Freddy. Just then Jason came storming out the doors.

"How about my wisdom, Derek? Stop feeling sorry for yourself and act like a man. Ian and Sophie need you right now."

Derek couldn't stop the incredulous look he gave Jason. "I hardly think Sophie wants to meet me right now, Jason. This is something she needs to work through with Ian alone. He is her husband now, for better or worse."

Jason made an impatient gesture. "Of course, you're right, I didn't mean that, although it certainly shows a level of understanding on your part that surprises me. I meant Ian needs you to act like his partner here. To take charge of removing these wedding guests from your house with as little upset as possible. To minimize whatever damage Sophie's outburst may have caused and to make sure they have the time and privacy they need."

Derek was horrified. "Handling the public is Ian's job, Jason. I am not good with people, you know this." He shook his head decisively. "If you need someone beaten up, I'm your man. Avoiding scandal and soothing ruffled feathers? Not on my best day."

"I'm sorry, Derek, but it's time to grow up." Brett finally spoke. He was sympathetic, but firm. "I don't know what's going on, and I don't want to. This is obviously something that distresses Sophie in the extreme, and Ian as well. Even before Sophie's tearful exit, I could see that Ian was very upset. Like it or not he has someone else who needs him now, perhaps in some ways more than you ever did. He needs you, Derek. Be there for him."

"You're right, all of you." If the situation hadn't been so serious, Derek might have been amused at the expressions on his friends' faces. "You needn't look so shocked. I've been doing a great deal of soul-searching lately." He narrowed his eyes as Freddy opened his mouth to speak. "Yes, Freddy, I do have a soul. I realize I've made this whole situation worse with my behavior, and I told him last night I'm going to make a sincere effort to live with Sophie." He straightened his shoulders, and then he shot his cuffs and checked his cravat. "And so I shall go and play peacemaker and dutiful host, two roles that do not sit well with me. But I shall do it for Ian."

Without looking at his friends again, Derek walked purposefully back into the drawing room. The next two hours were grueling, but he smiled until his face felt stiff, grinding his teeth all the while. It seemed as if he had to answer the same questions about Sophie and Ian over and over. He wasn't a good liar, so he stuck as close to the truth as possible. He told everyone that Sophie had been nervous about the wedding and meeting all of Ian's friends for weeks, and that the pressure simply got to the poor girl. She was, after all, a country-bred girl who had never been away from her father's house. He could feel his bile rise over all the things that went unsaid in that explanation, but it was no one's business but theirs, even if all these people were their friends.

When the door finally shut on the last of the wedding guests, Derek breathed a huge sigh of relief. He leaned back against the wall next to the stairs, too tired to climb them.

"Sir," Montague said next to him, and Derek nearly jumped a foot in the air he was so startled.

"How on earth do you do that?" he snapped at the butler.

"Do what, Mr. Knightly?"

"Sneak up on a person so quietly. The War Office could have used you against Napoleon."

Montague didn't even crack a smile. "Shall we prepare a light supper for Mr. and Mrs. Witherspoon? Neither of them ate much after the ceremony."

Derek's eyes closed briefly in resignation. More decisions. "Ah, yes, all right. That sounds good. Yes."

"Very good, sir. Where shall we serve it?"

Jesus, couldn't they make any decisions themselves? "Christ, I don't know. Her sitting room, the one attached to her bedroom? I'd think she'd feel a little less conspicuous there about now. She wasn't feeling all that, ah, well after the ceremony."

Montague smiled at Derek and Derek almost fell over in shock. He'd always assumed the butler didn't like him very much. He rarely addressed Derek directly and exuded an air of disapproval whenever Ian deferred to Derek's preferences.

"If I may say, Mr. Knightly, you did very well with the wedding guests today." Derek looked up warily, expecting to see the sky falling at Montague's unheard of praise.

"Thank you?" Derek responded, his confusion evident.

Montague cleared his throat. He seemed uncomfortable, but continued the discussion in spite of it. "Mrs. Witherspoon needs all the support and companionship that we can offer her at this time, I believe."

Derek was reduced to blinking wordlessly at Montague. The butler sighed. "I recognize the source of her distress. I sincerely believe that you and Mr. Witherspoon will help her overcome it."

"You recognize what?" Derek asked suspiciously.

Montague's eyes refocused on a spot over Derek's left shoulder. "My daughter experienced something similar, if I am not mistaken."

Oh God, Derek thought, horrified. What do you say to a man who's just told you his daughter was raped? "I'm sorry, Montague." He *was* truly sorry, he realized. "Is she all right now?"

Montague still refused to look at him. "I hope so, sir. She's dead."

Derek felt the color drain from his face. "Oh God, Montague, I'm sorry. I didn't know. Was it the…the attack?"

Montague finally looked at him and Derek flinched at the desolation in his eyes. "No sir, it was by her own hand afterward."

Derek couldn't contain his gasp of horror. Involuntarily he reached out and gripped the other man's arm. "We won't let that happen to Mrs. Witherspoon, Montague."

"No sir. We won't." He turned and walked several paces before he stopped and turned back. "I shall have a light supper served in one hour's time."

Derek nodded mechanically. "Yes, thank you. That would be fine."

"You'll find them in the nursery." Derek just nodded again. He was beyond surprise at the man's intuitiveness.

He started up the stairs before he realized he had no idea where the nursery was. He hadn't even known they had one. What the hell were they doing in the nursery?

* * * * *

Ian raced up the stairs after Sophie, calling her name. When he got to the first floor, she'd disappeared. He looked in every bedroom and couldn't find her. As a last resort he climbed the stairs up to the little-used second floor, where an empty nursery from previous owners took up most of the space.

"Sophie?" he called from the top of the stairwell. He heard the faint sound of crying and walked quietly down the hall to the closed nursery door. He pushed it open and saw Sophie immediately. She was sitting on the floor in front of the window directly across from the door, her arms resting on the window seat, pillowing her head as she cried softly. Her legs were curled to the side and she managed to look elegant even in her misery. Did she understand her appeal? Ian didn't think so.

He walked into the room, his steps echoing in the emptiness. The nursery was half as long as the house itself, its wood floor gleaming. The whitewashed walls glowed in the fading evening light. The room's only furnishing was a small painted rocking horse in one corner, sweet and sad in its loneliness. Somehow it was the perfect setting for Sophie's tears. Ian's heart cracked a little more as with blinding clarity he realized Sophie had never had a haven like this in her own childhood.

"Will you send me back now?" Sophie asked in a raw, husky voice that made things in Ian clench, things that had no business clenching in the current situation. He'd liked her voice the first time he heard her speak and had grown more enchanted with it with each successive conversation. The ragged sound of it now made him think of sweat and heat and breathless abandon, and he ruthlessly tamped down his attraction.

"Never." He spoke forcefully, clearly, and his voice seemed overly loud in the echoing chamber. He watched as Sophie turned her head quickly to look at him, her shock evident. He crossed the room in long strides and went to one knee next to Sophie. He ignored her slight flinch at his nearness. He understood it now, and he believed the only way to overcome it was for her to grow accustomed to it. Unbidden, Derek's words from last night went through his mind. "Let her get used to it," he'd said. At the time Ian hadn't thought them useful.

"I will never send you back, Sophie, or send you anywhere you don't want to go for that matter. Nothing you've ever done or may do in the future will make me send you away. You are my wife, and I'm glad. I want you with me. Will you stay?" He resisted the urge to reach out to her, understanding she wasn't ready for that.

Sophie closed her eyes and bit her lower lip. "You don't understand. I'm not a virgin, Ian. I know that's what every man wants. Harold told me so. He told me you wouldn't want me if you found out."

Ian stopped resisting and gently wrapped his hands around Sophie's shoulders. She shuddered but didn't pull away. "Harold was wrong, and so are you, Sophie. Rape doesn't make you experienced. It merely makes you a victim." Another thought occurred to Ian. "Have you been with a man voluntarily, Sophie?" He hastened to reassure her. "Not that it matters. Whatever happened is in the past. But have you been with someone since you were attacked?"

Sophie shook her head violently. "Never! Why would I? It was horrid. Why would anyone want to do that?" She started crying harder. "I'm sorry, Ian. You deserve someone who doesn't hate the idea of being with you, who isn't afraid to let you do that to her. I can't be like that. I know how awful it is, I know."

Ian tried to pull Sophie into his arms, but she stiffened and pulled back sharply. He let her. Instead he sat on the floor next to her, his legs stretched out and his back leaning against the window seat. He didn't look at her.

"It doesn't have to be awful, Sophie. It can be quite wonderful actually." He rubbed his chin with a forefinger. "Tell me what happened, Sophie. Who was it?"

She was silent and he glanced at her to see her shaking her head again.

"Why won't you tell me?" He kept his voice soft so he merely sounded curious. Inside he was a seething mass of rage. He would find out, and if the man wasn't dead yet, he would be.

"I can't," she whispered. "I can't tell you who it was. He'll…" She stopped to lick her lips nervously. "He'll kill me. I know he will."

Ian fisted his right hand at his side where Sophie couldn't see it. "No one will touch you now, Sophie. You're mine, and I protect what's mine."

"Please, Ian," she pleaded.

Ian sighed. "All right, for now. But can you tell me what happened? When it happened?"

Sophie lay her head back down on her arms. "The first time was when I was sixteen."

Ian's heart stuttered in his chest. The first time. Good God, how many times had there been?

"The year I left for the war." He didn't realize he'd spoken out loud until Sophie answered.

"Was it? I didn't know."

Ian turned sharply to her. "Didn't you get my letter? I sent one, telling you I'd bought a commission."

Sophie raised her head slightly and looked at him. "No, I never received it. I just assumed you were too busy to bother with me. We weren't to be married for another two years, after all."

"You must have been shocked then to receive my letters from the Peninsula. Why did you never write back? I would have helped if I could." Ian hadn't realized until that moment that her failure to reply to his letters had hurt him. While he'd been callous about her feelings when he went to war, he'd wanted someone to care that he was there.

Sophie straightened further, her eyes wide. "I never received any letters, Ian."

Ian looked at her in dismay. "Not one? I must have written a dozen, every time I moved to a new camp. I can understand one or two going missing, but all of them?"

Sophie just shook her head.

"What about the letter I wrote two years ago, informing you I had returned?"

Sophie squeezed her eyes shut. "You've been back for two years?" she whispered.

Ian hated himself at that moment. He hated the selfishness and self-absorption that had made him cavalierly dismiss Sophie's long wait as irrelevant compared to his own war sickness and happy obsession with Derek. "I thought you knew." He cleared his throat, not wanting Sophie to know how upset he was.

Sophie shook her head. "No." She opened her eyes but refused to look at him, instead laying her forehead on her arms. "I assumed you only returned right before you sent for me."

Ian ran his hand roughly through his hair. "God, Sophie, I'm so sorry." He let his hand fall to his lap and asked the question he really didn't want to know the answer to. "Has it happened again, since I've been back?" He didn't need to explain what he meant.

"Yes," Sophie said softly, confirming his worst fears.

Ian could hardly breathe through the guilt constricting his chest. "Sophie…" He was alarmed at the roughness of his voice. He closed his eyes against the burn of tears.

"What was it like?" Sophie asked, her voice almost normal.

"What?" Ian couldn't follow the question.

"The war. What was it like?" Sophie clearly wanted to change the topic, and Ian, coward that he was, let her.

"It was bloody awful." Just saying the words freed Ian in a way he hadn't been for a long time. Most of his acquaintances did not wish to discuss the war except in terms of who won what battle. Even Derek tended to avoid talking about their experiences at war, not including the development of their relationship. But then Derek had nightmares that made him wake shaking and sweating. "I hated every god-awful, stinking moment of it."

Sophie raised her head and looked him in sympathy. "Did you? I thought men liked war."

Ian laughed, but not with humor. "What's not to like? The blood, the guts, the screams of men and horses. Smelling like the gutter because you haven't been able to have a bath for weeks on end. The fear of losing friends and lovers in a well-placed French artillery attack, or on the end of a French saber. Or, oh yes, the endless, boring days of sitting and sitting with nothing to do but dread the next call to arms. Yes, war is certainly entertaining, isn't it?" He winced at the bitterness he heard in his voice.

Sophie turned and sat with her back against the window seat and her legs out, imitating Ian's position. "Who did you lose?"

Her tone was as sympathetic as her look had been, and it was Ian's undoing. He laid his head back on the bench behind them and closed his eyes too late to stop the tear that ran down his temple into his hair.

"I lost more than one."

He was shocked to feel Sophie's hand tentatively touch his, and then her fingers loosely entwined with his own. He forced himself to relax and not frighten her away.

"Tell me," she told him, and he did. The words poured out of him, about friends lost to death, others to life-altering injury. And he told her about Dolores, holding nothing back. Her hold on his hand got tighter and tighter as he spoke.

"Oh, Ian," she sighed when he finally stopped talking, "I'm sorry, so sorry. I didn't know. You loved her, both you and Derek." Her voice was so sad, as if she'd seen all the misery in the world and none of it surprised her anymore.

"No, I didn't love her. I don't think Derek did either. But she was a dear friend." He was looking at their entwined hands, and he risked tentatively running one finger of his free hand over the strong tendons on the back of hers. When she didn't protest, he ran it around her knuckles and gently in between her fingers. She was silent so long that she startled him when she did speak.

"Just because you weren't in love with her doesn't mean you didn't love her. You can love a friend deeply and their loss can leave as big a hole in you as any." Ian could tell she spoke from experience.

"Who did you lose?"

Her hand squeezed his almost painfully at his question. "I lost the only friend I ever had. A servant, actually—a maid. She was kind to me when I'd forgotten what kindness was. She tried to protect me, and she paid for her kindness with dismissal and degradation."

"Sophie." Ian turned to look directly at her but didn't let go of her hand. "Is she dead?"

Sophie shook her head. "No, at least, I don't think so. But she was from an impoverished family and going back to them was not an option, particularly after being let go without a reference." She was looking out into space. "According to Harold she had no choice but to become a whore at the local tavern until one day she left and never returned."

"Sophie, look at me." She did and her expression was bleak. "Tell me about your life, Sophie. All this time I've thought of you as a child, even the last two weeks when I can see perfectly well you are not. You have grown into a woman who fascinates me. I must know, Sophie. I must know all about you."

She blushed and looked down and jerked slightly, almost as if just realizing they were holding hands. She tried to pull away, but Ian wouldn't let her.

"No, Sophie, please," he pleaded, "don't pull away. Tell me, tell me something, anything, whatever you like. I won't pry, I swear." She still seemed unsure. "What is your favorite color? I think it's blue. Am I right? Have you ever had a puppy? Would you like one? I can't spell very well. Can you?" Sophie was starting to smile, her lips curving up on one side self-consciously. "I hate tripe, and soup, but I love beef and ale. Derek says I have peasant tastes." He winced, worried that he oughtn't to have brought up Derek's name, but Sophie seemed unperturbed by it.

She held up a hand, stopping him. "Enough!" she cried with a little laugh. Ian cherished that laugh. He wanted to make Sophie laugh forever. "Um, let me see. Yes, blue, and no, but I have always wanted a puppy. How did you know? And how can you not spell? Everyone can spell. I am particularly good at unusually spelled words—for instance, ululation. Isn't that a wonderful word? And goodness, does anyone like tripe?" She shuddered. "But soup? I love soup. I could slurp it all day, every day. And I don't care if you have peasant tastes. I shan't be so embarrassed about what I like, I suppose." She grinned shyly at Ian. "I also have a very good memory."

Ian laughed out loud. "I will endeavor to remember that. In ten years time will you still nag me about the time I spilled wine on the drawing room rug?"

Sophie looked aghast. "I would never nag you! Never!" She looked stricken with fear. "I didn't mean it that way. I will never anger you by complaining about your behavior—"

Ian cut her off, cursing himself for forgetting to tread lightly around her. She still had a long way to go toward trusting him. He tried to speak lightly. "Well, that is a disappointment. What good is a wife if she doesn't nag? How will I know how to behave, or whether or not I'm tricked out properly if you won't tell me? I daresay if you treat me too well, people will begin to think I made a bad bargain." He grinned wickedly. "They may even, heaven forbid, start speculating you married me because you liked me, and what would the world be coming to then, I ask you?"

Sophie looked bewildered for a moment, and then she snorted inelegantly. "Well, we can't have that, can we? I shall reserve Monday morning at nine o'clock, before going over the week's menus, for nagging you. That way you shall have a fresh start with improving goals for the week."

Ian wanted to shout with joy. She had a sense of humor! His young, beautiful, fragile wife had not been broken. He would make her strong. He would nurture her, shower her with love and affection, passion and humor, and she would never know fear or abandonment again. Very slowly he raised her hand to his lips and kissed it, and Sophie's smile only faltered a little.

Derek quietly got up from where he'd been sitting beside the nursery door. He was stiff and sore, and realized with a start that the sun was setting. He must have been there for quite a while listening to Ian and Sophie talk. He didn't feel guilty at all for eavesdropping. How else was he to figure out how to live with this virtual stranger? He'd been more shocked by Ian's conversation than Sophie's. He'd never heard Ian talk about the war like that. Listening had been hard, so hard Derek had almost crawled away. But when Ian finished, Derek felt a lightening somewhere inside. Yes, he'd known exactly what Ian was talking about. He'd seen and felt the same things, lost the same people. He rubbed his chest absently, still feeling the ache that had gripped him when Ian had talked of Dolores' death. Sophie had been wise when she'd said Ian and Derek had loved Dolores. Derek knew it wasn't the kind of love he shared with Ian, but it was love just the same.

He heard the two still murmuring in the nursery, and Sophie laughed. That one sound made him hesitate. He'd had to bite his knuckle when she'd said the first time she was raped was when she was sixteen. He'd wanted to curse and punch the wall. No young girl should have to go through that. And it would make things so hard on Ian. That laugh meant perhaps she wasn't completely broken, and Derek was surprised by how much that pleased him. He went down the stairs stealthily, not wanting to disturb the intimacy between them. It was hard, but Derek was trying to be what Ian needed. And right now he needed Derek to help make his wedding night a success. As far as Derek was concerned, that meant staying the hell away.

Chapter Nine

ಐ

Very stood in the library and looked out the window into the back garden. The room behind her was lit only by the small fire on the far wall. She could make out the little Greek folly in the far corner of the garden, a dark shape in the moonlight. She loved to sit out there on warm days and read, or chat with companions. Had Sophie ever been able to do that, to relax with friends? She'd seemed so awkward at it the last two weeks, and Very had attributed it to her hideous father. But apparently there'd been more, as Very had suspected yesterday. She went to brush a strand of hair out of her eyes and found her hand was shaking. God, she was so full of anger. She'd wanted to scream at Aunt Kate for not telling her, and then she wanted to hunt down Mr. Middleton and cut his prick off. Aunt Kate said Sophie had denied he was the one, but who else? Most of all Very wanted to cut her own tongue out. How could she have teased Sophie that way? God, how could Sophie stand her? She couldn't stand herself.

She spun suddenly and grabbed a pillow from the chair near the window. She beat it against the chair arm with all her might, holding back a scream of rage until it came out as a growl. She raised the pillow and tore at it and beat it against the chair again until it finally came apart and feathers flew around her head. She stopped then, panting with her exertions, frustrated that there was still anger inside her in spite of her violence.

"Well, I'm glad that I'm not the pillow," Kensington's voice drawled from behind her.

She turned to glare at him. "Shut up. I'm not pleasant company tonight. I don't have the patience to put up with your supposed wit."

Kensington sighed and walked over to her warily. He reached up and tenderly plucked a feather out of her hair. "I know I'm going to regret this, but what's the matter, little Amazon?"

Very stared at him in disbelief. "What's wrong? What's wrong? I just found out a dear new friend was raped as a child, I ruined her wedding day and you ask me what's wrong?"

Tentatively Kensington stepped closer and wrapped his arms loosely around her. Suddenly he was all that held her together. She clutched him desperately and he responded by wrapping her tighter in his embrace. God, how she had missed this! He'd hardly touched her in almost a year, not since that unforgettable first time they met, when he'd dragged her into an alley and gave her her first woman's pleasure. She buried her nose in his neck and breathed deeply of his beloved scent. Spicy and exotic and all male, it made her blood thicken and heat.

"Very," he said, and she thrilled to hear the roughness of desire in his voice. He took several deep breaths and spoke again, his tone almost normal. "You did not ruin Sophie's wedding day. You can hardly blame yourself for her rape. In a sad way it's only natural that those memories surface the day she married. She's expected to share Ian's bed tonight. I can only imagine what fears she has about it."

Very turned her head to rest it on his shoulder. "Exactly, and I exacerbated the whole thing with my teasing. She was fine until I joked about being too drunk to enjoy her wedding night. If only Aunt Kate had confided in me sooner! I would never have said that."

Kensington ran his hand down her back in what was supposed to be a soothing motion. Instead it set every nerve aflame. Her pussy actually throbbed with desire for him as his hand came to rest on the rise of her rump. She couldn't control the small, unsteady gasp that broke from her. Kensington froze and then tried to pull away.

"No! Kensington, please." Very knew she was begging, but her pride was nowhere to be seen. She needed him tonight. Needed him to show her again what love felt like, to help wipe out the image of Sophie being raped that was trapped in her head.

"Very, I can't." His voice was harsh and he put his hands on her shoulders and tried to shove her back.

"You can, you can," she told him, pressing closer, wrapping her arms around his neck in a death grip. She placed kisses along his jaw and bit his chin gently, eliciting a moan from him. "You see, you want me. You can't deny it, I can hear how much. I can feel your cock, hard for me." She rotated her hips, feeling the hard length of him rubbing against her stomach. She placed an openmouthed kiss against his neck and sucked the skin lightly and suddenly his hands were grabbing her ass roughly and grinding her in to him. She laughed triumphantly and Kensington groaned.

"God damn it, Very. I promised myself I would leave you alone. You're so young, so innocent. Tell me to stop, tell me to leave you alone." He was kissing her wildly, his lips on hers for one moment and then running over her face and neck. He licked a path upward from her shoulder to the soft spot behind her ear and then bit her earlobe. Very shivered with unconcealed lust at the sting.

"Don't stop, don't ever stop, Kensington. I want to feel it again, that wild drop off a cliff that made my heart race and my breath catch. Show me what it means to love a man. Make me forget just for a while about what happened to Sophie. Show me how it feels when you want it, when you desire a man and he makes you his."

Kensington groaned aloud at her words and dragged her to the floor. "You make me throw all my principles to the wind, Very. I have no resistance to you, no way to fight when you tell me how much you want me. You are the ruin of me." He fell on top of her and Very had never felt such a delicious weight. She wrapped one hand around his head and pulled him to her for a kiss as her leg encircled his waist and yanked his erection down to her aching, damp mound. Though separated by layers of fabric, the contact was exquisite and she cried out into his mouth. He ground himself against her and she bit his lip sharply. The copper tang of blood made her pull back.

"Oh God, Kensington, I'm sorry. I'm just mad, as if I have some kind of brain fever. All I can think of is you and how wonderful you feel. You're so hard and heavy and mine. I want to taste you, to eat you up. Is this normal, this raging hunger for you?" Her voice was breathless and eager and she smiled to hear herself that way. It was glorious, everything about this was glorious.

Kensington was licking the blood from his lip as he tugged wildly at Very's bodice. "I don't know and I don't care. Just knowing you're dying for me is driving *me* mad. You've infected me with your fever." She heard her bodice rip and then she felt the cool air on her overheated breasts. "Yes," Kensington hissed. He dove into her breasts like a starving man, licking and sucking and biting and Very writhed beneath him. He rammed an arm under her back and yanked her chest high as he suckled one nipple ruthlessly, and Very thrust her hips into him, his cock rubbing against her in such a way that she felt the shudders of arousal through her whole body.

Reality became disjointed, as if time and place had no meaning for them. The heat and roughness of his touch, the feel of supple muscles flexing above her, the wet, smooth glide of his tongue on her skin seemed to be so natural, as if Very's whole life had led to this coupling.

"Touch me, Kensington, like you did before." She was like a woman possessed, wrapping her arms and legs around him and kissing him as if she might swallow him whole.

"Michael," he told her roughly, peeling himself away from her. He grabbed her shoulder and shook her. "Call me Michael. I want to hear my name on your lips when I'm loving you, Very. Say it."

"Michael," she pleaded, and the intimacy of his given name made her heart beat faster and her breathing grow ragged. "Michael, love me, please. I need you so much." His blond hair had turned to molten gold in the fire's light, his eyes dark and fathomless in the shadows. She shuddered at the fleeting fear that gripped her at his inscrutable expression. For one endless moment they were frozen there, she laid before him like an offering, he towering over her, her conqueror. The dramatic nature of the image as it formed in Very's mind broke the spell. "Michael," she whispered, arching into him, and Michael's hands came to her waist, gripping her almost painfully as he held her to him.

"I'm not strong, Very, not where you're concerned. I haven't trusted myself to be alone with you these last months. I've tried to leave you, but I'm weak, so weak. I keep crawling back—for this." He leaned down and kissed her hard and possessively. When he pulled away, Very gasped and thrust her hips at him. He reached out and touched a fingertip gently to the curve of her breast. "I crave this like an opium eater craves the drug, Very. I need you." She rose to her elbows to see his face as he stared at her. Those eyes closed in distress as he pulled his finger away, balling his hand into a fist. "Tell me to stop, Very."

"Never," she whispered. "I will never tell you to stop."

When the library door opened, the crack of light from the hallway split the floor like an arrow that ended at Michael's feet. Very gasped as Michael quickly tried to shield her from the intruder.

The door closed quietly with a click. "I'm sorry. Am I interrupting?" Wolf's voice was a low purr of surprised delight, and Very released the breath she was holding.

"Wolf," she whispered. Without thinking she reached out for him, and he came as if pulled by invisible strings. When he reached her side he dropped heavily to his knees.

Wolf Tarrant was not a large man. He was tall and lean, with the whipcord muscles of a fencer and the elegance to match. His face resembled his namesake with its sharp angles, long nose and square jaw. In the firelight his thick, wild dark blond hair took on the hues of the fire itself, red, gold, orange and black. He was always so composed, so self-contained, and yet Very suspected that there was a great deal of fire inside him as well, beneath the façade. She longed to see him burn — burn for her. She had never thought much of Wolf in sexual terms. She had accepted that he came with Kensington. But here, now, she realized with relief and excitement, she wanted him. She wanted to touch him and be touched by him and the happiness this brought her made her giddy. She brushed his strong cheekbone with the pads of her fingers as her thumb caressed his lower lip. "Wolf," she said again, her new sexual awareness of him as an individual clear in her voice and her touch.

Wolf closed his eyes and dipped his head into her caress. "Very," he said, his voice breaking, "Very." He bent down to kiss her and she rose from the floor to meet him halfway. The kiss was a tender exploration, a first kiss in every way. It ignored the fact that she was spread out on the floor half naked, caught in the throes of passion with another man. In that kiss it was only Very and Wolf and the wonder of their discovery of one another. He passed his arms gently around her until he was supporting her, until she was wrapped tightly against his chest, their hearts beating together. Her arms were around his neck, one hand on his shoulder the other buried in his untamed hair.

Wolf's tongue slipped into her mouth so gently that Very whimpered at the sweet sensation. He was so different from Michael, who devoured her like a starving man. Wolf savored and gentled her until she could take no more tenderness. She broke the kiss with a sob. "Please, please," she begged, her body once again on fire. Her nipples were so sharp they ached for a soothing touch, and she could feel the heat of her pussy as it was bathed in the cream of her sex. She clutched at Wolf's arm, dragging it from around her and he was forced to lower her to the floor. She took his hand in hers and guided it to her breast, pressing it against the aching point there. "Yes," she cried out her back arching. "Michael," she whispered, wanting him to share this feeling. Wolf was kneading her breast as he nuzzled her neck.

"No." The word was harsh and anguished. Wolf froze against her, and Very looked past his shoulder at Michael. He was still kneeling between her legs, but somehow he seemed apart, separate from her in a way he hadn't before. He was very carefully not touching her. He was looking at Wolf with dawning horror, at his hand on Very's breast, his face pressed to her neck. Very didn't know what to do. She was aching and burning and she was finding it hard to think of anything but the ecstasy that was just out of reach.

"Please, Michael," she begged, arching into Wolf's hand, which had resumed its pleasurable caresses. She moaned as Wolf sucked gently on her neck. "Oh God, please."

"I...I can't," he whispered brokenly, and Very watched him through a fog as he crawled backward away from her and Wolf. "What have I done?" His question didn't seem to be directed at her so Very didn't answer.

Wolf shuddered as Very pressed his hand harder against her breast. He lay down beside her, his warmth a delectable pressure against her side. "Michael," he said, his voice rough, and he kissed the delicate skin above Very's collarbone. "Don't, don't ruin it, Michael," and his voice broke. He cleared his throat. "Don't run away from this."

"I can't," Michael said again. "What are we doing, Wolf? She's a child." He turned his head away and covered his eyes as if he couldn't bear to look at them. "I can't do this to her."

"I am not a child," Very told him, and Wolf pulled back to look at her. She gazed into his face and saw none of the guilt that seemed to beleaguer Michael when he touched her. Wolf looked at her like a woman, a desirable woman. His gaze was possessive and arrogant and proud, and Very wanted to purr and roll all over him until she was covered in his scent. "I want this," she whispered, and hardly recognized the sinful voice as her own. "I want to touch and be touched, I want to come and I want a man to come for me." She looked at Michael. "I want to be a woman and not a child. I want to be wanted by a man without seeing guilt and shame in his face afterward."

"I can't, Very," Michael said brokenly, "I can't."

"I can," Wolf said firmly in her ear.

Very turned back to Wolf and with slow deliberation pulled his head down to hers and kissed him. She released all her desire into that kiss, tried to tell him all she wanted and needed with her lips and tongue and teeth, and he heard her and understood. He moved closer to her and slid one arm under her until her neck rested on it. He ran one hand down her stomach to rest between her legs. Very groaned and thrust against him.

"What do you want?" Wolf asked against her mouth. "Do you know?"

"I want you inside me," Very demanded wantonly. "I want you to take me over the edge, Wolf. Will you take me?"

"Oh, Very," he said wickedly, "I will take you any way you want." He pressed his lips to hers again and his tongue danced in her mouth deliciously. Very became breathless and had to break the kiss. She was panting but there was no embarrassment at her arousal. What she felt with Wolf was elemental, as if she had been stripped down to the bare essentials and there was only breathing and wanting and the touch of his flesh on hers, the beat of his heart against hers.

He broke the kiss slowly. "You are so wonderful, Very. Do you know how precious you are to me?" he whispered and then he kissed her again tenderly.

"Wolf, oh God, Wolf," she said, suddenly on the verge of tears. She'd never bothered to really see him before, accepting his presence as necessary if she were to have Michael with her. How long had he felt this way about her? Had she hurt him with her indifference? She was such a blind fool. Today had been eye-opening for her in so many ways. She was dizzy with the emotional highs and lows.

"How could you?" Michael's voice whipped out of the dark. "What are you doing to her, making her?"

Wolf sighed and rested his forehead against Very's temple. She ran her hand softly through his hair.

"I want to give my woman pleasure, Michael. I am not the kind of man who will tease her and leave her wanting out of some misplaced sense of offended moral righteousness." Wolf's voice was as angry as Michael's.

"No matter what she says, she is still a child, Wolf. She doesn't understand what you'll demand of her." Michael's voice was filled with accusation.

"I will force her to do nothing." Wolf angrily pushed to his feet, the mood clearly ruined. "But I will not deny her what she wants either." He reached down and pulled Very to her feet. She was still a bit unsteady and clung to him. "And do not attempt to place the blame on me. I have never forced anything on you, either."

"Stop talking about me as if I'm not here," she said, annoyed. She pointed at Michael. "And stop talking about me as if I'm an idiot. I know very well what I'm getting myself into."

"Do you?" Michael asked bitterly. "Do you really know what Wolf and I are to each other?"

Very busied herself with straightening her clothing. There was a slight tear in the fabric of her bodice that she was afraid couldn't be fixed. She sighed. She hadn't exactly wanted to have this conversation tonight, but she was not one to run from a challenge. "Of course. You're lovers. Look, I said it and didn't run shrieking into the night." She didn't even try to keep the sarcasm from her voice. Wolf chuckled beside her and she smiled up at him.

"And do you understand what that means?" Michael wouldn't let the subject drop. "Have you considered that?"

Very shifted uncomfortably. Oh, she had considered it all right. Just about every night in her lonely bed she thought about exactly what that meant. "It means that you will both come to my bed, at the same time." She was rather proud of how steady she sounded.

Michael snorted. "Yes. But it also means that we fuck each other, Very. It means that when Wolf looks at me the way he looked at you tonight—and yes, he does look at me like that—I can't pull my pants down and bend over fast enough. That cock that is even now hard for you, Very," Michael pointed crudely at Wolf's erection, "is buried in my ass at every opportunity, and I'm not above returning the favor just as often. Is that what you want?"

"Stop it, Michael," Wolf ground out.

Very felt herself blanch at his crudity. She'd had a vague idea about how men made love to one another, but thanks to Michael her education on the subject was now complete. She straightened her shoulders. "No, it's all right, Wolf." She looked at Michael. "If that is what you want, then yes, I want it too."

Michael growled in frustration and pulled at his hair as he spun away from her. "What must I do to save you from yourself, Very? You throw yourself into trouble at every turn, and I am the catalyst! This…" he made a motion between the three of them, "this is unnatural, do you understand? Whether your aunt enjoys the same relationship or not, it is not natural nor is it accepted." He paced away. "You are young and you have the chance to live a normal life." He shook his head. "But not with me. Not with us." He walked quickly to the door.

Wolf took two steps toward him. "Don't, Michael. Don't run again."

Michael stopped but didn't turn around. "Goodbye, Wolf. Goodbye, Very. I—" He broke off and opened the door. "Goodbye." He left, pulling the door closed behind him.

Very huffed and stalked over to the couch. She threw herself down on it in disgust. "Why does Michael have to turn everything into the great drama? I don't understand why he refuses to accept that I am a fully grown woman who knows exactly what I want." She crossed her arms stubbornly. "He can just stay away this time until he's ready to apologize. I shan't forgive him easily this time." It took a minute for Wolf to turn back to her. His smile was bittersweet.

"Well, he's right."

"What?" Very was shocked at Wolf's admission.

The handsome man smiled at her, but she was disconcerted by the aloofness of his expression. "You are young, Very. And we wouldn't have a normal, accepted relationship, the three of us, as much as we might wish otherwise." He sighed and walked over. He held out his hand to her and she automatically took it and let him help her to her feet. "Let's not discuss this now, all right? Come on, I've got to sneak you upstairs and into bed."

Very couldn't stop the flirtatious little smile that crooked her lips. That definitely sounded like a lovely plan. Wolf saw her smile and shook his head with a little laugh. "Michael is right, you have a habit of throwing yourself in front of trouble. I meant go to bed to sleep, alone. But don't think I'm not tempted." When they got to the door, Wolf turned to her and tried to straighten her clothes but gave up when he found the tear in her bodice. "I'm going to have to speak to Jason and Tony about keeping a closer eye on you," he mumbled.

"You wouldn't," Very breathed, horrified.

"No," Wolf admitted, "I won't, because I don't want to lose the chance of getting you alone again." He put his hands on his hips and looked at the floor for a moment, shaking his head and laughing self-deprecatingly. He peered up at Very through his eyelashes. "Which only, of course, reinforces that I am a very bad man and you should stay far away from me."

Very opened the study door cautiously and peered up and down the hall to see if anyone was there. When the coast was clear she stepped out lightly, motioning Wolf to follow her. She stopped suddenly and Wolf bumped into her, grabbing her arms and hauling her close to keep them both from falling. Very grinned wickedly over her shoulder at him. "I can't help it if I'm attracted to trouble, Wolf. And the best trouble is to be found with very bad men." She winked at his amused smile and slipped out of his grasp to run down the hall and up the stairs.

Chapter Ten

ജ

After their groundbreaking emotional confidences in the nursery, Ian and Sophie had gone to their rooms to change out of their wedding attire. Ian was going to see about a late supper but was informed by his valet that one awaited him and his new bride in her rooms. Less than an hour after he left her, Ian found himself knocking on her door.

"Come in," Sophie called pleasantly, and Ian opened the door. Sophie was sitting at her dressing table brushing her hair.

"Oh, Mary, I'm so glad you're back. Would you please ask Mr. Witherspoon to join me in a few minutes for supper?"

Ian froze, not sure what to do. Sophie obviously didn't realize it was him. She was *en dishabille*, wearing nothing but a light dressing gown over her chemise. The gown was open and parted as she raised her arms to try to pin up her hair. He could see the outline of her breasts, the shadow of her nipples. He felt like a voyeur as his cock stirred. This was the first time Ian had seen her hair down and it was a glorious spill of copper fire down her back in the light. It was heavy and thick, the ends curling. As he watched her try to put it up he couldn't stop his protest.

"Please leave it down."

Sophie shrieked and leapt to her feet. Her response was so out of proportion to Ian's softly voiced protest that he jumped as well.

"Ian! What are you doing here?" Sophie gasped, grabbing the edges of her dressing gown and holding them together.

"For God's sake, Sophie!" Ian clutched his chest and leaned against the wall. "You nearly gave me a seizure! What the devil did you scream for?" He saw Sophie relax slightly at his overly dramatic reply. She smiled in embarrassment.

"You frightened me. I was expecting my new maid and instead a man's voice answered. I'm sorry." She shook her head and laughed ruefully. "It's going to take me some time to get used to being here, and the way things are here."

"Sophie—" She trampled over his sympathy with her nervous babble.

"I was going to send Mary, my new maid, to get you for supper. Isn't it nice?" She gestured to the simply set table across the room in the sitting area by the fireplace. "But, oh!" She looked down at herself in horror. "I'm not dressed!" She spun around, giving Ian her very shapely back, lovingly outlined by the thin material of her dressing gown which was pulled tight by her grasping hands in front. "Don't look! I must look a fright. I meant to be more presentable before you came. I'm so sorry! Oh, this isn't going at all as I had planned." She looked up and suddenly realized that Ian could see her front in her dressing table mirror and reacted almost like a child, slapping her hand over her eyes as if blocking Ian from her sight would block her from his.

Ian couldn't help it, he laughed. Sophie peeped out at him from between two spread fingers.

"Are you laughing at me?" she asked suspiciously.

Ian shook his head. "Yes. I mean no. I'm just laughing at the whole thing." He casually walked over and fell into one of the chairs arranged around the table. "And honestly, it feels very good. I'm not sure I've laughed at all today. Thank you."

Sophie sniffed, still suspicious. "Well, all right then. I can live with that." She began edging toward the screen in the corner. "I'll just dress and then we can eat." She was fussing with her hair again as she turned and took two quick steps before Ian's voice stopped her.

"Please, Sophie, don't get dressed on my account." Ian was hardly dressed himself, having donned only pants and a shirt. "I'm not very presentable myself." Sophie looked over her shoulder at him and he held up one bare foot. "I just wanted to be comfortable."

Sophie chewed her bottom lip a moment and then nodded as if coming to a decision. She fumbled with the rather elaborate ties on her dressing gown and then turned back to him. "You're right, it does feel nice to be comfortable for a change." She looked down and Ian followed her gaze to her bare feet. She wiggled her toes. "I don't think I've dined barefoot since I was in leading strings, however. Don't you dare tell anyone."

Ian laughed again and Sophie came over and sat down opposite him. Ian didn't have the heart to tell her her hair was pinned up partially on one side, giving her a lopsided appearance. He wanted to reach over and pull the offending pins out, freeing her beautiful hair. Had he really thought it a boring brown when he'd met her two weeks ago?

"Shall we send for Derek, do you think?" Sophie asked innocently, and Ian promptly dropped his fork against his plate with a clang.

"I…no, I don't think so. Not tonight." Ian picked up his wayward fork and served Sophie a slice of cold ham. Without looking at her, he continued. "How did you know who Derek was today, during the ceremony?"

Sophie sighed as she took some more food from the serving dishes on the table. "I saw him sneaking out of your room this morning."

Ian was beyond surprise at this point. He could only shake his head in wonder. "After the ceremony, in the drawing room, you seemed very concerned that I go to him. Why?"

Sophie put down her own fork and fussed with the napkin in her lap, avoiding looking at Ian. "I don't wish to be a wedge between you, Ian. I understand how Derek must feel. I think he's very scared of losing you. I only want to reassure him that I have no intention of driving him away." She picked her fork back up and deliberately took a bite.

Ian sat back in his chair staring at Sophie, trying to decipher her. "Why? You must admit not many new brides would be so understanding."

Sophie still refused to look at him. "I don't ever want you to feel that you can't...can't be with Derek whenever you want."

And just like that, Ian understood. "You think that with Derek here I won't want to make love to you, is that it, Sophie?"

Her telltale blush answered for her. Ian sighed. "Sophie, you are my wife and I want to have a normal marriage. I wish for us to share a bed often. I hope we will be blessed with many children." He studiously avoided mentioning that if he had his way, some of those children might be Derek's.

Sophie noticeably flinched. "Yes, I assumed you wanted children. That could have been the only possible reason for marrying me."

"No, it couldn't. I wanted to marry you. I like you and I desire you. If we are very lucky, we will have children. But once I got to know you...I would have married you even if I knew you couldn't have children, Sophie."

Sophie didn't bother to pretend she was interested in eating anymore. "But initially, before you knew me, you were spurred by a desire for children."

Ian leaned his elbows on the table and rested his chin on his raised, entwined fists. "Yes, I won't lie to you, that is what prompted me to finally write to your father."

"What about Derek?" The question was asked in a small, quiet voice as Sophie looked down at her hands in her lap.

"I love Derek. He will always be a part of my life and, I hope, a part of yours."

Sophie looked up at him shrewdly. "But Derek did not desire a wife."

Ian sat back again. "No, he did not wish for me to marry."

"I would have done anything to make you marry me," Sophie said fervently, "anything." She looked at Ian in confusion. "But knowing how you feel about Derek, and how he feels about your marrying, I don't understand why you did. Marry me, I mean." She looked down again with a self-deprecating smile. "I'm not much of a prize, I fear."

Ian came out of his seat and went to his knees next to Sophie's chair. "Sophie, you must not think that. I think you are beautiful." He reached up and pulled the offending pins from her hair and then gently tucked the warm, thick fall of hair behind her ear. "You are also sweet, intelligent, kind — need I go on? You are everything that a man could wish in a wife."

Sophie bit her lip and looked at him with tears in her eyes. "You left out passionless."

"Sophie," Ian said with a shake of his head, and he laid his hand over hers where they were wringing in her lap. "If you don't wish to make love tonight, I'll understand. We can wait — "

"No!" Sophie's denial was surprisingly adamant and Ian pulled back slightly, shocked. She clutched his hand with both of hers. "No, please, Ian. I know we won't really be married if we don't consummate it tonight. I won't be able to relax until then, until I know there's no going back."

"Sophie, you can't think that I would send you back? Don't you know me at all? Rest assured you will never go back, no matter what. We could never consummate the marriage, you could shriek on the corner of Bond Street that you hate me and I would never send you back. You believe me, don't you?" It was suddenly vitally important that Sophie believe him, that she trust him.

Sophie closed her eyes in despair. She knew what Ian was asking of her, but she wasn't capable of trust. Not yet. She chose not to answer. She looked at Ian again. "Please, Ian, make me your wife in every way. I'll feel better, safer. Please."

Ian smiled sadly at her. "You won't enjoy it, will you?"

Once again Sophie couldn't lie to him. He had been so nice to her, a champion actually. He deserved better, but Sophie couldn't be so unselfish as to set him free, not now, now that *she* had the chance to be free.

"Sophie, I don't want to make love to you if it will frighten or hurt you." Ian sounded pained. "I want you to enjoy making love with me, to want it as much as I do."

Sophie looked at him in genuine surprise. "That's impossible, Ian. Women just don't enjoy sex. I'm sorry, but there's nothing pleasurable about it for us."

Ian closed his eyes and raised their joined hands to his forehead for a moment. When he looked at her, sympathy warred with amusement in his gaze. "You're wrong, Sophie. With the right man, or men, it can be very pleasurable for a woman. Someday you'll understand."

Sophie looked at him skeptically. "Well, I think you must be misinformed, Ian. Have you ever actually done that to a woman? Certainly it's different for men, and with Derek —"

Ian cut her off. "I think that's enough about Derek for tonight. And yes, I have made love to a woman, several in fact. And to anticipate your next comment, no, I don't believe they were lying to me when they said they enjoyed it."

Sophie closed her mouth as she had indeed been about to say that.

Ian sighed. "I can see that you are going to make this difficult."

Sophie cringed inside. It was that very difficulty that had gotten her beaten on a regular basis at her father's house. "I shall try not to," she said in a small voice.

Ian cocked his head as he looked at her. "You may be right, Sophie. If we put off making love I'm afraid that your fears will grow completely out of proportion." He stood decisively and held out his hand to her. "Come on then."

Sophie gulped and felt her eyes grow wide. "Now?" she squeaked, suddenly terrified. "Shouldn't we eat first?" She had no appetite left, but he didn't need to know that.

"I couldn't eat a bite," Ian said as he grabbed her hand and pulled her to her feet. He practically dragged her across the room to the door of the dressing room that separated their suites.

"Where are we going?" Sophie asked, alarmed at the rising panic in her voice.

"We are going to my bedroom," Ian said, stopping so abruptly that Sophie slammed into his side. He put his arm around her possessively. "Are you all right? Yes? Good. I thought my room might be better if you choose not to stay the night with me. Then you can return here, afterward."

Sophie could only blink at him in growing terror. Ian placed both hands on her shoulders and looked her in the eyes. "Breathe deeply, Sophie. One, two, that's right." When she had her breathing back to normal, Ian continued. "I will be gentle, Sophie. It will be nothing like what happened to you before."

Sophie clutched his upper arm and squeezed it in distress, distantly noting how large and firm his muscles were. "How can it be different? Doesn't it work the same? Don't you put it in the same place?" Ian winced and Sophie had her answer. "You say it won't be the same, but it's always the same, Ian, it is."

"No, it is not." Ian pulled her into him and hugged her tightly. Her initial reaction was to fight his hold, but his warmth and gentle strength permeated the fog of fear and she collapsed into him.

"Yes, that's it, Sophie. Trust me," Ian said softly, kissing her on the top of her head. She came only to his chest, her cheek resting on the strong, broad plain of it. His arms were loose and she knew she could get away if she really wanted to, but strangely enough she didn't want to. She couldn't ever remember being held like this, as if she were precious and wanted. Her arms snaked around Ian's waist and she clung to him. She turned her face into his soft linen shirt and breathed the scent of him in, sandalwood and linen water and a soft, elusive musk that she realized was the bare scent of him. It was a heady fragrance and she let herself become drunk on it.

She wanted to trust this man so much. She felt as if she were walking on the edge of a high cliff, one misstep and she would plummet to her death. Was trusting Ian that misstep? If he betrayed her now... She closed her eyes tightly. She couldn't stand that, she couldn't. Always before she'd known she had a rock inside her that couldn't be crushed no matter how hard they tried. Ian could crush her.

"You're strong, Sophie, I know you are, and brave. If you weren't you never would have survived all that you have. Surely making love with me is one of the less onerous duties you've had to endure?" Ian's voice was teasing. Sophie wasn't ready to be teased.

"It could destroy me, Ian," she whispered.

His arms tightened. "I don't understand, Sophie. I swear I won't hurt you. I won't do anything that you don't wish me to."

Sophie rubbed her cheek against his chest, surprised at his indrawn breath and the way his heart raced in response. Did he want her then, desire her as he claimed? She experimentally ran her hand down his back, lightly. She had no wish to be aggressive, to spark that animalistic rutting response that would make him throw her down and hurt her. Maybe Ian could control that. She'd seen women who weren't afraid of their men, particularly in the last two weeks. There must be men who wouldn't hurt you. There had to be, or Sophie's survival was for naught.

"Do you promise, Ian? Do you promise you won't hurt me? I think if you of all people hurt me, then that will be the end of me. I don't think I can take any more."

"Oh Sophie," Ian said softly, rubbing his hands up and down her back, "I promise. I swear no one will ever hurt you again."

He sounded so sincere, and Sophie wanted, no, needed to believe. She desperately wanted to trust. "Then make love to me, Ian. Show me how different it is."

Ian led Sophie into his room. He hoped she'd want to stay here, to be with him all the time. He hadn't figured out how that would work with Derek, whom he also wanted with him, but time would settle that, he was sure. He wouldn't worry about that now. Tonight was for Sophie.

It took a bit of work to get her dressing gown off. In her nervousness she'd knotted the ties so tightly Ian thought for a moment he'd have to cut her out. Sophie wasn't much help, her hands were shaking so badly. Once she was standing before him in nothing but her short chemise, it was Ian's turn to shake.

She was gorgeous, every luscious, creamy inch of her. Her coppery hair was dark against skin the color of buttermilk. Her shoulders were heavily covered by freckles and Ian loved them. He's seen some on her arms, which she tried to hide, so he'd suspected she had them all over. He wondered if she had them on her breasts. He hoped so. He wanted to kiss each and every freckle. Her breasts were not large, but they weren't small either. Just right, so perfectly proportioned they looked like peaches with hard, dusky nipples at their peaks. His mouth watered at the shadow of them under their thin covering. Her waist was curved deliciously and flowed into full, soft, womanly hips and thighs, the kind every man dreamed of wrapped around him. Her feet were beautifully arched and capped with the sweetest toes he'd ever seen curl into a carpet. That thought made him smile.

"Are you smiling because I please you or because something about me is funny?" Sophie asked in a little, unsure voice.

Ian's eyes slammed back up to her face. "You please me very much," he rushed to reassure her. "You're beautiful, absolutely beautiful." He reached to lift her chemise over her head, but Sophie balked.

"No! I…I'm not ready for…for that." Her arms crossed in front of her defensively and her toes curled harder. Ian dropped his hands.

"All right." He wasn't sure how to proceed. God! Last night when he'd talked with Derek about this he'd never imagined it would be this hard. Last night he'd feared normal maidenly jitters. Now it seemed as if his entire future hinged on his ability to make proper love to his bride tonight. No pressure, surely, Ian grimaced to himself. The daunting ramifications shouldn't affect his performance, of course not. He grimly tamped down those thoughts. "Would you like me to undress?"

"No!" Sophie practically jumped out of her skin. "I mean, can't we proceed without either of us being…" she vaguely ran a hand up and down between them, "unclothed?"

Ian sighed inwardly. "For now," he agreed softly, "but eventually some nudity will be required." He smiled gently to soften his words.

Sophie nodded jerkily. "All right. Eventually." She looked around. "Should we get on the bed? I think I would prefer it on the bed. I've never done that."

Ian's hands fisted at his sides but he managed to keep his face pleasantly arranged. Someday he would have the story out of her and someone would pay. Again he reminded himself tonight was for Sophie, and gentleness. "If you want. That sounds like a splendid idea to me. I'd rather hoped for the bed myself."

Sophie climbed awkwardly onto the bed, trying to keep as much of her covered as possible. The chemise was short, however, and Ian got glimpses of her full, round ass and dark pubic hair, glimpses that had him hard and aching in seconds. He took several deep breaths, telling himself it would be a while before he could see to his own needs. He climbed up after her. She'd lain down and was stiff as a board, her hands resting on her chest so she looked disturbingly like a corpse. Ian immediately lay down beside her, leaning on one elbow, and propped his head on his hand. He reached for one of her hands and she jerked slightly. He ignored it and clasped her hand in his.

"Now what?" Ian asked with a grin.

"W-what do you mean?" Sophie looked back at him, all big, wide amber eyes and lips pale with fright.

"Wellll," Ian drawled, "I promised I wouldn't do anything you didn't want me to, but that means I've got to know what you want me to do. So, direct me. Order me around. I think I might like that." He said the last with a little suggestive waggle of his eyebrows and Sophie's eyes got bigger.

"Order you around?" She sounded so incredulous that Ian laughed.

"Yes, order me around. Haven't you ever wanted to order anyone around? I personally love it. It's one of my favorite things to do." Ian was very pleased with the way things were going. Sophie looked intrigued. He flopped down onto his back and crossed his ankles negligently, spreading his arms in an expansive gesture. "Here I am. Use me."

Sophie literally looked speechless. She stared at him, opening and closing her mouth. She licked her lips nervously and Ian felt his gut clench. He tried to control his breathing so Sophie wouldn't be alarmed. Finally she spoke.

"I…I would like to be kissed. I've never been kissed." She couldn't look directly in his eyes when she spoke; instead she stared at a spot somewhere past his head.

"Well, I can do that," Ian said cheerfully. He rolled over onto his elbow again and leaned over her with a smile. "Kissing is an excellent place to start. But be warned, this will be nothing like your mother's kisses."

Sophie blinked at him. "I don't remember my mother."

Christ, Ian thought, *how am I to do this without crying over her? She's like a motherless orphan from a maudlin novel.* "Has anyone ever kissed you, Sophie, anyone at all?"

"The stablemaster tried once, but he was drunk and just slobbered on me. That doesn't count, does it?" She wrinkled her nose in disgust. "I did not like it, not at all." Then she looked at him hopefully. "I'm rather hoping you're better at it. You seem like the type who would be good at that sort of thing." She put a hand on his chest and looked at him warily. "However, if it will turn you into a rutting beast, then we can forego the kiss."

Ian snorted inelegantly as he tried not to laugh. "Ah, I think I can control my rutting beast tendencies if you can. As for whether or not I'm any good at it, well, you can be the judge." He started to lean in to her.

"What does Derek say?" Sophie asked ingeniously. "I saw you kiss him this morning."

Ian stuttered to a stop and closed his eyes. It was beginning to feel as if there were three of them in this bed even if Derek was not actually present. Sophie's curiosity about his and Derek's physical relationship was making Ian as lustful as Sophie's dreaded rutting beast.

"Derek is rather fond of my kisses." Ian could hear how hoarse he sounded, desire clogging his throat. He hadn't even kissed her yet, had hardly touched her and his cock was hard and throbbing. He'd never been with anyone as innocent as

Sophie, and he found the idea of being the one to educate her incredibly arousing.

Sophie looked up into his eyes, unconsciously acting the coquette. "Kiss me, Ian. Let me see."

Ian began to move again, closing the distance between their lips quickly, before Sophie could change her mind. The first touch of his mouth on hers was tentative, soft, tender. She held very still, her lips pliant. Ian ran his lips over hers, nibbled on them by gently pulling one of her lips between his and sucking. He explored every inch of her lips without using his tongue or teeth in any way. The kiss was as innocent as he could make it, and Sophie's entire body relaxed next to him in response.

Sophie's surrender encouraged Ian to deepen the kiss. "Open for me, Sophie," he whispered against her lips, "open your mouth for me so I may kiss you like a lover."

Sophie's eyes opened slowly and she blinked as if she'd been in a daze. "What? How," she stopped and licked her lips and Ian had to stop the groan in his throat, "how do lovers kiss?"

"With their whole mouth, Sophie." Ian softly kissed her jaw and Sophie unconsciously arched her neck to give him more access. "I want to taste you, put my tongue in your mouth and rub it on yours, explore the sweetness and the texture of you."

Sophie gasped. "I don't know," she said, her voice wavering.

Ian kissed her cheek tenderly, then pressed his own cheek to it. "Please, Sophie, please."

She turned her head toward him and her lips parted as they stared into each other's eyes. It was all the invitation Ian needed. He pressed his lips to hers hard enough to force her lips farther apart and then swept his tongue into the warm cavern of her mouth. Over the years he had learned a great deal about kissing from Derek, who was a connoisseur. Very slowly Ian moved his tongue around Sophie's mouth, tasting her and letting her taste him. He didn't give her too much tongue, he didn't wish to frighten her. But he gave her more than he might give another inexperienced virgin. He wanted her, and he wanted her to know that. He was showing her that desire was not something she needed to fear, but something that she should embrace and explore with him—something that would give her great pleasure.

Sophie tasted fresh and clean, with a hint of wine and mint. Her mouth was soft, and Ian hummed appreciatively as he ran his tongue over the soft flesh of her inner cheek. After the velvet softness of her cheek he felt the sharp edges of her teeth and unexpectedly imagined those teeth biting into him in her passion. The image burned a shiver of lust down his spine. As he tried to rein in his passion, Sophie's tongue suddenly moved tentatively against his. Ian squeezed his eyes shut against the hot burst of excitement that made his cock twitch. He fisted his hands until his fingernails bit into his palms, but he managed to keep the kiss from escalating into the forceful passion his body was demanding.

By the time Ian broke the kiss, Sophie was a willing participant and had proven to be an apt pupil. It seemed as if they'd kissed for hours, but the slow torture of the wait was worth it. Sophie was completely relaxed, and if Ian were any judge of a woman's desire, and he thought he was a good one, she was becoming aroused. When he pulled his mouth away, Sophie came up slightly off the bed, her lips following his. He lessened the abruptness of his departure from her mouth by bestowing small, wet kisses across her jaw and neck, kisses that had her arching her neck again.

"What now, Sophie?" he asked softly as he nuzzled behind her ear. "What do you want to do to me now?" Ian asked the question very deliberately. He wanted Sophie to feel that she was in charge. He could feel her surprise at the question, but released his held breath when she didn't tense up in fear at what they'd done, or what they might move on to.

"I'm not really sure where to go from here, Ian," she said breathlessly as he nibbled her earlobe with his lips. "I'd certainly entertain any suggestions you might offer."

Ian hid his smile in her neck. "Well, I'd like to feel your skin, Sophie. Would you like to feel mine? Taste mine?"

"T-taste yours?" Sophie stuttered. "What do you mean?"

"Like this," Ian whispered and then he ran his tongue down her neck to her shoulder, nudging the strap of her chemise slightly down onto her arm. He rested his lips on the exposed skin in an openmouthed kiss, his tongue swirling teasingly against the sharp bone there. He sucked gently and Sophie shifted uncertainly beneath him. "You taste salty and sweet," Ian whispered into her ear, "a little like the jasmine perfume you wear. And your skin is so soft, it's like silk on my tongue."

"Oh," Sophie breathed.

"Taste me, Sophie," Ian pleaded softly, and he arched his neck over her mouth. He nearly wept with pleasure when he felt her tongue tentatively swipe his neck where his pulse beat so frantically.

"Like that?" Sophie asked, her uncertainty clear.

"Oh yes, darling, just like that," Ian told her fervently. "More, Sophie, taste me some more."

She licked over his neck, starting at that beating pulse, over his Adam's apple and down to the hollow between his collarbones, just beneath the opening in his shirt. She sucked the skin there and Ian couldn't stop his moan. Sophie instantly pulled back.

"Have I hurt you?" she asked worriedly.

Ian shook his head and came down lower over her until her lips were nestled in the soft, tender area behind his ear. He loved it when Derek licked him there. "No, Sophie, it feels so good. More. Lick me there, right below my ear. Yes, yes, Sophie, like that," he gasped as she did as he asked.

"You taste salty too," Sophie whispered in wonder, "and spicy. You smell spicy too. Oh, Ian, you taste so good." Her tongue swept the spot again and he shivered. "Your skin is so soft here," she moved her head and licked the hollow of his throat again, "and here. But your neck has beard stubble." She rubbed her nose against his neck and giggled, and Ian was completely lost.

He reared back and her hands fell away from him. She gave a little squeak and Ian tried to temper his frantic movements but he was hard and aching, he wanted her so much. At that moment all he could think was how much he wanted her mouth on more of him. He ripped his shirt open and tugged on it clumsily, trying to get it off.

"I want more, Sophie. I want to feel your mouth on more of me. Please don't be afraid." He finally got the shirt off and threw it away in disgust. He looked at Sophie and was so happy to see that she didn't look frightened that he visibly slouched down in relief with a sigh. "Please, Sophie." He lay down next to her and turned his head to look at her. "Please kiss my chest, taste me here." He rubbed his fingers over his nipples. "Suck me here."

Sophie came up on one elbow next to him with a small frown. "Well, all right, Ian, if that's what you want." She leaned down to kiss him but Ian stopped her with a hand on her cheek.

"Is it what you want, Sophie?" It killed him to ask, to give her the opportunity to pull away, but he had to. It was imperative she feel in control.

She looked surprised for a moment and then shyly looked at him from beneath her lashes. "Yes," she whispered. She frowned in confusion for a second. "Yes, I really do want to." She looked at Ian for another moment. "You know you're really beautiful, Ian. I thought this morning that Derek was the most beautiful man I've ever seen, but you are really quite beautiful too."

Ian closed his eyes in relief, but they flew open again as he felt Sophie lick his nipple. He clutched the bedcover beneath him. She inexpertly licked and kissed the aroused point, and then took it in her mouth and sucked on it. Despite her lack of expertise, Ian nearly came off the bed it felt so deliriously good. He bit his lip and moaned. Sophie pulled back to look at him, a frown furrowing her forehead.

"That means it feels good, right?" she asked him haltingly. "When you did that before it was because you liked it."

Ian choked out a laugh and tugged her head back down. "Yes, I definitely like it." He continued to like it as Sophie bent to her task with dedication. She licked every inch of his chest and stomach, her tongue following the lines of his muscles, tickling his ribs. Her teeth nibbled and her mouth sucked. She paid special attention to his nipples, and Ian was nearly thrashing with desire when she literally climbed atop him, her legs straddling his torso as she licked. She held back her hair with her hands as she assiduously tongued and sucked and bit his left nipple. He couldn't stop his hands from reaching for her legs, running up and down the smooth, muscled length of them while she loved him. Without thought his hands ran under the edge of her chemise and onto her lush hips until they cupped her full, round ass. Sophie froze.

They stayed like that for endless minutes, or so it seemed to Ian. He was looking at the top of her head, silently begging her not to run. Slowly she raised her eyes to his.

"Sophie," he said quietly, trying to tell her how much he wanted her, to promise not to hurt her, to beg her to let him love her, all in that one word. She closed her eyes and swallowed nervously. "Sophie, let me taste you," he whispered brokenly. "I want to taste you." Her eyes flew open.

He gently nudged her off him and she slid down to the bed. The slide of her bare legs on the skin of his stomach made his muscles clench and his cock jerk. He rose up on one arm as Sophie sank down to lie next to him. He reached for the tie on her chemise and Sophie grabbed his hand. He looked at her and was relieved to see that she seemed only somewhat nervous, as any young bride would be, not terrified as he had feared. "I'll only open it, Sophie, not take it off." She visibly relaxed.

Ian slowly undid the tie and parted the soft material, pulling it down slightly to expose her breasts. Her chest flushed and Ian watched the blush travel up to color her cheeks. Her eyes were closed. "Open your eyes, Sophie. Watch me." She obeyed, her eyelids fluttering as she shyly met his eyes. Ian looked down at her breasts and his breath caught in his throat. "You're so beautiful, Sophie." He let his fingers lightly graze the rounded underside of one breast, smaller than he had at first thought, but no less perfect. Sophie gasped at his touch, and he watched, fascinated, as her nipple puckered. Her nipples were a work of art. Soft brown in color, excitement had given them a pink blush. Her areolas were large, covering nearly half her breast. Constellations of freckles adorned the creamy skin surrounding those wondrous nipples. "I wondered if you would have freckles on your breasts. I hoped you would, so I could kiss each one," Ian told her as he bent over and did just that.

He lost track of time as he worshipped Sophie's breasts, nuzzling them, sucking them, licking them. He spent as much time on her nipples as she'd spent on his, and it was worth every minute. He realized at some point that Sophie was arching into his mouth, her hands clenched in his hair and little mewling sounds coming from her throat. He felt like a triumphant conqueror and all because a shy, beautiful girl was enjoying the way he suckled her breasts.

"Sophie, Sophie," he murmured, rubbing his cheek against her hard, pebbled nipple. "Let me touch you, Sophie," he begged, stopping to suck the nipple, swirling his tongue around the hot, hard flesh, savoring it. "Let me touch your pussy, Sophie."

Sophie tensed, her whole body suddenly stiff and unyielding. "Don't call it that!" she cried out and tried to push him away.

Ian wouldn't let her. Instead he moved up and buried his face in her neck as he held her tight. "I'm sorry, I'm sorry, darling. Sweet Sophie, don't push me away. I just want to love you, Sophie, please." She relaxed against him them and clung to him.

"I'm sorry, Ian. I...please, just don't call it that." He could tell there was more to this than maidenly modesty.

"Is it what he called it?" he guessed quietly, softly stroking her hair as he kissed her face tenderly. She nodded jerkily. "Then we shall call it something else." Sophie looked at him askance.

"Like what? Doesn't it just have one name?" She sounded curious and Ian relaxed.

"Oh no, my sweet innocent, it has as many names as there are stars in the sky." He pulled back to smile at her. She smiled back, disbelieving.

"I ask again, like what?" she said teasingly, and she tenderly brushed a lock of Ian's hair off his forehead. That gesture more than anything made his heart soar. She trusted him. He knew it, even if she hadn't said it yet.

"Well, we could use a euphemism, such as flower." She wrinkled her nose in distaste. "Yes, I'm in agreement, I don't care for that one either."

"What real names does it have? No euphemisms." Sophie was concentrating very hard. Clearly this was important to her.

Ian licked his lips. His preferred name for it was not one generally used among well-bred young ladies. "I call it a cunt," he said tentatively, ready to move on if she wasn't amenable to that.

Her eyes widened almost imperceptibly, her pupils dilating. Oh yes, Ian thought with a flare of desire, she liked that one. He bent down and whispered hotly in her ear. "Shall we call it cunt, Sophie? Your hot little cunt?" Her breathing hitched.

"If that is what you like, Ian," she responded breathlessly.

Ian laughed wickedly in her ear. "Oh yes, Sophie, I'm going to like your hot little cunt." He nipped her ear and she yelped. "Let me touch it, Sophie," he demanded. He was done asking, he was ready to take. Even as he spoke, his hand was inching up her chemise, delving under it to caress her smooth thigh. "Is it wet, Sophie? Does it ache for me?" Sophie's head was shaking. "No? Not yet? Shall I make you wet and aching for me?"

"Ian," she said in a strangled voice. Her hips thrust up, and Ian could tell she hardly realized she'd done it, or what it meant. He moved his hand up to cup her mound and she moaned, her back arching as her legs clamped together.

"You're wet, Sophie," Ian told her harshly, lust lowering his voice, deepening it.

"Oh God," she cried, "am I bleeding?"

Ian was taken aback for a moment. Then he realized she'd never felt desire before. She didn't know what it did to a woman's body. "No, Sophie. It's your body's way of preparing for me, preparing you to be fucked."

Sophie was panting with a mixture of fear and excitement. "I don't understand, Ian," she cried. "What is it?"

Ian removed his hand and grabbed one of Sophie's, pulling it down and cupping it around herself. "Feel, Sophie, feel what desire does to you. It's your cream, your juices. This too has many names. But it's good, Sophie, so good. It means you want me. It means your body will welcome me." Sophie cried out again, and Ian let her pull her hand away. He put his back in its place. "I'm going to make you come, Sophie. And then I'm going to fuck you, and you'll come again for me." Her head was shaking, but her hips thrust, pushing her wet mound into his hand. "Yes, Sophie. Just follow your body's lead, my love, it knows what to do." He moved his hand long enough to spread her legs farther apart.

Ian ran his fingers along the slick, wet folds of her cunt. Christ, she was dripping, and Ian's mouth salivated at the thought of licking the cream up. That was a lesson for another time, however. He fit his finger at her entrance and felt her tense, but he pushed it in slowly, separating the walls of her tight channel gently. She relaxed and lay back, breathing erratically. He worked his finger in deeply, watching her bite her lower lip. He had only a moment to wonder if it was in pain or pleasure before her hips bucked and her neck arched. Definitely pleasure then. He pulled his finger back until only the tip remained in her, then pushed in deeply again. Sophie shuddered. After several more thrusts, Ian introduced a second finger. Sophie let a small sound of pleasure escape.

"Yes, talk to me, Sophie. Tell me how it feels." Ian fucked his two fingers in and out, increasing the pace. Sophie grabbed on to his wrist with a trembling hand. "Tell me Sophie," he commanded.

"Ian," she groaned out. "Ian, I...I've never felt anything like it. It feels...God!" She arched up uncontrollably as Ian rubbed her clitoris with his thumb as he fucked his fingers into her. Ian's laugh rumbled in his chest. Impatiently he reached down with his free hand and pulled her chemise up to her hips so he could watch her fuck his fingers. Sophie's tremors increased. "Ian, what's happening?" She sounded frightened, but the fear couldn't stop her hips, couldn't stop her cunt from clutching at his fingers.

"You're fucking my hand, Sophie, and loving it," he told her with satisfaction. "Come for me, baby. Come apart in my arms." She shook her head, uncomprehending. "You're going to come, Sophie, climax. An orgasm is the pinnacle of pleasure during sex. It feels amazing, and I'm giving it to you. It will help relax you when I fuck you if you come now. Just do what comes naturally, fuck my fingers hard and deep and let it take you." She fucked down hard on him and cried out, jerking against his hand. "Oh yes, we've found it, Sophie," Ian murmured as he rubbed his fingers against that spot deep inside her. He pulled his fingers out and drove them deep, then rubbed them inside while he rubbed her clitoris outside, and Sophie came apart, just as he'd promised her she would. Her orgasmic cry was the most beautiful thing Ian had ever heard. He tried to memorize every moment of her climax—the look of almost-pain on her face as she threw her head back and shrieked her pleasure, her neck and back arched, her toes digging into the bedcovers as her hand held his wrist, tightly pressing his hand into her cunt. He felt her vaginal walls pulsing against his fingers, squeezing them, and nearly came when he imagined them doing that on his cock.

When the spasms abated and Sophie was lying back against the pillows, sated, Ian slowly moved off the bed. He undid the buttons on his trousers and hissed with relief when his cock sprang free of the confinement. Sophie turned her head slowly to look at him. There was no fear on her face, only contentment, and Ian slid his pants down and stepped out of them. He climbed back on the bed and lowered himself down over Sophie.

"Is this all right?" he asked her gently. "Will it frighten you to have me on top?"

Sophie shook her head. "No, because it's you, Ian."

Her words had him closing his eyes against the tears that sprang up, tears of joy at her trust in him. He leaned his head down and kissed her tenderly. "Please may I fuck you now, Sophie?"

She nodded her head, wiggling her hips a little beneath him. "I want you to, Ian. I want to be your wife in every way."

Ian adjusted his hips, spreading her legs wider. His engorged cock found her entrance unerringly. Before he penetrated her, he rubbed the length of his erection along her wet lips, coating it and building up her excitement again. "Do you want me, Sophie?" he whispered, looking down at her. "Do you want my cock inside you?" He'd learned quite a bit this evening about what Sophie liked, and he already knew she liked rough talk during sex. That was fine, he did too.

She moaned and licked her lips, biting the bottom one as she arched her back and pressed the head of his cock against her sweet, hard clit. Ian moaned with her. "Say it, Sophie," he ground out. "Tell me so I can fuck you."

"Yes, Ian," she whispered in that voice that so enchanted him, husky and breathless. "Yes, I want you."

That was all he needed, and he drew his hips back and thrust gently, the large head of his cock breaching her entrance and sliding halfway inside her in one smooth motion, lubricated by her hot cream.

"Oh God, oh God," Sophie chanted, clutching his back, her nails digging into his skin.

Ian barely heard her. She was so wet and tight and hot, and he'd been hurting for what seemed like hours. It was all he could do not to fuck her hard and furiously until he came, which, if he did that, wouldn't take long. But he was determined to make Sophie come again before he spent himself in her. He pushed all the way into her and had to stop for a moment to breathe deeply and pull back from the abyss. Sophie had no idea how close he was, and she writhed beneath him, her hips fighting against his hands, which were gripping them, trying to hold her still.

He let go and pressed all his weight into her, burying his face in her neck as he gathered her close. She wrapped her legs around his waist and her arms around his neck and held him so tightly Ian wasn't sure where he ended and she began. She was shaking and Ian ran a hand soothingly down her side.

"I'm sorry, Sophie, I'm sorry," he muttered, inwardly cursing his size. "I didn't want to hurt you, baby. I'm too big, I know it. I shouldn't have taken you tonight." His ramblings were interrupted by a small, choked laugh from Sophie. "Sophie?"

She pulled back and laughed joyously out loud. She buried both hands in his hair and kissed his face, his cheeks, his nose, his lips. "It doesn't hurt, Ian. Oh God, it doesn't hurt." She hugged him again, and he felt her tears on his shoulder. "It doesn't hurt," she whispered.

Ian was glad it didn't hurt, but since it was perhaps one of the most profound sexual experiences of his life, he was hoping for more from his bride than it didn't hurt. So much for his vanity. He kissed her on the temple. "Can I move then, if it doesn't hurt?"

Sophie nodded against his lips. "Mmm-hmm," she said, pressing a kiss against his neck, "if that's what you want, then yes." She amended her statement before he could ask. "I mean, that's what I want."

Ian smiled and began to move. He was determined that when he was done fucking her, she would be able to say more than it hadn't hurt. The glide of his cock in and out of her was exquisite torture. She was softer inside than anyone he'd ever felt, soft and smooth and tight. She seemed to pulse and thicken around his cock until he was cocooned in her wet heat and his heart beat in time to the rhythm of her cunt. Her legs were wrapped so tightly around his back that he couldn't pull that far out of her. His movements were more of a circular grind that soon had Sophie moaning. "Move your legs higher on my back," Ian ordered her, and Sophie asked no questions, she just did it. The small adjustment made Ian slide farther inside her, and he knew the exact moment his grinding cock brushed her sweet spot. She gasped and her nails scored deeply into his back as her hips jerked hard against him.

"Christ, Sophie," he murmured, blindly searching for her mouth. He found it and kissed her — deep, wet, never-ending kisses that helped focus his mind as he fucked her senseless. He pulled farther out of her with each pass, slamming his cock back in deep and hard, right into the most sensitive spot of her. He pulled his knees up until he was kneeling low, his legs spread wide, his weight braced on his fists as he used all his weight and power to fuck her as hard as he could, and Sophie took it and begged him for more with each whimper and moan and the clutch of her fingernails on his back and ass. She began a low, humming moan that never stopped, just rose and fell with her breathing and the thrust of his cock into her, and Ian knew she was close. He pushed his weight down on her again, the change in angle bringing him into contact with her clitoris with each thrust. She began to cry out in soft, little feminine grunts that drove Ian mad every time he pushed into her.

"Come on, Sophie," he urged her roughly, "come for me again. I want to feel you come on my cock, that sweet little cunt clutching it. Come on, baby."

Sophie cried out and fucked him hard, her hips meeting his with an audible smack of flesh on flesh just a few times before she arched her back and screamed. Her cunt squeezed down so hard on him that Ian cried out, and then he felt his orgasm burst over him, and he cried out again at the relief of his semen being released deep inside her. The feeling of his cock and her cunt throbbing in time with one another as spasms rode them was so marvelous that Ian's vision darkened and his voice became ragged with his cries.

When he could move again, Ian rolled off Sophie and pulled her against him. She snuggled into his warmth and wrapped herself around him uninhibitedly. Before he could speak, he heard her breathing deepen and a little snore. He hugged her close to him, cherishing her trust. He would tell her all the things chasing around in his head tomorrow—how wonderful she was, how passionate, how beautiful, how treasured. She was his now, and nothing and no one would take her away. She had been right to insist they make love tonight. Now he could rest easier as well.

Chapter Eleven

♋

Derek woke with a start when he heard the scream. He was disoriented at first, not sure what had awoken him, until the second scream split the night. These were different than Sophie's earlier screams. Those had been screams of pleasure. Those screams had ripped into his heart like barbed arrows until he bled into the whiskey he was drinking in copious quantities. This was a scream of terror.

"Noooo! No, no, no," Sophie wailed. Derek threw himself out of bed and just barely managed to pull on his trousers before he was out the door and running down the hall.

He slammed open Ian's bedroom door without knocking. Sophie was cowering in the far corner opposite the bed. She had on nothing but a flimsy chemise, half falling off her, her creamy skin shimmering in the guttering candlelight. She had her hands over her ears and her eyes were tightly shut as she muttered brokenly, her hair a wild tangle about her head.

"I'll be good, I promise I'll be good. No more, I'll be good..." she cried in a high-pitched voice.

Ian was naked, kneeling next to her and soothingly calling her name. "Sophie, it's me, Ian. It's just me, Sophie. Darling, don't be afraid. Sophie, speak to me." His voice was filled with fear though he was trying to hide it. He tried to touch her and she scuttled back to lean against the wall, her knees drawn up to her chin.

"What the hell did you do to her?" Derek snarled at him.

Ian turned panic-filled eyes to him. "Nothing! She had a nightmare and woke me with her thrashing about. I tried to wake her, but the minute I touched her shoulder she screamed and literally fell out of bed. When I called her name and tried to help her up, she screamed again and ran to the corner. I can't get through to her. Oh God, Derek, what did I do?"

Ian's harsh breathing cut through Sophie's wretched singsong chant in the corner. Both sounds tore through Derek's head, which was worse for drink as it was. "Cover her up. Throw a blanket on her or something and put some pants on. I'm going to get Mrs. Montague. She'll know what to do."

"Mrs. Montague?" Ian asked, bewildered. "The housekeeper? How on earth will she know what to do?" He grabbed the cover from the bed and gently placed it around Sophie's shoulders. She shuddered and stopped speaking, grabbing the edges of the blanket and pulling them tight around herself.

Derek was walking briskly to the door. "Their daughter was raped. They have some experience with the aftereffects, I believe." When he reached the hall he began running. He wasn't sure if he was running to the Montagues or from Sophie and her nightmares. When he reached the stairs he stumbled to a halt. Montague was rapidly climbing the stairs, a hastily donned robe over his nightclothes and a candle in his fist.

"Montague, thank God," Derek said loudly, not even trying to hide his relief. "Quick, fetch Mrs. Montague. Sophie's had a nightmare and she's very upset."

Montague stopped and visibly collected himself. "We heard the scream downstairs. Mrs. Montague sent me to investigate. Shall I have her bring some laudanum?"

"Laudanum! Of course, why didn't I think of that? Yes, laudanum should help her get some rest and settle her nerves. Please, Montague, and do hurry."

Derek didn't wait to see Montague back down the stairs. He turned and suddenly felt a desperate need to get back to Ian and Sophie. What was happening? He ran back to Ian's room.

He came skidding to a halt a few feet inside the room. Sophie was still in the corner, but she seemed calmer. Her arms were wrapped around her legs and her head rested on her knees as Ian knelt beside her, his hand rubbing up and down her back.

"Is she all right?" Derek asked a little breathlessly.

"She's back to herself," Ian said, "but still a little shaky."

Derek leaned against the wall, his head tilted back, and closed his eyes in relief. His head flew forward again and his eyes opened as he glared at Ian in accusation. "What the hell did you do to her? I told you to take it slowly and let her get used to it. Jesus Christ, Ian, what is the matter with you?"

Ian stiffened in outrage. "I didn't do anything she didn't want, Derek. I let her make the decisions. She was in control."

"Her? In control? Look at her, Ian! No matter what happened to her in the past, she was as good as an innocent virgin. You don't fuck an innocent virgin to a screaming orgasm without repercussions!"

"Stop, please." Sophie's voice was quiet, wavering, wounded. "Please don't fight." She raised her head and looked at Derek. He could hardly see her face in the room's shadows. "I'll be all right. It isn't Ian's fault, Mr. Knightly, really it isn't." She covered her eyes with a visibly trembling hand. "I've had these inconvenient episodes before, I'm afraid. I shall try not to disturb you again. I'm so very sorry."

Derek hated her at that moment. Hated her for making him care. Because he did, no matter all his denials and protestations, he cared. He didn't like to see her like this, didn't like to hear her apologizing so abjectly for her nightmares. How dare she take the guilt on herself? There was someone else who deserved it far more, and someday he and Ian would find out who it was and make him bear the burden. Well, at least until they killed him. Derek felt the comfort of his old friend, anger, and embraced it.

"Stop being sorry," he snapped, "and call me Derek. I won't be able to stand having you call me Mr. Knightly all the time, as if I'm an unwanted guest."

Sophie drew back in surprise at his tone. "I'm sorry. I didn't mean to imply any such thing. This is your home, of course, and I am the interloper. I do apologize if I've made you uncomfortable." Her voice was still weak and raspy from her screams.

"Derek," Ian growled in a warning voice, "this is hardly the time to take Sophie to task."

Before Derek could answer, Montague and Mrs. Montague knocked lightly on the bedroom door. "Mr. Witherspoon?" Mrs. Montague called out in a quavering voice. "Is Mrs. Witherspoon all right?"

"Yes, do come in, Mrs. Montague," Ian called out to her.

Mrs. Montague bustled into the room with a shake of her head and rushed to Sophie's side. "Are you all right, my dear? Shall I help you to your room?" She cast a baleful look over her shoulder at Ian, who drew back in disbelief.

"No, Mrs. Montague," Sophie told her quietly, "I'd like to stay with Mr. Witherspoon. I don't want to be alone." She sounded so bleak that Derek's heart clenched in his chest, and he gritted his teeth trying to suppress his empathy. He'd had enough nightmares of his own to recognize what she was feeling.

"I could stay with you, my dear," Mrs. Montague offered, clearly still distrustful of Ian.

"No, please. It was just a silly dream, that's all. I had too much champagne today and not enough food, I'm afraid. Hardly a recipe for a good night's sleep." Sophie was trying to make light of the episode and failing miserably.

"Take some laudanum, Sophie," Derek ordered her. "Mrs. Montague brought some and it will help you sleep."

Sophie looked at him oddly for a moment. "No, I don't like laudanum. I've been drugged before, and I don't like it."

Not *I've had it before*, but *I've been drugged before*, thought Derek with rage. He clenched his fists.

"Oh come now, Mr. Knightly's right, dear," Mrs. Montague concurred. "There's naught to fear here and the laudanum will bring you a good, dreamless sleep." She poured some in a glass and mixed it with a little water. "Here you go." She tried to give it to Sophie but Sophie resisted, turning her head away and shoving the glass with her hand.

Ian took it from Mrs. Montague. "Thank you, Mrs. Montague. I'll see she takes it. You've been most kind. I'll ring if we need anything else." Reluctantly Mrs. Montague turned and walked to the door. "Yes sir," she said uncertainly. Montague gathered her up and closed the door behind them as they left.

Ian turned back to Sophie. "Sophie, my love, take the laudanum. I'll not leave your side. Nothing will happen." She shook her head, not looking at him.

Derek had had enough. He'd gotten very little sleep the night before, the wedding had been a trial from beginning to end today, and now this. He grabbed the glass from Ian, sloshing a little over the side. He squatted in front of Sophie and grabbed her chin with his free hand, turning her to face him.

"Drink the damn stuff, Sophie," he commanded, putting the glass to her lips. He nudged her head back and Sophie's eyes widened. "I'm exhausted and you must be worse. You might be able to take more drama tonight, but I can't. So drink it and let's all get some sleep." She opened her mouth and obediently drank as Derek tipped the glass for her until it was all gone. Derek stood abruptly and put the empty glass down on a nearby table with a thud. "There. Christ almighty, is this what our life is going to be like from now on? One catastrophe after another? If so, I definitely need more sleep than I've been getting lately." He strode out the bedroom door, smiling as he heard Sophie muttering behind him.

Chapter Twelve

🔊

Ian and Derek were still at breakfast when Sophie came down late the next morning. They'd all slept later than normal after the previous day's—and night's—emotional turmoil. Ian was amazed at how calm Derek was about the whole thing. He'd expected to have to soothe his wounded feelings this morning, but Derek had entered with a rather cheerful greeting and settled in to a large breakfast. The cheerful greeting alone made Ian nervous. They chatted about inconsequential things and all the while Ian's nerves were on edge as he waited for Derek to finally quit acting so pleasant and release the angry barrage of words that seemed to be all he had for Ian lately.

Derek motioned Montague for more coffee right before they all heard Sophie offer a maid a shy good morning in the hallway outside the dining room. Ian cringed, expecting her arrival to be the catalyst that set Derek off.

She entered the room and Ian was struck by how enchanting she looked. Neither their prolonged, passionate interlude nor the nightmare that followed showed in her glowing cheeks or sparkling eyes. She looked sweetly alluring in her new sprigged muslin dress, cut just shy of too tight so she looked demure and yet seducible. Kitty was a genius, Ian decided as he watched his new wife hesitate barely inside the doorway. She was looking at Derek with trepidation.

"Good morning, Sophie," Ian said pleasantly. "Do come and have some breakfast, my dear." He motioned a footman to pull out the chair to his right, directly opposite Derek. Sophie came over slowly as Derek lowered the newspaper he'd been looking at to peruse Sophie instead.

"Good morning, Ian," she said softly. As inappropriate as it was, Ian couldn't help physically responding to her husky tones as he remembered her voice last night, telling him she wanted him, screaming in climactic abandon. He shifted uncomfortably in his chair and Derek gave him a knowing look with a raised eyebrow. "Good morning, Derek," she continued a little uncertainly, and Derek turned his scrutiny back to her.

She sat gingerly and accepted a cup of tea from Montague. "I would like to apologize again for any inconvenience I may have caused last night. I don't know what came over me—bridal jitters I suppose." She smiled weakly.

"Montague, might I have that coffee now?" was all Derek said.

Sophie stirred her tea and when she set her spoon down it clattered out of her hand to the saucer noisily. She went to grab it and knocked her teacup over, spilling it all over the table. She jumped out of her chair, knocking it over as well. "Oh! I'm so sorry," Sophie rushed to apologize again. Montague came over to help the footman clean up the mess.

"It's all right, Sophie," Ian told her as he picked her chair up from the floor and helped her back into it. The servants were clearing off the table linen efficiently and laying new.

Derek sighed. "I suppose this means no coffee?"

"Oh, I'm so sorry," Sophie gushed and looked around for Montague. "Do get Mr. Knightly some coffee, Montague." She looked back at Derek, all but wringing her hands. "I'm so—"

"Yes, sorry," Derek said flatly. "Could you, if it wouldn't be too much trouble, stop being sorry all over my breakfast? Hmm?"

"Derek," Ian said warningly, narrowing his eyes at the other man. He'd really wanted to be wrong about Sophie bringing out Derek's bad side this morning, but he knew him too well.

"Yes, Ian, don't upset Sophie, I know. You can stop growling at me." Derek shook out his paper. "But honestly, must she apologize for everything, even things that aren't her fault, for Christ's sake? She's going to start apologizing for the rain falling and the crops lying fallow if we let her go on this way."

"Oh," Sophie squeaked indignantly. "I never."

"Well, you'd better start," Derek told her as he leaned back in his chair with a sly smile. "Whatever it is you haven't done, I mean."

Sophie stood up again, her eyes wide and her lips thin with annoyance. Ian was torn on whether or not he should intervene. Sophie would have to learn to deal with Derek on her own, and while not ideal, this morning was as good a time as any.

"Oh, are you going to run out again? Ask them to get my horse on your way by if you're not crying too hard, would you?"

"Oh," Sophie seethed, "and to think I was actually worried about your welfare yesterday. I shan't make that mistake again!" She turned and moved briskly toward the door.

"Now she's leaving and she didn't even eat anything. Is she going to drop by each morning to spill things and ruin my coffee?" Was that a smile Derek was hiding behind his newspaper?

"Oh!" Sophie spun back around to face Derek, her cheeks red with anger. "You're insupportable," she hissed at him. "I wouldn't eat breakfast with you if you were the King of England!"

"If I were the King of England, no one would eat breakfast with me. That way I would be assured of getting my coffee."

Sophie growled furiously as she marched out the dining room door. "Insufferable," they all heard her mutter as she stomped away.

Derek tsked at Ian. "That one has a temper, Ian. You shouldn't provoke her like that." He was grinning devilishly.

Ian sat stunned for a moment. He was at a complete loss as to what to do. He'd never seen Sophie like that. She'd actually growled at Derek. Sophie. Growled. It was so inconceivable that he wouldn't have believed it if he hadn't seen it. And Derek actually seemed happy about it. Derek. Happy. Ian pinched himself. "Ow!"

Derek looked at him strangely. "What the devil are you doing? Did you just pinch yourself?"

"I was just checking to make sure this wasn't a dream. Would anyone here care to tell me what's going on? You seem quite delighted that my bride just insulted you and stalked out of the breakfast room. And Sophie...I don't even know where to start. I've never seen her say boo to a mouse, and yet she just gave you a rather firm dressing-down." Ian lowered his head to his hands. "Should I follow her? Should I smooth her ruffled feathers? Or should I let her be good and angry at your impossibly rude behavior, to which she has every right?"

Derek sighed contentedly. "Poor Ian." Ian tilted his head and glared balefully at Derek with one eye. Derek placed an elbow on the table and took a sip of coffee. "I thought Sophie needed to gain a little confidence. But she can certainly hold her own against me, and, after all, let's be honest, I do tend to drive most people to madness. She will have no trouble with the harridans who stalk the salons of London." Derek relaxed back into his chair, smiling. "I believe I may bring out the worst in your little bride, Ian." He laughed out loud. "I have decided I'm going to like living with Sophie."

"Oh good Lord," Ian moaned, flopping back in his seat. "You what?"

"Mmm, you heard me. I believe I shall torment young Sophie until she is a match for any bounder, cad, bitch or raping mongrel she may have the misfortune to come across." Derek's face had grown dark with anger, and Ian couldn't have loved him more than at that moment. Even though he felt threatened by Sophie, professed to dislike her and was in general an ass about most things, he was moved by her and was willing to offer her his protection. Ian slid forward in his chair and reached out to lay his hand over Derek's where it rested on the table.

"Thank you." He couldn't express what he was feeling. The servants were still about, and he didn't want to descend to an emotional outburst, which might very well happen any moment.

Derek returned the pressure for a moment, then moved his hand away. He gave Ian an evil grin. "You say that now, but when lovely Sophie is railing against me, you may grow tired of smoothing her feathers."

Ian grinned back. "I am a rather firm adherent of smoothing. I enjoy a good smooth as often as I can. Don't let my sensitivities stop you, by all means."

Derek shook out his paper once again, and raising it stopped just short of covering his eyes. He raised his eyebrows at Ian. "Yes, we heard you smoothing half the night, which is why some of us got so little sleep. I'm a growing boy, you know. I need my sleep."

Ian leaned in close and motioned Derek forward. In a low-pitched whisper he drawled, "That's not what you say when I want to smooth you all night long."

Derek's pupils dilated and the sheer wickedness of his look made Ian's breathing deepen and his pulse speed up. The moment was broken when Montague cleared his throat. Ian sat back with a sigh. "Yes, Montague?"

"If I may be so bold as to offer my advice, Mr. Witherspoon?" Ian nodded with surprise. Montague had never offered advice before. "I believe some smoothing of Mrs. Witherspoon's ruffled feathers may be in order. She is not, ahem, familiar with Mr. Knightly's conversation."

Ian laughed as he pushed his chair back and stood. "Familiarity hardly makes Derek's conversation any better, Montague."

Derek spoke from behind the paper. "I shall choose to ignore that remark. I'm rather enjoying this whole taking the high road business. For now."

Ian laughed again as he exited the dining room. He agreed with Derek's observation that the other man seemed to bring out the worst in Sophie. That and her comment last night about how beautiful she thought Derek was encouraged Ian. She had strong feelings about him already. If only Ian could channel those feelings into affection and desire.

Now where could Sophie have gone? He stopped in the hallway and looked around. The footman stationed outside the room indicated with a small quirk of his head the left turn off the hall, which led to a back door into the garden. With a smile of thanks Ian took off in that direction. When he turned the corner, he nearly ran Sophie down. She was leaning against the wall with her hand covering her mouth and her eyes wide.

"Sophie?" Ian asked, alarmed.

Sophie moved her hand. "Oh, Ian, I'm so sorry. I don't know what came over me. I can't believe I talked to Mr. Knightly in such a fashion! What you must think of me, and, oh, what he must think." She dropped her head back against the wall and closed her eyes with a groan. "I was unconscionably rude. I am never rude. Rudeness simply opens you up to all manner of retaliation. I must apologize." Her head came up and she straightened from the wall. "Yes, I shall apologize. I'm so sorry, Ian, so sorry. Please forgive me." She turned back in the direction of the breakfast room.

Ian took her hands in his. "Sophie, you needn't tolerate that kind of behavior from anyone, including Derek, especially

Derek. You most certainly will not apologize for taking him to task, which he so richly deserved. You mustn't be afraid to speak your mind here, Sophie. This is your home now and you are safe here." He pulled her into a tight hug, and after a moment's hesitation, Sophie returned it. Ian realized sadly that Sophie would probably always hesitate. She was completely unfamiliar with open affection, and a lifetime of misuse was hard if not impossible to overcome.

After a too brief minute in his arms, Sophie pulled back, but Ian wouldn't let her get too far. She couldn't look at him as she spoke. "I'm still hungry."

Ian couldn't stop the laugh the burst out. Between Derek and Sophie, he'd laughed more today than he had in the previous week. He took this as a good omen for his marriage. "Well," he said, chuckling, "we shall just have to go beard the lion in his den and get you some breakfast."

Sophie wrinkled her nose. "Is there nowhere else? I do not wish to disturb his coffee." She said the last word scathingly and Ian found himself anticipating Sophie and Derek's next exchange.

"I've just the one breakfast room, darling. And it is of course your breakfast room now. Perhaps you could redecorate it so that it gives Derek indigestion?" While he'd been speaking, he'd guided Sophie back to the room she'd exited with such aplomb earlier.

"Oh, do you think so? That would be delightful," she agreed with relish, narrowing her eyes as she saw Derek still sitting at the table. Derek looked up as if he sensed her enmity. He smiled beatifically.

"Back so soon? Admit it, it's my stimulating conversation."

"I'm hungry," Sophie ground out.

"Yes," Derek said with a sage nod. "One generally is when one comes to breakfast. You might even say it was a requirement. Which makes your earlier departure all the more incomprehensible, since you came but didn't eat. And now you're back. The mind boggles."

Ian had to cover his mouth to hide his grin. Sophie was not nearly so amused.

"Do not let my breakfast plans detain you, Mr. Knightly," she said with a tight grin. "I've called for your horse."

"Why on earth do you want my horse?" Derek asked in astonishment.

Sophie's eyes widened as she breathed heavily, gripping the back of her chair with one hand. "You asked me to call for your horse. I assumed you were going out."

"Oh! You're absolutely right. So I am." Derek bounded out of his chair and headed for the door. "I shall be back for dinner. Ian, don't let Sophie spill it all before I get some."

"Oh, you—" Derek closed the door smartly on Sophie's retort. Sophie spun around and yanked out her chair. She sat down hard and stirred her fresh cup of tea so vigorously Ian was afraid for the new table linen. He made his way to the head of the table gingerly. Sophie turned a narrowed eye on him. "I shall make the effort, Ian, I shall, even if it kills me. For you I shall make the effort."

Ian was absolutely fascinated with this new side of Sophie. He loved her when she was timid and sweet, had loved her shy surrender last night. But this termagant, the thought of taking her to bed had Ian so hard it was all he could do not to drag her back upstairs. What would it be like to fuck Sophie when she was wild and angry? Heaven, he thought with a grin. To dominate and command this woman would be heaven.

* * * * *

When Derek returned that afternoon he found Ian in his study looking over some paperwork. Derek was a little self-conscious about the errand that had kept him away half the day. He didn't want Ian or Sophie to read too much into it. It was a peace offering, that was all.

Ian looked up and his eyes widened when he saw what Derek was holding. The silence stretched for a few interminable moments, and Derek spoke defensively. "It's a wedding gift for your peahen of a bride. And I don't want to hear one fucking word about it. It means nothing. It's a bribe to get her to trust me, then I'll strike when she least expects it."

Ian just shook his head. "Oh, Derek, what have you done?"

They found Sophie in the garden. The day was beautiful, not too warm with a light breeze that ruffled the hair and cleared the air. Sophie was on her knees pulling weeds.

"Don't we have gardeners for that?" Derek asked, genuinely perplexed as to why anyone would willingly dig around in the dirt if other people were around to do it for them.

Sophie's head jerked up at Derek's voice and she spoke without turning to look at them. "I've always wanted to have a garden of my own. To plant things and watch them grow. To have the freedom to be outside whenever and for as long as I wish. If you think Ian won't like it, I'll stop." Her shoulders were stiff and her voice only wavered a bit.

"Why the hell would Ian care? After last night I daresay you could spit in the coal shuttle and call it art and Ian would trip over himself to hang it in the hall." Derek was more amused than anything.

Sophie gasped and turned to him, her eyes wide. "What do you know about last—" She stopped when she saw Ian there. "Ian," she said lamely, "I'm just…" She struggled to stand, her skirts making it awkward. Ian stepped over quickly and helped with a hand on her arm. She tried not to touch him with her dirty hands, and when she was standing she frantically tried to dust them off.

"Sophie," Ian said, grabbing her hands in his to hold them still, "feel free to pull every weed on the property if you wish, darling. Tomorrow you can take Timmins, the gardener, and the two of you can pick up everything you need for the garden." He kissed her grubby hands. "Including gloves."

Derek arched an eyebrow. "See?" he said knowingly to Sophie. "I told you."

Sophie's attention was once again diverted to Derek. "I do wish you wouldn't—" She stopped again. "What is that?" She pointed at Derek's gift with a shaking hand.

Derek walked over and unceremoniously dumped the squirming, golden-haired spaniel puppy in Sophie's arms. "Your wedding gift." He backed away, not sure how Sophie would respond.

She hugged the puppy for a moment, looking at Derek in astonishment. The dog began joyously licking her face, and Sophie had to close her eyes and hold it away from her. But then she opened her eyes and hugged it close again, as if she couldn't get enough of it. She looked at Ian. "Look, Ian, he got me a puppy." She sounded all choked up, and Derek became uncomfortable.

"Well, if you don't like him, feel free to give him away." He spoke carelessly, not wanting Sophie to know how important it was to him that she accept his gift. He didn't understand it himself. It had started out as almost a joke. Who on earth got a puppy for a wedding gift? But suddenly, inexplicably, it had grown beyond that.

"I love him," Sophie whispered, clutching the dog to her until it whimpered. Sophie immediately put him down, and the puppy raced over to sniff at the pile of weeds on the ground, then raced back to Sophie to dance about her feet. When she bent to pick him up, he raced away and sniffed at a tree, only to race back to Sophie again. He did this several times and Sophie laughed in delight. Her laugh did strange things to Derek's insides. He told himself it was only relief that she was over her nightmare, and that Ian would be pleased at

Sophie's happiness. The look Ian gave him said as much. Filled with gratitude and love, it did the same thing to Derek's insides as Sophie's laugh.

Derek cleared his throat. "Well, aren't you going to give him a name?"

Sophie looked surprised. "I assumed he had one already. I don't know what to call him, I've never named anything before."

Derek almost cursed aloud at the reminder of Sophie's godforsaken childhood. Then he had a brilliant idea. "Well, actually, he does have a name, but I don't know if you'll like it." He turned and began to walk away, hiding his smile.

"Wait!" Sophie called after him. "What's his name?"

"Derek," Derek called back over his shoulder. He laughed out loud at Sophie's less than pleased exclamation. He knew she was the type who couldn't change the dog's name once she'd heard it spoken out loud. Her next words confirmed it.

"Oh, Ian! Now he shall always be Derek. Drat that man!" Ian laughed and laughed, and the last thing Derek heard as he went back in the house was Sophie laughing with him.

Chapter Thirteen

∞

The next few weeks were heaven for Sophie. She rose in the mornings as late as she wished and no one chastised her. She ate chocolate at least once a day, and as often as three if she wanted it! She worked in the garden every day, if only a little, and her efforts were showing. Mr. Timmins the gardener was a dear old gentleman who didn't mind digging up his own work in the least to replace it with Sophie's flowers. She tried to train Derek, but he was an ungovernable mongrel despite his breeding, much like his namesake, Ian joked. Sophie adored the puppy. She adored Ian. She adored everything about her new life, except perhaps Derek Knightly.

Derek was as unpredictable as he was disagreeable. She could never count on him for luncheon or dinner, but if he did show up, woe to both she and Mrs. Montague if there wasn't at least one of his favorite dishes on the menu. When she borrowed a book from Ian's library, it was always the one that Derek wanted to read next. His bed linens weren't fresh enough, he never had enough coffee, he hated gardening and he had beaten her at chess seven times in a row. She now owed him one hundred pounds, which was laughable since she had no money whatsoever. He'd actually made her give him an IOU! The nerve of him. He was driving her to distraction. She hated to admit that she rather looked forward to their confrontations. He was wickedly clever, and when she was able to hold her own with him in their little war of words, she felt inordinately proud of herself. He was also so handsome he nearly made Sophie forget she didn't like him very much.

But by far the best thing about her new life as Mrs. Ian Witherspoon was her new husband. Ian was the most wonderful person Sophie had ever known in her life. He was handsome, dashing, kind, generous, honest, intelligent and gentle. He was everything she'd dreamed of and more. At night he made love to her so sweetly she sometimes cried. It was frightening how perfect he was. Nothing in Sophie's life had prepared her to be loved by Ian Witherspoon. And she thought maybe he did love her a little. Sophie had been ready to settle for friendship and affection with Ian. She knew he loved Derek, he'd told her so. She hadn't thought it was possible to love more than one person. But with each kiss and caress in the heat of the night, Ian seemed to tell Sophie that what he felt for her went beyond paltry affection. She worried that perhaps she was reading too much into his lovemaking. Men didn't need to love a woman to make love to her. Sophie knew that very well.

Lying in the shelter of Ian's warm embrace one night several weeks after their wedding, Sophie found herself wondering when Ian and Derek found the time to be...together. She blushed and turned her face into Ian's shoulder. Intimate, she amended and then grimaced at her choice of words. Oh for heaven's sake, couldn't she even say it to herself? Fuck, when they found the time to fuck. The thought made her squirm.

Ian shifted onto his side and slid down until they were looking into each other's eyes. Sophie blushed again.

"What are you thinking about?" Ian asked softly, turning his head and closing his eyes as he rubbed his cheek against her hair spread out on the bed around them.

"Nothing." Her answer was too quick and sounded nervous to her own ears. Ian stopped and opened his eyes, quirking an eyebrow at her.

"That doesn't sound like nothing." He scooted closer to her and wrapped an arm around her, pulling her flush against him with a hand on her back. "It sounds like something I'd like to hear."

Sophie swallowed in embarrassment. "No, no, I'm sure not."

Ian laughed softly and the reverberations went through Sophie everywhere Ian was touching her. It sent a wave of desire crashing through her and Sophie was startled. They'd just made love and she wanted to do it again. Every time she felt aroused with Ian, she was surprised and a little alarmed. He made her forget the past and trust him, and those were two things Sophie had at one time sworn never to do. Ian made her forget that too.

"Tell me, angel. Now you've got me burning with curiosity." Ian nuzzled her neck and undulated his hips against her and she gasped as she realized he was getting aroused again as well. "Is it something that's going to make me want to fuck you more than I do already? That, I would definitely like to hear."

"Ian!" Sophie had thought she was beyond embarrassment when it came to bedding Ian, but she still blushed. He said the most wonderfully wicked things to her in bed, things that made her throb and ache and drenched her with want. Part of the reason she was blushing now was because of the direction of her thoughts. She had no doubt that knowing she was thinking about him fucking Derek would make him want to fuck her. The shameless woman he had unleashed inside her reveled in the knowledge. The outward, shy Sophie, however, found herself unable to tell him.

Ian's hand wandered down from her back to caress her bottom. "You have the most glorious ass, Sophie," he sighed. He ran his fingers lightly along the crease between her plump cheeks and Sophie closed her eyes and had to bite her lip to stop her moan. Lord, she loved it when Ian played with her ass. He was always effusive in his praise of that particular part of her body. He lavished attention on her breasts and had even recited a very bad impromptu ode to her nipples one night, but it was her ass he couldn't resist. Ian shifted again and suddenly Sophie felt his tongue swipe across the lip she held between her teeth.

"Don't hold it in, love. I want to hear you. Moan for me." He slid farther down the bed until his face was even with her breasts, and he took a nipple between his teeth. This time Sophie did moan. Ian took his hand off her ass and pushed it between her legs from the front. He moved the hand back up to her ass, but now his forearm was pressed intimately against the lips of her vagina. Sophie couldn't stop the little thrust of her hips against it. Ian moved the arm up higher until his biceps was rubbing her clitoris and Sophie groaned in delight. God, it was heaven to fuck those muscles of his. Unbidden, an image of Derek's naked upper body as she'd seen it that morning weeks ago flashed through her mind. His muscles were huge, his upper arm nearly as big around as her thigh. The thought of fucking against that made Sophie squirm against Ian's arm.

Ian pumped his arm against Sophie's drenched delta a few times, but it wasn't enough. It made her ache and she felt more moisture seeping from her body until his arm was slick with it, but the pressure only aroused, it didn't appease. All the while Ian nipped and sucked on Sophie's sensitive nipple and she dug her nails into his back in protest. Ian pulled away after one last nip. "I'll give you what you want if you tell me what you were thinking about." His tone was sly and tempting and Sophie's groan was as much from frustration as desire. Ian rubbed his hard muscle against her and she knew she was going to give in. At this point, she'd do almost anything to get him to fuck her.

"You and Derek," she gasped, closing her eyes in mortification.

Ian froze for what seemed endless minutes, but in reality was only a few seconds. To reward her, he pulled his arm back until he could run his fingers along the crease in her ass again, and then down through the swollen, wet valley adjoining it. He repeated the motion over and over until Sophie's ass was as wet as her cunt, and Sophie squirmed and moaned for him.

"What about us?" Ian finally asked, licking a path around her breasts, gently nibbling on the firm globes with his lips. Sophie was wild, she didn't even think about what she was saying anymore. She would answer all of his questions, she wanted to reveal all to him, to hold nothing back.

"When…" Sophie had to pause to lick her dry lips and she buried her hand in his baby-soft hair as his mouth played with her breasts. "When do you find time to fuck? You're with me every night."

Ian pulled away from her breast with a groan and buried his mouth against her side, biting her tender skin. Sophie cried out and bucked against his hand. Ian tore himself away and Sophie found herself roughly flipped over onto her stomach and then Ian was straddling her thighs, his hands holding her arms stretched above her head as he whispered in her ear. "Is that all you want to know, Sophie? Just when do I fuck Derek? Not how? Would you like me to tell you how? Would you like to hear all about how I fucked Derek in my study today?"

Sophie whimpered. She'd thought she knew desire after weeks in Ian's bed, but this, this lust slamming through her with the force of a whirlwind, was elemental and frightening in its magnitude.

Ian misinterpreted her whimper. He let go of her hands and pulled back. "God, Sophie, I'm sorry. I lost my head. Don't be afraid, darling. I won't hurt you."

Sophie's freed hands clutched the bedcovers as she thrust her hips back at Ian. "Tell me," she growled. "Tell me."

Ian placed his hands on the dimples right above her ass and slowly ran them up the length of her back. It was a sensuous move, meant to arouse rather than soothe. Sophie arched her neck and groaned. When he reached her shoulders he moved his hands to rest on the bed and leaned over her. "Shall I show you as well?" His voice dripped with sexual intent, rough and deep and Sophie shivered.

"Show me?" Sophie asked breathlessly. Ian was licking her shoulder, and at her question he bit it. Sophie clutched the covers tighter, her need so great she truly hurt from it. Ian didn't answer. Instead he leaned over and grabbed a bottle of scented oil from the bedside table. They had used the oil on one another before. Sophie shivered again in anticipation of Ian rubbing her back with it.

"Derek came to see me in my study today," he began, his voice low.

Sophie tensed and then moaned. Oh God, oh God, he was going to tell her. Ian poured a generous amount of oil in the small of her back. He rubbed the oil over her lower back and then he shifted down her legs to have freer access to her ass. He rubbed his oil-slick hands over her cheeks and kneaded the tight muscles, and Sophie groaned at how good it felt.

"He had one thing on his mind. He wanted to fuck. I was more than happy to oblige him." Ian grabbed the pillows piled at the end of the bed and stuffed them under Sophie's hips, raising her ass in the air. Sophie nearly purred in approval. He'd fucked her from behind several times and she liked it. She liked how deep he could go, even liked the almost helpless feeling of being covered by him in that fashion. Ian continued his story. "I knew what he wanted the minute he walked in and slammed the door. Derek gets this wild look in his eyes when he's horny and craving a good, hard fuck."

Sophie buried her face in the bed and moaned. Ian poured more oil, this time directly on her ass until it ran heavy down her crease and across the star of her anus. Ian had rubbed her there before when they made love, and it had been thrilling and wonderful, like everything Ian did to her.

"Without a word, he stripped off his clothes. He was stark naked in my study with a raging erection, and all for me, for my pleasure. I like Derek to strip for me, to be naked when I am clothed. He likes it too. He told me once it makes him feel a little like my sex slave. It is a game I enjoy." He smoothed a finger over the tight entrance to her ass. "Would you enjoy it as well?"

"Yes," Sophie whispered, aroused almost beyond endurance at the thought of Derek stripping for them both. He was so beautiful. Ian paused at her answer, and in the stillness Sophie could hear how ragged his breath had become. "Yes," he whispered in response, then seemed to come back to his senses.

"I hadn't moved. I was sitting behind my desk and the sight of him, so big, so male, so aroused, made my cock stand hard against me. I wanted him, and I knew he'd do anything I asked." Ian leaned over her, his mouth at her ear. "Will you do anything I ask, Sophie?" Sophie could only nod, her voice stolen by desire. Ian kissed the tip of her ear tenderly. "Good girl."

Ian ran his fingers down the crease of her ass again, but this time he stopped at the entrance there. Sophie felt one finger rub her and then slip inside. The feel of his finger in her ass was so shocking Sophie reared up off the bed. "Ian!"

"Shh, Sophie," Ian crooned, gently pushing her shoulders back down with his free hand. "This is what I'm asking. You'll let me, won't you, darling? You'll do anything I ask, and I promise you will like it." He wiggled his finger slightly and Sophie gasped at the pleasure. Of course she would like it, she liked everything Ian did.

"Derek came to me. I didn't have to say a word. He knew just by the look on my face that I wanted him to come to me. He stood between my legs while I sat in my chair. Can you picture it, Sophie? His hard cock was right in front of me." Ian pulled his finger almost out of her ass, just the tip teasing her, and a little sob of desire hiccupped out of her. The he pushed it in farther than before and she swallowed her cry of delight. Ian laughed softly. "I ran my hands over his wonderful body. Doesn't Derek have a wonderful body, Sophie? His hard biceps bulging, his broad chest with that thick pelt of dark hair, his flat stomach and tight ass, all supported by rock-hard, thick thighs."

Sophie could hear the lusty throb of Ian's voice as he described his lover. Clearly Derek aroused him. The thought should have made Sophie jealous, or at least uncomfortable, but instead she found it exciting. The image of the two men together stirred her in a wicked way. Ian licked a path down her spine and she felt him press back into her ass, only this time it was fuller and almost painful. The sting and stretch there disturbed her, but it also thrilled her. She made a distressed sound and Ian smoothed a hand down her back soothingly.

"Shh, darling. I've just put in another finger is all. I want you to feel what Derek feels when I fuck him, Sophie."

"Oh God," Sophie moaned, rubbing her flushed cheek on the soft bed linen.

Ian was placing small kisses over her back as he slowly fucked in and out of her, constantly stretching her with wiggling movements of his fingers. "I toyed with his nipples, plucking and rubbing them while I leaned over and took his cock in my mouth. I took the whole thing in one breath, right down to the root until I could feel it in my throat. Christ, he's sweet, the taste of him, his skin and the cream that leaks from his beautiful cock when he's hard for me."

"Ian, Ian," Sophie whispered, moved almost to climax by his words and his fingers. She was so close her orgasm burned in her. Ian stopped talking and pulled his fingers out of Sophie, to her dismay. He lay over her back, most of his weight on his forearms, and gently bit the nape of her neck. They lay that way for a minute or two, until Sophie felt back in control. Ian let go of her neck and licked the spot.

"Better?" he whispered hoarsely. Sophie nodded, and her head hadn't even stopped moving before Ian pushed his fingers back inside her. She moaned and thrust back on them. "Yes, yes, baby, fuck me like that," Ian murmured. Sophie's temperature rose at the approval and excitement in his voice.

"Tell me the rest, Ian," she whispered, fucking his fingers slowly, controlling her breathing and her desire. She knew Ian wanted her to wait, to ride the edge with him.

"I sucked his cock, Sophie. I sucked him hard and fast because I knew that was what he wanted. And while I sucked him, I pressed my fingers into his ass just like I have them in yours. He's so tight there, I can't get my cock in unless I work him like this." He wiggled his fingers and Sophie's breath became harsh in the quiet of the room. "I sucked him until he came in my mouth, Sophie, and I swallowed every last sweet drop." He leaned down until his voice was a mere breath in her ear. "Would you like to do that, Sophie? I would like to watch you do that someday."

Sophie's breath hitched. She'd done it to Ian already. He had taught her how. Did he mean he wanted to watch her do it to Derek? Her heart seemed to stop and then speeded up unbearably. The thought was deliciously arousing, but Sophie pulled back from it, horrified at her own perversity. It was bad enough enjoying listening to her husband talk about fucking another man. She couldn't believe she was fantasizing about sucking his cock. And Derek, of all men! He tormented her, how could she want him?

When her breathing hitched, Ian's free hand clamped down on her wrist. "Oh yes, I can see you do. Someday, Sophie, someday." She couldn't answer him, mortified at the anticipation coursing through her. He waited a moment. "All right, Sophie, take a deep breath." Sophie immediately obeyed. Suddenly Ian pressed what felt like another finger inside her. She bucked in protest at the painful thickness now pressing in and out of her. "Relax, Sophie, that's right," Ian crooned to her and she concentrated on her breathing, relaxing into the motion of his fingers. Before long the pain began to recede and the pleasure bloomed again. She felt Ian drizzle some more oil over his hand and her ass and the friction became a hot glide that left shivers in its wake.

"After I sucked his cock I stood and pushed him roughly down, so he was bent over my desk. I opened my trousers and put some cream on my aching cock. I keep some in my desk for just those occasions. You see, Derek likes my study very much." Sophie could hear a wet sucking sound behind her and she tensed. She recognized that sound. Ian was massaging the oil onto his cock behind her. His fingers were pressed deeply inside her ass, tickling her as they moved and wiggled. "Then I pressed my cock against that sweet, tight hole and pushed in, Sophie, just like this." Ian's fingers pulled out and were replaced by a hot, thick presence pushing against her. She felt her anus give and bloom as his cock forged slowly inside her. The feeling was indescribably erotic and enthralling. She felt full and fucked in a way she'd never felt before. "Yes, yes, like that." Ian continued until he was buried deep in her ass. "I filled him like this, and then I fucked him, hard. He wanted it, he was wild to be fucked. I slammed my cock into him over and over, Sophie, and it felt so *good*." Ian practically hissed the last word as he began to stroke in and out of her, not hard, not fast, but deep and steady, and to Sophie it felt so intense that her eyes burned and filled with tears. "I fucked him until he begged, Sophie. Until he begged me to let him come again, and I wrapped my hand around his cock and pumped at the same time I fucked into his sweet ass until he came, his cum all over my hand and my desk. And then I grabbed his hips and thrust so deep in him I thought I'd come out his throat. God," Ian growled as Sophie moaned. She pulled her knees up until she was on all fours, her ass in the air with her head and shoulders on the bed. The new position allowed Ian to go deeper and harder, which was what Sophie wanted.

Ian pulled his own knees in between Sophie's and spread her legs wider until she could hardly move. She was completely vulnerable, the position allowing her to do nothing but lie there and be fucked, and she gloried in it. There was no fear, no shame, only love and pleasure and Ian. Ian reached for her hands and spread them out to the sides, their fingers entwined. He controlled her, controlled her passion, her pleasure, her body, and Sophie rode the current of his lust.

"God, God, Sophie. I've wanted to fuck your ass since the first time we were together. No, before that. This is what I love the most. Let me do this, Sophie, let me." Ian's words were a plea, but his tone was a harsh command.

"Derek," she choked out.

"I fucked him until he cried, Sophie. I went deep and long and he trembled with the feel of my cock in his ass. When I came I was so deep, and it was tight and hot and Derek was begging me to come inside him, to own him, and I did, I did. I want to own you, Sophie," he growled, his fingers tightening around hers. "I want to come in you here, in your ass, Sophie's ass. I want to claim it."

"Yes, Ian, yes," Sophie sobbed. God, she hurt, she burned and ached and her climax was just out of reach.

"Are you going to come, Sophie? Are you going to come from the feel of my cock fucking your soft, sweet ass? Come for me, Sophie, now." Ian let go of one of her hands and reached beneath her to push two fingers into her clasping sheath, and it was as if Ian pulled a lever and sent Sophie soaring. She arched and bucked and cried out his name, the spasms of her orgasm ripping through her so that even her fingers and toes clenched. Ian roared as he ferociously drove into her hard and deep and came apart. She felt the hot scald of his semen in her rear passage and cried harder.

When it was over they lay panting, unable to move for several minutes. Sophie had collapsed to the bed beneath her. Ian had both arms wrapped around her waist, his forehead resting on her back. Eventually Sophie felt Ian shaking behind her. It took a moment to realize he was laughing weakly.

"Well, Sophie darling, now you know. That is how I fuck Derek."

* * * * *

217

Ian was sitting at his desk the next day, going over some correspondence when Derek casually strolled in. He didn't say anything to Ian, just walked over to the open French doors and looked out at the garden. Sophie was out there digging in the dirt again. Derek seemed fascinated by Sophie's gardening.

Derek leaned negligently against the doorframe and Ian took a moment to appreciate his rugged profile and his hair gleaming in the sunlight. He let his gaze travel down that long, hard body and felt his blood stir as he remembered what had happened on this same desk yesterday, and describing it to Sophie last night. Suddenly Sophie's puppy barked and ran from the garden to the man leaning in the doorway. Derek bent down to pet the dog that was jumping on his leg.

"Derek, behave," Ian scolded.

"I haven't done anything yet," Derek drawled with amusement.

Ian laughed. "I was talking to the dog. You do realize that people are going to comment on the fact that you are named after a dog."

Derek straightened immediately and sent Ian a perturbed look. "I came first. The dog is named after me."

"Yes, and our friends are known for their tact and their ability to pass up a perfect opportunity to bait you."

Derek scowled. "Damn. What the hell was I thinking? Can we change his name?"

Ian grinned devilishly. "Absolutely not, Sophie won't hear of it. Derek he was named and Derek he shall remain." He leaned back in his chair with a chuckle. "I believe she realized the possibilities immediately and is looking forward to years of jokes at your expense."

"Hmm," Derek said noncommittally and turned back to look into the garden. "Care to tell me why your little wife can't look me in the eye this morning?"

Ian felt his smile turn sly and hot. "Noticed that, did you? Why I suppose it's because I told her in vivid detail last night about how well I fucked you here yesterday."

Derek turned slowly to look at Ian. His face was inscrutable, neither happy nor upset, just...mildly interested. "For your pleasure or hers?"

"It turned out rather nicely for both of us, thanks." Derek saluted him with a jaunty tip of his hand. "That's it? You don't want details?"

"Why? Are you burning with the desire to do me a favor in kind by describing in vivid detail how you fucked your wife last night?" Derek's voice was neutral and Ian still couldn't gauge his mood.

Ian got up and walked over to stand next to Derek as they both watched Sophie. She dug a small hole in the earth, and then she placed a little flowering plant of some kind in the hole and gently patted dirt in around it. She had a whole box full of the little flowers, whatever they were. They came in all different colors and Sophie was planting them with no rhyme or reason. Ian liked it much better than the solid mass of flowers of only one color he'd seen in other gardens. He looked around and noticed she'd planted quite a few different types of flowers all over, wherever she found room, or made room. Ian didn't care as long as it made her happy. He could hear her humming softly. Obviously it did make her happy.

"Why does she do it?" Derek was still perplexed. "Why does getting dirty make her happy?"

Ian shrugged. "I don't know and I don't care, as long as it does."

"But don't you wonder? Don't you want to know what makes her tick?"

Ian tilted his head as he looked at Derek. "She tells me what she wants me to know and that makes her comfortable. I don't press her for anything. I don't have to. What she doesn't tell me I can usually guess." He leaned against the doorframe opposite Derek, facing him. "As for what makes her tick, no, not really. I like not knowing, I like the mystery. Just like I like that element of surprise that you have, Derek. I'm never sure what you're going to say or do, except that nine times out of ten it will be inappropriate." Derek turned to him with a half smile. "And I even like that. I love it actually, that you refuse to play polite when everyone is trying to stuff you into that box. I like being the one who takes the lid off and sets you free."

Derek glided across the space that separated them and leaned against Ian, pinning him to the wood frame behind him with his hips. He held the frame with both hands above Ian's head, dwarfing him, but Ian just smiled. Derek leaned in and licked the smile from his lips, then kissed him lingeringly. Ian put his hands on Derek's hips and kissed him back without hesitation. When Derek pulled away, his eyes were heavy with desire. "What if Sophie sees us?"

"Isn't that what you want? Why you kissed me here?" Ian asked softly with a faint smile as he watched Derek lick the taste of him from his lips.

Derek pulled back slightly, his face showing his shock. "I don't know. I didn't think about it. Maybe." He turned to look out at the garden again and Ian followed his gaze. Sophie was still busy with her flowers and hadn't seen the kiss. "How did she react last night? When you told her?"

Ian leaned in and rubbed his nose on Derek's neck, breathing him in. "You mean you didn't hear her?" His voice was smug and amused.

Derek moved away until he was leaning against the opposite wall again. He didn't look at Ian. "I haven't been going upstairs until the house is quiet lately."

Ian felt a tightness in his chest. "Come back. Come back to our room. I miss you at night." He tried to be casual but he could hear the longing in his voice.

Derek smiled crookedly. "And where will Sophie sleep?" He finally turned back to Ian. His face showed amusement, but his eyes were sad.

"With us. My bed is big enough for us all." There were layers of meaning in his words.

Derek's expression didn't change. "Yes, but I'm not big enough to share it."

"She asked me, Derek. She asked me how I fucked you. And I showed her." Ian stood away from the wall, unconsciously bracing for whatever Derek was going to throw at him.

"Don't," Derek said, his voice low and somehow defeated.

"Don't what? Don't talk about it, or don't do it? I fucked her in the ass, Derek, and she loved it. She loved every minute, every inch of it. You know what that means." Ian let himself get angry. Derek wasn't far behind.

"Don't." Derek's voice was harsh this time.

"Don't what? Answer me, Derek." Ian rarely used that voice on him, except perhaps when they were having sex. He saw Derek's eyes flare as his lips thinned.

"Don't tell me how I'm obsolete now."

Ian was thrown into confusion. "What are you talking about?"

"You fuck her now the way you used to fuck only me. She sleeps in my bed, now she takes you in the ass. I'm losing ground here, Ian, and I don't know how to get it back." Derek pushed angrily away and paced into the room. "God damn it! I hate how fucking pathetic that sounded." He spun back to face Ian. "Are you happy now? Look at what you've turned me into!" He held his arms out dramatically as if to display his lowered state.

"What I've turned you into?" Ian was incredulous and let it show. "I haven't done a damn thing and you know it. I've bent over backward to show you that I love you, that I accept you as you are, that I want you. If I had the power to change you in any way, I damn sure wouldn't make you a recalcitrant pain in the ass. I'd give you the common sense to realize that sharing a bed with Sophie and me is a good thing. That making love with both of us would be the best damn thing you ever experienced in your whole misbegotten life, you ungrateful cur." Ian stalked back to his desk and threw himself into his chair. "I want you back in my bed, Derek, with Sophie. It will happen, so you'd better get used to the idea."

"You snap your fingers and I'm supposed to jump, is that it?" Derek snarled. "I'm no one's lapdog, Ian, not even yours. I'll join you and your wife in your marriage bed when I'm good and ready, if I'm ever ready, and not a minute sooner. Until then you can damn well play the stallion at my convenience since you can't seem to keep your fucking hands off me."

"Make up your mind, Derek. Either I don't need you anymore or I can't keep my fucking hands off you. You can't have it both ways."

"I never said I was rational, just pathetic."

Sophie's voice broke into the argument from the doorway. "Well, I'll certainly agree with that assessment, if we're having a vote, that is. But shall we ask the neighbors as well? I'm quite sure they heard most of that enlightening little spat." She strolled casually into the room, taking off her gardening gloves as she went. She stopped and looked around in consternation when she couldn't find a spot to put the dirty gloves.

"Oh for Christ's sake, just drop them on the floor." Derek covered up his obvious embarrassment with the sharp command.

Sophie glared at him. "I will not. They are dirty and would make a mess that someone else would have to clean up." She marched back to the door and threw the gloves outside with an almost violent motion. She spun back to face

Derek. "And stop telling me what to do. I'm no one's lapdog either."

"Sophie—" Ian began placatingly, but she cut him off at the knees.

"Don't you dare try to soothe my temper, Ian. I'm angry at you as well. If you wanted Derek in our bed, don't you think you might have mentioned it to me? Or don't I get to have anything to say about it? And I must tell you, it does wonders for a woman's vanity to have a reluctant man ordered to make love with her."

Derek looked smugly at Ian. "I told you," he said. Sophie turned on him.

"You did nothing of the sort. You told him you'd come to our bed when you were good and ready. Well, nobody's coming to my bed until I'm good and ready. What do you both think of that?" She marched self-righteously to the hall door and yanked it open before turning back to them with another glare. "I think it only prudent to tell you that I feel a headache coming on. I shall have it all night." She sailed through the door past a startled footman who quickly recovered and reached in to close the door.

Ian was speechless for a moment. Then he started to laugh. She was magnificent, by God, bloody magnificent. She'd flown in here and given them both what for and not once had she faltered or doubted herself. She'd trusted them enough to get angry at them.

"What the hell are you laughing about?" Derek asked irritably. "Your wife just threw you out of your bed."

Ian smiled at him. "She did, didn't she? She was more than pissed, and she crawled right down our throats about it, as well she should."

Derek's smile broke slowly across his face. "She did, didn't she?" He sat down in his favorite chair and picked up the book he'd been reading lately, getting comfortable. He looked back up at Ian with the smile still on his face. "She was rather spectacular, wasn't she?"

"She was absolutely magnificent," Ian replied proudly. "A regular shrew."

A couple of hours later, Ian and Derek were idly playing chess when a knock came at the study door. Montague entered at Ian's summons.

"A letter for you, sir," Montague said, holding out a tray with a rather impressive-looking letter on heavy vellum with an ornate seal sitting on it.

Ian raised an eyebrow inquiringly. "Why didn't you give it to Gibbons?" Ian's secretary usually handled all his correspondence first, sending those deemed worthy on to Ian and handling the rest himself.

"It is from the Earl of Wilchester," Montague said tonelessly.

Ian sat dumbfounded for several seconds. He hadn't heard from or been received by his family for the last two years, not since he'd taken Derek home with him right after the war. They'd refused to accept his relationship with Derek, recognizing it for what it was in spite of Ian's admittedly halfhearted attempts to disguise it. What the devil did Wilchester want? He looked at the missive on the silver salver as if it were a particularly venomous snake.

It was Derek who reached out and plucked the letter from the tray. "Thank you, Montague," he said politely, throwing the letter in Ian's lap. "Could you see about some tea? Perhaps some of those little lemon cakes Cook makes?"

"Very good, Mr. Knightly," Montague said as he turned smartly and left the room.

Derek studied the chessboard silently for several minutes. He spoke without looking up as he made his move. "Are you going to read it, or are you going to continue to look at it as if it might jump up and bite your nose off?"

"It very well might," Ian said contentiously. "My family is not known for forgiveness or fair play. Ergo, it may indeed contain some type of poison."

"Only of the pen variety. Open it, for God's sake." Derek whipped it up off Ian's lap and tore it open.

Inexplicably panic-stricken, Ian grabbed it from Derek and fell back in his chair, his heart racing. Derek just laughed at him. "If they were going to do away with me, or you for that matter, they would have expeditiously taken care of it two years ago. Read it."

Ian took a deep breath and began to read. Just a few sentences into the letter his panic turned to incredulity and he felt his jaw drop. He got up and walked over to the window as he continued to read. When he was done Derek was already munching on Cook's lemon cakes.

"Well?" Derek was licking the frosting from one finger, and Ian had to smile at the boyish gesture. Derek did love his sweets. "You're smiling. It must not be that bad."

"I'm not sure what to make of it. Don't eat all those cakes, I want some." Ian went back and sat in his chair, reaching for one of the treats. "I have been summoned."

"Summoned? To your execution?"

"Hardly. To celebrate the prodigal's return at my uncle's knee." Cook really was excellent. He'd have to make sure and comment to Montague on it. Good servants were hard to find.

"Whose return? And are they actually going to make you sit on his knee?"

Ian laughed and Derek smiled at his own witticism. "I am the prodigal. Apparently they are overjoyed at the news of my recent nuptials. Everything is forgiven—that's reading between the lines—since I am now a respectably married man, and to the very woman my dearly departed father betrothed me to."

"Families are such a delight, when they're not stabbing each other in the back for the unentailed jewels, of course. So

225

they're thrilled about Sophie, are they? They think you've given me the heave-ho?"

"Apparently. I've been summoned to the family seat to be welcomed back into the fold." Ian didn't pretend to be happy about it.

Derek looked thoughtful. "I think you should go."

"What?" Ian was completely shocked at Derek's remark. He'd expected Derek to say to hell with them all.

"He's the Earl of Wilchester, Ian. If he acknowledges you and Sophie, no one can touch her." Derek's voice was low and hard. He didn't like it, but what he said was true. He was thinking of Sophie.

Ian sighed dismally. "You're right, of course. But I'm not going to bring Sophie with me. She doesn't need to meet that pack of wolves yet. They'd eat her alive." He looked over at Derek. "Will you be all right here with Sophie?"

Derek shook his head wonderingly. "All right how, exactly? Will I behave myself and not make her cry? Will I resist all her efforts to seduce me? Will I let her win at chess, finally? I'm afraid we'll have to iron out the details before I agree to a blanket statement like that."

Ian chuckled abashedly. "You're right, it was a foolish question. Just…take care of her, won't you?"

"You're going to Kent, Ian, not the Crusades. How long will it take to kill and eat the fatted calf, for God's sake? Surely you won't be more than a couple of days."

Ian sighed, disgusted with himself for being such a worrier. "You're right, you're right. I'll make sure to be back by Thursday."

"Thursday? You mean you're leaving today?" Derek reared back in surprise.

Ian laughed. "No, tomorrow. The sooner it's over the better."

There was another knock at the door and Ian called out, "Enter."

Montague came in and Ian could see the smile in his eyes. "The flowers are here, sir."

Ian jumped to his feet, rubbing his hands together. "Excellent, excellent." He hurried over to the door.

"Flowers? What flowers?" Derek followed him to the foyer. The footmen were bringing in bouquets of nearly every kind of hothouse flower Derek could name. There were brilliant explosions of color all around them. "What is all this?" Derek exclaimed.

Ian took a huge bouquet of blood-red roses from a footman and carried them over to Derek. "An apology," he told him. "Red is your favorite color, isn't it?"

Derek narrowed his eyes as he took the bouquet. "These are not all for me, and I don't require a nosegay, thank you." He set the flowers down on the nearest table.

"Of course they're not for you," Ian said, picking up the roses again. "They're for Sophie. She won't be able to resist them, particularly since several of them can be transplanted in the garden."

Derek laughed. "You have always been good at apologies, Ian." He started for the door. "I'll leave you to it."

"Derek!" he called out. "Wait." He walked over to him so he wouldn't be overheard. "Be back tonight, please."

Derek cocked his head. "Why?"

"Because I want to make love to you in a bed again." He shook his head as Derek started to answer. "No, in your bed. For now." He backed away, smiling at the heat that flared in Derek's eyes. He kept smiling as he climbed the stairs to Sophie. Oh yes, he was more than good at apologies. He was the best damn penitent in London.

Chapter Fourteen

𝕾

Ian didn't find Sophie in her bedroom, or anywhere in the house for that matter. So he grabbed one of the flowering plants that had just been delivered and sought her in the one place he knew she found solace—the garden.

When he walked out the doors onto the terrace he saw Mr. Timmins immediately.

"Timmins," he called, "is Mrs. Witherspoon out here?"

Timmins laughed. "Course she is, sir." He pointed to the far north corner. "Over there sir, tearing up some bushes I put in last year."

Ian paused as he was walking down the steps to the path that led into the gardens. "Do you mind, Timmins, that Mrs. Witherspoon is digging up your garden?"

Timmins shrugged good-naturedly. "Not my garden, sir, it's yours and the lady's." He scratched his head sheepishly. "And truth is, sir, it looks a sight better these days than when I was doing it alone." He shook his head. "She's got an eye for color and light, and a way with the flowers to be sure, sir. And it makes the lady so happy that I dare not complain." He smiled as he said the last.

Ian gazed at the far corner, though he couldn't see Sophie that far away, beyond the trees. "Yes, it does," he agreed in a murmur. He looked back at the gardener. "That will be all today, Timmins. You may take the rest of the afternoon for yourself."

Timmins' eyes widened in surprise. "Sir?"

Ian smiled conspiratorially at the older man. "I need to apologize to my wife, Mr. Timmins. I require privacy to do so."

Timmins' cheeks turned ruddy and he suddenly couldn't look at Ian. "Oh, well, yes sir, course, sir. I'll be on my way then." He chanced a glance in Ian's direction. "Shall I be back tomorrow then, sir?"

Ian chuckled. "Yes, Mr. Timmins. I fully expect to be done apologizing by tomorrow."

Mr. Timmins snorted softly as he gathered his tools. "It's clear you haven't been married long, sir."

Ian choked in astonished amusement as Timmins shuffled off down the path and out of the garden.

Ian found Sophie exactly where Timmins said she'd be. She was kneeling on the ground digging up what appeared to be some roses in their death throes. Her spade was viciously biting the earth around a small bush whose leaves were covered with white spots.

"What are those spots?" Ian asked conversationally as he leaned over her shoulder.

"Ahhhh!" Sophie gave a little scream and dropped the spade. "Ian! Where on earth did you come from?"

Ian had fallen back a step in surprise at Sophie's scream. "You have got to stop doing that," he told her breathlessly, "or you really are going to give me an apoplexy." He sat down on the ground beside her as she patted her heart in agitation. "I'm sorry, I thought you heard me. I wasn't trying to sneak up on you."

Sophie started to smile then frowned ferociously at him. "I'm still mad at you."

Ian nodded in acceptance. "And you have every right to be." He pointed at the plant he'd brought with him which he'd set down next to the spotted rosebush. "But I come bearing a gift of apology."

Sophie quickly moved the plant away from the bush she was digging up. "Don't put it there. You don't want to infect it."

Ian curled his lip in distaste. "Infect it? What the devil's wrong with it?"

Sophie picked up her spade and resumed her digging. "Mr. Timmins says it's called powdery mildew."

"You can't catch it, can you?" Ian asked in alarm, imagining Sophie covered in powdery spots.

Sophie giggled, and with that sound Ian knew she wasn't as angry as he'd feared. "No, silly. It's a plant disease, not a people disease. It is especially a problem with roses."

Ian reached out and ran the back of his index finger gently down her soft cheek. "Then you should be careful," he said softly. "You are by far the sweetest rose in this garden."

Sophie turned to look at him and he could see the melting warmth in her amber eyes. "Oh, Ian, why do you have to say such wonderful things right when I'm cursing you for being a selfish idiot?"

Ian scooted closer to Sophie on the grass. He took the spade from her unresisting fingers and set it carefully aside. Then he pulled her gloves off slowly, one finger at a time. "I am a selfish idiot."

Sophie shook her head and Ian saw her lip tremble. "No, Ian. I shouldn't have yelled at you."

Ian shook his head in response, and smiled ruefully. "Yes, yes I am, Sophie. I should have asked you properly. I should have told you from the start what I was hoping would happen. And I expect you to yell at me when I deserve it, as I did this morning."

Sophie bit her lip and Ian felt his insides tighten. He was shocked anew at how simple it was for her to arouse him. "You mean asked me about what you said earlier? About Derek in our bed?"

Ian had to close his eyes and take a deep breath at the shot of pure desire that arced down his spine at Sophie's words. He nodded and opened his eyes. "Yes. That was always what I wanted Sophie, how I envisioned our life together, the three of us."

Sophie shook her head. "But Derek doesn't want me, Ian, not like you do. Don't make him do something he…he doesn't want." Her hesitation showed her insecurity and Ian cursed both his and Derek's clumsy handling of this situation. His own clumsiness especially—he should have told her before they were even married and given her the chance to say no. He realized with sudden clarity that he hadn't told her for that very reason. He hadn't been willing to risk losing her. But to have her find out by overhearing a shouting match between him and Derek was unforgivable.

"I'm so sorry, Sophie. So sorry I didn't tell you before. This is not the way I wanted to introduce you to the idea."

Sophie had turned away, and Ian saw her wringing her hands in her lap. "So, I was for you and Derek, then?" She hung her head. "You didn't really want me, did you?"

Ian grabbed her by the shoulders and hauled her over into his lap. He buried his lips in her hair and spoke softly but fervently. "Don't believe that, Sophie. God, I've been such a fool and I've hurt you, which I swore never to do. I've always wanted you. From the minute the sunbeam hit your shining hair and sparkling eyes, I've wanted you."

Sophie was shaking. "What are you talking about?" she whispered, her hands tentatively moving to rest against his chest.

"That first morning, in the drawing room, when you looked up to greet me. The sun came through the window and you were beautiful. I began to want you then. I was thrilled that I wanted to fuck the woman I was going to marry."

Sophie collapsed against him. "Oh, Ian," she choked out. "You are just awful."

Ian hugged her close, hating himself for her tears and wishing he could make everything perfect. "Awfully wonderful?" he teased.

Sophie nodded, sniffing. "That too."

Ian held her for a few minutes, stroking her hair and back and Sophie settled into his lap, her arms around his neck, her fingers caressing the hair on his nape. It sent shivers along his skin, and he felt his cock grow hard. He wanted to take her here, in her garden, where she was so natural, so much a part of what she was creating. He wanted to reassure her in the only way he knew that he cared for and desired her. He began to touch her with the intent to arouse rather than to soothe. When he heard her breath catch against his shoulder he knew he'd succeeded.

Before he made love to her, however, he wanted to sort out the situation with Derek. "Sophie," he said quietly. She answered with a small hum as she arched her back into his caresses. "Do you think that someday you might welcome Derek in our bed?"

Sophie stilled, and it seemed as if the air had left the garden. "I don't know, Ian," she finally said. Her voice was quiet and breathless. Ian recognized the desire in it. She may not realize it, but she wanted what he was offering. "I don't know what that means."

Ian took a moment to adjust their positions. He set Sophie off his lap and moved back about a foot to lean against a tree. Sophie followed on her knees, holding his hand. When he was settled against the trunk he pulled her over and helped her straddle his lap. She tried to remain on her knees, not touching him, but Ian wanted her as close as possible. He grabbed her hips and lowered her so the damp heat of her cunt covered his hard cock through their clothes. Sophie let out a little mew of pleasure with a catch on the end that made heat surge through Ian's cock, and he felt it move against her. She involuntarily thrust her hips down slightly and Ian let his head fall back against the tree trunk in pleasure.

When he spoke he could hear the jagged edge of arousal in his words. "I want to fuck you with Derek, Sophie. Both of us, at the same time."

Sophie was breathing hard. "But, how? I couldn't possibly, Ian. You're too big for both of you to fit in there."

Ian laughed weakly and lifted his head to look at her. She was flushed and there was perspiration on her forehead and lip. She had a smudge of dirt across her cheek that he inexplicably wanted to lick off. "Remember last night, Sophie? I fucked you in the ass. With Derek, one of us would go in your ass, and one of us would fuck your sweet cunt."

"Oh my God," Sophie whispered. She began to shake her head as her eyes widened. "I don't...I mean, would that hurt?"

Ian pulled her down so that he could nuzzle her neck. "Did it hurt when I fucked you last night, Sophie?" he whispered. "When I came deep in your ass?" Sophie moaned in answer. "That's how it will feel, but better, because one of us will be filling your cunt as well. Both those pleasures, Sophie, at the same time."

"Ian," she moaned, lowering her head to bite his ear. He shuddered.

"I've got to fuck you, Sophie. Now." Ian could hear his own desperation as he began yanking her skirts out of the way completely. He had to be a part of her and make her a part of him. He reached back and undid the ties on her dress and pulled it off her shoulders to pool in the crook of her arm. She sat astride him, her eyes slumberous, and as he watched she licked her lips. His fingers fumbled on the front tie of her chemise for a moment, but he managed to get it open and pull her chemise down as well. The motion was stopped by her hands over her breasts.

"Ian!" she cried out in a frantic whisper. "We're in the garden! Mr. Timmins."

Ian laughed. "Now you remember Mr. Timmins?" He shook his head and pulled her hands away. "I gave him the afternoon off."

Sophie put her hands back again. "You mean you planned to fuck me when you came out here?" Indignation was creeping into her voice. "Even though you knew I was angry at you?"

With a sigh Ian leaned over and kissed the soft, smooth upper curve of her breast pressing out above her hand. "I always plan to fuck you, Sophie, if you'll let me. Everywhere we are. I can't be sorry for that."

"What?" she squeaked. "Ian, that's scandalous!"

Ian couldn't stop his snort of laughter. "And for some reason you thought a man who had a wife and a male lover wasn't scandalous?"

Sophie looked surprised for a moment and then burst out laughing. "That is a very good point, Ian." She removed her hands to cup his face. "I always want to fuck you, too." Her whisper was shy, as if she were revealing a great secret.

Ian grinned at her conspiratorially. "Good. Keep that thought." He pulled her chemise down to reveal her tempting, freckled breasts. God, how he loved them. He leaned over and sucked a tender nipple into his mouth.

Sophie gasped as Ian took her nipple into his mouth. She was shocked and excited by what they were doing. The warm air on her exposed breasts combined with the suction and wet heat of his mouth hardened her nipples painfully. She gripped Ian's head, her fingers tangled in his soft, fine hair, and without thinking she moved him to the other breast, to lave her neglected, aching tip there. Ian breathed deeply and took her nipple hungrily, sucking and licking. His tongue swirled over the hard nub, and then flicked it mercilessly. Sophie moaned at the sensation.

Ian's hands went between her spread legs and Sophie heard a ripping sound. His fingers touched her weeping center and Sophie knew he'd torn her drawers to get to her.

He pulled off her breast and spoke, his mouth still so close his breath tortured the wet, aroused nipple. "Don't wear these anymore, Sophie." His voice was low, ragged and it sent a wave of desire crashing through her. She did this to him. He may love and want Derek, but he wanted Sophie as well. She tried to focus on what he was saying. "I want to know that no matter where we are I could pull you aside and thrust into you without any impediment."

"Ian," she moaned. God, he said the most wicked things, and she loved it. And she'd do it, too, she'd do as he asked and stop wearing her drawers so he could fuck her whenever he wanted. A little voice in the back of her head added, *whenever I want*, and Sophie thrilled to the knowledge that it was true, he'd fuck her at her command.

Ian brushed his fingers along her damp nether lips and she could feel the slick wetness as he spread it around. He delved into her folds and Sophie jerked her hips in response, begging him without words to touch her on her tight, throbbing clitoris. He obliged, but the touch was soft and fleeting. She cried out in disbelief, and Ian's laughter was hot and suggestive.

"Do you need something, Sophie?" he whispered. "Do you need me to touch you here?" He pressed his finger against the ache, making her shudder in pleasure. Before she could move, before she could work on his finger to a climax, he pulled back again. Sophie growled and he laughed. "Tell me, Sophie," he tempted. "Tell me what you want."

"Make me come, Ian," she demanded in a shaky voice. "Do what you want, but make me come."

"Sophie," he ground out, and he pushed her up so he could free his cock. Sophie pulled her skirts out of the way so she could watch. His cock was beautiful, long and thick and hard. The veins in the side throbbed to the same beat she felt in her sex, and she wanted them to make music together. Ian barely had his cock out before Sophie was trying to lower herself onto it.

"You are as eager for it as I am, aren't you?" Ian murmured as he guided her hips down with one hand and she felt the tip of his smooth, firm head part her folds. She watched as he brushed the tip along her slick, swollen lips, dipping into the creases, coating it with her cream. With each brush of his cock against her his breathing grew more ragged. He was barely holding on to his control, and Sophie loved it. She began to undulate her hips, caressing him with her lips, kissing him with her cunt. Ian groaned. He reached with the fingers of both hands and gently parted her so her inner lips were exposed. When she continued her movements and caressed him with that tender inner flesh it was her turn to groan.

"Fuck me, Sophie," he told her roughly. "Let me watch you take my cock, all of it."

Sophie didn't hesitate. She reached down and grasped his shaft, moving him to her opening. She lowered herself and caught the head there, then let go to grab his shoulders for leverage. They were both breathing heavily. She closed her eyes and tightened around the plump, hot tip of his cock sitting just inside her. Ian cursed and she smiled, savoring the feel of him.

"Damn it," he growled, "fuck me."

Sophie opened her eyes to look at him. He was gorgeous. His hair was mussed from her hands, his cheeks flushed, his lips red and wet from suckling her. His look was thunderous, full of potent male desire, and Sophie wanted him as she had never wanted him before. He was hers. At least part of him. The unwanted thought brought Derek to mind, and an image of the three of them fucking as Ian had described flashed through her head. The thought made her cunt cream around Ian, and he gasped.

"Sophie," he cried out raggedly.

Sophie leaned down. "Kiss me, Ian. Kiss me while I make you mine."

"Yes," Ian said on a breath, and then he was kissing her. She lowered herself down on his magnificent cock as his tongue danced heatedly with hers, his mouth devouring her.

He was heaven inside her. She hadn't realized how she'd been aching inside, empty, until he was filling her with his heat and hardness. She swiveled her hips slightly, trying to take more of him and he groaned deeply in her mouth. When Sophie felt him hit that spot inside her she cried out.

Ian broke their kiss with a gasping breath. "Yes, there, ride it there, sweeting. Come apart for me."

Sophie thrust her hips, grinding on Ian's cock without lifting off it. It was so good Sophie felt tears prick the back of her eyes. Sophie kept grinding and Ian's hands gripped her hips hard, his roughness only adding to her pleasure. His head had fallen back on the tree again, and his eyes were closed. His face was pinched in concentration and Sophie knew he was feeling every move she made as intensely as she was. Suddenly he opened his eyes and one of his thumbs moved to rub her aroused clitoris and Sophie shrieked with the pleasure as she ground down on his cock.

"That's right, Sophie," Ian encouraged her, his voice thick with lust. "Fuck me, baby. Fuck me hard and tight. I want to feel you come, Sophie."

The feel of Ian's hard cock rubbing her inside so deliciously, his thumb pressing, pressing where she ached most for relief, and his hot, hungry eyes watching her pushed Sophie over the edge. She began to shiver, and the muscles inside her quivered around his cock as her orgasm raced to claim her.

"Yes, baby, yes," he whispered, eager, approving. "Like that, take it like that."

Sophie climaxed at the sound of his voice. She cried out his name and rocked against him, brushing his cock over that glorious spot that was sending pleasure in waves through her body. Ian kept the pressure of his thumb on her the whole time, whispering encouragement and wicked approval and Sophie spiraled in the pleasure.

When she collapsed against him, Ian held her tight. It took a minute for her to realize he was still hard inside her.

"Ian?" she asked, confused.

"I want more, Sophie," he whispered. "I'm not done with you yet."

His words were temptation itself. Yes, more, Sophie wanted more as well. Her body still clutching his in receding waves, Sophie sat up on him again. The movement made them both moan.

Ian reached out a hand and traced Sophie's mouth with a shaking finger. "I meant what I said earlier, Sophie. You are the most precious, the most exotic flower in this garden." She touched the tip of her tongue to the pad of his finger and watched him shiver at the caress. "Your lips are as soft as rose petals," Ian continued in a whisper. With surprise Sophie felt Ian pull out of her. Then the fingers of his other hand were on her nether lips. "Soft," he murmured tracing the lips of her mouth and her sex at the same time. Sophie was shocked at the heat that coursed through her. "Wet, like petals in the rain," Ian said, and dipped a finger into her mouth at the same time he pressed one inside her. Sophie gasped at the dual sensations. She sucked the tip of his finger as she clenched her inner muscles around the invader in her cunt. Ian's eyes lost focus for a moment before he pulled both fingers away. "Bloom for me, Sophie. I want to feel those petal-soft lips. You've kissed me with these," he traced his finger through her creamy folds, "now kiss me with these." He raised his hand and traced her mouth with the same finger he'd used below, leaving the taste and musk of her climax on her lips. Sophie gasped and Ian touched the tip of her tongue with his damp finger. It tasted warm and slightly sweet, and something else. Something that was different from Ian's taste. Her heart raced.

Sophie leaned in to kiss him, but Ian pulled back with a smile. "No, Sophie. I don't want your kiss there. I want it here." Ian took her hand and laid it on top of his cock, still hot and damp with her cream. She looked at Ian with wide eyes. He wanted her to suck him now, when he'd been inside her? She bit her lip and Ian's eyes darkened. He slid out from under her and stood up, his back against the tree. "Kiss me, Sophie," he whispered and he guided his cock to her mouth.

Sophie slid on her knees closer to Ian as she opened her mouth to take him, her mouth watering for the taste of him mixed with her own essence. Unfortunately a twig happened to be in the way and Sophie gasped and jerked back as it dug into her knee. "Ow!"

Ian immediately grabbed her shoulders to steady her. "Are you all right?"

Sophie laughed breathlessly. "Yes, I'll be fine." She grinned ruefully at Ian. "Well, I've certainly ruined the moment."

Ian grinned as he started to lower his back along the tree. "That was a bad idea, I'm—"

Sophie cut off his words by quickly leaning her hands on his thighs to stop him and taking his still-hard cock into her mouth.

"Christ," Ian groaned as he leaned back again.

Sophie couldn't answer. She tasted the salty flavor of the cum leaking from his tip as it seasoned the sweetness of her own cream. She sucked the plump, generous head of his cock softly, running her tongue over its contours. When she hit the slightly raised bump on the underside of his shaft, just below the crown, Ian groaned deeply. Sophie kept her tongue there, gently swirling it around and around.

"God, Sophie," Ian gasped as he shuddered with pleasure. "I love this, I love it when you do this." Sophie hummed with pleasure and grasped the base of his cock, angling it so she could take more in her mouth. "Tell me," Ian said roughly. "Tell me how it tastes, why it pleases you."

Sophie slowly pulled off his cock, giving the juicy head one last suck before letting go. Ian groaned and Sophie smiled. She was glad Ian had let her come already. She was able to concentrate on giving him pleasure now.

"Your cock is beautiful, Ian," she told him softly. She ran her finger up and down his shaft with a featherlight touch and watched it quiver in response. "The skin is so soft." She leaned in and rubbed her cheek along the shaft as she held it to her face with one hand. It was damp and hot. She thought she heard Ian whimper. Then she wrapped her hand around it and squeezed gently. Ian's breathing was ragged. "But under the softness is this glorious hardness, made for fucking, for loving."

"You, Sophie," Ian whispered. "Made for loving you."

Sophie's heart stuttered for a moment, and then she realized he meant making love, not being in love. Still, she refused to let it hurt her. It was enough. Ian liked her, desired her, and it was enough.

"And Derek," she couldn't resist adding, and then cursed herself. But Ian didn't take offense.

"Yes, and Derek," he whispered, and when Sophie looked up at him his face was stark with hunger. The sight tightened Sophie's insides and made that marvelous throbbing beat begin within her again.

"It tastes good, Ian," she whispered, watching him. His look became wild and his lips parted as he began to pant. "You taste salty and I taste sweet, and it's good together."

"Sophie," he rasped, grabbing a handful of her hair and gently but firmly pulling her mouth back to his cock. Sophie licked the end first, catching the drops leaking from him and Ian's hips jerked, fucking his cock into her mouth. She took it with a contented sigh. "That's it, Sophie," he praised her, "suck it like that, as if it's a delicacy to savor."

Sophie loved Ian with her mouth for the next few minutes. She sucked, and took as much of his length in her mouth as she could. But she also licked up and down the shaft and placed teasing little nibbling kisses along it, which made Ian groan and shake. She loved to suck the plump head. It was just the right size for her mouth, a soft, salty treat. Ian clearly enjoyed it as well, almost too much. When she was deliriously sucking on it yet again Ian pulled her off.

"Enough." His voice was low and hoarse and Sophie realized how close he was to losing control. The thought sent savage pleasure through her. Surely Derek couldn't do it better than she. "Move back," he ordered as he lowered himself to his knees, "and turn around."

Sophie did as he commanded. She felt Ian move in close behind her and her cunt clenched in anticipation. While she'd been sucking him she'd pulled her dress back up to her shoulders so she could move her arms to touch him. Ian now pushed it back down, pulling it off her arms. He pushed the dress to her waist. "Bend over," he told her roughly, "on your hands and knees."

Sophie's breath was coming in gasps. She was ready to come just from his orders. She leaned over and braced her hands on the ground. Ian spread her legs wider and pushed her skirt up around her waist. Then she felt a jerk and heard more ripping.

"These have to come off," Ian murmured as he tore her drawers off completely. "I want to feel that ass pumping back against me when I'm fucking you." Sophie shivered at his words and his rough treatment. She felt irresistible, wild and free, fucking Ian in the sun, the breeze a breath on her skin. She wasn't scared of his passion, she reveled in it. Reveled in the control he exerted over himself and her.

When her drawers lay in tatters around her, Ian spread the cheeks of her ass and she knew he was looking at her intimately. She spread her legs like a wanton and bent her arms, lowering herself further to the ground, offering herself without shame.

"Sophie, Christ yes," Ian moaned. "You want it, you want it so much." He moved in behind her and thrust gently, his cock spearing into her to half its length. Sophie moaned at the searing heat of the erotic impalement. She'd never thought she could enjoy this, never, yet Ian had made her want it, every time. Would it be like this with Derek? Sophie gasped at the traitorous thought even as she felt a gush of cream bathe her cunt and Ian's cock there.

"Yes," Ian murmured, as if in answer to her question, and Sophie tightened on him in response.

"Sophie, I'm sorry, I'm sorry," Ian gasped, "I can't wait. God, you're so good, darling, you feel so good." He was fucking into her hard and deep, and Sophie was riding his cock, thrusting back on him in a wild, furious fuck, wilder than they'd ever been before. Sophie heard her own gasps and moans and grunts, and didn't even feel embarrassed by them. She wanted to scream each time he slid over that sensitive spot, to shout out how wonderful Ian felt inside her. Ian was just as loud in his pleasure behind her, his vaunted control lost in the throes of their passion.

"Sophie," he shouted and she felt him ram home, deep and hard, and then she felt his cock jerk and the hot wash of his cum bathing her inside. It was enough, it was more than enough, to push her into another orgasm, pleasure so profound that Sophie was unable to speak at all as wave after wave washed over her.

When it was over Sophie was dazed. She realized that she was lying on the ground, her head cradled on Ian's shoulder where he now lay next to her. He was breathing heavily, she could feel his chest rising and falling, the hot puffs of his labored breaths in her hair. Ian's arms held her tight and Sophie felt the warmth of belonging with him, a belonging she had never felt before in her life.

"Ian, I …" She wanted to tell him she loved him, but the words stuck in her throat. What if he didn't want her love? What if it ruined the relationship they had now? He loved Derek, he'd told her that. He didn't want or need Sophie's love.

Ian lifted his head and looked down at her, puzzled. "What?" he asked softly, and he brushed a stray curl from her forehead. The caress was so intimate, so tender, that Sophie forced herself to sit up before she blurted out her feelings.

"Why am I nearly naked, and you are nearly fully clothed?" she asked instead, her voice unsteady. She began to fumble with her dress, trying to put her shaking arms in the sleeves. Ian sat up next to her with a wicked grin and started to help her.

"Because I like it. I like to strip my lovers while I remain clothed." He shrugged. "I just like it. I can't explain why."

Sophie turned her back quickly so he wouldn't see the tears in her eyes. His lovers! He'd included her in the same category as Derek. Surely that meant he did feel something for her? She bit her lip and the sting helped her regain her composure. "Would you tie me up?" she asked. She heard Ian choke behind her, so she turned to look at him in concern. "Are you all right?"

Ian laughed, but Sophie wasn't sure why. At least not until he leaned in and whispered in her ear.

"I would love to tie you up, Sophie." He ran a finger down her spine through the back of her open dress. "And I'll do up your dress, too."

Sophie gulped. "Ian," she squeaked. He just laughed again, making Sophie imagine all the things he might do to her if she were tied up. The thought should frighten her, but instead she felt herself growing hot and tight with arousal. She was shocked again at how she could want Ian so quickly after they'd just made love.

Ian leaned in and kissed her shoulder and her breath hitched. "Is there a rose named Sophie?" he asked softly, his hands still on the ties of her dress.

Sophie swallowed. "I…I'm not sure."

Ian pulled back and began to do her ties. "Surely in all of England there is a rose named Sophie, as fair as you."

Sophie smiled gently. "You're not going to burst into iambic pentameter again, are you?"

Ian made a disgruntled sound behind her. "I knew my 'Ode to Sophie's Nipples' was woefully unappreciated."

Sophie couldn't stop her laughter. "Derek's 'Ode to Sophie's Execrable Chess Playing' was far more amusing."

Ian's hands had gone still again. "So you like him, don't you?" She couldn't miss the hope in his voice.

"Yes, Ian, I like him," she answered softly. It was true. Without her realizing it Derek had become an important part of her new life.

"It's a start, then," he replied before going back to her ties. "I'm not going to do this up properly," he told her matter-of-factly. "For one, I'm not sure how. Undoing it is much easier. And second, I'm planning on spiriting you up to our room and making love to you several more times, so there's no reason to make more work for myself once we're up there."

"Ian Witherspoon!" Sophie cried out in mock outrage, but she ruined the effect by laughing. "Could you at least do it up enough so that I don't expose myself to Montague?"

Ian nipped the nape of her neck and Sophie shrieked, swatting blindly at him behind her. Ian's laughter rang out in the garden. "Saucy wench," he grumbled playfully. "As if I'd let you expose yourself to anyone."

Not even Derek, Sophie almost blurted out. But she managed to rein in her unruly tongue. She wasn't ready to think about what Ian wanted. Not yet. For now, she wanted to enjoy having him all to herself for a while.

* * * * *

The following morning Sophie walked Ian to the door as he was leaving. Montague and the footmen had mysteriously disappeared in order, Sophie suspected, to give her and Ian time for a private goodbye.

Ian had spent most of yesterday afternoon in Sophie's bed after delivering his heartfelt apology and more flowers—a roomful of flowers that she couldn't resist. She knew that he'd spent most of the night in Derek's bed. She supposed she should be jealous, but honestly he'd loved her so well in the afternoon all she'd wanted to do last night was sleep. And Derek had been so pleasant at breakfast this morning it was worth it. Sophie had been surprised that she felt almost no embarrassment around Derek after overhearing him and Ian arguing about her yesterday. She wasn't sure what that meant.

"You'll be all right?" Ian asked for the umpteenth time, and Sophie smiled at him sweetly.

"Of course, Ian, I'll be fine. Derek is here, and Montague and a houseful of other servants as well. I'll be perfectly fine." She bumped her hip against his as they walked slowly arm in arm. "But I shall miss you terribly, you know."

Ian wrapped his arm around her waist tighter. "I shall miss you too. I don't relish a night sleeping alone."

Sophie laughed. "I see. So you're worried about carnal deprivation."

Ian laughed. "Hardly. Between you and Derek, I need the rest." He talked about sex with Derek as if it was perfectly normal, and Sophie supposed it was, for them. She was actually relieved Ian had made it so casual and straightforward. It would have been impossible to pretend he and Derek were anything but lovers, and the pretense would have made her so uncomfortable.

"Well, I don't know about Derek, but you, sir, are wearing me out," Sophie teased as she stopped and turned to him. She smoothed the collar of his jacket, suddenly nervous about his leaving. "This will be the first night since we were married that we'll be apart."

"I wasn't with you last night," Ian said quietly. "I'm sorry. I should have been. I—"

Sophie placed a finger against his lips to stop him. "You were with me. I knew you were close, and even that, if I needed you, I could go and get you in Derek's room. I felt perfectly safe. There's no need to apologize."

"What will you do while I'm gone?" Ian kissed her finger and swept a stray curl off her cheek.

"Oh I daresay I shall indulge all my wildest sexual fantasies with the costermonger, redecorate your study and have a nude portrait painted."

Ian reared back in horror. "My study? What are you going to do to my study?"

Sophie burst out laughing. "I was teasing you, Ian. I'm not going to touch one single threadbare rug or worn-out chair, I promise."

"You idiot, I'm more interested in the nude painting. Can we hang it directly across from the entryway? I want everyone to see it first thing when Montague opens the door." Derek strolled casually out of the drawing room to their right, startling Sophie. He was always so quiet, especially for a big man. He was so graceful he made Sophie feel like a clumsy schoolgirl. Derek waggled his eyebrows. "And what is this about the costermonger? I had no idea he fulfilled the lewd fantasies of not-so-innocent ladies."

"Well, I guess you don't know everything about everything," Sophie said with a superior sniff. "If I told you all I knew about the butcher, you'd have an apoplexy."

Derek laughed and Sophie felt a thrill of victory. She was getting rather good at making him laugh.

"I concede that I know very little about a little of everything," he said with a smile, "but I don't know a lot about anything."

Sophie frowned as she puzzled that out. "Is that a riddle that requires coffee in the morning? Because I've not even had my tea."

Derek laughed again, and Ian joined him as he hugged Sophie. She wrapped her arms around him tightly, reluctant to let go because then he would leave. *He's coming back, he's coming back.* She squeezed her eyes shut to stop the sting of tears.

"Here now, Sophie, don't cry," Ian whispered to her, kissing her cheek. "I'll return, love, before you know it." He ran his thumb along the curve of her cheek. "Open your beautiful eyes, Sophie." She did and his beloved face was smiling softly at her. "Not even the king himself could keep me from you, darling, for more than one night." He looked over her shoulder. "And Derek will be here to keep you company, won't you, Derek?"

"Today? Do I have to keep her company all day? I was going to Tattersall's to look at a new filly."

Ian frowned at him, and Sophie smiled as she rubbed her nose in his coat, soaking up his delicious smell. "Well, take Sophie with you."

Sophie peeked around her shoulder and giggled at the look on Derek's face. "A woman at Tatt's?" Derek exclaimed. "Are you mad?" He took the sting out of his words by winking conspiratorially at Sophie.

"Derek—" Ian sounded angry and Sophie interrupted him.

"Oh Ian, he's teasing. I'm crying because I'm going to miss my new husband, not because I'm worried. Well, perhaps I'm a little worried. You are leaving me with Derek, after all."

Derek snorted behind her. "It's a good thing I have a high opinion of myself or I'd be completely unappreciated around here."

Sophie laughed and sniffed loudly as she stepped back from Ian. "It's only because your opinion is so high, Derek, that I don't feel the need to compensate."

Derek gasped in feigned distress. "Ian, she wounds me!" He spun around and pretended to look over his shoulder at his back. "Quick, look, did that rapier wit come all the way through after it pierced my heart?"

Ian sighed dramatically. "Perhaps I shouldn't leave you two alone. You cannot be trusted to behave yourselves."

"I didn't do anything," they both chorused at the same time, and Sophie went into peals of laughter while Derek smiled.

"Come, kiss your bride goodbye, Ian. The sooner you leave, the sooner you'll come back to us."

Sophie felt her heart lurch at Derek's words. It was the first time he had conceded any ownership in Ian to Sophie. She got a lump in her throat and wanted to throw her arms around him in gratitude. Instead she threw her arms around Ian and kissed him. He quickly took control and the kiss was as thorough as it was demanding, as satisfying as it was arousing. By the time he pulled slowly away with a nip on her lower lip, Sophie was clinging limply to him.

"Not fair," she whispered. "You are leaving and now I am aching for you already. You are a cruel husband." She placed her hands on his chest and laid her cheek between them, listening to his rapid heartbeat. He was not unaffected by their kiss.

"I merely want to make sure you are thinking of me when the costermonger comes to call," Ian teased as he stroked a hand down Sophie's spine.

His remark made her lean back and smile at him. "I shall close my eyes and think of you and England."

Ian chuckled softly. "Oh, I do adore you, Sophie." He kissed her nose and turned to Derek, so he didn't see the absolute joy she felt radiating from her face. He adored her. That was close to love, wasn't it?

"Goodbye, Derek. I shall see you day after tomorrow. No later than Thursday." Ian held out his hand around Sophie, who was still loosely in his embrace, and Derek took it slowly.

Sophie was startled and hurt on Derek's behalf. "Aren't you going to kiss him goodbye?" she exclaimed. Both men looked at her in surprise.

"I wasn't sure how you'd feel about that," Ian said slowly.

Sophie pulled completely out of his arms and rolled her eyes. "Well, it isn't as if I don't know you two are lovers, now is it? And I've certainly never said anything to indicate that was a problem for me, have I? I'd like to think that I'd be no more affected by watching you kiss Derek than Derek is watching you kiss me."

Ian hesitated, but Derek stepped over to him and pulled his jacket lapel so Ian faced him. Derek placed a hand on Ian's cheek and leaned down and kissed him on the lips. It wasn't a quick kiss, but a lingering one, and Ian's arms snaked around Derek, one going up so he could bury his hand in Derek's thick, dark hair. Sophie could see Ian open his mouth and Derek did the same. She could see their tongues glide along one another before their lips locked. It affected her far more, and in a far different way, than she expected. She was shocked by the intensity of the desire that swept through her as she watched the two men kiss. It was the most arousing thing she had ever seen, even though they were both clothed. Was it because she knew what they wanted? Knew that she could see more than this if she agreed to let Derek share their bed?

They pulled apart and Derek ran his hand down Ian's cheek to his jaw. He rubbed his thumb along Ian's lower lip sensuously while he bit his own plump lip. "Goodbye," he finally whispered. Ian just pulled his head down again until he could lay his forehead against Derek's, then he let go.

Ian cleared his throat and turned to Sophie again. She could hardly speak over the pounding of her pulse in her throat. Her nipples were hard and aroused, her mound wet and throbbing. She tried to hide her reaction from the two men, but the look Derek gave her made it clear he knew. It was her turn to clear her throat. "Well, then. Goodbye, darling. You'd better leave now or you'll never get there before nightfall with all the traffic out of the city." She leaned in and kissed Ian on the cheek quickly. His look spoke volumes as well.

"We'll talk about this when I get home." Ian moved briskly to the door. "Montague!" he called, and the butler materialized from the other end of the foyer. "Keep an eye on things here while I'm gone, Montague. I shall be home no later than Thursday. If something important comes up, bring it to Mr. Knightly's attention."

"Very good, sir," Montague said as he opened the door. Ian stood silhouetted in the morning light for a moment as he looked back at Sophie and Derek. Then he turned and bounded down the steps to the carriage. Sophie's heart gave a small lurch as Montague closed the door with a soft thud.

Chapter Fifteen

ဆ

He didn't make it all the way to Tattersall's before guilt had him turning around and heading for home. Damn Sophie and her sense of humor, and the odd glint of defensive vulnerability in her twinkling amber eyes. God damn the fact that he was actually starting to like her. He sighed. The truth was an afternoon defeating her at chess and winning ludicrous amounts of money from her sounded infinitely better than an afternoon at Tattersall's. He didn't need another horse anyway, damn it.

He wouldn't love her. He refused. Loving someone was too dangerous. He'd never meant to love Ian. Ian had been safe when Derek had sought him out that day so long ago. A man who couldn't, wouldn't, die. Derek had never planned on Ian becoming the center of his universe, it just happened. And loving Ian had been so wonderful, Derek had been vulnerable. Then he loved Dolores—perhaps not like he loved Ian, but he'd loved her all the same. And she'd died, horribly, like so many others in Derek's life. He wouldn't go through that again, couldn't. There was nothing he could do about loving Ian, but by God he could protect himself from Sophie. He refused to love her. But liking her wasn't love. They were going to be living with one another for a good, long time. It would certainly make life more bearable if he and Sophie were at least friends.

Derek was startled to find himself home already. Once a man started that kind of self-reflection it was hard to stop. He'd been doing far too much of it lately. It wasn't healthy. It implied that he was a deep kind of fellow with myriad buried emotions and motivations. Derek prided himself on being exactly the man he projected to the world. There was no pretense in him, no hidden agendas. What need had a man like that for self-indulgent self-reflection? Derek didn't need it, not at all. He dismounted and climbed the front stoop indignantly. This was all Sophie's fault. Perhaps he didn't like her as much as he thought.

Montague opened the door before he reached the last step. "Good morning, Mr. Knightly."

At his tone, Derek looked at him sharply. "I've only returned because I realized that I do not need a new horse. I feel a great deal of loyalty to Hunter and wouldn't want to hurt his feelings by bringing a newcomer into his stables."

"Of course, Mr. Knightly. Horses are well-known for their extreme sensitivity and jealousy."

Derek narrowed his eyes at Montague dangerously. "Are you mocking me?"

Montague merely lifted his brows.

Derek let it drop. "Hmm," was all he said. He handed the butler his hat and gloves. "Where is Mrs. Witherspoon?" He started walking down the hallway to the study before Montague could answer. It only took the butler a moment to hand off his things to a footman and follow.

"Mrs. Witherspoon is in the drawing room—" he began and Derek cut him off.

"Splendid. I'm famished. Send in some kind of tray, would you?"

"Mr. Knightly." Montague's voice was firm and Derek slowed down to look over his shoulder inquiringly. "Mrs. Witherspoon's brother came to call—a Mr. Harold Middleton."

Derek immediately changed course, turning and heading in the opposite direction. "Why didn't you say so?" he said irritably. "Is he still here?" Chances were good that the son was as bad as the father. Sophie had never mentioned a brother, not once that Derek could remember. That did not bode well.

"Yes," Montague said, diverting his course to follow Derek once again. "There is also a problem with the roof that was only brought to my attention this morning. There is some work that needs to be done immediately, but it will be extensive and requires your approval."

Derek was taken aback. He'd never been consulted about any work around their townhouse before. He found he rather liked it. "Well, if it must be fixed, then do so. As soon as I've checked on Sophie I shall head out there and see what the problem is. Have you mentioned it to Gibbons?"

"Yes sir. He directed me to you. If you approve the work, you will need to sign a work order. I believe he has it all in order."

"Excellent. Now tell me—" He stopped abruptly at a noise coming from the drawing room still several doors down. The door was closed, muffling the sound, but it set the hair on Derek's nape prickling. He ignored Montague and quickened his pace. The noise came again and he ran the last few steps. That was Sophie's voice crying out.

* * * * *

Sophie nearly threw up when Montague informed her Harold was here. How had he found her? When had he returned? She had to sit down for a moment when she realized neither Ian nor Derek was here. She would have to see Harold by herself. As she walked to the drawing room she felt as she imagined a prisoner on her way to the gallows felt. Her life here was dying a slow death with each step. He was here. He had infected her perfect home and her perfect life, and it would sicken and die as her childhood had.

She stopped and leaned against the hallway wall with a hand on her heart to slow its pounding. Deep breaths, in and out, and again, in and out. *He can't touch me here. He can't touch me here. I hate him. I hate him. I hate him.* Sophie was reduced to the old chant as she resumed walking toward the drawing room. The footman standing outside the room gave her an odd look before he opened the door. Clearly he'd seen her stop back there in the hall. She sent him a tremulous smile as she passed him, deliberately looking down at the carpet so as not to have to look at Harold yet.

"Good morning, Sophia." Harold's voice cut harshly through the stale air of the little-used room. It made Sophie's back twitch reflexively in self-defense.

"Harold," she said quietly, still not looking at him as she moved to place the sofa between her and Harold.

"Are you so ashamed of what you've done you cannot even look at me?" he said indignantly.

Sophie was so incredulous she couldn't prevent her head from jerking up and she stared at him. Her, embarrassed? It should be Harold who was embarrassed, not she. Ian had taught her that. She'd always known what Harold did to her was wrong, but now she knew how wrong, how horrible, how awful. But his face was the same as always, accusatory, hateful, gleefully evil.

"You should be ashamed, you ungrateful girl. Sneaking off while I was away to marry that horrendously perverted Witherspoon. Father said you voiced nary a protest and practically threw yourself at him when you arrived here."

Harold stalked toward her and Sophie unconsciously shrank away from him. He paid her no mind, instead going past her to the door and shutting it firmly. He spun around to confront her and Sophie assessed him dispassionately. He was still trim and fit, his dull brown hair continuing to recede on his prominent forehead. His eyes were perpetually narrowed with meanness, his lips thin. Some might say he was not an unattractive man in his way, but to Sophie he was all that was ugly in the world. He's just a man, Sophie told herself, trying to shore up her courage. *This is my home and he cannot touch me here.*

"What do you want, Harold?" Sophie was proud of the calmness of her tone as she straightened her shoulders.

Harold stopped and stared at her long enough for Sophie to get uncomfortable and nervous once again. She began to wring her hands and had to grip the back of the sofa to stop. Harold saw her weakness and smiled cruelly.

"How dare you speak to me like that," he said conversationally. "When I get you home I shall have to teach you obedience and meekness once again."

Sophie flinched, she couldn't help it. Harold's lessons were hard-learned. She wouldn't go through that again. She thought of Ian, and Derek, and took a deep breath to settle her nerves. She was safe here. "I am never going to your home again, Harold. This is my home now. And you are not welcome."

He stalked her slowly around the sofa, and as much as she wanted to stand her ground, Sophie couldn't. She backed away, always keeping the piece of furniture between them.

"I'm going to petition the court, Sophia. It shall be a simple thing to prove Witherspoon's cruelty to you. After all, he does keep a male lover here, in your home, and probably forces you to service him as well."

Sophie's pulse leapt in fear and her eyes widened. Could he do that? Was Ian in danger? Surely the Earl would protect him. But would he? He'd cut Ian off from the family before because of his relationship with Derek. Harold's look was calculating, so Sophie didn't know whether to believe him or not.

"If you come with me now, Sophia, there needn't be the unpleasantness of a court proceeding. Your husband's perfidy need never be revealed." He began to walk again, and again Sophie backed away from him. "He could be imprisoned, Sophia. Homosexuality is a crime, you know."

"We are married." Sophie's voice was dry and reedy with fear. Ian couldn't go to prison! Surely they wouldn't throw a man in prison for loving someone?

"You and I both know that has not changed his relationship with that uncouth ox he beds. But you could protect him, Sophia. All you have to do is come home." Sophie hesitated and Harold stepped closer. She stumbled as she backed quickly away. "I'm only thinking of you, Sophia. This can't be a pleasant place for you."

"This is my home now. You must leave and never come back, Harold."

Harold retreated, much to Sophie's relief. He sidled back around the sofa until they were opposite one another. "You know I can't do that, Sophia. You are my responsibility. What kind of brother would I be if I let you stay here, suffering? What the—" Harold turned quickly to the door and Sophie followed his gaze. She let out a small scream when he suddenly lurched across the back of the sofa and grabbed her arm. "I've got you now, Sophia!" he crowed in triumph. "You should have known better than to try to get away from me."

Sophie struggled, panting with terror. She couldn't break his hold! She clawed at his hand mindlessly, barely hearing his hiss of pain as her nails scored the back of his hand. He let go and she tried to scramble away, but she was lightheaded with fear, memories crashing through her mind into one long, endless session of pain and degradation. She stumbled around the end of the sofa and screamed again as Harold suddenly loomed in front of her. With a snarl he grabbed her arm again with one hand and fisted the other in her elegantly upswept hair, pulling it ruthlessly until her head was bent at an unnatural angle.

"You filthy little whore. Fight me, will you? Are those the kinds of games your perverted new husband likes to play? Do you fight him every night before you let him fuck you? You should never have come here, Sophia. Do you remember what I promised you, if you ever told anyone, if you ever left me for someone else?"

His voice was the same terrifying whisper that haunted her nightmares. Of course she remembered. He said he'd kill anyone who tried to take her away, and if she ran, he'd kill her. Everything started to turn black as Sophie collapsed inwardly as well as physically. Harold jerked her head roughly and all Sophie could do was moan in anguish. He'd kill her now and then he'd kill Ian. She couldn't fight him, she'd never been able to fight him.

Suddenly the door flew open and Derek burst into the room. Sophie focused on him as if he were air to a drowning woman. "Derek!" she cried, and was surprised at how strong her voice was. She wasn't dying then, she wouldn't. "Derek," and this time she couldn't stop the sob in her voice, the note of complete and absolute relief that he was here, he would save her.

Derek moved so quickly even Sophie was unprepared when he suddenly appeared next to them. He was furious, his teeth clenched as a growl spilled from his lips at the same time his hand wrapped around Harold's throat. "You fucking bastard," he ground out, and Sophie saw Harold's eyes narrow as his face started to turn red. He increased the pressure on Sophie's hair, nearly pulling it out at the roots and she cried out at the pain, tears springing to her eyes and running down her cheeks.

"Let her go or I will kill you," Derek told him in a quiet, lethal voice. Sophie managed to turn enough to see his face and its very calmness was more frightening than the fury that had been there moments before. She didn't doubt for one moment that he meant it, and she cried harder. She cried not for the pain, but for this man who would protect her even though he didn't like her, for Ian, who cared for her and wanted to protect her from everything, for Montague hovering in the door, worry etching his features, for Thomas and Peter, the two footmen who flanked Montague in the doorway, for this house, this life, this sanctuary. She cried because for the first time in her life she felt safe and loved, and because she knew she would never be afraid again.

Harold's hand released her hair abruptly and she fell back, tripping over the corner of the sofa to fall in an undignified heap on the floor. Rather than soothing Derek, her freedom seemed to kindle his rage. He shook Harold by the throat effortlessly as if he was some macabre doll, and Sophie felt her bile rise. Derek threw Harold into the wall and the smaller man's shoulder hit with a resounding thud, the side of his head connecting with a crack against the delicate picture hanging there. The picture fell and shattered and Harold stumbled upright with a snarl.

"You'll regret that," Harold said, and his voice no longer had the power to frighten Sophie. Derek started for him again, his fist raised, and Harold retreated toward the door with a curl of his lip. "I won't lower myself to brawl with you. But I shall be back."

"Montague, see that this rat is removed from the premises. He is barred from this house, do you understand? He is never to set foot here again."

"Very good, Mr. Knightly," Montague replied, his relief evident. He motioned the two footmen over and they grabbed Harold by the arms. He tried to shake them free, but they dragged him from the room.

Derek stood with his back to her. Sophie began to tremble. Her hands shook so badly she couldn't stand. She heard a whimper and covered her mouth when she realized it came from her. Derek spun around to face her at the sound. For one endless moment he stood and stared at her, his face a frozen mask. Sophie was cold and her trembling became violent shivers that shook her whole body.

"Sophie," Derek said quietly, and the kindness and compassion in his voice were her undoing. The tears that had slowly been running down her face became a torrent and a sob was ripped from her chest almost painfully. Once she began, she couldn't stop. "Sophie," Derek cried and he hurried over, falling to his knees next to her. He grabbed her and hauled her into his arms, onto his lap, and he rocked her like a child. "It's all right, Sophie. It's going to be all right," he murmured, and Sophie believed him.

* * * * *

Harold Middleton stalked into the library of his rented townhouse and immediately went to the sideboard to pour a generous whiskey for himself. He threw the drink back expertly and slammed the empty glass down. Only when he was done did he turn to his houseguest.

"That little bitch of a sister of mine had her husband's lover throw me out of the house. Can you believe her gall? She's forgotten who her betters are. I was gone too long. If I'd returned when I originally planned, this farce of a marriage would never have been allowed to take place." He pointed a rigid finger at the man lounging in a sunny corner of the room. "I blame you. You convinced me to stay in Europe, financing your schemes and providing for your comfort. Now how am I to get her back?"

Middleton, as far as Sir Albert Robertson was concerned, was a vile, obnoxious, perverted worm. His money, however, was a delightful asset that made the man bearable. He could almost feel sorry for the sister he'd abused all her life and was obsessed with retrieving, but she had married one of Lord Jason Randall's perverted boys, so she deserved whatever she got. Because of Randall and his friends, Robertson was forced to rely on dregs like Middleton for the very bread he ate. Well, he had been forced. Fortunately Harold Middleton was as stupid as he was pernicious and Robertson had been able to "borrow" quite a bit of Middleton's money without the other man knowing.

Robertson had been hiding in Europe for the better part of a year, after he almost killed Lord Randall in a duel when Robertson fired early. The ensuing scandal had turned him into an exile, and his creditors had fallen on his meager assets like vultures on carrion. Not only had he toadied to men like Middleton, but he'd sold his youth and vigor to wealthy old women willing to pay for it. If he had to fuck another wrinkled old crone and pretend to like it he was going to go mad. He had gone a little mad when he'd made one ill-advised foray back to England. He'd nearly killed one of Randall's friends' wives. She wouldn't have been a great loss. She too was married to a couple of his soldier boys, so Robertson figured one less slut would hardly have been noticed.

Unfortunately Randall had quite a few friends who were making Robertson's life a nightmare. He was being hunted like a common criminal. He hated Randall and his homosexual lover, Tony Richards, but their whore of a wife, Kate, had a special place in his rage. She'd been Robertson's mistress. It was the prerogative of a man to share his mistress with his friends if he so chose. He paid for the privilege. So what if his so-called friends got a little rough one night with Robertson's encouragement? She'd willingly sold her body to him, and he used it as he saw fit for his amusement. Admittedly he'd used her to try to even an old score with Randall and Richards, but again that was what he paid her for. They acted as if he'd desecrated some holy vessel.

Well, he'd learned something from his last aborted visit to England. He'd learned what the best form of revenge was. And Harold Middleton had given him the means and the opportunity. He swirled the brandy in his glass and watched it gleam in the sun as Middleton ranted for a few more minutes, getting drunker and drunker. When he felt Middleton was drunk enough to be pliable, but not so drunk he could deny responsibility should his plan go awry, Robertson stood. Middleton immediately stopped talking. Robertson sighed at how easy he'd been to train.

"My dear Middleton, you are absolutely right." And the idiot in his blinding conceit believed it. "I've said it before and I'll say it again, your dear Sophia is in mortal danger. Any man who would force her to service his homosexual lover, who would teach a young, innocent girl to enjoy the perverted pleasures of the flesh would surely not stop there. Who's to say his…pleasure won't get out of hand some night? She could be seriously injured, not to mention the mental anguish the poor thing is suffering as we speak." Robertson was disgusted at the gleam of indecent lust shining from Middleton's eye. Any man who would fuck his young sister was beyond redemption. He had to turn away to hide the nauseated curl of his lip. It took only a moment to control his reaction and he turned back. Middleton was hanging on his every word. The fool was the perfect scapegoat.

"If I may be so bold, Middleton, I believe I know how we can rescue your dear Sophia. And perhaps you'll be able to teach her a valuable lesson about defying you in the process."

Chapter Sixteen

ဢ

Ian schooled his features into a pleasant, bland mask as he was ushered into the earl's private study. His Uncle Victor had become the Earl just five years ago, while Ian was in the Peninsula. His grandfather had been a rather cold, remote man. Ian had always been nervous in his presence and happy when he was able to leave it. His Uncle Victor had been kind to him, he did remember that. He hadn't seen him often, his uncle had been away at school or too busy to see his youngest brother's small children. But Ian had a vague recollection of candies and toys and a gentle demeanor. When he'd last been ushered into his presence, however, all traces of that kind uncle were gone, replaced by another cold, remote man who issued ultimatums about dubious life choices. Ian had once again fled an earl's presence with great relief.

That had been two years ago. Ian had defied the earl's displeasure at his association with Derek in the intervening years, essentially choosing Derek over his family. Now he was married to the woman whom his family had chosen for him. He hadn't done it as a means to get back in the earl's good graces. Had it been viewed that way? If so, was Ian willing to let the misunderstanding lie in order for Sophie to be further insulated from hurt by his family's influence? Yes, yes he was. He'd made that decision when he answered the earl's summons.

"Ian, my dear boy, how good it is to see you again. You've stayed away far too long." His uncle stood up behind his desk and held out his hand. He was a tall man, bordering on gangly, but still quite distinguished with his blond hair turning a shimmering gray, his blue eyes dark and intelligent in an angular face.

Feeling like a hypocrite, Ian shook his hand. He compounded his sin with a pleasant greeting. "My lord, it is good to be back. I'm sorry if you've misconstrued my absence. I've been terribly busy reestablishing a life here after the war." He smiled benignly and felt a stab of unease when he saw the shrewd look his uncle gave him.

"Yes, so I've heard," was all the earl said in response. He let go of Ian's hand. "Drink?" He indicated an intimate grouping of chairs near the sideboard and Ian followed him over. Ian remembered this now too, how self-contained his uncle always seemed. He was a man who kept his own counsel well, rarely letting anyone close enough to know what he was really thinking. Two years ago that had intimidated him. Now he was merely impressed with his self-possession. The intervening years had taught Ian that what his uncle did or did not think had only as much influence on Ian as Ian allowed it to. With that in mind, he took the offered seat.

They didn't speak again until his uncle had poured drinks for them both and sat down opposite Ian. The seating arrangement was less adversarial than Ian thought it ought to be—almost companionable, really.

"Did you bring your new wife with you?" The earl's question was asked casually, but Ian sensed so much more behind the words. He chose his own just as carefully.

"I came alone this time." He kept his face in its neutrally pleasant mask. If things were going to go badly, he intended for his uncle to fire the first volley.

"That's a shame. I am eager to meet her, as is the countess." A polite remark that required no response. Ian offered none but a smile. The earl sighed expansively, and Ian raised his brows in surprise at this show of emotion. "This is the girl your father picked?"

"Yes," Ian confirmed. He said no more, once again masking his suspicion behind a smile.

The earl put his drink down on the table beside him. "Ian, we'll get nowhere if you refuse to answer my questions."

"Where are we going?" Ian asked, his voice a little harder, his smile a little sharper.

"I am merely trying to find out what you've been up to these last two years. The news of your marriage was a complete surprise to the entire family. None of us were there to represent your family, Ian. That showed a lack of respect for your bride that, at least on our part, was completely unintentional."

Ian tilted his head and looked at his uncle. "Meaning?"

The older man leaned back in his chair and steepled his fingers, pressing the two index fingers against his lips for a moment as he studied Ian. After a moment he lowered his hands to the chair arms. "Meaning," he drawled in reproof, "that we support this marriage and would have liked the opportunity to affirm it."

Ah, thought Ian, this was about saving face then. "I'm sure no one took much notice of it, and a word here and there on your part now will suffice."

"Will that be sufficient for your wife, or is that immaterial?" The earl's tone had gotten decidedly cooler.

Ian was again taken aback at the display of emotion. "Sophie could not care less. Family is not that important to her, as hers is bloody awful. We are more than enough family for her." Ian inwardly winced at his use of the word "we". He had hoped to get this interview over without mentioning Derek's name. The earl must have seen some tiny flinch on his part and his eyes sharpened like a hawk's.

"We?" The tone was cool, but only mildly so.

"Yes, we." Ian would give him no more than was necessary. The earl sighed again.

"Whose idea was this marriage?"

The question took Ian by surprise. "My father's," he replied immediately, knowing that was not the answer his uncle wanted.

"Did you want to marry her?" The earl was tenacious, Ian would give him that.

"I wanted to marry." Ian could honestly answer that question. He had wanted to marry very much. That he was able to marry Sophie was a gift he greatly appreciated.

"Good, that's good," his uncle said encouragingly. "We had begun to wonder what we were going to do with that betrothed of yours, since it seemed you would never marry her. Her father had inquired of me about a possible breach of contract."

"What?" Ian didn't bother to hide his incredulity. "That bastard cares for naught but his money. I hope you told him what he could do with his breach of contract."

"Actually I inquired of him whether or not he had asked you about the marriage. Before I received a reply I got news of your marriage. I assumed he had indeed inquired of you, and the promised suit drove you to the altar."

"No." Ian was emphatic. "I was not forced to marry Sophie. I wanted to marry her, and I am glad I did. I will never regret this marriage."

The earl cocked a brow. "Never is a long time."

"I'm in love with her." The words surprised Ian as well as his uncle. He realized with startling clarity that he meant it. For a while now he'd been evading the truth, using words like adore and fond, but the fact was he loved her. He loved her humor and her strength, her vulnerability and her compassion. He loved her freckles and her willingness to trust him. He loved her as much as he loved Derek. The thought made him blink. How the hell had he gotten so damn lucky, to have two such amazing people in his life to love? "I'm in love with her," he said again, not even trying to hide his stunned delight at the wondrous revelation.

His uncle smiled wryly. "I can see that." He paused and gazed at his drink as he swirled the amber liquid. "Love doesn't solve everything, Ian." He looked up at him in consternation. "Well. For once clever ambiguities fail me. What about your Mr. Knightly? Will he be a problem?"

"Derek? Why would he be a problem? Granted, he and Sophie quarreled a bit at first, but I think they're becoming fond of one another." Ian was still too shocked by his recent epiphany to think about what he was saying.

"Do you mean to say that he is still with you?" The earl's tone was incredulous. As if realizing he'd overstepped his bounds, he coughed delicately into his hand. "I'm sorry, that's none of my affair, Ian."

Ian sobered at his uncle's words. "Why? You certainly made it your affair two years ago."

After taking another drink, his uncle put his glass down. "Marriage changes everything, my boy. Once you are married, what happens in your bed is no one's business but you and your wife. Society turns a blind eye to any…irregularities as long as you and your wife present a united front."

When he said no more it was Ian's turn to look at him incredulously. "And that's it? Because I'm respectably married now, you're willing to look the other way and let me fuck Derek, is that what you're saying?" Ian was getting angry, for his own sake, but also for Derek's. In his anger he forgot his determination to reconcile with his family.

His uncle refused to answer Ian's anger in kind. Instead he looked predictably inscrutable and picked up his drink again. "I was in love once." The earl's confession surprised Ian almost as much as his earlier declaration. "She was inappropriate, of course, for the future Earl of Wilchester." He looked at Ian sardonically. "My father's words, not mine. I went along because I imagined that I would be able to marry the countess and still keep my love as a mistress." He stood suddenly and went to the nearest window to stare out at the twilight. "Unbeknownst to me, my father made an arrangement with hers. She was summarily married off to a barrister from Wales and spirited away. She now has five children. We write often." He took a drink. "If I had been able to have both of them..." He left the thought incomplete.

"Why are you telling me this?" Ian asked quietly when it was apparent the earl was done sharing his past.

The earl turned to look at him, his face smooth, emotionless. "Because I see myself in you."

Ian thought he couldn't be shocked any more than he already had been, but he was. He shook his head. "How?"

The wry half smile that passed for amusement crooked his uncle's lips again. "I've learned quite a bit from you the last two years, you know."

"Uncle, at this point I know nothing. I am stunned by this conversation."

His comment caused his uncle to bark with laughter. "Oh yes, Ian. You didn't back down, you see. I played the autocrat to perfection and you threw it in my face. In all our faces. Then you marched off to London with your wholly inappropriate lover and proceeded to carve out a life separate from this family. You've become a wealthy man of property. In every way you have shown that you don't need us." He walked over and put a hand on Ian's shoulder. "And with each success I cheered you on, Ian, in my heart. How I wished I could march out and live my life on my terms." He squeezed Ian's shoulder. "Until one day I realized I could." Ian turned to look at him unsure of what he meant. "I cannot be what was, Ian. I can only be what I am, right now."

Ian gave his uncle a genuine smile. "You are lucky, Uncle. I had to go to war to learn that lesson."

The earl walked back over and sat down again. "We all worried about you greatly when you were there, Ian." He let his true feelings show, and Ian was moved by the sincere words.

"I know, Uncle Victor. I'm sorry. I'm sorry that when I came back...well, my return was hardly reassuring, was it?" He shook his head at his own foolishness. No matter what had transpired, he'd known they had worried about him, that they were truly grateful for his safe return. He'd not appreciated it at the time.

"It was concern for you and your future that drove me the last time we spoke."

"I know that now." Ian tried to find the words to convey what that concern meant to him and couldn't. He felt the empty hole that had been left behind when his family turned their backs on him filling up again, and it was a sweet relief. He could admit some of the fault had been his. He'd been defensive and hurt and still bleeding inside from the wounds of war that no one else could see. "Thank you," he finally said. "Thank you for that concern."

His uncle sighed and Ian could see that a great weight had been lifted from his shoulders as well. "The countess wishes to have a ball in celebration of your marriage. Will that suit you?"

Ian was taken aback. "A ball. I...yes, that would be fine. I'm sure Sophie would love it."

The earl smiled unreservedly and the expression made him look ten years younger. "Good, good. Shall we say in three weeks then, in London?" His uncle stood up and walked over to his desk and began flipping through the papers there.

"Yes, that will work out well." Ian stood and faced his uncle. "Derek will attend with us." He wanted to make absolutely sure his uncle understood what their relationship was, he, Derek and Sophie.

His uncle stopped and looked at Ian, inscrutable again. "Of course. I'm sure he can be discreet if he actually tries."

Ian couldn't stop his laughter. "He has been known to, on occasion. I'll see that this is one of them." He walked over to the desk. "Please do not invite Sir Middleton. He and Sophie are estranged, and we plan on keeping it that way until he dies a miserable death."

His uncle made a note on a piece of paper. "Hmm, that way is it? Just make sure you don't hasten his demise in any way." He looked up at Ian from his notes. "It would seem your bride is in need of family then, Ian. It's a good thing you have some to spare."

Ian grinned. "We are all in need of family, Uncle, whether we admit it or not. I'll be only happy to share my overabundance with Sophie." And Derek, he thought to himself, overcome with the understanding that he would be welcomed as well.

"Then I shall see you at dinner, Ian, and you can let your relatives welcome you back to the fold. Oh, Cousin Elspeth is here. For God's sake don't mention Derek. I don't want you to give her an apoplexy."

Ian just laughed and showed himself out of the room.

* * * * *

Derek awoke with a jerk, sitting straight up in bed, the echo of his cry reverberating around the empty bedchamber. He could feel the sweat on his forehead, his hair a damp mess on his head. A cold trail of sweat trickled down his spine as he heard footsteps running down the hall. He raised a shaking hand and rubbed it across his eyes, trying to erase the picture still lingering in his mind from the dream. He heard his bedroom door open, a quick click as the handle turned and a rush of air when the door was swung inward rapidly. She didn't even knock, he thought with a small grin that was as shaky as his hand.

"Derek?" Her voice was slightly breathless, emphasizing that certain huskiness that she always spoke with. With his eyes closed, it was a sultry voice, a voice that spoke of sex and forbidden pleasures and made him think she'd taste like rich chocolate. He felt his cock go hard, the lust slamming into him, shocking but not unexpected. After one of his dreams, Ian always soothed him with sex. His body was reacting on instinct. He quickly opened his eyes to dispel his rising desire, to show his body and his brain that it was Sophie not Ian—not a lover. There would be no sex tonight.

She was an illusion in the candlelight. An angel sent to comfort, a demon sent to entice. Her white gown was gossamer thin, clinging to her curves lovingly, giving teasing glimpses of long legs and dark, erect nipples, hinting at the warm shadow between her thighs. Her unbound hair tumbled around her shoulders and down her back, the flame catching streaks of red in its undulating waves. Derek would have, could have imagined her the angel of his imagination, a perfect vision of desire no more real than his fear, if not for the freckles. The freckles dancing across her shoulders and arms from her time in the garden pushed him forcefully into awareness. She was no vision, she was Sophie—flesh and blood and passion, and as Derek stared at those freckles his mouth watered with the need to taste them, to find out if they were as delicious as Ian claimed.

Lust made him weak and he sat and stared and trembled. Desire stole his voice and he watched her walk cautiously across the room to his bedside, all the while crying out a warning in his head to her to stay away. He was wild, out of control. He needed, God how he needed, and she was here.

"Derek, are you all right? I heard you cry out." She sounded so worried, so concerned for him. Why? Why did she have to care? It made it so much harder. She moved and a trick of the light made her gown diaphanous, a superfluous mist around her lusciously naked form. Derek had to gasp for breath around the fist that grabbed his gut and made his cock throb.

"Derek," she cried out softly, leaning toward him in alarm. He shoved his arm out, holding her away with a raised hand.

"Stay away," he growled, when all he wanted was for her to come closer, close enough to grab, to throw down, to cover, to devour. His lust for her was clawing its way through his body, eating him alive to get to her.

"It was a nightmare, wasn't it? Ian said you have them sometimes, like me. Let me help, Derek. How can I help?" She was practically begging. One small, sane corner of his brain wondered if she even knew what she was begging for. "How does Ian help?"

Her last question made Derek laugh, but it wasn't a happy sound. He wrapped an arm around his middle and leaned forward to rest his head on the sheets. "Just go, Sophie. Go." He turned his head to look at her, and her worry made him relent a little. "I'll be fine. You just need to…go. Go now, for both our sakes."

"Derek—"

"Damn it, Sophie, just do as I tell you! Are you always to be a thorn in my side? Can't a man even have a nightmare anymore without you hovering?" His words hurt her, he knew it and was grimly satisfied. He'd wanted to hurt her, to drive her away. He forgot how hard he'd worked to build up her confidence in the last few weeks, but she reminded him.

"No, no, I won't go, Derek. Don't shut me out. Let me help. Ian isn't here and I…I have to take care of you for him." She took a hesitant step toward him and he sat up with a curse.

"Ian fucks me blind, Sophie, until I can't remember my own name much less the dreams. Is that what you're offering? If you don't go, that's what's going to happen, Sophie. I'm on the edge right now. It won't take much to push me over. You need to leave. You need to leave now."

He watched the emotions fly across her face almost too quickly to catch. There, fright. There, sympathy. There, desire. No, no he must have mistaken that last one. "Why aren't you leaving, Sophie?" His voice was a harsh whisper. Every muscle in his body strained toward her, demanding he capture her and take her. He resisted, but for how long? He couldn't hold out much longer.

"If...if that's what you need, Derek," she whispered, and he was lost, lost god damn it.

"Sophie," was all he said, and he shuddered at the need in his voice, at the relief. He reached out and hauled her onto the bed, dragging her across his lap. He lay her down in the middle of the bed and rolled over to cover her. She was so small, so fragile, so breakable. He thought of her struggling to get away from that bastard this afternoon and felt the remnants of the boiling rage that had made him want to kill. Remembered her cowering and whimpering on the floor and his touch gentled. "Sophie," he whispered and she looked up at him, trust, desire and uncertainty all warring in the gaze of her warm amber eyes. "I will take care of you, Sophie," he told her softly and he watched those eyes begin to burn. He felt the heat that had almost banked flame to life inside him and he groaned as she parted her legs and cradled him in her thighs.

He grabbed a fistful of her soft hair and she gasped as her head arched back. Her reaction was the straw that broke his restraint. He thrust against her, trying to find her heat through the sheets and her nightgown as he buried his face in her neck, seeking that fragrance that was uniquely her, the scent that had been tantalizing and tormenting him for weeks. When he found it, he had to taste it and he licked it from her freckles, shoving the material of her gown out of the way.

Derek chased the flavor all across her shoulders and started down her chest, but again the cursed gown got in his way. He reared back and Sophie squealed in surprise. She had been running her hands all over his back and sides when he was on top of her. Now she lay shocked as he grabbed the edges of her nightgown and with a swift pull tore it open from neck to hem. He peeled back the material to expose her and he watched a shudder move through her. A quick glance at her face showed her response to be from desire, not fear. The thrill of her reaction shot through him and he felt his cock begin to leak. Christ, he hadn't wanted a woman this badly since that first time with Dolores.

He put his hands on her stomach, spanning it so his thumbs rested over her navel and his smallest fingers curved around her sides. The feel of such intimate flesh against his hands made Derek close his eyes as a wave of longing crashed over him. She was soft and smooth, so different from Ian. His touch was firm, not gentle as he ran his hands up her torso to her breasts. He stopped just below them, so his hands were pushing them high until her nipples stood straight up, hard and flushed with desire. She had glorious nipples, large and a soft brown that showed her blush to perfection and complemented her creamy skin and delightful freckles. He brushed his thumbs over them and she whimpered. At the sight of the freckles on the full globes of her breasts, Derek couldn't stop himself from leaning over and ravenously sucking a nipple into his mouth.

God, he'd forgotten the taste of a woman, the sight and sounds and flavors of a woman's passion. Was there any other woman who tasted like Sophie? She was sweet and earthy, like eating fresh-picked fruit, a juicy burst of flavor and texture. Sophie arched her back and moaned as he drew deeply on her breast, pressing her nipple between his tongue and the roof of his mouth to explore its texture and shape. Derek was straddling her hips, and he pushed both hands under her back to wrap his arms around her tightly, pulling her torso up and off the bed, bending to hold her breast captive in his mouth. He fed on her sweet flesh as she lay limply in his embrace, her arms flung out, hands resting on the bed, her head falling back. She was his, her utter trust and complete surrender pushing him into an almost violent state of arousal.

Derek moved one arm up Sophie's back and again grabbed a handful of her hair. He pushed her head up and Sophie's eyes fluttered open. They locked on Derek's as he lifted his head from her breast, and he saw his own desire mirrored there. He yanked her closer, until their lips were almost touching. He wanted to kiss her with a painful intensity. He wanted to see if her mouth tasted like the rest of her, wanted the heat and the wet of it, wanted to breathe her air into his lungs until he was full of her, and it scared the hell out of him. He knew in that moment he mustn't ever kiss Sophie. Some remnant of self-preservation told him that to do so would be the end of him. Sophie slowly raised her arms and rested her hands on his biceps, massaging them gently. The lightning of her tender touch shocked him. He pulled away, determined to make this about sex, about satisfaction, even about comfort, but not about he and Sophie. They were just a man and a woman satisfying one another—there was no Derek, no Sophie, no future.

Roughly Derek grabbed Sophie's upper arms and pulled her up. "On your knees," he ordered her, his voice harsh. He could see her confusion, but also her acquiescence. She struggled to her knees without a word of protest and Derek knew she'd do whatever he asked of her. She trusted him, and he hated himself because he wasn't worthy of it. Sophie saw something in his face and with a tender look reached up to touch his cheek. "Derek?" she whispered. He jerked away and pushed on her right arm to spin her around, pulling her ruined nightgown off her arms in the process. "Derek?" This time her voice was louder, startled.

"Put your hands up on the wall." He made his voice flat, almost impersonal. He could fuck her without losing himself. He had to. He had to learn how to, because Ian was right. He couldn't stay out of their bed forever. He had to prove to himself he could fuck Sophie without loving her. He didn't love her, he wouldn't.

Sophie complied, facing the wall beside the bed and placing her hands next to her shoulders. Derek moved directly behind her and spread her legs apart with a knee until she was wide open. Her breathing grew uneven and he could feel her heartbeat thrumming faster. Her excitement escalated his. He moved her hands until they were high over her head, still pressed against the wall. "Leave them there," he told her, and inwardly cursed the raspy tremor in his voice. Sophie nodded silently and leaned back just enough to touch the curve of her upper back to his chest. He wanted to push her away, to break that contact, but he couldn't. As far as arousing touches went, it was nearly innocent, but it was the emotions behind her movement that made him tremble. He could sense her need to connect with him, to feel him. He realized with frustration that no matter what he tried to make this encounter, for Sophie it was about the two of them. For Sophie it *was* about her and Derek.

He leaned in then and rested his mouth against the soft, sweet curve of her shoulder where it met her neck—that mysterious spot where a person's smell seemed to be concentrated, the unique essence of their physical self. Derek wanted to roll around in that smell, to coat himself with Sophie and in turn mark her with his scent. He shook his head with a wry chuckle and licked the spot until Sophie shivered. With a feeling of inevitability, Derek slid his hand from her hip and down the slope of her stomach until he met the wiry thatch of pubic hair that had been a mere shadow under her gown. He burrowed his fingers in it, and when he felt how wet she was he moaned out loud. She was dripping, the lips of her cunt swollen and hot and throbbing. "Christ," he murmured. "God damn it, Sophie. God damn you. Is this for me? Tell me this is for me." He slid a finger into her and felt his neck and shoulders tense at how tight and hot she was. Jesus, no wonder Ian fucked her night and day.

"Derek," Sophie murmured, and he wasn't sure if she was answering his question or responding to the invasion of his finger. He pulled it out and she moaned.

Derek bent his knees until he could maneuver his cock between her legs. He didn't thrust into her. Instead he slid forward, using his cock to caress the lips of her cunt until the head bumped into her hard little clit. He cupped his penis in his hand and pressed it against her and held her open with two fingers so she would feel his cock in the slippery valleys hidden there and fucked back and forth, torturing them both. "God damn you, Sophie," he murmured, kissing her shoulder. "Fuck me, Sophie, fuck me now."

If Sophie hadn't been nearly insensible with lust, she would have laughed. No love poems and gentle words from Derek. He fucked liked he did everything else, with curses and commands. God, she wanted him. She hadn't thought it was possible to feel like this with anyone but Ian. It shocked and thrilled and horrified her. She couldn't control the shiver that shook her whole body as he fucked his cock against her slippery, swollen folds again. Derek's cock, Derek's hard body bracing her from behind, Derek's breath hot and heavy on her cheek. She was lost in Derek, surrounded by him. He was so big, so male. His arms enfolded her and she felt like she was melting into his heat.

Sophie's fingers curled into the wall as Derek spread the lips of her vagina wider and pressed his cock against her at the same time he circled her clitoris with a finger. She loved what he was doing to her. Loved his rough handling and how vulnerable he made her feel, imprisoned between his body and the wall. She wouldn't move her hands, she couldn't, not until he told her to. It was unbearably exciting to be under Derek's control.

"Damn it," Derek growled, and Sophie literally felt the gush of warm liquid between her legs. Derek groaned and rubbed his cock in the new juice of her. "You like this? You want it?" Derek hadn't lost the growl and she shivered. "I'm going to give it to you now." He pulled away suddenly and grabbed Sophie's arm, pushing her down on the bed.

She landed on her side and Derek gave her no time to roll over. He picked up her top leg and lifted it, straddling her other leg. He moved forward, bending the leg he held until he could get close enough to push his cock into her. As the tip of his cock penetrated her, Derek cursed again, and Sophie flung one arm out to clutch the bedsheets, twisting her torso so she faced Derek while her hips and legs remained to the side. It should have been uncomfortable, but it wasn't. The position let Derek penetrate deep as he hugged her leg around his middle, her thigh pressed to his stomach. He felt...different than Ian, not as big, but hard and hot and just...wonderful. He pushed in deeper and Sophie felt her swollen channel part for him and then spasm around him, trying to hold him and suck him deeper. She gasped and it ended on a moan as Derek gripped her thigh hard enough to leave bruises and thrust fast and hard until he was all the way inside her, so deep she knew he could go no farther.

She looked at Derek and saw the tension in the muscles of his throat, his arms bulging with restrained power as he held her leg against him. He was beautiful. He was breathing heavily, and the look he gave her from hooded eyes was feral with sexual hunger. Sophie's breath caught in her throat with a little shiver of apprehension that only seemed to enhance her arousal. She was shocked at herself, shocked at how much she wanted him to fuck her hard and fast, to control her and use her. He loomed over her big and hard and frightening, and she had never wanted to fuck so much. Not make love, but fuck. Her desire was pagan and elemental and she closed her eyes and arched her back and ground herself down on his cock with a deep-throated purr that she hadn't even known she could make until just that moment.

"Jesus," Derek breathed, "you were made to fuck, Sophie. Tell me how you want it, because I know you do. Your cunt is so hungry it's eating me alive. Tell me." He pulled out slowly and pushed back in just as slowly. "Like this?"

Sophie was shaking her head. No, no, no, she was chanting in her head, harder, faster, but she couldn't make her voice work. Derek slid his knees closer to her, so close he couldn't even pull out all the way. He began a small, steady in and out movement, firm but short, as if he was mimicking the beat of her heart. Sophie cried out softly and tried to press down on him harder, her hips moving rapidly but erratically and Derek thrust in all the way as he pulled hard on her leg, fucking her down on his thrusting cock. His hard thigh brushed against her clitoris as he moved, and Sophie's cry was high as pleasure streaked through her.

"Liked that, did you?" Derek chuckled. He had one hand around her knee, holding her leg up, and the other at her hip where her leg joined her body. With the two hands, he was able to control her movements and he held her still. "Tell me. What do you want, Sophie?" His whisper burned her ears and set her blood on fire. "What do you want?"

She licked her dry lips and felt Derek's gaze on her mouth. Her voice was deeper, huskier than normal when she finally spoke the words. "Fuck me, Derek," she told him, "hard and fast and deep. I need you. I need you to fuck me now."

"Sophie," he growled as only Derek could, and then he began to give her what she wanted.

Derek couldn't have controlled himself if he tried, so he didn't bother. He let loose all the raging lust inside him for this slight, beautiful girl. All the anger and hatred and fear turned into a need that consumed him, a need to fuck her so hard she'd never forget him, never forget that he'd possessed her so thoroughly. He wanted to brand his name on her womb as he thrust his cock into her again and again. And she took it. She took and took and begged for more. He hugged her leg to him and fucked her and watched her shatter as the first orgasm threw her head back and made her cry out hoarsely.

She sobbed his name as he continued to fuck her through the climax and beyond. He found a primitive thrill in her cries. He wanted to throw open the windows and the doors and let the sounds of her passion and satisfaction announce his prowess to the world, and warn others to stay away from her because she was his. He let his head fall back and closed his eyes as he thrust, thrust, thrust into her drenched cunt. He focused on the heat of her, the softness of her insides where she gloved his cock so tightly, the sound of her voice as she said his name. He wanted to remember it all perfectly. He began to shake and felt his balls grow tight. He wanted to come — no, he needed to come — to fill her with his semen so that tomorrow as she walked around it would leak from her and she'd remember too, remember the feel of him fucking her just like she needed him to, remember her own cries and how she'd come for him.

"Can you go again, Sophie? Will you come for me again? Come on my cock, Sophie." His voice was low and guttural, animalistic. That was what Sophie reduced him to, an animal who knew nothing but the fuck. Sophie didn't seem to care, as a matter of fact, she was wild for it and for him, a match for the animal in him in every way.

"Yes," she cried out, "please," and she came for him, just like that. He felt her cunt clamp down hard on him and he let himself go. He fucked into her as deep as he could go and let her climax milk him as his cock jerked and released spurts of hot semen in her channel, increasing her heat and wetness and making her cry out and spasm again. His cock was so sensitive by then he threw back his head and yelled her name as they rode out the intense pleasure.

Derek fell forward, catching himself on one arm, still holding her leg with the other. Sophie gave a little whimper and covered her mouth with her hand, her eyes squeezed shut. Derek was breathing heavily as if he'd run a race. His pulse was pounding and he felt so alive. He wanted to roar like the animal he was and proclaim his dominance over this woman, his woman. He wanted to gather her up in his arms and tell her how wonderful she was, how beautiful, how perfect. Instead he rolled off her and lay at a distance, not touching her. He threw an arm over his eyes, blocking her from his sight and tried to clear his thoughts. He was done, he was satisfied, as was she. He'd given her pleasure as well, he hadn't been selfish. It was enough. It had been about fucking, not love. To think otherwise would be a lie.

"Well." Sophie's voice was shaky, weak. He felt the bed move and the sheets rustle as she got up. He had to fist his hands to keep from reaching out and stopping her. She cleared her throat. "I don't know about you, but I feel better." She sounded awkward and self-conscious, and her joke fell flat.

Derek couldn't let her leave like that. He opened his eyes and raised up on his elbows to look at her while she searched for her clothes. He lifted his ass off the bed and pulled her ruined gown from beneath him and held it out to her silently. Her blush was so red it looked painful and she wouldn't look at him as she snatched it from his hand. She tried to cover herself with it, but it was beyond redemption and useless. It only made her more appealing, choice bits of her flashing out from between the torn edges, the silky cream of the material complementing the silky creaminess of her skin. "Take my robe," Derek told her, pointing to the chair behind her. She looked startled at his words, and he realized they were the first he'd spoken since he'd called her name while coming. She turned to get the robe and the sight of her lush ass made Derek grit his teeth.

"Thank you," he said quietly when she was struggling into his too-large robe. She froze for a moment and then stuffed an arm into the sleeve.

"You're welcome," she finally said, her voice so polite they might have been passing tea in the drawing room. Derek was surprised at the slight hurt he felt at her tone. With unusual insight he realized it must be worse for her, considering his words and tone.

He sat up with a sigh and moved over to lean his back against the wall. He pulled the sheet over his lap and raised his knee. "I didn't plan on that happening." He winced at the accusatory tone. Damn it, he couldn't even handle an apology well.

Sophie's back was still to him. "I didn't either." Her tone was still polite, impersonal. Suddenly she spun around to face him, and she looked so vulnerable lost in the folds of his clothing his chest ached.

"Sophie," he started, but she interrupted whatever he had been going to say.

"I love Ian with all my heart and soul," she said fervently, as if she had to defend herself. Didn't she realize he was the bastard here?

"I know you do." And that was the problem, wasn't it? Fuck, he hated wading through his own feelings. Sophie had given all her love to Ian, and Derek didn't like being a charity case. He was jealous and selfish and confused, and God, just so...wrong inside. He wanted her to love him, but he didn't want to love her. That was wrong, wasn't it?

"So do you." Sophie's voice was no longer impersonal. It shook with emotion.

"Yes." Speak, damn it, Derek cursed himself. Why can't you just talk to her?

"Don't ruin this for me, Derek, please."

Derek looked at her sharply. What was she talking about?

"He loves you so much, Derek. And I only need a little piece of him. You have his heart. All I'm asking is that you let me have one little corner of it. For someone like me...that's such an awful lot. Please, Derek, can't you let me have just that little?" Her voice broke at the end, and Derek's heart did too. So, she'd just fucked him to secure her position here. He couldn't stop his sarcastic laughter. She misunderstood. She thought he was laughing at her, but no, he was laughing at his own goddamn gullibility.

"Don't worry, Sophie. I'm pretty sure Ian's in love with you too. He'd be just as likely to put me out as you, and I certainly won't risk that." He shook his head and rubbed both hands over his face. Then he let out a loud, frustrated yell. When he looked at Sophie again she was backed up against the wall next to the door. "Christ almighty, Sophie, how the hell did Ian end up with two such pathetic misfits as you and I?"

Sophie looked taken aback for a moment and then to Derek's relief she smiled, although the smile was bittersweet. "I guess he's just lucky that way."

Sophie felt wrung out, as if she were a hollow shell collapsing in on itself. Her heart was breaking into little pieces and she was amazed she hadn't heard the jagged shards tinkling like broken glass as she'd walked across the room. She had thought this was the beginning for her and Derek, that Ian could have what he wanted, and what Sophie had secretly wanted as well—the three of them together, lovers, in love. She was in love with Derek. Oh God. And then he'd rolled away and treated her like a stranger. She could have been anyone tonight and he'd have fucked her. It was all because of the nightmare, not about any feelings he had for Sophie.

She'd panicked then. What if he used this to drive a wedge between her and Ian? Now she felt like a fool. Derek would never do that. He was too honorable. He pretended he was an amoral bully, but he wasn't. She knew him now, she knew things about him he'd rather no one did, no one but Ian, that is. She knew he was gentle and kind, funny and shy. He'd laugh at that description, but it was true. He hid his shyness behind rough language and cutting humor. He was also brilliant, something he hid from most of his friends. He memorized almost every book he read. He knew at least six languages that she knew of, and Ian said he thought in numbers. She wasn't quite sure what that meant, but it made him a devil at chess. He was also unquestioningly loyal to his friends. She'd heard him talk about that man, Robertson, the one who had hurt Jason and Kate and some other friends, and she knew he would kill him if he ever found him. No, Derek would never use their lovemaking against her.

Her thoughts registered, and she felt herself blanch. Oh God, it was true, she was in love with Derek. And he felt nothing for her, nothing.

"Well, for some reason he likes us. Perhaps it's not luck, but some perverse aberration in his character." Derek's voice cut into her thoughts.

Sophie had to think for a minute to remember what they'd been talking about. She couldn't do this. She couldn't stand here and talk to Derek as if nothing were amiss, as if her dreams weren't going up in flames around them. She turned away and walked quickly to the door. She fumbled with the long sleeves for a moment and finally wrenched the door open. She didn't turn back around as she rushed through it. Before she closed it behind her she spoke over her shoulder. "He's in love with you, Derek, the forever kind of love, because he's a very smart, very lucky man."

"Sophie!" Derek called out, crawling down the bed, but she closed the door firmly on him. "He's in love with you too, you little fool," Derek whispered to the closed door. "And God help me, I think I may be too." He fell back on the bed and covered his eyes, trying to block out the nightmare that had only gotten worse by making love to Sophie. It had been about Dolores, but it was Sophie's face in the flames, Sophie's face on the ruined corpse, Sophie's face staring up at him from the grave.

Chapter Seventeen

ɷ

Ian nodded at Montague as the yawning butler opened the door for him. He'd ridden all day to get home to Sophie and Derek. He'd told them he'd be home no later than today, and he didn't want them to worry. One thing after another had delayed his departure and then slowed him down on the road. He'd thought he'd never get here. Now all he wanted was a warm bed and an even warmer body to snuggle up to.

"Is everyone in bed, Montague?" he asked, handing over his hat and gloves.

"Yes sir, some time ago." Ian started toward the stairs only to be stopped by Montague. "We had a visitor yesterday, sir, a Mr. Harold Middleton."

Ian froze in his tracks and spun about to stare at the butler.

"Mr. Knightly took care of it. He had the footmen escort him out and gave instructions he was not to be allowed in the house again."

"What happened?" Ian's tone was clipped. Thank God Derek had been here.

"He assaulted Mrs. Middleton. She was able to stop Mr. Knightly from killing him, but only just in time." The last was said with a decided note of approval. Apparently Derek had risen in the older man's estimation.

"Good for Mr. Knightly. Please see that his orders are followed. Thank you, Montague." He started to turn away but looked back at Montague. "Is she all right?"

"A little shaken, but other than that I believe she is fine, sir."

Ian nodded again and this time kept going toward the stairs. He found his fatigue disappearing as he bounded up the steps to his bedroom. There was only a faint light coming from under the door, so he very quietly opened it and stepped into the room. Sophie was sleeping, her hand tucked under her pillow and her hair spread out behind her as she lay on her side. Ian slowly lowered himself into the closest chair, still watching her, his knees going a little weak at the thought of her being assaulted without him here to protect her. Again he thought, thank God for Derek.

"Derek?" Sophie's voice came low and sleepy from the bed, and Ian pushed to his feet and went to her.

"No, it's Ian, darling," he murmured, wondering briefly why she would think he was Derek.

"Ian?" Her voice was stronger and she sat up, squinting in the dim light until he reached her side and sat on the edge of the bed. "Oh, Ian!" she cried and threw her arms around him.

"I heard. I heard what happened yesterday," he told her softly. "Are you all right?"

Sophie's body went very still against his and he heard her indrawn breath. "You...you heard?" she asked, her voice tremulous. "Derek told you?"

"No, Montague. He said Derek took care of you."

Sophie pulled back and gave Ian a guilty look. "It wasn't Derek's fault, Ian, really. It was partly mine. No, mostly mine. I'm sorry, I'm so sorry."

"Of course it wasn't your fault, Sophie, or Derek's either. How could you have known?" He reached out and ran a hand down her soft, curling hair from her temple to her shoulder. Sophie flinched and Ian inwardly cursed her brother.

"We didn't know, Ian. We didn't plan it. You must believe me." Sophie was almost begging his forgiveness, and Ian's heart broke that she could think he would blame her for her brother's brutishness.

"Sophie, I know you didn't invite your brother here, for heaven's sake. He won't bother you again, I swear it. Thank God Derek was here to protect you."

"My...Harold? You're talking about Harold?" Sophie's confusion and then relief were obvious.

"Of course. What are you talking about?" Ian was the one confused now.

"Nothing! I mean," Sophie laughed self-consciously and shook her head. "Oh, Ian, I'd almost forgotten about Harold." She bit her lip and looked at her hands in her lap. Ian raised her chin with a finger.

"Sophie?" he asked quietly.

"Derek had a nightmare last night." Sophie spoke quietly as well, but her words came out in a rush.

"Damn," Ian said harshly and started to rise, determined to go to Derek. He stopped halfway to his feet and sat back down again. How could he leave Sophie? She was probably still upset about her brother's visit, no matter what she said. Damn it, why couldn't they all be in the same room? That would make his life so much easier. How hard was it to share a damn bed?

As if she sensed his inner turmoil, Sophie reached out and laid her hand on his. "Go to him, Ian. I promise I won't have any nightmares tonight. He needs you. Please." She smiled encouragingly at him and he smiled back.

"If you're sure, Sophie?" Picking them up, he kissed both her hands. "I don't want to leave you if you're still upset."

"I'm more upset by Derek's nightmare. He didn't say much, but he was very shaken by it, I think." She shook her head sadly. "I'm afraid I wasn't the one he needed to help him get over it."

Ian thought of how he usually soothed Derek with sex after one of his nightmares. Sophie could have helped him if only he'd let her. If only she'd offer. Ian sighed and got to his feet. "I'll be back, Sophie."

"No, Ian, really it's all right, you don't have to—"

Ian cut off her protest. "I said I'll be back," he told her firmly as he opened the door and then closed it softly behind him.

He didn't bother being quiet when he got to Derek's room. Somehow he knew Derek wouldn't be sleeping. When he opened the door, he found Derek sitting in a chair in the near dark, staring out the open window. Derek spoke without turning around.

"I saw you ride up. You look tired. Go to bed and we'll talk in the morning." His voice was casual, but he still didn't look at Ian and Ian's internal warning bell was going off. As he'd suspected, Derek was still upset about the nightmare.

"You had quite a day yesterday, didn't you, you and Sophie?" Well, that got a reaction. Derek swung around to look at him, startled.

"Sophie told you?" he asked incredulously.

"No, Montague did, but I just came from seeing Sophie."

"How the hell does Montague know?" Derek was indignant.

"Didn't you ask for his help?" Ian was confused again. Perhaps he was more tired than he realized.

"Good God no! Why the hell would I ask Montague for help with that?"

"He said you had the footmen throw him out and gave instructions that he wasn't to be allowed in the house again." Ian sat down on the bed and let his fatigue and confusion show. "However it happened, I'm just glad you were here, Derek. I don't know what would have happened to Sophie if you hadn't been here."

Derek looked at him for a moment and then he started to laugh. Ian didn't like this laugh. It was bitter and spoke more of unhappiness than amusement.

"Derek? Are you all right?"

Derek shook his head as his laughter died, leaving a sardonic smile behind. "Middleton. Yes, I had the bastard thrown out. I wanted to kill him. He had a hold of her hair and it looked like he was trying to break her neck. She was so white I thought for a moment he'd already killed her, until she saw me and screamed my name." Derek fisted his hands on the arms of the chair and Ian saw the slight tremble in one of them. Derek's description made Ian shake as well.

"I never should have left you two alone, never," he said, furious with himself. He was shocked when Derek laughed bitterly again.

"No, Ian, you really shouldn't have." Derek stood suddenly and grabbed Ian's arm. "Come on. Sophie needs you more than I do tonight."

Ian resisted. "Derek, stop. Sophie sent me to you. She told me you had a nightmare last night."

Derek cocked his head and looked searchingly at Ian. "Did she? What else did she say?"

"Just that she wasn't able to help you afterward. I'm sorry I wasn't here, Derek. Damn it, I'm just so…angry that all this happened when I was gone, when I wasn't here for the two of you."

Derek sighed and placed his hands on his hips, looking off in the distance for a moment before turning back to Ian. "You can't be here for us all the time, Ian. Sophie and I need to learn how to take care of ourselves."

"No you don't," Ian said sharply. "I don't mind taking care of you. It's why I'm here. You will always have me, and each other. Was she no help to you at all last night?" He'd hoped a little time alone would help the two of them grow closer, but apparently not.

"No, she wasn't, but not for the reason she thinks."

Derek's reply was enigmatic and left Ian more puzzled than before. "Derek, what the hell are you talking about?

Between you and Sophie, tonight I don't know what's going on."

Derek pulled on his arm again and Ian let him lead him out of the room and back down the hall. Ian just shook his head as Derek unceremoniously opened the bedroom door and dragged Ian in behind him.

"Here," Derek said, shoving Ian toward the bed, "you need him more than I do. I'm not a charity case."

Sophie sat up in bed at their arrival and glared at Derek while she covered her scantily clad breasts with the sheet. "Neither am I. You are the one who had the nightmare—you need him more."

Ian was beginning to feel like three-day-old fish. "What happened while I was gone?" he demanded, quite sure there was more to the story than he'd been told by anyone so far.

"Sophie and I—"

Sophie cut him off with a sharp cry. "Derek!"

"Sophie," Derek responded sarcastically. "He's got to know sometime." Derek looked at Ian with a carefully blank face. "I fucked Sophie last night, after the nightmare." Derek's mask crumbled and he let his frustration show. He shoved a hand through his hair and sighed. "It wasn't her fault. I was...upset. It was a bad dream, and Sophie came barreling in demanding to help, and wanting to know how you helped, and I told her you fucked me blind and one thing led to another..." he sighed again, this time sounding tired and broken, "and things got out of hand. I took advantage of her concern and compassion, and it won't happen again."

Ian didn't know what to say. He'd never have guessed that that was what had happened. Derek and Sophie...he was in shock. Not upset, but bewildered. He'd had no idea they were beginning to feel that way about one another. He'd hoped, of course, that one day...but so soon? His shock was quickly replaced by alarm. Neither Sophie nor Derek seemed happy about the new turn in their relationship.

"Don't be such a...a goddamn martyr." Sophie's voice was angry, and Ian was nearly as shocked by her language as by the actual fact she'd fucked Derek. "I don't need you to take all the blame. I was there too, and I certainly didn't tell you to stop or yell for help. It did not even remotely resemble rape."

"God damn it, Sophie, you had no idea when you came running to help me I was going to drag you into my bed."

Derek was clearly furious with her, but Ian didn't know what for. For trying to take some of the blame? That didn't make sense.

"No I didn't. But if you'll remember correctly, you told me what you wanted and gave me the opportunity to decline. I did not. I let you drag me into your bed, and what's more, I enjoyed it. If we're going to tell Ian, then let's tell him everything." Sophie was defiant and outraged and so incredibly desirable Ian wanted to drag himself into her bed right that moment, with Derek too.

Derek didn't respond, just stalked over to the far corner and back and then stood before Ian with his arms crossed, looking at the floor. The silence was uncomfortable, punctuated by both Derek's and Sophie's rapid breathing. Ian supposed he needed to say something now.

"Well," he said, at a bit of a loss, "I see. Um, are you all right, Sophie?" He looked at her, really looked at her. She didn't seem to be any worse for wear after her night with Derek, but Ian was willing to bet she had bruises. Derek could be a rough, demanding lover, particularly after one of his dreams. Ian tried to hide how arousing he found the thought of seeing Derek's bruises on Sophie's creamy skin.

Sophie's tone was clipped. "I'm fine." She looked blindly over Ian's shoulder and hugged her middle with both arms.

"All right," Ian said, nodding inanely, he was sure. "And you, Derek? Are you all right?"

"Of course I'm all right," he snapped. "I'm fine. Why wouldn't I be fine?"

"And you, Ian? Are you all right? I feel as if...as if we'd betrayed you." Sophie's voice was quiet and a little shaky.

Ian shook his head. "Absolutely not, no one betrayed anyone here. I love you both very much," at his words, Sophie gave a little cry and then sniffed loudly, "and if you had to find comfort from one another because I wasn't here, I'm not going to cast stones." Derek snorted, and when Ian looked at him Derek raised an eyebrow with a wry twist to his lips. "So we're all fine."

"Just fine," Sophie agreed with obviously false cheerfulness.

"Just fine," Derek agreed with a growl.

"Exactly so," Ian said, nodding again, "just fine." They stared at one another for a minute until Ian broke the silence. "So, where the hell am I supposed to sleep tonight?"

* * * * *

Ian ended up in bed with Sophie simply because he was already there. Sending Derek back to his own room seemed as hard for Sophie as it was for Ian. Derek had turned into a sphinx, so Ian had no idea what Derek was feeling, but he could guess.

Breakfast the following morning managed to be far less awkward than any of them anticipated. Ian filled Derek and Sophie in on the meeting with his uncle.

Sophie gripped his hand tightly when he was done. "Oh, Ian, I'm so relieved. I know how hard it was for you to be estranged from your family. It was very kind of you to forgive him."

Ian couldn't help but smile at her and kiss the hand that held his. "Sophie, my dear, most people would say it was kind of him to forgive me."

Sophie sniffed delicately. "Yes, well, most people would be wrong, wouldn't they?"

Derek gave a derisive snort. "Most people don't care whether they are right or wrong—they just care that they are not the source of gossip, merely the purveyors. The Earl of Wilchester included."

Sophie pulled her hand away from Ian's and fiddled with her teacup. She wouldn't look at Derek. "Yes, I know. Many people are small-minded and mean. But many are not. Naïve or not, I refuse to go through life hating everyone who is merely misguided. I've spent too much of my life on hate already."

Derek sat back with a huff. "Christ, Sophie, I didn't mean anything by that. Is everything I say from now on going to be misconstrued as an attack on you?"

Ian was sorry the truce was over so soon. "She didn't say that, Derek."

Derek glared at him. "*Et tu, Brute?*" He pushed his chair back from the table forcefully. "Well, I guess I can defend myself. I've certainly had enough practice."

"What is that supposed to mean?" Ian asked, exasperated. "I'm trying to avoid a fight, not start one."

"Stop, please," Sophie pleaded with them both, quietly desperate. "This isn't what I wanted at all, please. Ian, Derek is right. I'm being overly sensitive. Don't yell at him."

Derek turned on her with his glare. "I don't need you to defend me. Didn't I just say I can take care of myself?"

"Well I'm going to do it anyway," Sophie snapped at him, "so just be quiet and sit down."

Derek blinked at her in astonishment. "Did you just order me to be quiet?"

Sophie nodded briskly. "And sit down."

Ian laughed at Derek's consternation. "Well, she certainly knows how to stop a fight in its tracks. Do sit down, Derek. She's right, we're all being overly sensitive." He sighed. "We're going to need to sit down and discuss what happened." At Sophie's protest, Ian raised a hand in a conciliatory gesture. "Later, we'll discuss it. But did you not hear what I said earlier? My uncle wishes to have a ball in celebration of our marriage in three weeks time. I thought we might go over to Lord Randall's today and invite them all personally. You can talk to Kate and Very about it. I'm sure you'll need all new frocks and fripperies and whatever else it is that women need for these things."

Sophie's complexion turned pale. "A ball? You mean we have to attend?"

Derek sighed and sat back, shaking his head. "Of course you have to attend a ball in your honor, you widgeon. You and Ian are about the only two people who absolutely have to be there."

Ian smiled devilishly. "Mmm, yes, well, I told my uncle you would be coming as well, Derek, so he will be expecting you. That makes you the third person who really has to be there."

Derek looked utterly astonished. "He's going to let me come? I know you said he recognized our relationship, but that was in private. Surely he won't want you to flaunt it in public."

"No, he doesn't. But I did promise that you would be discreet, as will Sophie and I and Uncle Victor, so there should be nothing untoward in your attending." As Derek started to shake his head, Ian sent him a look that told him in no uncertain terms there would be no arguing. "I wish you to be there, Derek."

Derek narrowed his eyes for a minute, then nodded grudgingly. "Fine. But don't expect me to dance attendance of any of the little husband-seeking vultures I'm sure your uncle will throw my way. I will not be palmed off to placate his social obligations."

Ian gave him a crooked grin. "I'm actually quite sure the purpose of the ball is to celebrate my marriage to Sophie, not marry you off, Derek."

"Humph," Derek muttered, "I wouldn't be too sure of that. Your uncle is a wily bastard."

Sophie had been noticeably quiet during their exchange, and Ian looked at her. She looked vaguely sick at the thought of the ball. "Come now, Sophie, it will be a very grand affaire. You shall meet some nice people and some not-so-nice people. They will look you over and declare you unfit for a Witherspoon bride, lie to our faces, eat my uncle's food and then leave. Then we shall come home and never think about them again."

His last comment managed to make Sophie sputter with nervous laughter. "Promise?" she asked.

"I won't even think about them while we're there," Derek muttered in disgust, and that made Sophie laugh outright.

* * * * *

They arrived at Lord Randall's that afternoon to a chorus of delighted greetings. There were already several other gentlemen there visiting, and they all greeted Sophie warmly. She remembered most of them from the wedding, but wasn't given the opportunity to be embarrassed about her dramatic exit from the wedding breakfast. It was laughed off as bridal nerves and she let the impression stand.

Ian announced the coming ball and invited everyone there to attend. There was much discussion of who else might attend. Sophie was shocked to learn that Kate had yet to be out in society since her marriage to Jason, and Very had not been introduced to society yet.

"Well, we are not exactly welcome in most *ton* drawing rooms, my dear," Kate said with a blush. "Our...situation is well-known among the *ton*, and universally frowned upon."

"You mean the fact that you live with both Jason and Tony? Well, I hardly think that signifies. According to Ian's uncle, as long as the husband and wife present a united front, what goes on behind closed doors is no one else's business.

Now that Ian is married, the earl assured him that no one will look askance at Derek in company with us." Sophie's tone was so matter-of-fact that silence greeted her announcement. Sophie looked around nervously. She had to force herself not to wring her hands. "Did I say something wrong?" she whispered to Kate.

Kate was blinking at her like an owl but shook her head at Sophie's question. "No, no, Sophie, you're right, of course, it's just that we never thought about that. I think perhaps we have been fooling ourselves about why we hide here. Perhaps it's not what the *ton* will think, but what we think." She looked disturbed, and Sophie felt awful for upsetting her.

"Oh Kate," she cried, "don't be silly! I would have been afraid too, if Ian's uncle hadn't told him that. Was he wrong?" Sophie started to panic, and she could feel her breathing become erratic.

Suddenly Ian was there and Derek was frowning at Kate. "Breathe, Sophie," Ian told her quietly as he sat down next to her, "nice and slow. That's it."

"She hasn't had one of those nervous attacks in weeks, Kate, and now you've gone and upset her. If Wilchester says no one will care, no one will care. They all bark like dogs if he tells them to, so if he tells them to ignore it, they will," Derek growled at her.

"Don't you dare yell at Kate," Jason growled right back, marching up to confront Derek, standing right in front of him.

"Then tell your wife to quit upsetting Sophie," Derek barked at him, taking a menacing step forward.

"Derek," Sophie said breathlessly, "I'm all right, really. It's not Kate's fault. You said it yourself, I'm a little widgeon. But I'm not. See? I'm fine." She sat up straight and tried to breathe normally. She was mortified that she'd made another spectacle of herself, and Derek was making it worse. He narrowed his eyes at her. "Look, breathing," she told him, taking three exaggerated deep breaths. "See? I'm fine."

"Derek," Ian said mildly, and after looking at the two of them, Derek stepped back.

"My apologies, Kate," he said grudgingly.

"Oh Derek, that's all right. You're quite right. If Wilchester tells them to they'll ignore a white elephant in the ballroom." She turned to Sophie and smiled. "You're very lucky to have Ian's family, Sophie. They care for him a great deal, and I'm sure those feelings will be extended to you." She looked over at Derek, stricken. "I mean…I'm sure they feel that way about Derek too." Her voice trailed off at the end, as everyone within hearing was aware that Ian's relationship with Derek had caused the rift with his family.

Derek smiled wryly. "Well, that would be something to see, wouldn't it? Now you all must come to the ball, if only to see me clasped to the bosom of Ian's family."

Ian sighed and relaxed next to Sophie. "See, Sophie, didn't I tell you a ball would be great fun? Look how much fun we're having already and it's still weeks away."

Sophie burst into laughter at Ian's sarcasm. "Oh, great fun. Why, I eagerly anticipate the fun escalating to at least a maiming or a good press ganging before I get to dance in front of hundreds of slavering *ton* critics, all barking like dogs." The entire room burst into laughter at Sophie's rejoinder, and even Derek smiled approvingly at her.

"Well, Ian, your wife's idea of fun may be a little unorthodox, but I do like an Original," an amused voice drawled from the drawing room door.

"Freddy!" Kate cried, holding out her hand as he came forward to greet her. "And Brett too, how lovely to see you. You're back from Ashton Park so soon?"

"A minor unpleasantness that took very little time and ended in a wedding," he told her with a kiss for her hand. "There are things that require my attention there soon, however. But enough of that, what is this I hear about a ball?"

He turned and kissed Sophie's hand and she smiled shyly at him.

A duke was kissing her hand! She blushed as the quiet Mr. Brett Haversham followed behind him.

"You positively glow, Mrs. Witherspoon," Mr. Haversham said with a smile that transformed him from plain to breathtakingly handsome. "Marriage seems to agree with you." He looked at Ian and then over his shoulder at Derek, who was thumping the duke on the shoulder and laughing about something. "It seems to agree with all of you."

Sophie blushed harder. "Thank you, Mr. Haversham," she replied politely. "I quite find it to my liking." She gave Ian a pert look and Mr. Haversham laughed.

The duke sat gracefully in a delicate armchair and smiled warmly at the gathering. "So tell me why dear Mrs. Witherspoon will be dancing before barking dogs," he inquired politely, and Sophie laughed, her nerves at being in such lofty company evaporating. He was quickly filled in on the proposed ball.

"Well," he exclaimed, astounded, "of course there will be no problem. Wilchester commands a great deal of respect among the *haute ton*."

"You will attend, won't you, Freddy?" Kate asked. "As Duke of Ashland you wield as much if not more power than Wilchester."

"I do?" Freddy asked. "Well, yes, I guess I do—just never thought to use it in such a fashion. If it is what you desire, dearest Kate, then I shall wear my most fashionable dancing slippers and lop off heads if anyone so much as frowns at you or Mrs. Witherspoon. Will that make you happy, my dears?"

"You shall have to dance with Very, Your Grace. It will be her bow in society, and it would quite make her the envy of all." Sophie looked around the room. "Where is Very?"

Kate and Jason looked uncomfortable. Tony sighed and Wolf looked out the door into the garden. "She's out in the garden, Sophie," Kate said. "Why don't you go and say hello?" Sophie cocked her head inquiringly at Kate, but the other woman subtly shook her head and indicated Sophie should go out, so she stood and excused herself. She felt several pairs of eyes follow her as she left the room.

She found Very hiding at the back of the pretty, informal garden. She was sitting in a little Greek folly, crying piteously. It was so unlike Very that Sophie stood in shock for a moment before hurrying over to her. "Very, darling, what's wrong?" she cried, sitting down next to the miserable girl and pulling her into her arms.

"Oh Sophie!" she wailed. "It's all my fault. And now we are to be separated." She sobbed into her sodden hanky. The poor dear was not a good crier. She was red and splotchy and sounded as if her nose was stuffed with cotton.

"Shh," Sophie soothed. "You must settle down, dear, and tell me everything."

Very sniffed loudly a time or two and looked askance at her ruined handkerchief. Sophie fished one out of her reticule and Very took it gratefully. "Well, I've had a good cry, so I guess you're right, it's about time to stop." Sophie almost laughed. How like Very to refuse to linger in the depths of misery for long. With a final sniff and a delicate swipe of her nose, Very looked at Sophie and Sophie could see how unhappy she was.

"It all started when I let Wolf make love to me," Very began, as if telling a fairy tale. She got no further because Sophie interrupted with a gasp.

"You what?"

"Well, not make love exactly. We did not actually have sexual congress." Very made a face and then sighed. "Actually, we were also fully clothed. And neither of us climaxed. So perhaps made love is not the right phrase."

Sophie's shock had turned to suspicion. "What exactly is the right phrase?"

Very looked at her lap as she twisted the handkerchief in her hands. "He kissed me. We kissed." She looked over at Sophie then. "Michael was there."

"Kensington?"

Very nodded. "I was kissing Michael, you see, and well, perhaps a bit more than kissing, when Wolf walked in on us. It seemed the most natural thing in the world to include Wolf, as he and Michael are lovers."

Sophie gaped at Very. "They are?"

Very looked at Sophie in bemusement. "I don't know why that should surprise you. After all, it's the same situation you are in."

Sophie shook her head. "Of course. I'm sorry, I just hadn't realized. Do go on." Part of Sophie was shocked at the revelation, part titillated, and part, the biggest part, vastly relieved that someone else could understand her predicament.

"Well, after Wolf kissed me," Very paused, shaking her head, "no, after I kissed him, Michael had another of his attacks of conscience and stormed out." A tear leaked out of Very's eye and she dabbed at it impatiently. "And now it appears that Michael has left. No one knows where. Apparently he makes a habit of it every few months, when the guilt over his relationship with Wolf becomes more than he can bear." She sounded so miserable, Sophie squeezed her hand.

"Are you sorry you kissed Wolf?" Sophie asked her gently, hoping the answer was no.

"Oh no," Very said emotionally. "It made me realize I have deep feelings for him as well. It's always been Michael, you see, and Wolf was just there, just part of Michael. But that night, well, I wanted Wolf. I wanted to kiss Wolf. I saw him, really saw him, for the first time, and I saw how he feels about me, and I wanted him, with or without Michael." Very turned anguished eyes to Sophie. "But Michael got very upset. Not out of jealousy, but because he thinks it's wrong, the three of us together."

"How does Wolf feel?" Sophie was no fool. She clearly saw the parallels between Very's problems and her own. Perhaps if she understood Wolf's feelings she'd understand Derek's?

"He cares for me, deeply, but he agrees with Jason and Kate and Tony."

Sophie shook her head, confused. "They were there as well?" This might be a little more than Sophie could handle right now.

Very looked at her in horror. "Good God, no! Jason and Tony would have thrashed them both. No, this was the day of your wedding. They asked Wolf and me to take things slowly between us. They think I'm too young to make such a momentous decision. They actually believe I may change my mind after I'm out in the world a bit more and entertain a few more suitors. More? I haven't got but Wolf and Michael. Where am I supposed to get more suitors?"

With a start Sophie realized that Very knew nothing of the ball. Quickly she caught Very up on the latest news.

"Oh, Sophie, that's marvelous!" Very was overjoyed as she grabbed Sophie's hands. "You shall be so happy now that Ian's family has accepted you and welcomed him back. And a ball! I would love to go. Did Kate say I could go?"

Sophie laughed. Very looked much better now than she had when Sophie came out to find her. She was getting her color back and her eyes were regaining their sparkle. Sophie was glad—she didn't like to see her friend so unhappy.

"Yes, yes, you are to make your bow at my ball, Very. Isn't that wonderful?"

Very wrinkled her nose. "I suppose so, but I shall be expected to dance with all those mythical suitors, I'm sure." She gasped and looked at Sophie in awe. "Oh Sophie, you and

Ian will probably be expected to dance a waltz together. How divine!"

Sophie's eyes widened and she felt her earlier illness return over that thought. "Very, you must help me," she begged the quite recovered girl as she gripped her hands.

Very looked at her in concern. "Of course, Sophie, whatever you need. Tell me how I can help."

Sophie bit her lip and then blurted out her secret. "I can't dance."

Very scoffed. "You can't be that bad, Sophie. I myself tend to stumble a bit because I'm a little taller than most men are used to."

Sophie looked at her measuringly. "But you can dance?"

Very looked affronted. "Of course I can dance! I may not be out in society yet, but we occasionally dance here at the house when we have guests, and as there's usually a shortage of women, I have my pick of partners."

Sophie took a deeply relieved breath. "Then you can teach me."

Very's eyes grew round as saucers. "You mean you don't know how?" Sophie shook her head.

Very grabbed her hand and dragged her down the steps of the folly and across the garden toward the house. "Come on, no time like the present. We've a drawing room full of available partners. You shall dance like a princess by the end of the day."

Sophie tried to tug her arm free with a protest. "Very, no! Can we not do this quietly, so no one knows? Please?"

Very snorted. "Absolutely not. The sooner we start, the better you shall be in three weeks time." She spared a glance behind her. "Don't worry, Sophie, no one here will make sport of you simply because you don't know how to dance." Very suddenly snapped her fingers. "Of course! Derek. Derek dances divinely. I'm sure he won't mind teaching you."

Sophie was shaking her head frantically. "No, Very, not Derek. Anyone but Derek, please."

Very furrowed her brows in irritation. "Is he still being unpleasant? I shall box his ears, Sophie, and make him behave."

Sophie closed her eyes. "We are friends, are we not, Very?" she asked quietly and a little desperately. "Please do not make me dance with Derek."

Very sounded exasperated. "Sophie, don't be a ninny. Derek isn't so bad."

"I made love with Derek two nights ago, Very." Sophie blurted out the confession, her eyes flying open in shock even as the words came from her mouth.

"What?" Very squealed loudly. "Oh my God, Sophie!" She pulled Sophie over to the nearest bench and shoved her down. "How was it?" she asked with avid curiosity.

Sophie blinked at her and couldn't seem to stop the flow of words. "It was wonderful, Very, incredible. And I think I may be in love with him." She slapped a hand over her mouth to stop herself from saying anything more.

"Very? Are you all right?" Wolf appeared on the path a few feet away, his expression guarded as he watched the two women.

"Go away," Very snapped at him. "We are having a private conversation." Wolf looked startled at her words, but immediately turned to comply. "And make sure no one else disturbs us, darling," she called out blithely, and Wolf's back stiffened before he turned to flash a smile at Very and then disappeared as he went back toward the house.

Very looked at Sophie with narrowed eyes. "You will tell me everything, Sophie. Every little detail." And Sophie pulled her hand away from her mouth and let everything pour out of her.

"Well, is everything all right?" Derek asked Wolf impatiently when he stepped back onto the terrace.

Wolf grinned at him. "Girl talk."

Derek rolled his eyes. "What's wrong with Very?"

Fortunately Wolf was used to his blunt ways and didn't even bat an eye before answering. They had both retreated to the terrace, tired of the speculative looks being cast their way by well-meaning friends. "Kensington's gone again."

"Bloody hell. I'm sorry, Wolf." Inwardly Derek had a few more choice words for Kensington's desertion. Wolf just shrugged, but Derek had known him long enough to sense the pain behind his nonchalance.

"It's not the first time, nor the last, I suspect. But it has hurt Very."

"It's hard to love someone who doesn't want you to." Derek turned to see that Freddy had stepped out on the terrace in time to hear their conversation. Derek knew he was talking about Brett. Freddy's devotion to the taciturn older man was well-known, and they had all spent endless hours speculating on why Brett denied Freddy when he so obviously cared for him.

Derek sighed. He was not without his own problems in that area, so he didn't feel qualified to offer advice. Without thinking he spoke aloud. "It's hard to let people love you."

Freddy gave him a measuring look. "Yes, but it's their choice, isn't it? You can't make it for them."

Derek looked away. He really didn't want Freddy crawling around inside his head, trying to find out what made him tick. He didn't like crawling around inside his own head, thank you very much.

"How are you and Sophie getting along?" Freddy asked casually, and Derek winced.

"Fine," he ground out without looking back at Freddy.

"Just fine," Ian agreed jovially from behind him, and Derek spun around.

"Bloody hell, is anyone else going to creep out here and eavesdrop on my conversations?" He glared at the other three men on the terrace.

Wolf just raised his eyebrow and smiled politely. "I was here first."

Ian laughed. "It's not as if I'm skulking about in dark corridors, Derek. I walked out an open door onto an equally open terrace in broad daylight. Very stealthy of me, to be sure." Ian spoke dramatically and waggled his eyebrows and Freddy and Wolf laughed, which irrationally pissed Derek off more.

"Derek and Sophie are getting on extremely well these days, wouldn't you say, Derek?" Ian continued conversationally.

"Ian," Derek warned with a growl.

Brett limped casually out the door onto the terrace. "Oh, are we talking about Sophie? I quite like her."

"Fuck," Derek said flatly. He knew Freddy and Brett together were nearly impossible to shake off once they got their teeth into something. It seemed that today he was the bone.

Ian laughed again, having a marvelous time it seemed to Derek. "Oh, Derek likes her just fine now too, don't you, Derek?"

"Ian, don't make me silence you," Derek said menacingly.

Ian was all innocence. "What? I can't tell our friends how much you like my wife?"

"Why are you doing this?" Derek was torn between anger and exasperation. What was Ian doing? Why was he pushing Derek like this?

"Doing what? Talking about how well you and Sophie get on? It's the truth, isn't it? You talk to her and about her endlessly. You watch her when she's in the garden. You almost let her win at chess. You bought her a puppy. You let her comfort you. You were ready to pummel Jason because she was upset. Don't you like her, Derek?"

Derek grabbed Ian's arm and roughly pushed him back against the brick wall. He stepped forward, close enough to growl into Ian's ear. "Why are you doing this?" he repeated.

"Is there a problem?" Tony asked slowly from the open door behind Derek. Derek turned to regard him for a moment, but before he could answer, Ian spoke.

"Is there a problem, Derek?" His tone was mocking, and Derek had had all he could take. He pushed away from Ian in disgust.

"I don't know, Ian. You're the one who all but told our friends here that I slept with your wife. Is there a problem?"

Tony quickly closed the door behind him against the curious stares they were receiving. "Keep your voices down." Tony was glowering. "Sophie deserves better than to be talked about as if she were a common tavern wench."

Ian looked at Derek and sadly shook his head, all his earlier bonhomie gone. "I'm trying to tell you that there aren't any problems, Derek, except the ones in your head." He took a step toward Derek and Derek retreated. Ian frowned and followed. Derek stood his ground and Ian wrapped a hand around the back of his head and pulled him down until their foreheads were touching. "Damn it, Derek, why can't you admit you're in love with her? Why?"

"I am not in love with her, Ian. You just wish I were." Even as he said it, he knew it for the lie it was. By the look on everyone's faces they knew it too.

"Ian?" Sophie's voice came from the bottom of the stairs that led to the garden. Derek spun around, horrified that she may have heard their argument. Sophie saw the look on his face and she raised her skirt to rush up the stairs. "Derek? Are you all right? Is something wrong?"

Derek and Ian stood frozen, but all the other men on the terrace stepped forward at once to reassure her.

"No, no, nothing's wrong," Tony told her as he met her at the top of the steps and tucked her hand into the crook of his arm.

Tony gave Derek a look that commanded without words, and Derek smiled crookedly at Sophie. "No, nothing's wrong. I was just being my usual disagreeable self."

Sophie grinned back in disbelief. "You're admitting you're disagreeable? Now I know something's wrong."

Derek heard Ian snort in amusement behind him. "Well, if you are all done amusing yourselves at my expense..." Derek drawled as he made a movement toward the doors to the drawing room. He needed to get away from Sophie before he gave up and gave in to the desire to snatch her hand away from Tony and press it to his side.

Ian laughed. After years of sharing Ian's every mood, Derek was able to hear the unhappiness hidden in that laugh. "No, nothing's wrong except the usual." Derek saw immediately that Sophie recognized Ian's mood too, but as she started to say something, she was interrupted by Very.

Very was climbing the stairs much slower than Sophie. "There certainly is something wrong," she announced dramatically as she reached the top of the stairs. "Sophie cannot dance."

"Very!" Sophie cried, spinning around to confront her. "I thought you weren't going to say anything!"

"Well, I certainly never promised that," Very said smugly. "And even if I did, why ever would you believe me?" She marched over to Derek and pointed a finger at his chest. "You are going to teach her."

"Sophie darling, why didn't you say anything?" Ian asked. He stepped up to Derek's side. "Is that why you've been so upset about the ball?"

Sophie nodded miserably. Derek had been about to refuse Very's command, but at the distress on Sophie's face he just couldn't do it. He grabbed Sophie's hand. "I'll be damned if you're going to embarrass us in front the entire *ton*. If they're going to talk about us behind our backs, it won't be because of your dancing." He started to drag her inside. "Where can we go?" he called over his shoulder as he threw open the doors. He marched inside the drawing room.

"Derek," Ian said menacingly from behind him.

"Don't worry, Ian, it's only dancing. I promise to be sweet and patient. By the end of the day she'll dance, or my name isn't Derek Knightly." He tried to be amusing, but he could hear the desperation in his voice.

Sophie sputtered behind him, trying to tug her hand free. "Clearly you are not Derek Knightly because he doesn't know how to be sweet and patient. Oh!" she cried out as she slammed into Derek's back when he stopped abruptly.

"We need music." Derek didn't know why he was so determined to teach Sophie to dance. His heart was still pounding from the scene with Ian, and his fear that Sophie may have heard what he said. Buried deep inside, where he refused to examine it, was the awareness of the lie he'd told. He kept layering them one on top of the other, lie upon lie, as if he could pile enough of them on top of the truth until they smothered it.

"Music for what?" Kate asked with wide eyes as she watched the grim procession troop in from the terrace.

"Derek is going to teach Sophie how to dance," Very informed the room in general. "Come along. The piano is in the library. Who's going to accompany the dancing? You know I frighten birds and small animals with my playing. And I want to dance. So who's going to play?" She blithely blew through the room past Derek and Sophie as if she expected everyone to follow her, and they did.

"I shall play," Ian said solemnly. Derek jerked to a stop and looked at him. Ian smiled at him tenderly. "He is teaching my wife to dance, after all. It's the least I can do."

Derek's heart seemed to stop for a minute, and then resumed at twice its normal rate, making him struggle for breath. Did Ian know what he was doing to him? Did he know what he was offering? The idea was tempting, to be loved by Ian and Sophie, to love them, to lie with them—to live a dream. But dreams weren't reality. He blinked to clear his vision. The reality was that loving people was a gamble. When they died they took a little of you with them. Some took more than others. He was already at risk, loving Ian. He wouldn't gamble with his heart again. He didn't have that many pieces left to lose.

Chapter Eighteen

જી

Sophie stood breathlessly next to Derek in the library while some footmen cleared the furniture out of the way and Ian chose some music from the sheets Very brought him. Derek was as still as a statue next to her, refusing to look at her and clutching her hand so tightly it hurt. She was confused and frightened. What was wrong with Derek? Why did Ian look so sad? What had happened while she'd been in the garden with Very? The questions spinning around in her head were making her dizzy.

"I thought dancing was supposed to be fun," she said quietly to Derek.

He jerked his head around almost as if he was surprised to see her next to him. His hold on her hand loosened and then fell away. She felt lost at the abandonment. "It is." His voice was flat, impersonal.

"Then why are you so grim?" Sophie asked, her tone as flat and impersonal as his. The question, or her tone, seemed to anger him.

"I am merely thinking about the steps," he informed her dismissively.

Sophie moved slightly away from him. "Really?" she said dryly. "If you have to concentrate that hard, perhaps you're not as good as everyone thinks. Perhaps I should find another teacher."

Derek's eyes narrowed on her, and she caught a glimpse of heated emotion in them before he hooded them and hid it from her. "No one else is going to teach you to dance, Sophie. Only me."

The dark promise of his voice caused memories of their night together to flash through Sophie's mind. He'd commanded her in just that voice, had loved her with the same rough timbre and hooded eyes. Her heartbeat raced and her breathing became erratic. "Why? Why only you?" she whispered. Before he could answer, Ian called to them from the piano.

"It shall be a waltz first. It is a relatively simple dance, and as Very has pointed out, Sophie and I will most likely be expected to dance one together for everyone's enjoyment." Sophie looked over at Ian and shivered a little at the inscrutable look on his face. What was going on? She looked back to Derek and he was grim again, also staring at Ian.

"Fine. A waltz," he answered, and he swung Sophie into his arms. He put one hand on her waist and held her other hand high. Sophie automatically grabbed his upper arm with her free hand and felt the muscles bunch and tremble beneath her hand. Sophie looked up at him, and it was as if she'd been punched in the stomach as desire slammed through her and she fought to breathe. His beautiful hazel eyes were staring at her, stark and hot with an emotion she could clearly recognize, a desire equal to her own. Derek's eyes with their green and gray depths made her think of the forest. The dark heart of a great forest, sunlight filtered far above by the trees, casting a soft green-tinged light on the dark earth forest floor. When he looked at her like this, so intense, so dangerous, it was like the air in that forest, still and quiet and full of teeming life, wild things watching and hunting just out of sight. Life poured off Derek, life and heat and a wildness that was barely contained.

"Put your hand on my shoulder." Sophie blinked several times as Derek's voice penetrated her thoughts. "Sophie," he repeated impatiently, "put your hand on my shoulder, not my arm."

"Oh," Sophie said and quickly complied. She winced inwardly at her wayward thoughts and less than intelligent response. No wonder Derek didn't love her, she was an idiot.

"When you dance, no matter whom you are dancing with, keep a respectable distance between you and your partner. The high sticklers will pounce on you if they sense any impropriety in your dancing." Derek's voice was detached, lecturing, and Sophie couldn't help being just a little hurt at his dispassionate treatment. His comment made her snort inelegantly.

"Yes, I'm sure it's the impropriety in my dancing that will set tongues wagging." She saw Derek fight a grin at her comment and felt a small thrill of victory. Then Ian began to play and Sophie was utterly amazed at the musical magic his clever hands were making at the piano. The piece was beautiful, slow and sensual with a lyrical, dreamlike quality. She'd never heard it before.

"I didn't know Ian could play the piano," she said, staring over her shoulder at Ian sitting there concentrating completely on the music, as if no one else was in the room.

Derek tugged on her hand and she turned back to him. "Ian is the consummate lover, Sophie. He excels at all things romantic, including music. It is one of his passions, although he has rarely indulged it the last two years."

"Why?" she asked breathlessly. The combination of Ian's sensual music and Derek's physical presence was arousing Sophie tremendously. Her skin felt tight and hot and ached with a yearning to be stroked. Her breasts felt heavy, her nipples hard, her sex wet and swollen. Why? Why now, in front of a room full of people? She bit her lip and unconsciously gripped Derek's hand tighter.

When Derek answered, his voice was low and filled with the gravel of desire. He had to stop and clear his throat, but it was too late. The sound had traveled down Sophie's spine and lodged inside her where it throbbed in time to Ian's music. She stared helplessly at his mouth as he answered. "He won't say. I think it makes him too emotional to release himself in the music. He has a lot of things stored away behind a locked door inside him, and music unlocks the door that he wants to keep closed." The look he shot Ian was almost painful in its naked adoration and concern.

"You love him so much," Sophie whispered, awed by the depth of Derek's feelings, dismayed that anyone could think him cold or unfeeling or a bully. Derek felt things so deeply. He understood Ian's closed door because he had so many of his own.

Derek looked down to her again. "Yes," was all he said. Then he moved and Sophie followed.

Derek gave her very little direction. He used his body to guide her and taught her the steps by demonstrating them instead of explaining them. Sophie was glad. She'd always learned better this way, by doing rather than being told what to do. Somehow Derek knew that. She wasn't surprised. In her experience so far, Derek knew everything.

There were several couples dancing. Very and Wolf, Kate and Tony, and a pretty girl named Rachel who was here with one of Jason's friends. She was dancing with the Duke of Ashland and looked as if she couldn't believe her good fortune. The duke just laughed and swung her around, his dancing as boisterous and happy as the duke himself. Sophie saw them all as if through a fog. Almost all her concentration initially was on learning the steps of the dance. Eventually her awareness was less on the steps and almost exclusively on Derek.

Dancing with Derek was extraordinary. He moved as if the silly rules that applied to other people had no meaning for him. He was a big man, but when he danced it was as if he floated above the ground, and Sophie floated with him. She stopped looking down at her feet and simply stared into Derek's eyes, lost in them, and he stared back equally transfixed. He was so beautiful, so big and strong and wonderful.

I love him. I love him. Sophie's thoughts kept tempo with the dips and swirls of the dance. Even as her desire deepened, her heart grew heavy. He didn't want her. He'd come to her bed, with Ian, because of Ian, but he didn't want her, Sophie. She could be any woman as long as Ian was there. She wanted to cry at the injustice of it. All her life she'd wanted someone to love. Now she loved two men. She was being greedy. Ian loved her. He'd said he loved her. It had to be enough. And even if she couldn't have Derek's love, she could have his body, and give hers to him. And during those times she'd pretend he loved her. She'd pretended most of her life, but this would be the most precious lie she'd ever told herself. *I love him.*

Ian looked up from the music to watch Derek and Sophie dancing. They looked perfect together, he so big and strong and Sophie tall and slender and moving to the music like a willow in the wind. The two of them were amazing to watch. They gazed into each other's eyes as they spun and whirled around the floor, oblivious to everyone else in the room, including him. He didn't mind. He was secure in their love and affection for him. The sight of them like this made his heart pound and his hands tremble on the keys as he poured all his love into the music he made for them.

Slowly all the other dancers stopped and stood off to the side to watch them, as mesmerized by their grace as Ian. Derek had pulled Sophie close so that their bodies were pressed together from chest to thigh, moving as one. Her arm was around his shoulder, her hand on his nape as she tipped her head back to look deeply in his eyes. They were born to dance together, to be together. Derek may try to lie to himself, but the proof of his love was there on the dance floor, in the way he held her and the way he looked at her.

Sophie wore her heart on her sleeve. It was obvious to all that she was desperately in love with Derek. Her eyes were dreamy, her lips parted as if in anticipation of his kiss. She clung to him and followed his every move, letting him lead her, guide her, completely trusting him with everything she was. Ian ached for her. How many times would Derek hurt her before he admitted he loved her? Ian wanted to protect them both from hurt, but how could he? He was only a man, and all he could do was love them both. He had to look away and, closing his eyes, released that love into his song.

Derek was under a spell and he wished never to awaken. Sophie felt like a dream in his arms as they floated around the room. She was fire and heat and passion as the sunlight danced in and out of her flaming hair as they glided past the open windows. He knew he had pulled her too close, but he needed to feel her pressed against him, to feel each breath she dragged into her chest, each beat of her heart in her breast. Her fire called to something in him, something that had lain dormant for so long. He felt a great love and passion for Ian, but this was different. This feeling was mixed up with protectiveness and possession in a maelstrom of emotions that had him off balance and he didn't like it, but there was nothing he could do.

He was drowning in the depths of her glittering amber gaze. He couldn't pull his eyes away, as if she'd bewitched him. But he knew the fault was his own, the weakness of his own making. He hadn't protected himself well enough from her. He craved her. He craved her kisses, her moans, her laughter and her quick wit. He craved the earthy, sunshine smell of her after she came in from the garden, and the scent of her sweet tea over the breakfast table. He craved the taste of her freckles and the strength of her legs around his waist, the feel of her hair against his chest.

How? How had he let this happen? He felt his heart beating a rapid, panicked tattoo in his chest as if to remind him that it was fragile. He hoped it wasn't too late, that he'd be able to pull back from this pathetic needing. With a sinking heart he suspected it was already too late. He was in too deep now with no way out. To walk away meant leaving a big part of himself behind with her, not to mention what it would do to Ian. What was he going to do? Christ, he loved her. He loved her. The thought frightened him so much he felt his hands tremble as they held her.

The music stopped and Derek glided Sophie to a standstill. They didn't release each other immediately, but blinked slowly as they continued to stare into each other's eyes. The desire in her gaze was obvious, but there were other emotions hiding behind it. Gradually Derek became aware of the utter silence in the room and the deserted dance floor around them. He reluctantly took a step back from Sophie, but they'd been so close he was barely at a respectable distance. The urge to flee was nipping at his heels, his fear and confusion clouding his mind.

"Are you going to break my heart, Derek?" Sophie whispered brokenly as he let his hands drop. The question pierced him like an arrow. He shook his head, whether in denial of her question or of his feelings he wasn't sure. He turned and walked from the room without a word, the silence he left behind more deafening than words.

* * * * *

Ian and Sophie left Jason's right after Derek. They came home hoping to find him there, but he was nowhere to be found. Sophie was very quiet through dinner and excused herself to go to bed early. Ian joined her soon after, determined to talk about what was going on and what Sophie wanted. Ian realized that he was at fault in the whole situation. He'd been holding back his hopes and fears from Sophie, and it was time to stop. If they were truly to make a life together, they needed to be honest with one another. She was already in bed by the time he got to her room. Without a word he climbed in beside her and pulled her into his embrace.

"Sophie, we must talk. About Derek, about us, about what's going on." No sooner had he broached the subject than Sophie broke down and began crying on his shoulder. "Oh, God, Sophie," he murmured, kissing her head gently as he stroked her back, her gulping sobs echoing in his head. He'd done this to her. He'd been so focused on what he wanted and what Derek needed, he'd ignored Sophie's needs. It took him a moment to understand what Sophie was trying to say through her tears.

"I'm sorry, Ian, I'm sorry," she cried. Ian's heart clutched painfully. "It's my fault, I drove him away. I pushed him today, and now he's gone. Gone! How you must hate me. I'll leave, Ian, I'll leave and Derek will come back to you. I'm sorry. I'm so sorry."

Ian held her tightly to him, trying to absorb her pain. "Sophie, no! You mustn't believe that, you mustn't. It was me, always pushing him, telling him what to do. Why didn't I leave him alone?" Ian closed his eyes and tried to gain control. "He'll be back. He always comes back. Derek...oh, Sophie. There's so much you don't understand about Derek."

Sophie pulled away violently, her fists wrapped in the sheet. "I understand he loves you, Ian. I understand that. How could he not? And I understand he doesn't love me. He desires me and he hates himself, and me, for it."

"Sophie, no—"

"Yes! Yes!" Sophie was shouting. She was getting hysterical.

Ian sat up and leaned over her where she was curled up in a sobbing heap. He grasped her shoulder firmly. "No. Sophie, listen to me. You must stop crying and listen to me, darling. Please."

Sophie's sobs quieted after a moment, though she continued to hiccup and sniffle into the bed, refusing to look at Ian.

"Sophie, I don't hate you, and neither does Derek. Sophie, I love you. I've told you that. I think Derek could love you too, if he'd let himself. He won't tell me what's wrong. Derek doesn't like to talk about what's going on inside his head, not even with me. I have to drag it out of him most of the time. Eventually he'll tell us, when he's ready. You have to learn to be patient with Derek, Sophie. He's so fragile. No one else sees it, but I do. Don't you? Don't you see how he's breaking?" Ian bit back his own sob. "He's breaking. I thought we could fix him, you and I, Sophie, but what if it's too late?"

Sophie turned to him and stared at him with her beautiful eyes red-rimmed and swollen and still damp with tears. Ian searched the table next to the bed for a handkerchief. He found one and turned back to hand it to Sophie, who wiped her cheeks and blew her nose. "What do you mean, Ian? I don't understand. How is he breaking? How can I help fix him?"

Ian lay back down and placed his forearm over his eyes to hold back the tears. "The nightmares, Sophie, they're getting worse, not better. And Derek, did you know he used to laugh at everything? He was a devil, with a brutally sharp wit. When we were with Dolores we laughed all the time, even when hell was waiting right outside our tent. But he hardly laughs now, Sophie." Ian moved his arm and looked at her, letting the bleakness he felt at losing Derek show. "I've never known him to sleep through the night. He avoids people, avoids attachments. His rudeness, his bullishness, it's gotten worse in an attempt to drive people away. He won't plan for the future, Sophie. It's as if he doesn't believe in a future."

Sophie crawled back over to Ian and laid her head on his chest, curling up at his side. Ian wrapped his arm around her and held on as if she were an anchor in storm-tossed seas. "How did you think I would help, Ian?" she asked quietly.

Ian ran his hand through Sophie's silky hair, smoothing it across her scalp. "Derek and I began in the war, Sophie, and in some ways, for Derek, that hasn't ended. I'd hoped that you would be a new beginning for us, the start of the rest of our lives. Something good and lasting that wasn't rooted in that fucking Peninsula." He turned his head and buried his face in the warmth and sweetness of her hair. "You were always for both of us, Sophie. You were going to save us, you see. You were going to give us a home, children, a family, a place to belong. And peace, God, how I wanted you to bring us peace."

Ian shook his head and spoke roughly. "I'm such a fool. What a burden to place on you, my love."

"I love him." Sophie's voice was quiet and quavering. Her words pierced Ian with happiness, but also with sadness. Sophie had never said those words to Ian. He hadn't realized that he needed Sophie as much as Derek did. She gave him all that he thought he'd lost in the war—joy, laughter, hope. When she continued with a sniff, Ian's heart stopped beating for a moment, and then nearly pounded out of his chest. "I love him as much as I love you, Ian. I never thought I'd have anyone to love, or that anyone would love me. Loving you has been the most wonderful gift I've ever received. I'm selfish and greedy. I want to love Derek, too. I want him here with us, loving with us, sharing with us."

With a sob Ian hugged her tightly. "Yes. Yes, Sophie, that's what I want too. What I've always wanted, for all of us."

Sophie tenderly stroked his cheek. "We'll find him, Ian, and we'll fix him. We'll fix us. I will save you, Ian, you and Derek. We'll have everything we've dreamed of. I will give you children, and I will bring you peace. If I have to drag Derek back screaming and kicking to do it."

She held Ian and he held her as they both cried. As Derek would say, Christ, what a fucking mess they all were.

* * * * *

They didn't have to drag him back. The next morning Ian looked out the window of his study and saw Derek sitting on a bench in the garden looking pensive. How like him to suddenly appear and act as if he hadn't gone missing in the first place. Ian couldn't be angry. He was just so glad to see him. Sophie had gone shopping with Very and Kate, which was probably why Derek had come out of hiding.

Derek looked up at him when Ian sat on a bench across from him. "Hello." Ian spoke casually, trying not to spook him. Derek seemed in an odd mood.

Derek gave him that crooked little grin that always made Ian forgive him and want to fuck him. Derek knew exactly which cards to play in this game. Ian hardened himself to resist. It was past time they talked. "You ran yesterday." Ian's words were deliberately provoking.

"Yes." Derek surprised him by agreeing, not only readily but calmly. Derek got up from the bench and Ian tensed, anticipating another flight, but Derek just leaned against a tree trunk bordering the path and stared at the ground. Ian's heart began to pound. Derek wasn't running or ranting defensively. Did this mean he was ready to talk?

"Why?" Ian started simply. He had a million questions, a million things he wanted to tell Derek, but he forced himself to go slowly.

"Because she scares the hell out of me." Derek looked up at him through his lashes, his face relaxed in spite of his words.

"Sophie?" Ian asked in shock. "Why?"

"I'm afraid, Ian. I'm afraid to love her." Derek paused and looked away again, and Ian almost spoke, but he sensed Derek had more to say. "I loved Dolores, you know."

Ian was a little taken aback at the change of topic. He felt his way blindly through the conversation. "I suspected as much, although you never said the words."

"She was...sweet. I'd never met a girl like her before, sweet and easy to be around, so accepting of who I was. And then at night, she'd let us do anything we wanted, she loved it, every minute of it. She was wild and hungry and wanted us and didn't think it was wrong."

Derek's voice was so low Ian could hardly hear him, but he could hear the emotion in it. "I know," Ian agreed. "She was unlike anyone I'd ever met."

"But you didn't love her." It was more of a statement than a question, but Ian responded.

"I loved her, in a way. Not like I love Sophie, but Dolores was important to me."

"No," it was Derek's turn to agree, "not like Sophie." He turned his shoulder so he was leaning facing away from Ian. "Do you remember how she used to dance?" He was talking about Dolores again. "Day, night, it didn't matter, Dolores danced. She'd hum and dance around the tent, swirling her skirts."

"I remember." Ian couldn't keep the sadness out of his voice.

"I dreamed it was Sophie." Derek's voice was harsh, as if confessing some sin.

"Dancing? That's not so unusual, Derek. You danced with her yesterday."

Derek was shaking his head vigorously. "No. The night you were gone. The nightmare."

"I don't..." Ian's confusion cleared with sudden gut-wrenching clarity. "Oh God, Derek."

Derek turned back to face Ian, his shoulders slumped against the tree. He covered his eyes with a shaking hand. "I can't get it out of my head, Ian. What if she dies?"

"Derek," Ian said gently, "Sophie isn't going to die."

"Dolores did." Derek's voice was bleak, his posture dejected. He was breaking Ian's heart. He had never let Ian or anyone else inside him like this, never shown his weaknesses. He always had to be strong, belligerent even. Ian loved him even more now that he'd seen him humbled and trembling.

"It was war. We were...stupid, monstrously stupid not to consider the possibility. But there are no French cannon here, Derek."

Derek laughed reluctantly. "No, no French cannon, but there are other things that could take her."

Ian couldn't fight that logic. "Yes, yes there are. Just as they could take you or me. Death is a part of living, Derek. You can't let the specter of it shadow your life."

Derek thumped the heel of his hand against his forehead in frustration. "I know that here. But it doesn't stop me from wanting to throw up at the thought of loving and losing another woman."

"You don't let it stop you from loving me."

Derek looked up at Ian in shock. "Nothing could stop me from loving you. I did almost from the first moment I saw you."

Ian chuckled at the memory. "I was hardly at my best. Thank God for young, scavenging lieutenants."

"I knew when I saw you that the rumors were true." Ian stopped laughing and looked at Derek, dismay and resignation flooding him.

"I guess I always knew that was why you came, why you stayed. But the rumors were just superstitious nonsense, Derek. I can die, just like everyone else. If you love me because you think I'm invincible, then you are bound to be disappointed."

Derek smiled thinly. "I thought at the time that anyone who looked as you did, so strong, so beautiful, a golden Adonis with the mouth of a dock worker and the fighting skills of a pirate—if anyone was going to survive that war, it would be you."

Ian laughed disbelievingly. "You thought I couldn't die. Why was that so important to you? I mean, men were dying all around, it was war. Why search for the one man who wouldn't die?" Ian shook his head. "Never mind. That's an idiotic question."

"I was at Talavera."

"Christ, Derek." Ian was so shocked he didn't know what to say. Derek had never told him that. He'd had no idea he'd lived through that nightmare. Three thousand British against ten thousand French, and a grass fire had swept over the wounded on the battlefield when it was over. "You never told me."

"Well, today is the day for confessions, isn't it?" Derek smiled grimly. "By the time I found you I'd spent nearly two years without any sleep. Being with you let me sleep." Derek rubbed his face tiredly. "For a while anyway."

"Is that why you seduced me that night? Because you thought I couldn't die, that I would never leave you? Is that why you're here today?" Ian's chest was tight.

"Don't be an ass." Derek's tone was back to its normal acidity. "I seduced you that night because I wanted you, had wanted you for quite some time, since before Dolores. I just wanted you, Ian. I wasn't thinking about death then, just you and me."

"Why are you here now?" Ian wasn't sure he wanted to know. If the answer would drive him and Derek farther apart, he'd gladly let the matter drop. He would live never knowing as long as Derek was here with him. He almost told Derek that, but Derek answered his question.

"I'm here because I love you." The look on Derek's face was intent as he regarded Ian. "I may have come to you because I thought I'd never lose you. But I stayed because you made me strong enough to survive even if I did. I love you because you love me, warts and all. I've never dissembled with you, never lied about who I am. You've never made me pretty myself or my manners up, and you've defended me to all comers. You encouraged me to be what I wanted, to pursue my interests, and you've never asked for anything in return. You showed me what sex could be between men and women, and then between us." Derek straightened so he was no longer leaning against the tree. "I love you because of who you make me when I'm with you. I love you because we have a history together. When I'm with you there is no me, just us. You are the other half of my soul, Ian. Do not ever forget that."

Sometime during Derek's impassioned speech, Ian had risen. He didn't remember doing it, but suddenly he was there before Derek, pulling his head down, kissing him. Derek wrapped an arm around Ian and clutched a fistful of his jacket in his hand as he opened his mouth and accepted Ian, begged for him, reveled in him. This was part of why Ian loved Derek so much. He had always accepted him like this, as if their passion was the most natural, wonderful thing in the world. Ian knew how precious that was, that acceptance. It was the way Sophie accepted him too. He slowly pulled back from the kiss and rested his lips against Derek's jaw. Derek tilted his head to give him more access.

"Sophie is in love with you," Ian murmured, kissing the soft spot along Derek's jaw just below his ear.

"I didn't mean for it to happen," Derek murmured back, pulling Ian closer as he shivered at Ian's kisses.

"But it has. Will you deny her?" Ian relaxed back away from Derek enough to see his face. Derek looked scared, bewildered and unsure. Ian had never seen Derek like that before, and his vulnerability made Ian ache to take him right there.

Derek shook his head in confusion. "How can I deny her when I love her? And how can I love her when I'm so afraid?"

Derek was pulled from his thoughts and Ian's arms by shouting in the house.

"What the hell?" Ian muttered. He let Derek go and turned to stride quickly back toward the study doors. Before he arrived, Very appeared in the doorway. She was disheveled and in an unaccustomed panic.

"Ian! Derek! It's Sophie! Hurry, we've got to find her!"

Derek's insides twisted violently in fear. Sophie, oh God, Sophie. What was wrong? Derek ran to Very, but Ian was there already. Ian held the terrified girl by the shoulders as he questioned her. He was trying to soothe her, but in his own panic, Derek didn't see her trembling or the blood on her lip. He shoved Ian out of the way and grabbed Very, shaking her roughly. "What are you talking about? Talk sense, Very! Where is Sophie?"

Derek's rough handling seemed to bring Very to her senses. She slapped his hands away. "We were coming out of a shop and two men grabbed her. I'd sent the footman ahead to the carriage with packages, and when I tried to stop them, one of them hit me. Thank God Aunt Kate stayed back! They knew Sophie, Derek. They called her by name. Well, they called her Miss Middleton. The big one, he threw her over his shoulder and ran down an alley out of sight, I could hear her screaming! I tried to follow and that's when the little one hit me. It knocked me down and he ran off too, and I lost them! I lost them!" She was on the verge of hysteria again and Derek shook her, more gently this time. She calmed down. "I rushed Aunt Kate to the carriage and we drove up and down the street several times but saw nothing. We decided to come here first. Aunt Kate dropped me here and now she's going home to tell Jason and Tony." Very started to cry and shake. "I'm sorry. I'm sorry, I should have stopped them."

Derek pulled her against his chest and hugged her desperately. Very clung to him as she cried. "It's not your fault, Very," Derek told her, numb with disbelief. He looked at Ian and the other man was white as a ghost, pale and drawn.

"What street, Very? Could you show us?" Ian spoke faster than he normally did, his words slurred with a fear Derek could see reflected in his eyes.

Very nodded against Derek's chest. "Yes, yes, I'll take you there."

Ian turned, but Montague was signaling a footman already. "Get Mr. Witherspoon's carriage immediately!" He turned back to Ian. "Is there anything else? Shall I send several of the footmen with you?"

"Yes," Ian nodded, sounding once more in control. He strode through the study, calling behind him. "Come on,

Derek, and bring Very. We'll search high and low. Someone certainly saw something."

Derek followed, practically dragging Very in his haste. They had to find Sophie. They had to. He couldn't lose her. He knew that now. It was already too late for him. He was in love, and he would search heaven and hell to find the girl that was his heart as surely as Ian was his soul.

They wasted precious time combing the streets near the point of Sophie's abduction. By the time they admitted defeat, the sun was setting. Very was beside herself with guilt and grief. Ian was stoic, but his fear and frustration rolled off him in waves. Derek was drowning in his own guilt and regret and fear. If only he'd just admitted he loved her. If only he hadn't run yesterday, he might have been with her today to stop the kidnapping. If only she were still a timid little mouse afraid to leave the house instead of a newly self-confident and independent young woman, for which he could also share some of the blame. His head was awhirl with horrific scenarios whose end results were all the same—Sophie, dead. He was making himself sick with dread, but he couldn't stop.

They arrived at home with the intention of sending the carriage on with Very to Jason's. It was clear when they arrived, however, that Jason and Tony and quite a few others were already there waiting for them.

"Did you find her?" Jason demanded as he bounded down the steps to the carriage as a footman opened the door. Derek saw Ian shake his head as he climbed out.

"No. There's no sign of her or the men who took her. No one saw a thing. It's impossible! How could a woman be kidnapped in the bright light of day without a single soul as witness, except Very?"

Jason pushed Ian out of the way and Very fell out of the carriage into his waiting arms, bursting into tears again. Tony came rushing down the stairs to their side.

"Very, sweetheart, are you all right?" Tony ran his hand down the back of her head soothingly, speaking to her like a child, and for once Very didn't object. She hiccupped miserably as she clung to Jason and nodded dejectedly.

"We...we didn't find her," Very stuttered through her tears. "I was useless! I can't tell them anything! One big and one small, that's all I remember! Why can't I remember anything more?"

Very's tears tore at Derek's conscience. They shouldn't have pushed her, shouldn't have dragged her with them to search for Sophie. It was too much for her. She was still so young. He still sat on the carriage seat, his elbows on his knees, his hands clasped. He looked up and met Jason's eyes over Very's head.

"I'm sorry, Jase. We shouldn't have brought her with us. We weren't thinking. We were just so worried...I'm sorry." His voice broke and he had to look away.

"Come out, Derek. It's all right. Knowing Very, she would have insisted on going anyway." Derek turned back to Jason and realized he meant what he said. Beyond his shoulder he saw Ian looking at him, riding the edge of panic, trying to stay in control but Derek could see his fear. Ian needed him. Sophie needed him. He pushed out of the carriage.

The drawing room was filled with their friends. Christ, Derek had taken the friendship of these men for granted. He would never do so again. They were here when they needed them. Hadn't they always been? Kate and Kitty were in the center of the room on the sofa. Kate held out her hand to them and Ian and Derek went to her.

"I'm so sorry." Kate's voice was rough with tears, her eyes red-rimmed from crying. "I couldn't stop them. I was worried about the baby. I couldn't do anything. I'm so sorry."

Ian sat next to her as Derek went to one knee before her. Derek took her hand. "Don't Kate, don't blame yourself. You know Sophie won't like it. She'd have wanted you to protect the baby at all costs." He patted her hand. "We'll find her. She'll be fine, you'll see." He stood up and turned to the room, but his mind went blank. Where did they go from here?

Ian was thinking the same thing. "Who? Who would take her? And why? First we've got to figure that out before we can search anymore." Ian closed his eyes and rubbed his hand across his forehead as if it ached. "Why take her?"

"They called her Miss Middleton." Very spoke up from a chair near the door where Wolf was handing her a glass of brandy. "They knew her, or knew of her. It wasn't random."

Derek growled with impatience. "God damn it! Sophie doesn't know anyone who's not in this room." He stalked over and punched the wall, leaving a small dent. "I'll kill them, I swear, if they've harmed a hair on her head."

Daniel Steinberg spoke from the far corner. "What about her family? Her father was at the wedding. Is there any reason he would take her?"

Derek spun around to stare at Ian incredulously. Ian had the same look on his face.

"Harold." Derek spit out the name distastefully. "Her brother, that whoreson. This is something he'd do." He began to stride toward the door, but Ian jumped up and grabbed his arm.

"Let me go." Ian shook his head at Derek's protest before he could voice it. "No, you're too angry. You'll kill him before we find Sophie." Ian moved to the door. "We know whoever took her was not Harold. But they were probably hired by him. Derek, you need to track those men down." Ian turned back to look at him. "In case Harold refuses to talk."

"I can be very persuasive," Derek said menacingly.

"We need him alive." Ian turned away and continued out the door.

Jason watched Ian leave and turned to the room. "Freddy, Brett, Daniel, come with me. We'll accompany Ian to Mr. Middleton's. Surely one of us can be as persuasive as Derek."

His smile was feral as he said it. He looked at Derek. "We'll find her, Derek, and if he's responsible he'll pay."

Derek nodded once and they left. He looked around. "Now, how do we find the bastards who took her?"

Kitty spoke for the first time since Ian and Derek had come home. "I may know someone who can help."

Chapter Nineteen

ဢ

Devlin O'Shaughnessy looked up from the papers on his desk when he heard the commotion in the hallway outside his office. He reached for the pistol in the drawer just as his office door flew open.

"'Ere now, you can't go bargin' in there!" his right-hand man Rufus Gallagher hollered at the young man forcing his way into Devlin's office.

"The hell I can't," the tall gentleman growled and slammed the door in Rufus' face. He spun around to glare at Devlin, who just raised his eyebrows with a less than pleasant grin in response.

"Are you here for a lesson in manners?" Devlin asked politely as he very deliberately set his pistol down on the desk in front of him. He didn't know this man, but that could mean he was more, not less, dangerous to Devlin. In his line of business his competitors eliminated the competition with a funeral. The young man was obviously tough. He'd managed to get through at least four of Devlin's bodyguards and he had barely a hair out of place. He was huge, tall and muscular.

"Kitty Markham said you could help me." He spoke grudgingly but sounded almost desperate.

Devlin relaxed slightly at the mention of Kitty's name. They'd been lovers now for months, after knowing one another long ago in different lifetimes. He refused to let Kitty tell anyone about their association. She was turning respectable now, she didn't need the taint of an illicit love affair with one of London's most notorious crime lords to drag her down again.

"How do you know Kitty?" Devlin growled.

"My name is Derek Knightly, and my w —" he stuttered awkwardly. "The wife of a good friend has been kidnapped."

Knightly? Devlin knew that name. He must be one of Kitty's soldiers, the ones she was always talking about. Suddenly the name clicked into place.

"Who has been kidnapped, Mr. Knightly?" he demanded, his back tensing.

"Sophie, Sophie Witherspoon," Mr. Knightly said miserably, collapsing into the chair across from Devlin.

Devlin swore viciously. Kitty adored that little Witherspoon bride, she'd talked endlessly about the wedding dress, the wedding, the groom, the little girl's painful past. Just the other night she'd been almost tearful as she talked about how well Sophie was doing in her new life. "Who took her?"

Mr. Knightly just shook his head. "We have some idea of who may be behind it, but no solid evidence. Very Thomas was with her and could only give us a minimal description of the men who actually took her."

"Tell me." Devlin leaned forward. He knew just about everyone who operated out of London.

"They grabbed her on Church Street, from an alley next to a little confectioner's where they were shopping. One big man who did the grabbing and carried Sophie off down the alley, and a smaller man who seemed to be calling the shots. The small one hit Very when she tried to stop them." Mr. Knightly suddenly jumped up from his seat, as if he needed to go somewhere or do something but was trapped here instead. "God damn it! We're wasting time. Can you help us or not?"

"Rufus!" Devlin shouted. His office door flew open and Rufus stood there with two of the bodyguards looking a little dazed behind him.

"Yes sir?" Rufus asked, glaring at Mr. Knightly.

"A friend of Mr. Knightly's has been kidnapped." Devlin leaned back in his chair. "One big man who carried the lady off down an alley off Church Street and one little man who seemed to be calling the shots. Oh, and the little one smacked down another woman when she tried to stop them. Any ideas?"

"Well, guv," Rufus started slowly, "I'm not sure that we'd be knowin' those types of gents—"

Devlin cut him off. "We're going to help."

Rufus looked at him in surprise, but nodded and immediately became efficient. "Well now, that sounds like it'd be Lukey and Jack, Mickey and Mike, or Ivy and the Duke. Is it just kidnapping, or is they wantin' her dead?"

Mr. Knightly grew pale and leaned against the desk. "Christ almighty, I don't know. I...I don't know why they'd want her dead. I think he just wants her back."

Rufus nodded sagely. "Well, then, Lukey and Jack'd be your best bet, guv." He shook his head sadly. "If it's Ivy and the Duke, the lady's dead already."

Mr. Knightly covered his mouth with a trembling hand as if he were going to throw up or scream.

"That's what I thought too, Rufus. I just wanted to check to make sure they were still working out of London." Devlin stood up and came around the desk, walking over to a table in the corner. He spoke as he walked. "Find them all, even Mickey and Mike. I want the lady back. Her name is Sophie Witherspoon." He paused and looked at Rufus. "She's a friend of Kitty's." Rufus' eyes got huge and he nodded. "Get the word out. There's money in it for good information."

"Middleton." Mr. Knightly spoke, his voice hoarse. "They called her Miss Middleton, her maiden name. Very said when they took her they called her Miss Middleton."

Devlin nodded at Rufus and the little redheaded man scampered out the door, already shouting as he closed it behind him. Devlin poured a generous glass of scotch from a bottle on the table and brought it to the pale young man. He grabbed the drink and tossed it back without even a shudder. Devlin wasn't sure if that was because he was numb or because he was used to strong drink. He mentally shrugged. It wasn't his business.

"Would you like to go home? I can have someone take you, and as soon as I know anything I'll contact you."

Mr. Knightly was shaking his head before Devlin was done speaking. "No, I'll wait here. I don't want to waste any time once we get some information."

Devlin wandered back to his chair behind his desk. "Suit yourself. Have another drink or two. It may be a while."

After an hour of watching the other man pace his office and nurse another scotch, Devlin set his pen down on his desk. He couldn't get any work done, not with Knightly's pacing and his own worry over Sophie Witherspoon's well-being. Kitty would be devastated if anything happened to her. Devlin didn't want to disappoint her. She'd sent her friend here hoping Devlin could help. He was determined to succeed.

First things first. He set out to distract Knightly. "You're Ian Witherspoon's lover."

The other man stopped pacing and turned to Devlin with a blank face. "Yes." His answer was straightforward, yet gave nothing away.

Devlin smiled. "And Mrs. Witherspoon's?" He was guessing, but he could tell he'd hit the nail on the head by Knightly's expression.

"Yes." Again, no hesitation, no embarrassment. Devlin liked this young man.

"Convenient, that," Devlin commented slyly.

"We like it," Knightly said neutrally. His tone was belied by the tensing of his shoulders and neck, the fist at his side.

"Kitty told me," Devlin supplied, and he watched the other man relax.

"Kitty is very important to us," Knightly said as he lowered himself into the seat across from Devlin again and took a drink before setting his glass on Devlin's desk. "We'd hate to see her hurt."

Devlin raised his eyebrows in mock surprise. "And you think I could hurt her?"

Knightly tilted his head to the side as he studied Devlin. His scrutiny made Dev want to squirm, but he forced himself to sit there negligently. "No."

His answer surprised Devlin so much he was unable to mask his shock. Knightly continued, satisfied at his reaction. "Not deliberately. She was reluctant to offer your help. I think she believes she is protecting you."

Devlin snorted with amusement. "That sounds like Kitty. The little housecat protecting the lion."

Knightly flashed a grin. "Sophie adores her."

Devlin smiled companionably at him. "Kitty feels the same about her."

There was a perfunctory knock at the office door a moment before Rufus opened it and stuck his head in with a grin.

"We've got 'em, guv," he said gleefully. "Just this morning Lukey and Jack were inquiring where one might sell a young lady quickly."

Devlin felt relief race through his veins. Thank God it was Lukey and Jack. Those two bumblers shouldn't be hard to track. He saw his relief mirrored on Knightly's face.

"Slavers? Are there any in port now?" Devlin asked as he buttoned his jacket and grabbed his pistol.

"Nah, but there's a ship in Dover with a captain whose not too particular how he gets a passenger or where he takes 'em. He'll do the sale on commission."

"They can't have made it to Dover yet," Knightly said, shoving Rufus unceremoniously out of the way. "I can catch them on the road."

Devlin grabbed his arm before he was out the door. "Do you need any help?"

Knightly grinned and Devlin realized he'd only scratched the surface of this man. He'd been right to assume he was deadly at first glance.

"I have some friends who might help." He looked at Devlin assessingly. "But I'm always willing to make new friends."

* * * * *

Ian glanced in the window at the dark drawing room, just visible through a break in the curtains. Middleton's townhouse was completely dark and echoed with emptiness when he pounded on the door. The knocker had been removed, indicating the owner was not in town at the moment. Ian didn't believe it. There was something about the house that slithered down his spine and made his senses come to attention. Someone was lurking in there.

He noiselessly motioned to Daniel to go 'round the back of the house and seek another entrance. Jason positioned himself next to the window, but out of sight, and Brett motioned that he and Freddy were going to go in the opposite direction of Daniel, looking for a way in along the other side of the house. Ian nodded quietly and the three men faded into the night, leaving Jason and him to find a way in here.

Ian silently felt along the window casement for a latch of some kind. He cursed inwardly when it became clear the window was locked from the inside. Suddenly a very thin, very sharp stiletto appeared in front of him and he reared back in surprise. Jason was grinning devilishly at him as he offered the unique knife. Ian took it with an answering grin and slid the blade upward between the windows, pushing the inner latch up. The window glided open a few inches once it was unlocked, creating a big enough gap for Ian to grab one side and pull it open. He hoisted himself inside and turned to hold up a hand, stopping Jason from following him. He wanted to check out the house before the others entered. Jason slid back from the window and waited patiently from his earlier position, out of sight but with a clear view into the house.

The drawing room was empty, of that Ian was sure. He cracked the door open and walked quietly out into the hallway after ascertaining it too was clear. His head whipped around when he caught the very small flicker of a candle coming from an ajar door down the hall. He leaned back into the drawing room and pointed, showing Jason where he was going, then he turned and tiptoed toward the light.

When he was still a few steps from the lighted doorway Ian heard an unmistakable click behind him. He froze at the sound of a pistol being cocked.

"Well, Witherspoon, fancy seeing you here." The voice was such a shock Ian forgot the danger and spun about to face the other man.

"Robertson! What the devil are you doing here?" He froze again when Robertson raised the gun menacingly, his eyes gleaming with intent.

"Why, I'm going to kill an intruder at my dear friend Middleton's house, of course." Robertson stepped into the light and Ian knew a moment of true fear.

"I meant what are you doing in Middleton's house? We thought you were back on the Continent." Ian spoke slowly and kept his voice evenly modulated. He had to keep Robertson talking.

Robertson motioned Ian into the lit room behind him with a sharp jerk of the pistol. "Get in the study."

Ian reluctantly turned and walked into the study, anticipating the burning blast of a bullet in the back at any moment. Robertson followed and pulled the door closed behind him, although it didn't latch. Robertson didn't seem to notice. He motioned toward a chair placed in the middle of the room. "Sit." Ian obeyed, trying desperately not to antagonize the other man. All he had to do was stay alive until Jason and the others were able to rescue him. He wanted to be rescued above all things. Thoughts and memories of Derek and Sophie flashed through his mind, and his heart stuttered in his chest at the thought of what might happen to them were he to die.

Robertson arranged himself on the edge of the desk, his face glowing in the light of the candle there. He lit the others in the candelabrum without moving the gun off Ian. The brighter light chased the shadows away from the corners of the room, and Ian saw a flicker of movement outside the window behind Robertson. When he looked back at Robertson the man had picked up a second pistol from one of the desk drawers.

"It's a brilliant plan, you see," Robertson told him, his voice chillingly reasonable.

Ian looked at him in bewilderment. What was he talking about?

Robertson shook his head disdainfully at Ian's lack of response. "My plan," he said slowly, as if explaining to a child. "Honestly, I don't know why Middleton was so afraid of you."

Ian shook his head. He had to get back into the moment, keep Robertson talking so he wouldn't notice the others closing in. "Tell me. What is your plan?"

Robertson looked amused at Ian's sudden interest. "I'm going to kill you all, of course. I came up with it after my botched attempt on Phillip Neville's slut. I was overly emotional or I never would have failed with her."

Ian was sickened at Robertson's tone. He sounded disappointed. Ian had been there after Robertson attacked Maggie. He'd seen her beaten and bloody face, the bruises around her neck. He'd seen the emotional carnage left behind. Ian fought and won the battle to keep his emotions in check. "I see. Why kill us? And who is 'all'?"

Robertson looked at him coldly. "You mean nothing to me. But your death will weigh quite heavily on Randall and Richards and that whore." He got up and began to pace. "They ruined my life, and now they're going to pay. I can't get close enough to spit at them, but the rest of you are easy pickings. And how much sweeter my revenge will be as I watch from the shadows as they beat their breasts and lament the deaths of their friends one by one."

"*You* want revenge?" Ian was dumbfounded at the man's audacity. "You are the one who fired early in the duel, Robertson. You nearly killed Jason. You knew what the consequences of your actions would be. *You* ruined your life, Robertson. Jason and Tony and Kate were merely your victims."

"Hardly," Robertson hissed in anger. "Randall never should have forced the duel. Over a whore! A mistress! What utter rubbish. He acted as if she were a virgin, when everyone knew very well she was far from it."

Ian was sickened. "A gentleman takes care of his mistresses, Robertson. You should have looked after Kate, not tossed her to your pack of dubious acquaintances and watched them rape her as you stood by laughing. You used her to assuage your petty jealousies against Jason and Tony. As Kate was his future wife, Jason had every right to call you out."

"Loyal to the end, aren't you, Witherspoon?" Robertson's smile was frighteningly calm. "That very loyalty is what will make your death such a blow for them." Robertson chuckled darkly. "I suppose it's only fitting that my banishment to the Continent provided the means of my revenge. It was there I was able to earn the blind loyalty Middleton gladly gives to me."

"How did Middleton get involved?" Ian was truly puzzled about that connection.

Robertson sneered. "That misbegotten, incestuous bastard? He was a hanger-on in London, before Randall's accusations drove me to the Continent. When he turned up there, his money was greatly appreciated." Robertson laughed coldly. "He disgusts me. He pants after that little sister of his like a dog in heat. Do you know he's been fucking her for years? Disgusting. I can almost see how you and your lover might seem like a change for the better for your little wife. Almost. But she likes fucking the two of you too much to be considered a victim here." Robertson shrugged negligently. "Apparently her brother gave her a taste for the perverted."

Ian almost ruined everything at that point. How dare this pathetic worm talk about Sophie like that? He spoke through gritted teeth. "He raped her. Sophie was never willing. All she learned from him was violence and fear."

Robertson shrugged again. "I don't really care, to be honest. She's inconsequential except as a way to make them pay. As she's probably dead already, it hardly matters. I told those two thugs I hired to kidnap her to kill her, I didn't care how and I didn't care what they did with her first."

"You bastard!" Ian roared as he came out of his chair and lunged for Robertson. He saw Robertson raise his gun and didn't care.

"Ian, no!" Freddy came at him from the shadows and knocked him aside as the report of the gunshot echoed around them. It happened so quickly Ian didn't have time to react. He heard a dull thud and Freddy cried out as they hit the floor together.

"Freddy, are you all right?" Ian asked frantically as he rolled over. Freddy was on his back with his eyes closed and Ian could see blood seeping onto the floor from a wound in his shoulder.

"Damn it!" Robertson screamed. "What is he doing here? Now you've done it! You've made me kill a duke! Where is he?" he demanded, quickly crossing the distance between them until he pointed the second pistol at Freddy, the first still smoking in his other hand. "Where you are, that limping sycophant isn't far behind. I know you didn't come here alone. Where is Haversham?" He pressed his forehead with the spent pistol as if he had a headache. "I'll have to kill all three of you. Tell me where he is and I'll at least make it quick."

"Over here." Brett spoke calmly from the open doorway. "You have one pistol, Robertson. You can't kill us all with it." He walked slowly into the room, his limp more pronounced than usual. He spared a glance for Ian and Freddy on the floor. "How is he?"

"I don't know." Ian had ripped off his cravat and was pressing it to Freddy's shoulder, but Freddy had yet to move. As Ian looked down at him, he saw Freddy's eyelids crack open slightly and Freddy looked furtively at Robertson. He was pretending to be gravely hurt. Ian wasn't sure he'd get a chance to take Robertson by surprise, but it was a good move on Freddy's part.

Brett spoke again in the same calm voice. "You must know you can't kill all of us, Robertson. It would be smarter to leave us alive. You'll have a better chance of escape then. If you kill a duke you know they'll hunt you down."

Robertson looked at Brett with narrowed eyes. "Always so smart, aren't you, Haversham? Well, it hardly matters who I kill now. You know I had the girl kidnapped and murdered. You know I shot Ashland. That's enough to put a noose around my neck, particularly if I let Ashland give testimony against me. A duke's word, no matter the company he keeps, is enough to hang innocent men."

"You are hardly innocent," Ian growled from the floor. "You've murdered my wife, you bastard, and I will see you dead." Just saying the words made Ian's chest ache so painfully he could barely breathe. His vision was blurred by tears as he thought of Sophie dying far away, scared, alone, at the mercy of hired killers.

Robertson kept the gun pointed at Freddy. "Shut up," he growled at Ian. His narrow look became triumphant. "Clearly my original plan must be altered a bit. I begin to think I shot the right man. If I kill the duke, you all lose a very powerful friend, don't you? Someone who could smooth the way in society for your tawdry little three-way marriages." His eyes were gleaming. "He's so young, so full of promise. Yes, killing Ashland will make Randall and Richards and that slut suffer."

Robertson stiffened his arm as he prepared to shoot Freddy at close range. Ian was primed to leap up and take the shot when Brett roared, "Stay down!" A shot rang out from the window where Ian had seen movement, which now stood open. Robertson cried out and jerked forward, taking two steps in their direction as the bullet hit him. He didn't fall, however. Instead he raised the gun yet again, his hand shaking slightly but not enough to miss at this range. Ian was trying to scramble to his feet as he looked over at the window. He saw Daniel there, climbing over the frame into the room, but he was too far away to reach Robertson in time. Suddenly another shot rang out from the open door. Robertson's body toppled sideways as he was hit. The gun fell from his hand and Ian reached over and snatched it up. He spun toward the door and saw Jason lowering his gun.

Brett was crawling frantically across the floor to Freddy. "Freddy! My God, Freddy," he cried out.

Freddy sat up quickly and then had to lie back down. "I'm fine," he said, his voice a little weak. "I'll be fine." Brett reached his side and pulled Freddy into his arms, hugging him tightly.

"One last kiss before I die," Freddy murmured melodramatically from where his face was pressed into Brett's neck.

"Freddy," Brett laughed shakily, chastising.

"Well, it was worth a try," Freddy mumbled as he pulled away. "Ow! Why didn't you ever tell me how much it bloody hurts to get shot? Damn!" He grabbed his shoulder and let Brett support him.

"Is he dead?" Jason asked from the doorway. He still stood where he'd fired the shot. Ian and Daniel walked over and Ian looked away as soon as he saw Robertson was dead. He'd been shot in the head and there wasn't much left of him.

"He's dead all right," Daniel said cheerfully. "I say, Jason, good shot. I'd have had him if he hadn't jerked at Brett's warning."

Jason slumped against the doorframe. "I hoped I'd gotten him. We were running out of bullets and he seemed to be impervious to them."

Ian took two steps and stumbled. He fell to his knees and then curled himself into a ball as the tears came. Daniel and Jason came running. Jason hauled him into his arms. "Ian, Christ, Ian," he said.

"She's dead. She's dead," was all he could say as he felt his world crashing around him. How was he going to tell Derek?

Chapter Twenty

ം

Sophie was tired and hungry and dirty. She missed Ian and Derek so much she ached inside almost as much as she ached outside. Lukey and Jack were a couple of incompetent fools, but Sophie was still no match for their superior strength. They'd managed to catch and drag her back two different times today, and the second time they'd not bothered to be polite about it. The ropes that bound her wrists now were painfully tight, and her jaw was still sore from the gag that Jack had put on earlier when he tired of her shouts and complaints. He'd removed it when they reached these secluded woods, but she'd kept quiet, afraid he'd put it back on.

They had traveled most of the day and well into the night before stopping. That was Sophie's fault. Partly because she'd slowed them down today, hoping to give Ian and Derek time to find her, but mainly because she'd told Lukey and Jack in vivid detail what Ian and Derek were going to do to them when they found them. The two men were jumping at shadows now. Sophie grinned in malevolent satisfaction at their fear, which only aggravated them more.

"My husband will pay you just as generously to return me to him as my brother is paying you to kidnap me," she told them reasonably for the hundredth time.

"You already said that," Jack snarled, "and I told you that he'd pay us first, see us hanged second. No sir, Jack and Lukey ain't that stupid. We'll take the money what was offered us first, it's the square thing to do. Wash our hands of you, little miss, and won't be sorry." Sophie didn't like the way he was looking at her. "You ought to be grateful we didn't slit your throat like that gen'leman told us to. We're too softhearted, we are. And he's not paying us enough. Murder's a sight more costly than kidnappin'."

"That's right, Jack," Lukey agreed. Sophie hadn't heard him say anything else all day. Just "That's right, Jack" every time the little weasel opened his mouth. It was beginning to grate on her nerves.

"Softhearted?" Sophie scoffed. "You have kidnapped me, humiliated me, tied me up, gagged me and now you are starving me. I hardly call that gentle treatment." She spoke with false bravado, her heart racing at Jack's offhand mention of murder. Harold wanted her dead? That didn't sound like him. He'd always threatened to kill her himself. She found it hard to believe he'd let someone else do it.

Jack wiped the dripping liquor from his chin as he lowered the bottle he'd been steadily drinking from since they'd stopped. He'd become more and more belligerent with each drink. "Ungrateful little bitch is what you are. Got you a carriage to ride in, didn't we? Let you stop to take a piss whenever you asked, didn't we? We ought to have something in return, I'm thinking."

"That's right, Jack," Lukey agreed, turning his piggish, vacuous face toward her, his little eyes gleaming evilly in the firelight.

"If you touch me, my husband will see you tortured until you beg for death," Sophie told him, disgusted at the thin thread of fear that ran through the words.

Jack heard the fear in her voice and grinned, making Sophie shiver at the black teeth that were revealed. "Not if he doesn't find you, or us."

"What do you mean?" Sophie asked, her panic starting to overwhelm her. She tried to breathe slowly as Ian had taught her, and she thought of Derek and how disappointed he'd be if she succumbed to the panic. The thought stiffened her back and she raised her nose disdainfully.

"Why, the reason we're takin' you to Dover, Duchess," Jack chortled. "You'll soon have a new husband, one who won't put up with your airs and naggin'. You'll learn obedience at the end of a whip if I don't miss my guess." His laughter grew at the horrified look on Sophie's face. "But don't you be worryin' too much, missy. In them harems you only got to fuck the master once in a blue moon, he's got so much pussy to choose from." He laughed so hard he fell off the log he'd been sitting on, and Lukey laughed with him.

Slavers. That's where they were taking her. Oh God, where were Ian and Derek? Why hadn't they come yet? Sophie closed her eyes as she tried to control her breathing, but her heart beat so fast it drowned out all her mantras until all she could hear in her head was a silent scream. She was brought back by the stench of foul-smelling breath in her face and a hand on her throat. Her eyes flew open and she saw Jack leering at her.

"So Jack and Lukey must be lookin' pretty good about now, eh? Might be your last chance for some good English cock, little missy. I wouldn't be so ungrateful if I were you." She tried to shrug off his hand, but Jack suddenly pushed her hard and she fell back on the ground. Before she could recover, he was on top of her. He raised her bound hands over her head and held them as he squeezed her breast painfully. She fought like a she-cat, but suddenly her hands were being pressed painfully into the ground and she looked up to see Lukey holding them down. Jack laughed. "Good idea, Lukey. You hold 'er whiles I fuck 'er, and then I'll do the same for you."

"That's right, Jack," Lukey said, and Sophie screamed as Jack ripped her bodice open.

*　*　*　*　*

They rode half the night before they found Sophie. They found the carriage first, behind some trees on the edge of the woods. The horses had been unhitched and their tracks led deeper into the woods. Derek and Wolf and another old friend,

Simon Gantry, took the point because they had experience with covert night maneuvers in the war. Devlin and Rufus and the two bodyguards, John and William, stayed back.

The kidnappers were camping in a deserted stretch of woods, after apparently riding most of the day to get here. According to several people they'd interrogated on the way, Sophie was making their progress painfully slow. The cover story the kidnappers were using painted Sophie as a young runaway from an aristocratic family who was being returned to her father's house after being rescued from a botched elopement. They had her incarcerated in a shabby carriage. At one stop they'd let her out to relieve herself and had to chase her through the coaching yard and livery before hauling her back yelling and screaming to the carriage. Several people had complained and were about to call the sheriff when the kidnappers drove recklessly away, nearly running down several occupants of the inn. When Derek heard the story he'd laughed appreciatively. "That's it, Sophie," he'd said, and then he'd nearly cried at how proud he was of her courage.

The trail led here, to this dark stretch of woods in the middle of nowhere. Derek could see the faint outline of a weak fire through the trees. The kidnappers were smart enough not to take Sophie someplace she could try to escape and attract attention again, but too ignorant to realize that a fire in this lonely stretch of woods would attract just as much attention from anyone passing by. Derek wanted to race through the woods and snatch Sophie from them, but he knew that could be dangerous. They didn't know for sure that Lukey and Jack were alone. And cornered, the two men might harm Sophie if given the chance. No, it was best to sneak up on them, but it was taking much too long. God help those bastards if they'd hurt her. Derek was going to have to beat them to a bloody pulp as it was. If he had to kill them too it could get messy.

He glided through the trees, just able to make out Simon on his left and Wolf on his right. The two smaller men had run some late-night forays with Derek on the Peninsula, so he was confident they knew what they were doing. They had decided to surround the camp and determine if Lukey and Jack were acting alone. If so, Simon and Wolf were to wait for a signal from Derek before moving in.

Derek could hear voices murmuring at the fire, but he was still too far away to make out the words. One of the voices was Sophie's, he was sure of it. When he first heard it, he had to stop and kneel on the ground he felt so lightheaded with relief. She was alive, and well enough to speak. *Thank God, thank God.* He rose again, and his progress became swifter, his heart beating fast as if calling out to Sophie. Suddenly Sophie's scream echoed through the night and Derek threw caution aside as he crashed through the woods to the campfire.

He didn't hesitate as he crossed into the small clearing. He registered the scene immediately, and dove for the little man on top of Sophie. He picked him off her and threw him to the ground several feet away. With hardly a pause, he spun about and kicked the big one in the jaw, sending him flying back into a tree. He felt the hair on the back of his neck rise and turned around in time to see the little one on his feet and running at Derek with a knife in his hand. Derek feinted to the right and then knocked the knife out of the other man's hand with a blow to his wrist. The man—Jack, Devlin had said—cried out and awkwardly tried to punch Derek with his other hand. Derek landed a fist on his jaw and the man went down, Derek on top of him. Derek straddled his chest and his hands wrapped around Jack's throat. Derek's vision was black on the edges, his focus narrowed to Jack as he choked and turned red. The image of Sophie being assaulted by this spineless bastard was burned in Derek's memory, and all he could think was that he had to die for touching her. Jack's hands clawed at Derek's, trying to loosen his hold so he could take a breath, but Derek just squeezed harder. Suddenly a hand on his shoulder was shaking him, and the killing rage receded. He let go of Jack's throat just as the other man began to lose consciousness. Derek turned his head sharply to see Devlin back away, his hands in the air.

"You'd regret it. Killing him in front of her," was all Devlin said in explanation. Derek knew he was right.

"I wish you had killed him," Sophie rasped from where she was kneeling a few feet away. She was spitting mad, and Derek had never seen anything so beautiful.

"That's my girl," Derek said approvingly, and Sophie's head jerked around so she could stare at him. Her eyes suddenly filled with tears and she began to tremble.

"Am I?" she asked in a small voice.

And suddenly they both lunged for one another at once, crawling across the ground that separated them, Sophie falling into Derek's arms. "Christ, yes, Sophie," Derek murmured as he kissed her cheeks, her lips, her eyes, all the while holding her so tightly it was as if he were trying to absorb her into himself. "Tell me you love me, Sophie," he demanded as he cupped the back of her head and held her lips to his.

Sophie's eyes were closed, tears dampening her cheeks. "I love you, Derek," she whispered desperately, "I love you."

He rewarded her with a passion born of fear and its aftermath. Their kiss was scorching in its intensity. Derek devoured Sophie's mouth only to be forced to give way to her demands as she licked and sucked and nipped his lips with murmurs of joy. Her body was pressed to his, her tied hands between them. Her breath was his breath, her heartbeat an echo of his own. The sound of a clearing throat finally brought Derek back to his senses. He slowly pulled away from Sophie's kiss as she moaned in disappointment.

"Um, sorry to interrupt, Derek old man, but don't you think we ought to get Sophie home? Or at least inside somewhere?" Derek slowly turned his head to Simon. He blinked several times before he was able to register the question.

"Home," he growled. "I want her home." He stood up and cut the rope binding Sophie's hands, throwing it away in disgust. Sophie stepped in and clung to him, and he lifted her into his arms and carried her toward the waiting horses. Only after she was settled on his horse with his jacket wrapped around her did he turn back and get an accounting of what was going on.

Simon and Wolf had made short work of the big and slow Lukey. He and a now-conscious but groggy Jack were tied to their own horses and ready to be transported back to London. The two bodyguards were watching them as the others caught and mounted their horses.

"Take her home," Devlin told Derek as his horse pranced under him, impatient to be out of the dark woods. "We'll take care of these two."

"What are you going to do to them?" Derek asked. "I need to know who hired them."

Devlin smiled. It was a wolfish grin, and it was clear he was going to enjoy meting out their punishment. "I'll get it out of them, don't worry. I'll send the information to Witherspoon's." He turned and nudged Jack's leg with his foot and the trussed kidnapper snarled at him. "Then, well, I heard His Majesty's Navy is recruiting again."

Jack's snarl turned to a whimper and it was Derek's turn to smile. "I like the way you think, Devlin," he said with a chuckle.

Derek climbed on his horse behind Sophie and gathered her close. Wolf rode ahead and Simon behind as they set out for London. He was exhausted and could only imagine how much worse Sophie felt. But he needed to get her home to Ian. Sophie snuggled against him and was asleep almost instantly. Derek marveled at the trust in that simple act, his heart swelling with gratitude for whatever deity had brought him to her side tonight just when she needed him most.

They'd been riding for quite a while when the sound of fast-approaching horses drove them off the road to hide behind some haystacks. Wolf dismounted and crept forward to get a glimpse of who was riding so furiously just before dawn. When the riders were almost upon them, Wolf suddenly jumped up and began shouting. There was a great flurry of activity as the band of riders stopped. Derek stole a glance from his hiding place and then rode slowly out to the road just as the early morning sun began to tint the sky.

Ian walked his horse toward Derek, his heart filled with joy at Wolf's news, but trepidation set in when he saw how still Sophie was in Derek's arms.

"Is she…" he croaked, his chest constricting with fear so he couldn't finish the thought.

"Sleeping," Derek whispered as he rode up next to Ian. "She's exhausted. Your arrival didn't even wake her."

Ian closed his eyes in abject relief at Derek's reply. He opened them quickly and surveyed Derek. "Are you all right?" he asked.

Derek smiled, clearly exhausted but also…content. Ian felt tears prick his eyes at the sight of Derek holding Sophie so closely, so intimately. Seeing them together like this completed Ian, as if the last puzzle piece had finally fallen into place.

"I'm fine, Ian," Derek told him, "now."

Ian turned his horse back toward London. "Then let's go home."

* * * * *

When Sophie awoke, she wasn't sure where she was at first. She sat up in bed alarmed and looked around. She sighed with relief and sank back down in the bed when she realized she was home. The last day ran through her mind and she shuddered in horror at the memory of Jack slavering over her and the painful grip Lukey had had on her arms. Then the image of Derek beating them both and nearly killing Jack in his anger made her smile. Then she giggled. Clearly association with Derek had turned her into a bloodthirsty wench.

She leaped out of bed and rang for her maid. Discreet questioning revealed she'd been asleep for a day and a night. She was aghast. Where were Ian and Derek? She had the quickest bath she'd ever had since marrying Ian, dressed and headed for Ian's study.

When she entered, Ian looked up from the papers on his desk. It was obvious he hadn't been expecting her from the look on his face. He rose from his chair so fast it nearly fell over behind him before he caught it.

"Sophie," he said softly, and she ran to him. He swept her into his embrace and held her tightly. She felt his arms tremble as they wrapped around her.

"Ian, Ian," she said, and then she inexplicably began to cry. He stroked her hair and back and murmured silly love words in her ear, but he didn't loosen his hold on her.

By the time she'd calmed down Ian had sat down again and pulled her on to his lap. "I'm sorry," she told him, taking his offered handkerchief and wiping her face. She discreetly blew her nose and looked up to see Ian smiling at her.

"What?" She could feel her face turning red in embarrassment. She must look a sight with her swollen eyes and tearstained cheeks.

"Are you also sorry for the crops lying fallow?" he asked with a quirk of his eyebrow.

It took Sophie a moment to remember Derek's words that morning after the wedding. She laughed and pushed off Ian's lap. "No, I'm not sorry for that. I did that on purpose." Ian laughed with her. "Speaking of which, where is Derek?"

At Sophie's question, Ian's smile was wiped from his face. Sophie felt the relief and expectation she'd been feeling melt away, leaving resignation and weariness behind. She wandered over to the back wall and kept her back to Ian. She didn't want him to see how disappointed she was. "You don't have to answer. He's gone again, isn't he?"

"I don't think so," was Ian's enigmatic answer. His voice was very carefully neutral.

Sophie laughed bitterly and leaned her head into the small corner created by the wall and the edge of the bookcase there. "What exactly does that mean?"

"It means I haven't seen him since we brought you home, but his things are still here and his bed has been slept in." Still neutral, he was hiding his feelings behind a dispassionate brick wall.

Sophie pulled her head up. "And what exactly does that mean?" She closed her eyes against tears.

"It means I don't think he's gone." Ian didn't seem perturbed by her determination in the slightest.

"I think it means he's just as far away from me as he was before, and he has no intention of closing the distance. I think it means he rescued me, but he still doesn't need me, or love me. I think it means he's a stubborn, selfish bastard who made me love him just to watch me suffer."

Sophie kept her face to the wall and her eyes closed. She was trying her damnedest not to cry. She wouldn't cry any more tears over Derek. She wouldn't.

"Sophie—" Ian began soothingly.

"Is that what you really think of me?" Derek's voice cut Ian off in mid-sentence and Sophie spun around to see Derek standing in the open French door that led to the garden. "The things you learn eavesdropping." He took two steps into the room and very deliberately turned back and closed the door behind him. When he swung to face Sophie again he wore a scowl. "I practically throw my fucking heart at your feet the other night and you have the audacity to call me a stubborn, selfish bastard."

Sophie stood her ground, though inside she trembled. "Yes, I do. Where were you? Do you love me?"

Derek looked startled at her rapid-fire questions. "You sound like a fishwife. I do have a life, you know. I had some things to take care of, and since you were doing a fairly good turn as Sleeping Beauty, I did them. And of course I love you. I said so, didn't I?"

Sophie's hand curled into a fist as she held it to her heart, her chest tight with emotion. She shook her head. "No," she whispered, "you never did."

Derek looked at her incredulously. "Of course I did. Maybe not in words, but in deed. In the way I need you, the way I can't breathe, eat, sleep, live without wanting you. In the way I held you the other night, as if I could absorb you into my body and never let anyone hurt you again. Did all that mean nothing to you?"

He loves me. He loves me. Sophie leaned back against the wall, weak with relief and joy. "I thought...I was afraid to believe." She licked her lips, her stomach fluttering with the beauty of Derek's words. With the matter-of-fact way he described how much he loved her. "I—"

Derek tore open his coat and placed his hands on his hips. "You were afraid? How do you think I feel? I'm jumping off the cliff here, Sophie. I didn't want to love you, or need you. But you wouldn't leave me alone. Night and day thoughts of you haunted me, and then you let me fuck you, Sophie. We fucked. And it was one of the most incredible experiences of my life. Did you feel it? Did you know then? I did, but still I ran." He stalked over and roughly pulled his coat off and threw it on the chaise.

"At the rate you've been ripping those off, you're costing a fortune in coats, Derek," Ian murmured. Sophie turned her head to look at him, and she could see Ian hiding a smile behind his hand. He couldn't hide the love and fierce joy in his eyes, however, as he watched Derek rant.

"I don't care about the fucking coats, Ian," Derek growled, never taking his eyes off Sophie. "What will it take to convince you, Sophie? I'm done running. I'm here now, and there'll be no getting rid of me. Is that what you want to hear?

Christ, I'm so hard I ache. I need you. I need to take you now, to be inside you, to claim you."

Derek had been stalking her as he talked and now he stopped in front of her. He placed his fists on the wall on either side of her and leaned close. He lowered his head to the sensitive spot on the curve of her neck and breathed in deeply but didn't touch her. "I'm like an animal, Sophie, a wild thing in the forest that hunts its mate. Your smell, your taste, your nearness, they bring every instinct I have alive. I want to mark you with my scent, my claim."

"Derek," Sophie whispered. He pulled his head back and she placed her hand on his cheek tenderly, overwhelmed by the love she felt for him.

"I own you, Sophie," he said softly, turning his head to kiss the palm of her hand. He looked back into her eyes. "And you own me."

Sophie heard a sound from behind Derek, and she looked over his shoulder to see Ian walking toward the two of them. He stopped and stared at them, not even attempting to conceal the desire flaming in his eyes. "Ian," Sophie said, her voice strange to her own ears, thick and pulsing with need.

"Don't you know, Sophie?" Derek leaned in and whispered directly into her ear. "Ian knows. Ian knows that he owns both of us."

At Derek's husky words, Ian smiled, and Sophie felt that feral smile deep in her womb as it wound tight and began to throb, sending moisture to her cunt and making her gasp. Derek chuckled. "Yes, you know it too, Sophie."

Suddenly Derek pressed his full length against her, dwarfing her with his heat and size and strength. He spread his legs wide so that Sophie was tucked between them and he wasn't so tall. His hands ran up her arms to her shoulders and then his fingers lightly traced the rounded neckline of her gown. He pressed his pelvis into Sophie's, and she felt his thick, hard arousal against her stomach. "Fuck me, Sophie," he whispered enticingly. "Fuck me like a wild thing in the forest, Sophie. Give yourself to me." One hand cupped her jaw and raised her lips to his. "Give yourself to me," Derek repeated and then his lips came down on hers.

Derek kissed as if there were no tomorrow, no yesterday, just now, just this hot, wet suction of mouth on mouth, tongue on tongue. He ate and drank at her mouth, shared his breath at the same time he took hers away. Sophie wrapped her arms around his neck and held on as her legs grew weak. He tasted of sunshine and coffee and spices, and Derek and heat.

Even though he'd tried to lower himself, Sophie's head was tilted back at an impossible angle to accept his kiss. His shoulders were so big her arms ached to reach around them. She whimpered as he bit down lightly on her lower lip and then licked the sting away. She felt like juicy prey to his predator and a thrill shot down her spine.

"Christ, I've been dying to kiss you, Sophie," he whispered as he laid his forehead against hers. He pulled away and Sophie was caught in his heated gaze. "Say it, Sophie," he demanded roughly. "Tell me."

Sophie's breath was ragged, her control willingly relinquished. Without hesitation, she gave the answer she knew he was looking for. "I give myself to you, Derek. Take me. Take all of me." The next moment Sophie gave a little surprised scream as Derek ripped her dress open from the neck down to the hem. He pushed it off her shoulders. Sophie's heart was racing.

"Derek," Ian rumbled warningly.

"Tell him how much you like it, Sophie," Derek ordered. "Tell him how much you want to be taken."

Sophie shook her head mutely as it leaned against the wall, embarrassed by her arousal, by the warm rush of hot liquid that was even then leaking out of her slit at Derek's rough treatment. Another rip rent the air as Sophie's chemise met the same fate as her dress. Having dressed in a hurry that morning, Sophie wore no corset or drawers. She stood nude against the wall, wearing nothing but her stockings and shoes.

"Derek!" Ian's voice rang with command. Derek ignored him and thrust his fingers through the curls hiding Sophie's wet and swollen pussy. When he touched her drenched lips, both he and Sophie groaned.

"She's soaking wet, Ian. Christ, she's so aroused by what I'm doing she's going to come right here with just my fingers on her, aren't you, sweetheart?"

Sophie mutely shook her head against the wall as she bit her lip to keep her moan trapped in her throat.

"Don't lie, Sophie," Derek whispered wickedly, "or you may not get what you crave so much." As he spoke, Derek pressed one finger deeply inside her and Sophie couldn't stop her whimper, or the shiver of deep pleasure that danced down her spine.

"Yes," Derek murmured approvingly, "that's what I like to hear, Sophie, honest desire. Be honest with me, Sophie."

Sophie broke down and grabbed Derek's forearms. The muscles of his arms were tight with desire and Sophie realized Derek was holding back. The thought heightened her arousal and she thrust against his hand, down onto the finger that was penetrating her deeply over and over in a slow, intoxicating rhythm. Derek's laugh was a low rumble of satisfaction.

"Did you see that, Ian? See how our girl loves what I'm doing?"

"Yes." Ian's voice had deepened into the growl that he always used in the bedroom, the one that made Sophie's nipples hard and her cunt wet without a single touch from him. "Yes, I saw her. Are you going to fuck Derek here, Sophie? Now?"

"Ian," Sophie whimpered as Derek thrust his finger in again and pressed his thumb against the hard bud of desire nestled in her curls.

"I want you to fuck him, Sophie. I want to watch you fuck each other, right here, right now."

The words and the image they inspired coupled with Derek's long, clever fingers and Ian's deep growl drove Sophie over the edge. She came apart with a cry and pressed hard against Derek's hand, trying to hold his arm steady as she rode out the intense climax.

"Oh Christ, Christ, Sophie, yes," Derek told her roughly, pressing his fingers against all the right places, pushing the pleasure higher. She sobbed his name right before his mouth came down on hers again.

Chapter Twenty-One

ဆ

When Sophie came Derek felt his cock jerk, felt a drop of moisture seep out of the end. He blindly sought her mouth, and the warm welcome he received there helped to temper his raging lust slightly. It was imperative he gain control. He wanted to do this right, this first time with the three of them. Somehow fucking Sophie here in the study, where he'd first seen her, in his and Ian's favorite room, seemed right. The thought made him smile and he pulled back and watched Sophie's eyes flutter open as she panted, her breath blowing hot against his cheek.

"Are you ready for more?" he asked her quietly. "There is so much more, Sophie. So many things I want to do to you, although I don't think I have the control to do them all right now. Right now I may just have to fuck you."

Sophie's eyes met his and the heat in her gaze made Derek's stomach clench. "I want it all, Derek. I want whatever you care to do with me."

Derek could do nothing less than reward her with a kiss for that. She tasted like heaven, sweet and lemony with a hint of chocolate and a heat that melted his heart and made his cock throb. She did this little thing with her tongue, wrapping it around his and sucking it into her mouth, and he growled like the animal she made him and pressed her hard against the wall. He felt her fumbling at his chest and pulled back, his lips wet with the kiss. He looked down and she was struggling to undo the buttons of his waistcoat.

"Naked," she panted, "I want you naked for us."

When she said "us", Derek groaned. To be with Sophie and Ian...it was all Derek could do to hang on to his control.

He looked over his shoulder at Ian and had to close his eyes against the stark, hungry look on Ian's face. Suddenly Derek's clothes were an irritant, something hot and scratchy and loathsome. He stumbled back and nearly fell to his knees at the sight of Sophie leaning back against the wall, her legs spread, dressed in nothing but stockings with lacy garters, delicate shoes and freckles. He began ripping at the buttons on his waistcoat and two fell to the floor.

"Let me," Ian rumbled in his ear as his arms came around Derek and he deftly divested him of waistcoat and shirt. Ian's hands trailed slowly across his chest before he slid them down Derek's stomach to the buttons on his trousers. Ian nimbly undid the buttons and untied his drawers then pushed them over Derek's hips with another lingering caress, this time a stroke into the heavy nest of hair cradling his rigid cock. Derek's breath was ragged. Ian knew just how to touch him. And this unveiling felt almost as if Ian were unwrapping him as a gift for Sophie. Derek had to sit down on the chaise to pull off his boots and then he stood and kicked the rest of his clothes off. As he stood there, he felt a featherlight stroke on his back from his nape to the top of the cleft in his ass that made everything in him tighten in anticipation, then Ian gave him a gentle push toward Sophie.

"Fuck her," Ian told him, his voice soft but commanding. Derek was only too eager to obey.

Derek hesitated a moment after Ian's push, mesmerized by the look on Sophie's face. She was transfixed by his body, her pupils large, her lips parting slightly as her tongue darted out and licked them. Derek felt that swipe of tongue along his nerve endings. The rush of heat and blood to his cock broke the spell and he stepped forward to haul Sophie off the wall and into his arms. As their naked bodies pressed together from Sophie's breasts against his chest to his cock against the soft silk of her belly, Derek threw his head back and groaned. Finally, finally to feel Sophie's warm flesh on his again.

"Derek, Derek," she murmured as she nuzzled her face against his chest, "you feel so good. You are so beautiful." She kissed his nipple and Derek looked down in time to see her suck it gently between her lips. He caught his breath and raised a trembling hand to cup the back of her head and softly hold her to him.

"You are the beautiful one, Sophie," he told her with a tremor in his voice. "You've made me see that loving someone is worth the risk. I love you, Sophie. I love you so much."

Sophie pulled away and laid her cheek on his chest over his heart. "Oh Derek, I love you too. So very much." She ran one hand up his stomach and over his shoulder to wrap it around his neck and lifted her face to his. He saw the truth of it there, her love for him shining in her eyes, in the gentle curve of the smile on her lips, even in the shadow the sun cast against her cheekbone.

"Sophie, Sophie," he whispered, cupping her cheek, "you are my heart, my mate in every way. And while this outpouring of emotion is very touching, I really, really want to fuck you now."

Sophie burst out laughing and Derek heard Ian choke with laughter behind him. "God yes, Derek," Sophie laughed. "I thought we'd never get to the fucking."

"That's my girl," Derek said with a growl and she squealed as he dragged her to the floor with him. He was desperate not just to fuck her, but to taste her, to taste the sweet cream he'd felt on his fingers earlier, on his cock what felt like eons ago but was in reality only a short week before. He pushed Sophie until she was flat on the floor and, spreading her legs, lay down between them. Without preamble he leaned in and pressed his mouth against the damp curls covering her hot, juicy cunt and he licked a path over her swollen lips. Sophie gasped and her shoulders rose from the floor as her torso curled up and she fisted her hands in his hair to hold him against her. Derek laughed with his mouth still touching her and Sophie groaned.

"Liked that, did you?" he teased. He reached up and parted the lips of her cunt with his fingers revealing the hot pink valleys there. It was decadent and enticing and it was Derek's turn to groan as he leaned forward and began to feast on her. She tasted sweet, with just a hint of spice and Derek was instantly addicted. The folds of her tender flesh were so soft it was like licking silk. Her juices poured out of her as she moaned above him and he drank them down, thirsty for the evidence of her desire.

Suddenly he had to feel her sheath around his tongue. He thrust it inside her, and involuntarily his fingers holding her thigh tightened, digging into her tender skin. She gasped and arched into his mouth and he began to fuck her with his tongue, loving the feel of her impossibly soft flesh sliding along his tongue and clenching around it. God, she was so wet and hot and soft, and she was making him mad with the need to feel her come against his mouth. He didn't want to push her too hard, still needed to fuck her so badly, but he had to feel her come around his tongue inside her. He pressed a finger against her clitoris and rubbed softly, then increased the pressure until she arched again and trembled against his mouth. He kept up the motion and she began to moan. She was fucking against his mouth now, her hips thrusting her cunt down on his tongue and Derek was as wild as she. He worked her ravenously, until her feet dug into the floor and her back bowed and she screamed. He grabbed her hips roughly and held her hard against his mouth as he thrust his tongue deep inside her and flicked it, making her cry out again. Her vaginal muscles gripped his tongue so hard he could barely move it and he actually laughed with the wonder of her orgasm.

He didn't pull away until she collapsed back on the floor and weakly pushed his head to make him stop. His face was wet with her cream, and Derek started to wipe it off but was stopped by Ian's grip on his arm. He looked up as Ian knelt next to him. Ian leaned in and licked along Derek's jaw and chin and Derek shivered. Ian slowly licked Sophie's essence from his skin. Finally Ian licked across Derek's lips and Derek opened them, inviting Ian inside. Ian's tongue slid between his lips and tasted Sophie in his mouth. Derek felt Ian's fingers dig into his arm as Ian moved closer and grabbed a fistful of Derek's hair, kissing him hard and possessively. Derek moaned and let Ian have his way with his mouth.

"Oh God," Sophie whispered. Derek felt her legs, still spread around him, move restlessly, and he reached out blindly to run a hand soothingly down her thigh. Sophie sighed and a little moan escaped her as Ian's mouth moved on his, his tongue thrusting into Derek's mouth ruthlessly. After another minute, Derek broke the kiss breathlessly.

"Ian," he panted. Ian ran a hand down his chest, his fingertips brushing over his pebbled nipple. Derek shivered. "Ian, I still want to fuck your wife. But you may certainly join us if you like."

Ian's eyes were hooded and he crooked a seductive half smile at Derek. "Oh I shall, at the appropriate time. I just wanted to taste her on your lips, Derek. I love the taste of her. I want the taste of both of you in my mouth, and I want to drink the taste of her and me from yours. But that is for another day." Derek's heart stuttered at Ian's words, and from the look in Ian's eyes he knew the effect he had.

"Oh God," Sophie said again, and Derek turned to look at her. Her eyes were wide as she stared at them. "I never even thought about that," she whispered as if she were sharing a forbidden secret with them.

Ian's laugh rumbled through the room as he moved away from Derek with a possessive caress of his shoulders. Derek cocked his head to the side as he regarded Ian with narrowed eyes. "Don't worry, Sophie, Ian's thought of everything." Ian just laughed harder.

Sophie squirmed again, drawing Derek's attention. When he looked down at her he couldn't believe that he'd been able to look away for even one moment. She was sex personified laying there beneath him as if an offering from the gods. Her hair was a coppery tangle spread around her on the floor, framing a face flushed with satisfaction, but her eyes said she was not yet sated. Her lips were swollen from his kisses, and her glorious pink-tinged brown nipples were hard. Her legs were spread around him, her knees raised and her cunt open and begging. He was immediately, desperately, achingly hard. He leaned down and sucked a pebbled nipple into his greedy mouth.

"Ahh!" Sophie let out a shriek, clearly taken by surprise. Derek grinned around her breast in his mouth for a moment, then suckled her softly. Sophie's surprise turned to pleasure and she cradled him in her arms, her hands running down his back. She teasingly ran her nails along his spine and Derek shivered and pulled away with a gasp. What she had meant to be teasing was an unexpected spark that ignited a conflagration in Derek. No more waiting. He pulled out of her embrace abruptly and grabbed her thighs, spreading them wider and raising her legs to his waist.

"Yes," Sophie said, understanding what he wanted and not just granting permission, but proclaiming her need as well in that one word. She wrapped her legs around his waist and pulled him down until his weight was balanced on his forearms. "Yes, Derek, God yes." Again she matched him with her fire and need, and Derek sank his cock into her with one hard thrust, pressing deep until he felt her pubic hair on the base of his cock and his balls. The coarse caress was like kindling to the fire in his blood, and he pulled out and surged forward, harder, faster than before and Sophie matched his pace with a moan and a shiver that made him want to shout in exultation.

"Fuck," he groaned. "God damn it, Sophie, yes. You are the most amazing fuck." Why was it with Sophie his clever words deserted him? Why was it so hard to explain to her what she made him feel?

"Oh Derek, God, yes," Sophie moaned. "I am."

Derek couldn't stop the bark of laughter that escaped him, although it was slightly breathless. He heard Ian's laugh behind him.

Sophie covered her red face with one hand. "Oh God, that's not what I meant. I meant with you, you and Ian, it's always amazing. It's not like...it's wonderful. That's what I meant. I meant you make me amazing."

Derek had stopped moving, his cock buried deep in the tight confines of her heat and wetness. Being in Sophie like this was unlike any feeling he'd had before. He reached up and tenderly moved her hand away and looked into her beautiful amber eyes. "Yes, you are amazing. And yes, we are amazing. As for you and Ian, I can't wait to see how amazing you are. But the fact is, Sophie, everything about you amazes and fascinates and arouses me. It's an excitement I haven't felt for anything or anyone except Ian, and I love it. I love you." As he finished he pressed a little harder, a little deeper into Sophie and she gasped.

"More, Derek. I want more." Sophie squirmed and thrust, trying to drive him deeper and Derek laughed again. He couldn't remember the last time he'd laughed this much while making love. Before Dolores died, quite possibly. And suddenly he understood what Ian had been trying to tell him ever since he'd decided to get married. They *had* needed someone else. They needed someone who came to them in peace, and who brought peace. Peace and laughter and a joy for living that he'd lost somewhere along the way, despite his love for Ian. Sophie had given it back to him, to them, and he knew that the love he shared with Ian would be sweeter for what Sophie brought them.

Derek pulled up to his knees and gathered Sophie in his arms, trembling with his new understanding. What a bastard he'd been, and Ian had been right. He'd been so right. "Ian, you were right. I understand now, I understand how much I needed Sophie, how much we needed her. God, I'm so sorry, Ian. So sorry I was such an obstinate bastard."

Ian came to him then and again knelt beside him, brushing a lock of hair from his forehead. "It's all right, darling, it's all right. I always knew you'd give in, and eventually you'd see what I was trying to give you. I wanted this for us, Derek, but you've made it happen." Sophie's hands were smoothing along his back comfortingly as she snuggled in his arms. He was surrounded by their love for him, and he knew he was undeserving, at least for now. But he'd earn it, and they would never regret loving him. His eyes were burning with unshed tears and he closed them tight and buried his face in the curve of Sophie's neck, holding them back. Ian pressed a kiss against his nape and rested his cheek on Derek's hair.

After a moment Sophie moved tentatively on him, and the slide of her silken sheath against his cock reminded him why he was naked on the floor of the study with Sophie riding his lap. He pulled away from her neck with a moan and looked at Sophie's face. She was intensely concentrating on the pleasure of their joining, sliding slowly down his rigid shaft and back up at a pace that was just short of torture. When she saw Derek looking at her, she smiled tremulously. "While this emotional outpouring is very touching, Derek…" she said breathlessly, and Derek laughed as he finished the sentence for her.

"I really, really want to fuck right now. Yes, Sophie, I'm sorry. Fuck me, fuck me, Sophie, however you want. Use me, ride me, toy with me, torture me. I'm yours, completely."

"Not completely," Ian drawled from behind him. "Lie down, Derek. Let Sophie have her wicked way with you."

Derek somehow managed to lie down on the floor with Sophie on top of him while keeping his cock snug in the hot cocoon of her cunt. Their new position clearly delighted Sophie as she sat up tall astride him and began to move sensuously. She threw her head back and moaned as she swiveled her hips against him, rubbing his cock against that sweet spot inside her. Derek rubbed his hands over her stomach and up to her soft, freckled breasts, squeezing and caressing them as he gave her a moment to ride him.

He looked up as Ian walked over behind Sophie. Derek's breath caught as Ian slowly began to undo his trousers. Ian's eyes caught his briefly then closed in pleasure, and Derek looked down to see Ian had pushed his pants and drawers down enough to free his huge erection. As always the sight of Ian's hard cock made Derek ache with desire, and he felt his own cock actually quiver with anticipation inside Sophie. This was a new aspect of their lovemaking that Derek instinctually knew he'd come to crave, the thrilling uncertainty of which one of them Ian would fuck first.

As if reading his mind, Ian opened his eyes and looked directly at him. "Not this time, Derek. This is your fuck, yours and Sophie's. But I must put my mark on you both. I feel a little like your wild animal, Derek, claiming my mates." Ian gracefully dropped to his knees behind Sophie, who had gone still when she realized he was behind her.

"Ian?" she asked in a breathless, tentative voice. "You may fuck me too, if that's what you want." She was clearly a little frightened at the thought, but also excited.

Ian snuggled in close behind her and nuzzled the nape of her neck as his arms went around her. He cupped Derek's hands holding her breasts and Sophie made a small, mewling noise of pleasure, thrusting the soft mounds into their joined hands. "Is it what you want, Sophie?" he asked quietly in her ear. "Remember it's always only been what you want."

Sophie's head jerked in a shaky nod. "Yes, it's what I want." Her voice was so low it was almost inaudible, and Derek passed his thumbs over her nipples in a light caress in an attempt to soothe her. The heat in her eyes as she looked at him told him it had the opposite effect. He smiled at her smugly and she thumped his shoulder with a frown, making him laugh. "I do want it," she said with a newfound authority that Derek found utterly irresistible, and he thrust his cock into her in an involuntary reaction. Sophie's head fell back on Ian's shoulder as she moaned and thrust back.

Ian chuckled behind her and Derek could feel that laughter pass through Sophie and rumble sensuously along his cock. He arched his back, chasing that laughter inside her. Ian's hands pressed his against Sophie's breasts as he kissed her shoulder, his eyes watching Derek's reactions. As Derek settled back to the floor, his breathing agitated, he could see Ian smile against Sophie's shoulder. He pulled back to speak. "Not here, not now, Sophie. But soon. Tonight I think, in our bed, which by the way we shall all three be sharing from now on, and it's about damn time. We'll fuck you together tonight. I don't think the study floor is quite the right spot for that."

Derek could see and feel Ian move in closer to Sophie and suddenly he felt the unmistakable stroke of Ian's cock against his balls. His back arched again. "Ian, fuck! Don't stop. Christ, that feels good."

Sophie moaned and tried to grind down on Derek, but Ian held her hips and kept her from crushing him as he stroked between them. "Ian, oh my God, is that your cock? That feels wonderful. Damn, damn, damn, don't ever stop."

Ian laughed, and Derek was pleased to hear that he was slightly breathless. "Yes that's me, so be careful. God, Sophie, you're beginning to sound like Derek. I love it." He stroked between them again, his cock gliding over Derek's balls, sliding past the root of Derek's cock buried in Sophie, and judging by Sophie's reaction, up against her sensitive clit. "Christ, Sophie, you are so damn wet, you and Derek both. It's like gliding through wet velvet. You've soaked Derek's pubic hair with your cum." Ian shivered and thrust against them again and Derek had to bite his lip to keep from moving. "It feels so marvelous."

It felt so good, so goddamned good to have Sophie riding his cock and Ian stroking his balls with his thick cock. Ian pulled back and Derek felt the tip of his cock against the sensitive skin between his balls and his anus. "Soon, Ian," he gasped, "soon I want you in my ass while I fuck Sophie."

"Mmm," Ian rumbled, and Sophie moaned. "Fuck her now, Derek," Ian commanded in a rough voice. "Move again. Fuck, both of you."

And Derek and Sophie obeyed.

Ian needed them to get on with it. He wasn't going to last long after watching them together, and now the feel of them both beneath him, rubbing them both with his cock had him so close he could feel the heat of his orgasm as it rose up from his balls.

It was so hard not to separate the cheeks of one of the sweet, tight asses he was caressing and slide inside. Soon, soon, he told himself, but the image was in his head and he couldn't dispel it. Then Derek spread his legs wider to encompass both Ian and Sophie and thrust into Sophie and against Ian and Ian was completely in the here and now, his fantasies forgotten. He threw back his head and moaned at the exquisite feeling.

Derek was holding Sophie's hips, his hands just below Ian's. He moved one of his hands back to grip Ian's hip and pull him forward as he thrust into Sophie. The simple movement had so many complicated meanings and Ian savored it. He'd been afraid he'd be jealous when Derek and Sophie finally overcame their reluctance and came together. He found that his fears had been groundless. He reveled in their passion for one another. He felt omnipotent watching the love he'd fostered between them come to fruition. The two of them, their love for him and for each other, their acceptance of the relationship he'd thought at one time only a dream, made Ian feel invincible.

He had to bend his head and close his eyes and concentrate on his control to keep from coming right then with Derek's hand on his hip. He wanted to come on them both where they were joined. He wanted Derek to fuck into Sophie with a cock covered in Ian's cum. The thought made him shiver and he knew this was it, he couldn't hold back anymore.

"Stop," he told them with a growl, and he held Sophie's hips so she was suspended with Derek only half inside her. Ian pushed back between them and rubbed his sensitive head against Derek's wet cock and Ian exploded with a cry. The pulsing waves of his orgasm rocked through him, bowing his back and leaving him with shaking hands. He distantly heard Derek's curse and Sophie's moan as they were washed in his release.

He was breathing so heavily after his orgasm he found it hard to speak. "Fuck...now. Fuck with...me on you."

Sophie sobbed as she slid down Derek's shaft, her head still on Ian's shoulder. "Ah, yes, Ian," she said, her voice trembling. "I can feel it and it's so good."

Ian felt Derek's hands dig into Sophie's hips and slam her down hard on the next thrust and then Derek was coming, his head thrown back, neck and chest arched as he cried out Sophie's name. He was so beautiful. Did he know how beautiful he was? How much Ian and Sophie loved to look at him? As Derek forced her down on his cock, Sophie climaxed for the third time. She reached a hand back and gripped the back of Ian's head tightly as she rode Derek's orgasm, moaning with satisfaction. Ian could feel her jerk with each contraction of her release and raised his hands to cup her breasts and pinch her nipples. Sophie cried out and fought Derek's hold in the throes of another crest. Christ, Christ, they were so perfect. They were his. If he hadn't already come, Ian would have at that moment.

When it was over, Sophie collapsed against Derek's chest and he held her tightly as Ian ran a hand down the sensuously curved arch of her back.

"It wasn't the forest floor, but I think I did all right," Sophie mumbled. Both Ian and Derek laughed gently.

"I think you did better than all right, Sophie," Ian murmured with one more stroke of her back. He moved and lay down on his back next to them.

"I think our girl definitely has the ability to handle both of us, Ian," Derek said with a smile in his voice.

For a moment Ian was taken back in time, to a place before Salamanca, when Derek was young and eager and so happy. He had to close his eyes against the tears as he silently said thanks for returning that Derek to him. When he opened his eyes and turned his head, both Derek and Sophie were staring at him. He smiled, glad that he was able to do so without hesitation. "Yes, yes, I think our girl is bloody amazing, Derek. Bloody fucking amazing." And both Sophie and Derek laughed as Ian hoped they would.

* * * * *

Ian had to send for Montague and order him to keep all the servants downstairs until further notice so that Sophie could sneak back to her room wearing nothing but Derek's shirt and her stockings and shoes. The shirt covered her from her neck to below her knees, but Sophie was mortified that someone would see her.

Derek took his time getting dressed after he spent nearly ten minutes getting Sophie into his shirt. He kept kissing her and suddenly the shirt would be off and they'd have to start all over again. Ian had laughingly joined the game, and when Sophie left they were as aroused as they'd been before "fucking like animals on the study floor", as Sophie had described it with a blush.

Ian was reclining on his chaise watching Derek dress. There was little he enjoyed more than simply watching Derek move. The play of his muscles in the sunlight entranced Ian, and he could feel himself smiling. The look Derek gave him was grave.

"What is it?" Ian asked, his smile fading.

"We have to do something about that bastard, Middleton."

Ian relaxed. "It's already been taken care of, darling."

Chapter Twenty-Two

ဆာ

Derek had to wait at the door of Daniel's club while a footman went to see if Daniel was available. When he returned, Derek was shown to the far corner of a back room with great civility. Daniel had trained them well. Amazing really that a Jew was even a member here. But then again, Daniel defied almost every stricture of their society.

Daniel was drinking with Simon, heavily by the looks of it. Derek felt a stab of remorse because he knew the reason why.

"Derek," Daniel said congenially when he sat down across from him. You couldn't tell from his voice he'd been in his cups, just the glassy look in his eyes.

"Thank you," Derek said simply.

Daniel blinked slowly, then inclined his head with a raised brow. "You're welcome, although I'm sure I don't know what the thanks are for. The fabulous cut of my new coat?"

Simon laughed as if Daniel were the wittiest man in London. Suddenly Derek realized why Simon was also drunk. "I thank you as well," he told him. Simon stopped laughing and frowned at Derek.

"Do you? Well, that's original." Simon shrugged. "Daniel's little project, really. I was just along for the entertainment."

Daniel looked at him sharply. "Hardly. Why do you want everyone to think you're a bloody fool? I can't be the only man in England who sees through that ruse."

"No, you're not," Derek agreed, silently accepting the glass the footman brought him with a nod. He raised the glass.

"To successful projects, then. And the bloody fools who carry them out."

Daniel and Simon gravely raised their glasses and then took a long drink. Derek sipped his. He wanted to be sober tonight.

"Daniel." Jason's voice came from behind Derek and he started with surprise. Daniel smiled sardonically at him.

"Saw 'em coming," he told Derek. "That's why I swallowed the whole damned glass."

Derek looked at Jason, and Tony beside him. Both men looked grim. Derek knew why they were here and he narrowed his eyes at them warningly. Jason gave him look for look.

"You had damn well better not be drinking to what occurred last night," Jason growled. "He doesn't need that kind of encouragement, Derek."

Derek pretended ignorance. "What happened last night?" he asked innocently.

"Harold Middleton was found murdered this morning." Jason looked at Daniel accusingly. "You disappeared the other night right after you and Ian had that mysterious, hushed conversation. A day later Middleton is dead."

Daniel merely raised an eyebrow. "And you are suggesting…?"

Jason threw himself down in a chair at Daniel's right. "God damn it, Daniel. That's not who you are anymore. You are not that killer anymore."

Daniel casually poured himself a drink. "I am what I am, Jason. You can't erase the past. We are the sum total of our experiences. That said, I resent your assumption. I'm sure there are hundreds of people in London alone who wanted Middleton dead." He smiled wickedly. "He was a dead bore already."

Simon burst into laughter, again drawing Jason's attention. "And did you have to drag Simon into it? He's not like you."

At the look on Daniel's face, Derek intervened. "Shut up, Jason. This is none of your affair." Jason looked as if he were going to argue. "I mean it, Jason. You and Tony wanted Robertson dead. Ian and I wanted Middleton dead. I'm not sorry he met with an unfortunate accident. If he hadn't, I would have killed him. And that is the end of this discussion."

Simon's chair scraped back as he stood unsteadily. "And I resent the implication that I don't have the brains to make my own decisions." He turned slowly and walked over to pat Daniel's shoulder. "I'm off to Mrs. Moffat's. Care to join me?" At the mention of one of the most licentious brothels in London, Jason's look grew darker.

Daniel slumped lower in his chair. "Not tonight, Simon. I've had a little too much to be any good to anyone."

Simon chuckled. "I plan on letting someone else do all the work. As a matter of fact, I'm going to lie there and let several someones have a night to remember at my expense."

"Simon," Tony sighed in resignation, "that is no way to live."

"Tony," Simon sighed mockingly, "not all of us have the good fortune to have two bloody wonderful fucks waiting at home."

Jason's chair fell over as he stood abruptly. Suddenly all five of them were standing, Jason and Tony looking thunderous, Simon unrepentant and Daniel amused. Derek just wanted to go home to Ian and Sophie.

"I have the good fortune to have two excellent fucks waiting at home, so everyone settle down. If I don't leave this place able to fuck them both blind tonight, you will all pay, and I will make it extremely painful. Now sit down, all of you." Derek made a great show of sitting back in his chair and Daniel followed suit. Jason and Tony reluctantly followed while the few other members of the club in the room glared at them. Simon remained standing.

"I wasn't sitting to begin with, Derek, so fuck you and your wonderful new domestic arrangements. I am still off to Mrs. Moffat's, where I hope to be fucked blind as well. Good day, gentlemen." Simon doffed an imaginary hat and sauntered a little unsteadily out the door.

"Well, you certainly pissed him off," Daniel told Jason as he raised his glass for a sip.

Jason started to speak but Tony laid a hand on his arm and he sat back with a frown.

"Daniel, we're worried about you. What happened last night...you've worked so hard, Daniel, to forget. We don't want you to have to go through that again." Tony spoke eloquently, his genuine concern obvious.

Daniel relaxed in his chair and looked at them affectionately. "You needn't worry about me, Tony. I came to terms with myself a long time ago. That's all you can do. There is no forgetting. There's just moving on."

Derek's heart lurched at Daniel's words, at the truth of them. He stood up abruptly. "I'm grateful, Daniel. I know how hard it must have been for you, and I appreciate what you did for us. We will never forget. If you ever need anything..." Derek pushed his chair back to the table and then looked hard at Daniel. "You're right, there is no forgetting, and moving on is so bloody hard it's almost as painful. But once you do move on... Daniel, you have to. I feel more alive today than I have since we came back. I took the chance. Move on, Daniel. I appreciate what you did, but don't fall back to it. Move on."

Daniel looked at him with haunted eyes. "Go home, Derek. Go home to Ian and to Sophie. Help her move on too." He poured another drink with an unsteady hand. "I did it for her, you know, not you or Ian. For Sophie." He tilted his head back and threw the drink down his throat, then set the glass back on the table delicately. "If I have it in me, then I should use it for that, don't you think? For the things that really matter."

Derek walked over behind Daniel's chair and squeezed his shoulder. "It matters, Daniel. It really matters." He looked at Jason and Tony and knew that both men would stay with Daniel and make sure he was all right. Then he turned and headed home to Ian and Sophie and a new life.

* * * * *

Derek let his head fall back as he thrust deeply into Sophie's incredibly tight ass one more time. He felt Ian pull out of her cunt at the same time, their two cocks rubbing and pressing against one another through the thin barrier inside Sophie as they passed. The dual sensations of Sophie's tight heat and Ian's large, hard cock made him shudder. God, had it been this good with Dolores? Derek couldn't remember, he could only live in this moment, in the wonder of loving these two people and letting them love him. He moved forward on his knees, spreading his legs a little wider to penetrate Sophie's ass deeper as she rode Ian's cock. The movement made Sophie moan and she rolled her head against Derek's shoulder.

"Yes, Derek, more," she told him with a sob. "God, darling, more."

Sophie was truly amazing. When they came to her tonight she'd been eager and willing, pliant beneath their questing hands and mouths one moment and a tigress in her lust the next. She'd taken them both in her mouth, Derek while Ian stretched her ass for fucking and Ian when Derek first fucked into her ass. She'd loved every minute of it.

God, fucking into her ass while Ian watched had been so damn erotic Derek had thought for a moment he might come then and there. Ian had gripped his wrist so hard it hurt and the pain brought him back from the edge. He'd bit his lip until it bled to keep from coming when he helped to lower Sophie onto Ian's cock and felt that sensuous caress inside her for the first time. Ian had pushed up on his hands and pulled Derek's head down, licking the blood off his lip.

Sophie was moaning almost continuously, as if she couldn't contain the pleasure. She held both of Ian's hands, using them for purchase as she thrust back and forward, fucking them both in a perfect rhythm. Derek could see his ring on her finger, next to Ian's, the ring he'd been buying just that morning when Sophie had woken to find him gone. How she'd cried when he gave it to her tonight.

"That's right, Sophie," Ian softly encouraged her, "fuck us just like that. You are so good, Sophie, such a good fuck. I want to watch you come, Sophie. You have to come before Derek and I do. Come Sophie, come for us. Come around our cocks so deep inside you, loving you."

Sophie sobbed incoherently and pulled her hands from Ian's grip. She raised her arms and reached back for Derek, wrapping her arms around his head where it rested, chin on her shoulder. The movement altered their penetration and her ass became even tighter, making Derek groan.

"Sophie, Sophie." Derek heard the growl in his voice, recognized the animal she unleashed in him. He ran his hands up her stomach to her breasts and passed his palms tenderly over her aroused, sensitive nipples several times. She arched her back and then pulled her arms down and placed her hands on Ian's stomach. She began a hard, steady, fast rhythm, pressing her clitoris down on Ian with each thrust. Derek became fascinated with a freckle on her back and leaned down to suck on it. Sophie cried out his name with a tremulous sob. She had love bites all over from where he and Ian had feasted on her freckles. Christ, Christ he loved her. He loved them. His thrusts were hard and fast, matching Sophie's rhythm, pacing Ian's cock inside her.

Suddenly Sophie froze with a keening cry, Ian deep within her. She threw her head back, her mewl of pleasure endless.

"God, Sophie, yes!" Ian cried out. Derek gently pressed his cock all the way into her ass and he could feel the hot bursts of Ian's ejaculation through the thin wall of Sophie's cunt. The tight spasms of her muscles in climax wrung a cry from deep in Derek's throat and then he was coming too, coming with Ian and Sophie in a haze of tight, wet heat and indescribable pleasure.

Sophie collapsed on top of Ian, both men still buried inside her. Derek curled over her but didn't pull out. He and Ian stayed that way, stroking and kissing Sophie until they were both soft and sated and their cocks fell from her naturally. Then Derek lay down next to them on his side, facing them so he could still stroke and touch them both.

Sophie turned her face to him, her cheek pressed to Ian's chest. "Didn't we just do this? Only your positions are reversed." Her voice was hoarse, overused as she'd let them know her pleasure while they'd fucked her. The sound was music to Derek, sweet, sensuous music.

"We're going to do it again too," Derek told her with a soft smile, and Sophie smiled back.

"Oh good. Just give me a minute to rest," she told him, closing her eyes.

Ian's laugh rumbled over them. "I'm afraid I'll need more than a minute, sweetheart, but I'll do my best."

Derek snorted with gentle laughter. "You'll probably need less time than I. You usually do."

Ian turned his head on his pillow and looked at Derek heatedly. "You'll be fine. You always get hard when I fuck you."

Derek found his breathing growing ragged again. Yes, that's what he wanted, Ian in his ass and his cock in Sophie. Derek wanted to be in between them, fucking and being fucked. He slowly leaned over and kissed Ian. Without words he let his lips and tongue tell Ian how much he wanted him, wanted that.

Sophie's voice trembled between them. "Oh, we haven't tried that yet. I want to do that. Can we do that?"

Derek pulled back from the kiss with another laugh. "Oh, yes, Sophie, we are going to try that, that and so much more."

Sophie smiled enticingly. "Promises, promises." She reached out and brushed a lock of hair off Derek's forehead. "Who says I'll let you do more?"

"I do." Ian's voice was low and gravelly and both Derek and Sophie shivered at it. "I started this, and, if you'll remember correctly, I own you both." He suddenly turned and the motion dumped Sophie onto Derek's chest as he turned instinctively onto his back to give Ian more room. Ian snuggled in close against them both, his growing erection pressed to Derek's hip as he kissed the edge of Sophie's shoulder and then sank his teeth gently into it. Sophie shivered again and sucked in a little breath that for some reason was astoundingly arousing to Derek. Ian let go and licked the spot he'd bitten so lightly. "Now run and get a nice, warm cloth to clean us up, Derek, and let's start all over again."

Derek gently moved Sophie off him and rose from the bed with a smug grin. "As always, Ian, your wish is my command."

The End

Why an electronic book?

We live in the Information Age—an exciting time in the history of human civilization, in which technology rules supreme and continues to progress in leaps and bounds every minute of every day. For a multitude of reasons, more and more avid literary fans are opting to purchase e-books instead of paper books. The question from those not yet initiated into the world of electronic reading is simply: *Why?*

1. *Price.* An electronic title at Ellora's Cave Publishing and Cerridwen Press runs anywhere from 40% to 75% less than the cover price of the exact same title in paperback format. Why? Basic mathematics and cost. It is less expensive to publish an e-book (no paper and printing, no warehousing and shipping) than it is to publish a paperback, so the savings are passed along to the consumer.

2. *Space.* Running out of room in your house for your books? That is one worry you will never have with electronic books. For a low one-time cost, you can purchase a handheld device specifically designed for e-reading. Many e-readers have large, convenient screens for viewing. Better yet, hundreds of titles can be stored within your new library—on a single microchip. There are a variety of e-readers from different manufacturers. You can also read e-books on your PC or laptop computer. (Please note that Ellora's Cave does not endorse any specific brands.

You can check our websites at www.ellorascave.com or www.cerridwenpress.com for information we make available to new consumers.)

3. *Mobility.* Because your new e-library consists of only a microchip within a small, easily transportable e-reader, your entire cache of books can be taken with you wherever you go.

4. *Personal Viewing Preferences.* Are the words you are currently reading too small? Too large? Too... ANNOYING? Paperback books cannot be modified according to personal preferences, but e-books can.

5. *Instant Gratification.* Is it the middle of the night and all the bookstores near you are closed? Are you tired of waiting days, sometimes weeks, for bookstores to ship the novels you bought? Ellora's Cave Publishing sells instantaneous downloads twenty-four hours a day, seven days a week, every day of the year. Our webstore is never closed. Our e-book delivery system is 100% automated, meaning your order is filled as soon as you pay for it.

Those are a few of the top reasons why electronic books are replacing paperbacks for many avid readers.

As always, Ellora's Cave and Cerridwen Press welcome your questions and comments. We invite you to email us at Comments@ellorascave.com or write to us directly at Ellora's Cave Publishing Inc., 1056 Home Avenue, Akron, OH 44310-3502.

COMING TO A BOOKSTORE NEAR YOU!

ELLORA'S CAVE

Bestselling Authors Tour

MAKE EACH DAY MORE *EXCITING* WITH OUR

ELLORA'S
CAVEMEN
CALENDAR

☥ WWW.ELLORASCAVE.COM ☥

erridwen, the Celtic Goddess of wisdom, was the muse who brought inspiration to story-tellers and those in the creative arts. Cerridwen Press encompasses the best and most innovative stories in all genres of today's fiction. Visit our site and discover the newest titles by talented authors who still get inspired - much like the ancient storytellers did, once upon a time.

Cerridwen Press

www.cerridwenpress.com

Discover for yourself why readers can't get enough
of the multiple award-winning publisher

Ellora's Cave.

Whether you prefer e-books or paperbacks,

be sure to visit EC on the web at
www.ellorascave.com

for an erotic reading experience that will leave you
breathless.